For Anna and Jack

Name: Joe Jefferson

Occupation: Schoolboy

Hobbies: Football, TV, arguing with his sister

Favourite food: Anything not cooked by Norbert

Name: Randalf the Wise
Muddle Earth's leading wizard

Occupation: Um . . .
Muddle Earth's leading wizard

Hobbies: Performing spells (I think you'll find that's spell! – Veronica)

Favourite food: Norbert's squashed tadpole fritters

Name: Henry

Occupation: Joe's dog

Hobbies: Walkies, chasing squirrels, sniffing strangers' bottoms

Favourite food: Dog food, obviously

NAME:
Norbert the Not-Very-Big

OCCUPATION: Ogre

HOBBIES: Thumb-sucking,
cooking – especially
cake-decorating

FAVOURITE FOOD: Everything

NAME: Veronica

OCCUPATION: Familiar to the
great wizard, Randalf the Wise

HOBBIES: Being sarcastic

FAVOURITE FOOD: Anything not
cooked by Norbert

NAME: The Horned Baron

OCCUPATION: Ruler of Muddle
Earth and husband to Ingrid

HOBBIES: Ruling, and doing
whatever Ingrid tells him

FAVOURITE FOOD: Bad-breath
porridge

NAME: Dr Cuddles (Sshhh! Don't
say his name out loud!)

OCCUPATION: (SSHHH!
No one even knows he exists!)

HOBBIES: (Didn't you
hear what I just said?)

FAVOURITE FOOD: Snuggle-muffins

Book 1

Engelbert the Enormous

Prologue

Night was falling over Muddle Earth. The sun had set, the sky was darkening and already two of its three moons had risen up above the Musty Mountains. One of these moons was as purple as a batbird. The other was as yellow as an ogre's underpants on wash day. Both were full and bright.

The land was full of noises as the day creatures (such as tree rabbits, hillfish and pink stinky hogs) said goodnight to the night creatures (such as stiltmice, lazybirds and exploding gas frogs), who were just getting up. High above their heads, the batbirds had left their roosts and were soaring across the purple and yellow striped sky. As they bumped into each other, the air filled with their characteristic cry: '*Ouch!*'

In Elfwood, the trees bowed and bent as a chill wind howled through their branches. In the Perfumed Bog the oozy mud bubbled and plopped. In the far-off Ogrehills, there was the slurping sound of a thousand thumbs being sucked and a thousand sleepy voices murmuring '*Mummy!*'

Twinkling lights were coming on throughout overcrowded Goblintown and, as the goblins prepared their evening meals, the air was filled with the smells of bad-breath porridge and snotbread – and the sounds of too many cooks.

'Have you spat in this?'

'No.'

'Well, go on then, before I put it in the oven.'

By contrast, Trollbridge was cloaked in cold, dank darkness. The trolls who lived there could see nothing of the cabbages and turnips they were eating for supper. Their deep voices rumbled up from their dwellings beneath the bridge.

'Has anyone seen my mangel-wurzel?'

'It's over here.'

'*OW!* That's my head!'

As the purple and yellow shadows swept down from

Mount Boom to the Horned Baron's great castle below, a loud, piercing voice ripped from the windows of the highest tower. Another of the inhabitants of Muddle Earth seemed to be finding it hard to tell the difference between a root vegetable and a head.

'Walter, you turnip-head! WALTER! Where *are* you?'

It was Ingrid, wife of the Horned Baron himself, and she was far from happy.

'Coming, my sweet,' he called out as he climbed the circular stairs.

'I've just seen something I really want in this catalogue,' Ingrid continued. 'Singing curtains. It says here, "No self-respecting Horned Baron's wife should be without these enchanted window hangings to lull her gently off to sleep at night and sensitively wake her with song the following morning." *I* want to be lulled to sleep by singing curtains, Walter. *I* want to be woken with song. Do you hear me?'

'Loud and clear, love-of-my-life,' the Baron replied wearily. 'All *too* loud and clear,' he muttered under his breath.

The next moment the third moon of Muddle Earth – a small, bright green sphere which only seemed to appear when it felt like it – sailed up in the sky to form a perfect equilateral triangle with its yellow and purple neighbours. The three moons lit up the Enchanted Lake, which hovered high up above the ground, and the seven magnificent houseboats bobbing about on its glistening waters.

Six of the houseboats were dark and deserted. The seventh was bathed in an oily, orange lamplight. A short, portly individual by the name of Randalf was staring out from one of its upper windows at the configuration of coloured moons. A budgie perched on his balding head.

'Norbert,' he said at last to his assistant. 'The astral signs are auspicious. My pointy hat, if you please. I feel a spell coming on!'

'At once, sir,' said Norbert, his voice gruff yet well-meaning. As he stomped across the floor to the wizard's cupboard the whole houseboat dipped and swayed. Norbert the Not-Very-Big was a fairly weedy specimen, as ogres went – but he was still an ogre. And ogres, even weedy ones, are big and heavy.

'You feel a spell coming on?' said the budgie, whose name was Veronica. 'No, don't tell me. It couldn't be the spell to summon a warrior-hero to Muddle Earth by any chance?'

'It might be,' replied Randalf defensively.

Veronica snorted. 'Some wizard you are,' she said. 'You've only got one spell.'

'Yes, yes, don't rub it in,' said Randalf. 'I do the best I can. With all the other wizards . . . *errm* . . . away, I've got to hold the fort.'

'This is a houseboat, not a fort,' said Veronica. 'And the other wizards aren't *away*, they're—'

'Shut up, Veronica!' said Randalf sharply. 'You promised never to mention that dreadful incident again.'

The houseboat lurched once more as Norbert strode back across the room. 'Your pointy hat, sir,' he said.

Randalf placed it on his head. 'Thank you, Norbert,' he said, trying hard to overcome his irritation with Veronica. She was *such* a know-it-all! Why couldn't he have had something nice and sweet for a familiar like an exploding gas frog or a slimy bog demon? True, they might have been a bit smelly, but at least they wouldn't have answered back all the time. Not like this infernal budgie. Still, he was stuck with Veronica now, and he'd just have to do what he always did in these situations – make the best of it.

He carefully removed a piece of paper from the folds of his cloak, delicately opened it up and cleared his throat.

'Here we go,' came a muffled voice from under his hat as Randalf began to recite the incantation from the piece of paper. '*Hail, oh Triplet Moons of Muddle. Shine down on these Words of Enchanting, now I utter . . . um . . .*'

'That's all very well and good,' Veronica's voice broke in, 'but it's the last bit you need to concentrate on.'

'I know that,' Randalf muttered through clenched teeth. 'Be quiet now. I'm *trying* to concentrate.'

'That'll be a first,' Veronica commented, wriggling out from under the brim of the hat.

Randalf stared down at the spell miserably. Much as he hated to admit it, Veronica was right. He *did* need to concentrate on the last part of the spell. The trouble was, the bottom of the piece of paper had been torn off, and with it, the all-important words of enchantment for the warrior-hero-summoning spell. Once again he would have to improvise.

'*Creator of Wonders, Master of Intricate Arts, Possessor of Breathtaking Skills . . .*' he began.

'Don't overdo it,' Veronica cautioned. 'You said something like that last time you summoned a warrior-hero. Do you *want* another Quentin the Cake-Decorator?'

'No, you're right,' said Randalf. He rubbed his beard thoughtfully. 'All right,' he said at last, 'how about this?' He took a deep breath.

'*Strong . . . and loyal . . . and . . .*' He gave Veronica a dark look. '*Hairy. Oh, Triplet Moons, on these words shine clear.*

Let a mighty warrior-hero now appear!'

There was a bright flash, a loud crash and clouds of purple, yellow and green smoke billowed from the fireplace. Randalf, Norbert and Veronica spun round and stared, open-mouthed – and beaked – at the figure which appeared amidst the thinning smoke.

'What is *that*?' said Norbert.

Veronica squawked with amusement. 'I've just got one thing to say,' she chuckled. 'Come back Quentin the Cake-Decorator, all is forgiven!'

'Shut up, Veronica!' said Randalf, 'and stop sniggering. Everything's going to be fine! Trust me, I'm a wizard.'

Joe slammed down his pen angrily and clamped his hands over his ears to shut out the surrounding din.

'This is hopeless!' he bellowed. 'Hopeless!'

The noise was coming in from all directions – above, below, the room next door . . . It was like being stuck in a giant noise-sandwich.

On the desk in front of him, the title of his English assignment – 'My Amazing Adventure' – headed a blank piece of paper. It was early evening at the end of a sunny midsummer Sunday, and if Joe was to get the homework finished and ready to hand in on Monday morning then he needed to get down to work. But how *could* he, with that infernal racket going on all round him?

Joe Jefferson lived in a small brick house with his mum, dad, older sister, younger twin-brothers and his dog, Henry. To a casual observer, the Jeffersons seemed like a nice, quiet family. It was only when you stepped in through the front door that it became clear that they were anything *but*.

Mrs Jefferson worked in a bank. She was tall, slim, dark and fanatically house-proud. Mr Jefferson – a travelling sales-rep by day and a DIY freak at night, weekends, holidays and any other spare hour he could find – was short, stocky and never

more happy than when clutching a power tool in his hands.

Over the years, Mr Jefferson had constructed a garage, converted the loft, knocked rooms through, put up shelves and cupboards, built a conservatory, landscaped the garden and was currently working on a kitchen extension. At least, that was what *he* would say. So far as Mrs Jefferson was concerned, the thing her husband was best at was making a mess.

At this precise moment the electric drill was busy battling it out with the vacuum cleaner as Mrs Jefferson followed Mr Jefferson around the kitchen – attachment pipe raised high like a light-sabre – sucking up the dust from the air before it had a chance to settle.

As the noise vibrated up through his bedroom floor, Joe shook his head. He'd never get his homework done at this rate, and if he didn't, he'd be in serious trouble with Mr Dixon.

He wondered wearily why his dad didn't take up a nice quiet hobby – like chess, or embroidery – and why his mum couldn't be just a little less obsessed with cleanliness. And why his sister, Ella, who had the converted attic-room above his head, had to do everything – from flicking through a magazine to putting on mascara – to the accompaniment of loud, pounding music. And why the twins' favourite game was chasing-up-and-down-stairs-screaming.

Joe opened the drawer in his desk, pulled out his ear-plugs and was just about to shove them into his ears, when Henry let out a bloodcurdling howl and started barking furiously.

'That's it!' Joe yelled. He leapt up from his desk and stormed across the room. 'Henry!' he called. 'Come here, boy.'

The barking grew louder. It was coming from the bathroom. So were Mark and Matt's squeals of delight.

'He's in here, Joe,' they shouted.

'Henry!' Joe called again. 'Heel!'

Henry came bounding on to the landing and stood in front of Joe, tail wagging and tongue lolling. The twins appeared behind him.

'He was drinking the water from the toilet bowl again,'

they shouted excitedly. 'So we flushed it!'

Joe looked down at the water dripping from Henry's hairy face. 'Serves you right,' he laughed.

The dog barked happily and held out his paw. Upstairs, Ella's door opened and the music grew louder than ever. Ella's angry voice floated down.

'Shut that dog up!' she yelled.

From downstairs, the sound of the electric drill was abruptly replaced by loud hammering.

'Come on, boy,' said Joe. 'Let's get out of this madhouse!'

He turned and, with Henry at his heel, went down the stairs, grabbed the lead from the hook by the door and was just about to leave when his mum noticed him.

'Where are you going?' she shouted out above the sound of the vacuum cleaner and hammer.

'Out,' Joe replied. He opened the door.

'Out where?'

But Joe had already gone.

The local park was deserted. Joe picked up a stick and threw it for Henry, who chased after it, retrieved it and dropped it back at his feet for another throw. Joe grinned. However exasperating his life became, he could always count on Henry to cheer him up. He ruffled the dog's ears and tossed the stick a second time, then set off after Henry.

Across the grass they went, past a cluster of trees and down the hill. As they approached the stream, Joe whistled for Henry to return and clicked the lead into place. If Henry ended up splashing about in the dirty water again, his mum would go mad!

He patted the dog's head affectionately. 'Come on, boy, we'd better get back. That essay won't write itself.' He turned to go. '*My Amazing Adventure*,' he muttered. 'What a stupid title . . . Henry, what's wrong?'

Henry was standing stock still, the hairs along his back on end and his ears and nose twitching.

'What is it, boy?' Joe knelt down and followed the dog's intent stare.

Henry strained on the lead and whimpered.

'What can you see?' Joe muttered. 'Not a squirrel, I hope. You know what happened last ti . . . *aaargh*!'

Unable to remain still a moment longer, Henry suddenly bounded forwards. Head down and following his nose, he dashed straight for a massive rhododendron bush, pulling Joe along behind. The good news was that Henry was heading for a hole in the dark foliage. The bad news was that the hole was only dog-height.

'Henry! Henry, stop!' he shouted and tugged in vain at the lead. 'Stop! You stupid . . .'

The rest of the sentence was lost to a mouthful of leaves as Joe was dragged into the bush. He ducked down and tried his best to shield his eyes with his free hand as Henry dragged him deeper and deeper inside.

All at once, the branches and leaves began crackling with silvery strands of electricity, the air shimmered and wobbled and filled with the sound of slow mournful music – and the smell of burnt toast.

'What on earth ...' Joe gasped as, the next moment, he was pulled headlong down into a long flashing tunnel. The music grew louder. The smell of burning became stronger and stronger until ...

CRASH!

'Aargh!' yelled Joe. He was still falling, only now he could feel the sides of the tunnel grazing his elbows and bashing his knees as he continued to drop. And it was black – pitch-black. Joe cried out in fear and pain and let go of the lead. Henry disappeared below him. What seemed like an eternity later, he tumbled down out of the long vertical tunnel and landed with a heavy thump on the ground.

Joe opened his eyes. He was sitting on a tiled floor, bruised, dazed, surrounded by a thick cloud of choking dust and without the faintest idea what had just happened.

Had he fallen into a hole beneath the bush?

Had he cracked his head on a branch so hard he'd knocked himself silly?

As the swirling dust thinned, Joe found himself in a fireplace behind a huge pot, which was suspended on chains. He peered out into a dimly lit and exceedingly cluttered room.

There were tables against every wall, each one covered with pots, papers and peculiar paraphernalia. There were stools and cupboards and bookcases stacked high with boxes, bottles and books. Every inch of the walls was taken up with shelves and cabinets, maps and charts and countless hooks laden with bundles of twigs, roots and dried plants, dead animals and birds and shiny implements that Joe couldn't even begin to guess the purpose of. As for the floor, it was crowded with bulging sacks, earthenware pots and various angular contraptions made of wood and metal, with springs, pistons and cogs – and in the middle of all the chaos, two individuals with their backs turned.

One was short and portly, with bushy white hair and a blue budgie perched on the brim of his tall pointy hat. The other was hefty, knobbly and so tall that he had to stoop to avoid knocking his head against the heavy chandelier above his head.

'He doesn't say much, sir,' the hefty, knobbly one was saying.

'Obviously the strong, silent type, Norbert,' the portly figure replied.

'Unlike Quentin the Cake-Decorator,' said the budgie.

The portly one bent down. 'Now, don't be shy,' he said. 'My name's Randalf. Tell us your name.'

Joe climbed to his feet. This wasn't happening. You don't

take your dog for a walk one minute, fall into a bush the next and end up in somebody's kitchen. Do you? Joe closed his eyes and shook his head. Where was Henry, anyway?

Just then, the dog emitted a short, sharp bark.

'Rough?' said Norbert, puzzled. 'Did he say "Rough", sir?'

'Yes, Rough!' replied the short character, nodding enthusiastically. 'Of course. An excellent name for a warrior-hero, being both short and to the point.' He leaned down and added conspiratorially, 'Rough the Strong? Rough the Slayer? Rough the . . . Hairy?'

Henry barked again.

'Henry!' Joe called.

The dog appeared from behind Norbert, tail wagging furiously, and bounded over to the fireplace. Joe bent down and hugged him tightly. It was so good to see a familiar face, even if this was a dream.

'Who are *you*?' came a strident voice.

Joe looked up and stared back at the two individuals staring at him. The short one had a bushy white beard. The tall one had three eyes. Both of them were standing stock-still, eyes (all five of them) wide and mouths agape. It was the budgie who had spoken.

'I said, who *are* you?' it demanded.

'I . . . I'm Joe, but . . .' he began.

'Don't you see, Veronica?' Randalf exclaimed. 'That must be the sidekick,' he said, pointing at Joe. 'All good warrior-heroes have a sidekick. Mendigor the Mendacious had Hellspawn the goblin, Lothgar the Loathsome had Sworg Bloodpimple . . .'

'Quentin the Cake-Decorator had Mary the poodle,' Veronica muttered.

'Shut up, Veronica,' Randalf snapped. 'You'll have to excuse my familiar,' he explained to Henry. 'She's been getting a bit big for her boots recently.' He turned to Joe. 'I'm right, aren't I? You are Rough the Hairy's sidekick. His sword-carrier, perhaps? Or his axe-sharpener?'

'Not exactly,' said Joe, in a dazed sort of voice. 'And his name is Henry, not Rough. I was holding his lead when . . .'

'So you're his *lead*-bearer,' Randalf interrupted. 'Joe the lead-bearer. *Hmm.* Unusual, admittedly, but not totally unheard of.'

The budgie, who was wearing small yet sturdy lace-up boots, coughed. '*I've* never heard of it,' she said.

'Shut up, Veronica!' he said, and brushed the bird off the brim of his hat. 'We're forgetting our manners,' he went on, turning back to Henry. 'Let me introduce myself properly. I am Randalf the Wise, Muddle Earth's leading wizard.'

'Only wizard, more like,' said Veronica, settling on his shoulder.

'And this,' Randalf went on without missing a beat, 'is my assistant, Norbert – or Norbert the Not-Very-Big, to give him his full title.'

'Not very big!' Joe blurted out in astonishment. 'But he's gigantic.'

'Taller than you or me, I grant you,' said Randalf, 'yet for an ogre, Norbert is a small and rather weedy specimen.'

'You should see my father,' said Norbert, nodding. 'Now he *is* gigantic.'

'But back to the matter at hand,' said Randalf. 'I have summoned you here, Henry the Hairy, great warrior-hero, to . . .'

'Warrior-hero?' Joe interrupted, 'Henry's not a warrior-hero. He's my dog!'

Henry wagged his tail and rolled over with his legs in the air.

'What's he doing?' said Norbert, his three eyes open wide and panic in his voice.

'He wants you to tickle his tummy,' said Joe, shaking his head in disbelief. 'Any minute now, I'm going to wake up in hospital with a big bandage on my head.'

'Go ahead, Norbert, tickle his tummy,' said Randalf.

'But, sir,' said the ogre weakly.

'Tickle!' said Randalf. 'And that's an order!'

As Norbert bent down, the room gave a lurch. He gently stroked Henry's tummy with a massive finger.

'Go on, go on,' said Randalf impatiently. 'He won't bite.' He smiled at Joe. 'It seems there's been a slight misunderstanding,' he said, stroking his beard.

'There's always a misunderstanding with you,' chirped

the budgie.

'Shut up, Veronica. I was under the impression that Henry the Hairy was the warrior-hero I had ordered – strong, loyal and . . . errm . . . hairy. But if, as you say, he is in fact a dog, then *you* must be the warrior-hero . . .'

'He doesn't look very strong, or for that matter, very hairy,' said Veronica dismissively. 'If *he's* a warrior-hero, then *I'm* Dr Cuddles of Giggle Glade!'

'Veronica,' Randalf snapped, 'if I've told you once I've told you a thousand times *never* to utter that person's name in my presence!'

'Brings back memories, does it?' Veronica taunted, and flapped up into the air. Randalf tried to swat her.

'Ow, watch where you're flying,' Norbert shouted, taking a step back as the budgie booted him in the ear.

Joe clung on to the great hanging pot as the whole room seemed to tilt to one side.

'Button it, you great lunk!' Veronica shot back.

'You and whose army?' Norbert countered.

Joe watched in open-mouthed amazement as the wizard, the ogre and the budgie rounded on one another angrily. This was absolutely crazy. Who were they? Where was he? And most important of all, how was he going to get home?

'It's . . . it's been lovely meeting you all,' he shouted, interrupting the three shouting protagonists, 'but it's getting late and I've still got my homework to do. I really should be leaving now . . .'

The three of them stopped mid rant, carp and criticism, and turned to him.

'Late?' said Randalf.

'Leaving?' said Norbert.

Veronica jumped up and down on the wizard's head, feathers all fluffed up. '*You're* not going anywhere!' she squawked.

'O uch!' cried Joe, rubbing his arm.

'Again, sir?' asked the three-eyed ogre, bending over him.

'No, three times is quite enough,' said Joe ruefully.

There's nothing quite like an ogre pinching your arm to convince you that you're not in a dream, and Joe was now totally convinced that this was no dream. But if it wasn't, then where on earth was he? And how had he got there? Henry wagged his tail and licked the ogre's hand.

Before Joe had a chance to ask any questions, the clock on the wall above the fireplace erupted with insistent noise. There was coughing, the sound of a tiny throat being cleared and fists and boots battering on a small wooden door which suddenly sprang open. A little elf – dressed up in grubby looking underpants and with a length of elastic tied around its waist – jumped out and dived into mid-air.

'Five of the clock!' it screeched as it reached the end of the elastic, before rebounding and disappearing back inside the clock with a muffled crash.

'Five?' said Randalf wearily. 'But it's dark outside.'

The door sprang open a second time and the elf popped its head out. 'Or there-abouts,' it said, and disappeared again.

'Wretched clock's slow again,' Randalf grumbled. 'The mechanism probably needs cleaning.'

'I should say so,' said Veronica scathingly. 'Judging by the state of those underpants.'

'Shut up, Veronica!' said Randalf.

'"Shut up, Veronica!"' said Veronica. 'That's your answer to everything. Well, I won't shut up! Call yourself a wizard. You've only got one spell – and you can't even do that properly.' She flapped her wing at Joe. 'I mean, look at him,' she said. 'Is it just me or is our so-called warrior-hero a little on the short side? Not to men-tion puny – and gormless. And as for his hairy sidekick . . .'

'*Shush*, Veronica,' said Norbert, patting Henry on the head. 'You'll hurt his feelings.'

Henry wagged his tail.

'Ooh, look, his waggler's waving!' Norbert cried. 'Does he want his tummy tickled? Does he? Does he?'

He jumped up and down excitedly. The room lurched backwards and forwards alarmingly, and more books and utensils clattered to the floor.

'Norbert!' said Randalf, sternly. 'Behave yourself! Remember what happened with Mary the poodle. You don't want that to happen again, do you?'

Norbert stopped jumping, and shuffled to the corner of the room.

'Very nervous animals, poodles,' said Veronica, who was perched on Randalf's head. 'Ruined the carpet!'

'Shut up, Veronica!' shouted Randalf. 'That's all in the past. We have a new warrior-hero here and he'll be fine.' He clamped a hand on Joe's shoulder. 'Won't you, Joe? Just the job for the Horned Baron's purposes. Once he's kitted out . . .'

'Kitted out?' said Joe. 'What do you mean, kitted out? I don't want to be kitted out. I just want to know what's going on,' he added angrily.

'Temper, temper!' said Veronica.

'The fiery disposition of a warrior-hero,' said Randalf.

'Excellent!'

'What *are* you talking about?' Joe asked. 'I've got to get back for tea. And I've got this essay. I haven't even started yet . . .'

'Tea? Essay?' said Randalf smiling. 'Ah, yes. The mighty deeds of a warrior-hero – the great tournament of tea, the epic slaying of the monster essay! Of course you must get back for these tasks, but first, if you could just lend a hand with a tiny little task we have here . . .'

'I can't!' Joe insisted. 'I've got school tomorrow. I must get back. If you brought me here, you can send me back.'

'I wouldn't bank on it,' Veronica muttered.

'I don't think you appreciate the difficulty involved in summoning a warrior-hero from another world,' said Randalf solemnly. 'I mean heroes don't just grow on trees – well, apart from those in the Land of Hero-Trees that is. It's a long and painstaking process, I can tell you; by no means as easy as you seem to believe.'

'But—' Joe began.

'For a start, the three Muddle moons must be correctly aligned – and that doesn't happen often. If we'd missed this evening's triangular configuration, there's no knowing how long we'd have had to wait for the next one.'

'But—'

'Furthermore,' Randalf went on, 'because of a slight technical hitch with the actual spell—'

'What he means is, he's lost half of it,' said Veronica.

Randalf ignored her. 'You're only the second hero I've actually successfully summoned. The first one was Quentin—'

'The one with the poodle and the kilo of icing sugar,' Veronica butted in.

Joe became aware of a soft sniffing sound and looked up to see three big fat tears rolling down from Norbert's bloodshot eyes and over his lumpy cheeks. 'Poor, dear Quentin,' he sobbed.

'Cry baby!' Veronica mocked.

'Oh, but he never stood a chance!' Norbert wailed.

'That's enough, you two,' said Randalf.

'Sorry, sir,' said Norbert. He wiped his nose on the back of his sleeve, but kept sniffing.

'As I was saying,' said Randalf. 'First there was Quentin, and now I have summoned you . . .'

'But you had no right!' shouted Joe. 'I didn't ask to be summoned! I didn't ask to be pulled through a hedge, down a tunnel and into this, this . . . junk room!'

'Damn cheek,' came a muffled voice from the clock.

'I didn't ask to be kitted out by a stupid wizard! And insulted by a stupid budgie! And pinched by a stupid three-eyed ogre!' stormed Joe.

'Actually,' said Norbert. 'You did ask to be pinched. You said, "Pinch me. If this is a dream then . . ."'

'SHUT UP!' shouted Joe. 'SHUT UP!'

Norbert jumped back, his eyes wide with terror. 'Oh,

help!' he bellowed. 'Mayday! Mayday!' And he jumped up as high as the ceiling would allow, crashing back down on to the floor with both feet a moment later.

The room keeled to one side. Randalf fell, Veronica flapped up into the air, while Joe was catapulted across the room.

'*Aaaaaargh!*' he yelled as he hurtled past Randalf and Veronica and crashed into the wall opposite, missing the open window by a fraction. Dazed and winded, he slid to the floor. The room continued to roll back and forth, back and forth.

'Norbert, you bird brain!' shouted Randalf.

'How dare you!' screeched Veronica. 'Bird brain indeed!'

Randalf sighed as the room gradually righted itself. He turned to the ogre. 'Say "sorry", then,' he told him.

'I'm sorry, sir,' said Norbert miserably. 'Very, very sorry.'

'Not to me, Norbert,' said Randalf. Norbert frowned with confusion. 'To our guest here, our warrior-hero,' Randalf explained. 'To *Joe*,' he said, and pointed towards him.

'Joe!' Norbert cried out in horror. He saw him lying on the floor. 'Did I do that?' he said. 'Oh, I *am* sorry. So, so very sorry.' Tears welled up once again in his eyes. 'It's just that I panic when someone shouts at me. I have a very nervous disposition. In fact I was almost called Norbert the Wet-Trousers instead of Norbert the Not-Very-Big, because—'

'Yes, yes,' said Randalf. 'Pick him up, Norbert. Brush him down.'

'Yes, sir. At once, sir,' and he hurried back across the room.

Joe, by this time, was already climbing to his feet quite successfully on his own. As Norbert came lumbering towards him, the boat lurched again. Joe stumbled towards the open window.

'*What on earth?*' he exclaimed.

Randalf pushed past Norbert and placed his hand on Joe's shoulder. 'Not quite,' he said. 'Welcome to *Muddle* Earth.'

Joe stood stock-still as he stared out of the window. He was barely able to believe what his eyes were telling him. For a start, instead of the one familiar white moon in the sky, there were three: one purple, one yellow and one green. And the landscape! It was like nothing he'd ever seen before, with vast areas of fluorescent green forest and glistening rocky wasteland – and far in the distance, tall, smoking mountains.

Most curious of all, however, he realized that he wasn't underground at all, but rather in some kind of a boat. And there were others. Five . . . six others, all bobbing about on a lake which . . . But no, it made no sense. He closed his eyes, then opened them again.

There was no doubt about it. The lake was suspended high up in the air, without any means of visible support.

Joe turned to Randalf. 'The lake,' he gasped. 'It's . . . it's floating.'

'Of course it is,' said the wizard solemnly. 'The Enchanted Lake was raised up by the wizards of Muddle Earth many, many moons ago, and for a very good reason – only no one can remember what that was. Anyway, they raised it . . .'

Joe frowned. 'But, *how*?'

'By great magic,' said Randalf solemnly.

'And *that's* something you don't see round here much these days,' Veronica chipped in.

'Magic?' said Joe softly. He shook his head. 'But . . .'

'Don't you worry about it, young warrior-hero from afar,' said Randalf. 'You've got a lot to learn. Thankfully, I am an excellent teacher.'

'Yes, and I'm an exploding gas frog!' Veronica retorted.

'Shut up, Veronica!' said Randalf.

'There you go again,' said Veronica huffily, and turned her back on the proceedings.

'As I was saying,' Randalf continued. 'I shall teach you everything you need to know for the small task which lies ahead.' He smiled. 'Things are going to work out well this time, I can feel it in my bones. Joe, here, will see us proud.'

Veronica sniffed. 'I still don't think he looks like much of a warrior-hero,' she said.

'He soon will,' said Randalf. 'We'll set off for Goblintown just as soon as day breaks.'

Just then the elf sprang out of the clock. 'Half past twenty-six, and that's my final offer!' it shrieked.

'*Yip! Yip! Yip! Bibbitty-Bibbitty!*' came a shrill voice. 'This is your early morning wake-up call.' *Boing!*

Joe's eyes snapped open, just in time to see the elf disappearing back behind the little wooden doors of the clock.

Joe looked round, and groaned. Everything was exactly the way it had been when he'd curled up in his hammock the night before. The clock, the room full of junk, the floating lake ... What was more, it was still dark.

'What time do you call this?' Randalf demanded, emerging from the far end of the room.

The door of the clock flew open. 'Early morning!' snapped the elf. 'Or thereabouts.' The door slammed shut.

'What's going on?' squawked Veronica. 'I've only just tucked my beak under my wing.'

Norbert lumbered out of the shadows, yawning and stretching. 'Is it morning?' he said.

Randalf looked out of the window. There was a fuzzy

glimmer of light on the horizon. High in the sky the noisy purple batbirds were soaring back to the woods, to spend the day resting upside down at the top of the highest jub-jub trees. 'Almost,' he said.

'Stupid clock,' Veronica muttered.

'I heard that!' came an indignant voice from the clock.

'Never mind all that,' said Randalf. 'We're awake now, so we might as well make an early start. Come on, Joe. Stir your stumps. Today's your big day.' He turned to the three-eyed ogre. 'Norbert,' he said. 'Prepare breakfast.'

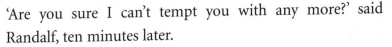

'Are you sure I can't tempt you with any more?' said Randalf, ten minutes later.

'No, thanks,' said Joe.

'You'll need to keep your strength up,' Randalf persisted.

'Such as it is,' added Veronica unkindly.

Joe looked at the ladle of slop hovering above his bowl. 'I'm really full,' he lied.

Without any doubt, Norbert had produced the strangest breakfast Joe had ever eaten in his life – lumpy, green porridge that tasted of gooseberries, a small cake iced with love-hearts and a mug of foaming stiltmouse milk.

'But you haven't touched your snuggle-muffin,' said Norbert, looking hurt.

'I'm saving it for later,' said Joe. 'It looks lovely, though.'

The ogre sighed. 'Dear Quentin taught me everything I know. He was an artistic genius with icing sugar.'

'Right, then,' said Randalf, clapping his hands together. He stood up and grabbed his staff. 'Let's get this show on the road.'

Relieved, Joe jumped up from the table, grabbed Henry by his lead and followed Randalf downstairs. Norbert stomped down after them.

'Eager to get started, eh, Joe?' said Randalf warmly. 'An excellent sign for a warrior-hero. We've summoned a good'un this time, Veronica.'

'You said that about Quentin,' the budgie was not slow in reminding him. 'And look how that turned out.'

'We must not look to the past,' said Randalf as he opened the door. 'But to the future.'

He stepped outside. Joe followed him, still none the wiser about what exactly was going on. He *seemed* to be on the lower deck of a houseboat, but it was difficult to know for certain.

Underneath the vessel, fat fish swam round and round in the crystal clear water. They reminded him of the goldfish at home and, for a moment, he thought that perhaps it wasn't so crazy here after all.

High above him, small fluffy purple clouds scudded across the sky. Below him – and attached to the side by a rope – was a small boat. At least that's what Joe thought at first. It was only as he stepped across from the rope ladder to the bobbing vessel that he realized it was not a boat at all, but a bathtub. Joe clapped his hand to his forehead.

'What was I expecting?' he said to himself. 'Of *course* it's not a boat. After all, this *is* Muddle Earth.'

The bathtub gave a wild lurch as Joe stepped into it. Henry jumped in beside him.

'Not there,' said Veronica. 'You sit at the other end where the taps are.'

'If you don't mind,' said Randalf, climbing in and sitting down. 'Just watch your head on the shower attachment if it gets a little bit . . . *errm* . . . choppy.'

'It *always* gets choppy with Norbert in charge,' said Veronica. 'You've sunk two boats, one wardrobe and an inflatable mattress. Now we're using our last bathtub. It'll be the kitchen sink next!'

'Shut up, Veronica!' said Randalf. 'Come on, Norbert. We're all waiting.'

The ogre climbed into the bathtub, which wobbled about dangerously on the water. Kneeling down, Norbert seized two objects from the bottom of the bath. One was an old tennis racquet, the other was a frying pan. He leaned forwards and began paddling furiously.

The bathtub reared up in a great swell of spray and froth, and sped across the surface of the lake. Norbert's arms were like pistons; up down, up down, up down they went. The edge of the lake came closer. Joe gasped.

'We're going to fall off!' he shouted.

'Trust me, I'm a wizard,' said Randalf. 'A little further left, Norbert,' he told the ogre. 'That's it.'

Joe looked up. He saw that they were heading for a waterfall.

'Hold on tight and watch out for that shower attachment,' the ogre smiled, and paddled faster than ever.

Closer and closer the waterfall came, louder and louder grew the sound of the raging torrent spilling over the edge.

'This is crazy!' Joe yelled.

'True,' said Randalf. 'But it's the only way down. Trust me, I'm a . . .'

'I know,' Joe muttered as he gripped the sides of the bathtub with white-knuckled ferocity, 'you're a wizard.'

'One last paddle should do it!' Randalf shouted.

Norbert obliged. For a moment, the bathtub see-sawed up and down at the very edge of the lake. Joe gasped as

Muddle Earth opened up before him in a broad, panoramic view.

'Brace yourselves!' came Randalf's voice above the raging cascade as the bathtub toppled over the edge. 'Here we go . . . *o-o-o-oh!*'

Veronica screeched. Henry howled. Joe screwed his eyes tightly shut. Only Norbert seemed to be enjoying himself.

'*Wheeeee!*' he cried as the little bathtub with its five occupants hurtled down the roaring, foaming torrent of water.

The wind whipped past so fast, Joe could barely breathe. Stinging water slapped his face. His head pounded, his heart was in his mouth, his grip was slipping . . .

SPLASH!

The bathtub struck the pool at the bottom of the waterfall with colossal force.

It sank.

It rose.

It bobbed around on the surface like a ball, until the current swept it down into the relative calm water of the river beyond. Joe opened his eyes.

'That was . . . terrifying,' he gasped.

Veronica snorted. 'You wait until the return journey,' she said.

'We've taken on water!' Randalf announced. 'Quick, Norbert, start bailing!'

Norbert looked down at the water swilling around the bottom of the bathtub. He picked up the frying pan, then paused. 'Don't worry, sir!' he said, reaching down into the water. 'I'll save us!'

'No, Norbert!' Randalf shouted. 'Remember last time!'

Too late. The ogre had already yanked out the plug and was holding it aloft.

'There,' he said. 'I've let the water out, sir!' He paused, and stared incredulously at the fountain of water gushing up from the plughole. 'Oops!' He looked up at Randalf. 'I've done it again, haven't I, sir?'

'I'm afraid so,' said Randalf.

'Abandon bathtub!' Norbert shouted.

With a gurgle and a plop, the bathtub abruptly disappeared beneath them. Joe kicked his legs, and headed for the nearest shore, with Henry doggy-paddling by his side. The pair of them dragged themselves up on to the bank. Veronica, who had decided to fly rather than swim, landed beside them, only to be soaked by a spray of water as Henry shook himself dry.

'Well, that's the last of the bathtubs,' she said. 'You'd think he'd have learned about plugs by now.'

Joe said nothing. The sight of the Enchanted Lake suspended in mid-air far, far above his head had left him speechless. As he watched, a fat silver fish dropped out of the bottom of the lake, fell down through the air and into the gaping beak of one of the waiting lazybirds clustered together beneath the lake.

Randalf and Norbert climbed out of the river, dripping with water. Norbert shook himself dry, drenching Veronica for a second time.

'Thank you very much!' she exclaimed indignantly. 'Now you're trying to drown me on dry land!'

'Sorry,' said Norbert meekly.

Randalf looked up at the sun, which was now peeking over

the distant mountains. 'No harm done. Quite refreshing in fact,' he said. 'Let's set off. With a brisk pace, we should arrive at Goblintown by midday.' He turned to the ogre. 'If you'd do the honours, Norbert, my good fellow.'

'Yes, sir,' said Norbert. He crouched down on his hands and knees.

With the budgie perched on his head, Randalf climbed on to one of the ogre's great, broad shoulders. He looked at Joe. 'Well, come on. We haven't got all day,' he said.

Joe climbed gingerly on to the other shoulder. 'Won't we be too heavy?' he said.

'Of course not,' said Norbert. 'I'm a two-seater. Now, my cousin Ethelbertha is a four-seater with an extra box-seat at the front and back . . .'

'Yes, yes,' said Randalf. 'If you're quite ready, Norbert.'

Norbert straightened up and climbed to his feet.

'Forwards!' ordered Randalf, and tapped the ogre on the head with his staff. Norbert lurched into movement and strode off, with Henry trotting along by his side.

On her lofty perch, Veronica tucked her head beneath her wing. 'I always get ogre-sick on long journeys,' she said weakly.

They were following a track which ran parallel to the Enchanted River. It was clearly seldom used, and had become totally overgrown. Tall jub-jub trees lined both sides of the path, their bendy branches heavy with sleeping batbirds. Norbert brushed past them.

'Ouch! Ouch! Ouch!' they cried.

Joe couldn't believe he was riding to Goblintown on an ogre's shoulders. About now, he should have been handing in his essay. He ducked to avoid a jub-jub branch and, with a thud, a batbird landed in his lap. Of all the excuses for late homework, 'Sorry, sir, I was too busy riding ogres and dodging batbirds,' had to be the weirdest. How on earth *would* he explain this to his teacher?

'It'll be easier once we hit the road,' said Randalf brightly. 'Not far now.'

'Liar,' muttered Veronica queasily.

By the time they did finally reach the road – or rather *roads*, since they had arrived at a three-way junction – Joe was feeling a little ogre-sick himself. Norbert had stopped at a signpost which stood by the side of the road.

To their right, according to the peeling gold lettering, was *Trollbridge (not very far)*. To their left was *Musty Mountains (quite a long way)* Joe craned his neck to check whether Goblintown was also marked. It was.

'Charming!' said Joe.

'Come on, then,' said Randalf, tapping Norbert on the head. 'Let's get going.'

Norbert shuffled about awkwardly. 'Which way, exactly, sir?' he said.

'To Goblintown, of course,' said Randalf impatiently.

'I know *that*, sir,' said Norbert, staring at the signpost with a perplexed frown. 'But . . .'

'Norbert,' said Randalf, 'when I took you on as an official Wizard Carrier, you assured me you could read.'

'Believe that, you'll believe anything,' said Veronica.

'I *can*!' said Norbert. 'Little words, anyway.' He nodded at the signpost. 'These are all so long.'

Randalf breathed in sharply. '*This way*, Norbert,' he said. '*A very long way away, so stop looking at this sign and get a move on, stupid*,' he read.

'Who are you calling stupid?' Norbert muttered in a hurt voice as he set off. 'My cousin Ogred the Dribbler,' he said, his pace increasing, 'now he *was* stupid. Did I ever tell you about the time he got his head stuck in a . . .'

'Snuggle-muffin,' Randalf mumbled drowsily, his head suddenly lolling on his shoulders.

'Typical,' said Veronica. 'Sleeping like a baby again!'

'Sir always falls asleep when he's travelling,' said Norbert. 'And usually right in the middle of my best stories.'

'Can't imagine why,' said Veronica testily.

'Well, it must be tiring being a wizard,' said Norbert, 'what with all that reading and spells and stuff.'

'I suppose so,' said Joe with a shrug.

'Oh, Randalf isn't a *real* wizard,' Veronica whispered into Joe's ear.

From up on Norbert's shoulders there came the sound of soft snoring.

'He isn't?' said Joe. 'But I thought . . .'

'Until the wizards – the proper wizards, the *Grand Wizards* – all disappeared, Randalf was just a lowly apprentice to Wizard Roger the Wrinkled,' Veronica explained in a hushed voice. 'It was only when they all went missing that Randalf started to pretend *he* was a Grand Wizard. He seems to have fooled the Horned Baron, but no one else is taken in. That's why he's so hard up. I mean, who wants to pay for the services of someone so useless?'

'Useless?' said Joe.

'Utterly useless!' said Veronica. 'Oh, the stories I could tell. The invisible ink that kept reappearing. The flying bicycle that fell to bits in mid-air. And all those poor goblins who ended up bald as an egg after trying his magic memory-cream. Not to mention Dr Cuddles.'

'Dr Cuddles?' said Joe. '*Who* is Dr Cuddles?'

'Only the baddest, meanest, most evil villain there ever

was!' Veronica told him. 'He won't rest until he's the ruler of Muddle Earth, with everyone under his thumb. Randalf is in a right mess. He needs help.'

'And he's expecting me, as a warrior-hero, to sort all this out?'

'Good heavens, no,' Veronica replied. 'You're just here to earn Randalf some money, though if I were you—'

At that moment, a loud clattering, banging noise echoed through the air, cutting Veronica off in mid-sentence. Joe looked up to see a flock of cupboards, their doors beating like wings, flying across the sky. 'What are *they*?' he gasped.

'They look like cupboards to me,' said Norbert.

'Do cupboards *normally* fly in Muddle Earth?' Joe asked, bewildered. He stopped and, with his hand shielding his eyes from the dazzling sun, peered into the distance. 'They're flying in formation – and they seem to be coming from that forest.'

'Elfwood,' said Veronica, nodding. 'That doesn't surprise me. There have been a lot of strange goings-on in Elfwood recently,' she added darkly. 'If you ask me, it's all to do with Doc—'

'*Aaargh!*' shouted Norbert as, still looking skywards, he failed to notice a large pothole in the road. He tripped, stumbled and crashed to the ground. Veronica flapped squawking into the air. Joe landed in a heap beside Henry. Randalf rolled over in the dust.

'My lovely snuggle-muffin,' he murmured. 'I . . .' His eyes snapped open. He found himself sprawling on the ground. 'What's *happening*?'

'Please, sir. Sorry, sir,' said Norbert apologetically as he climbed to his feet. 'I tripped in that pothole.'

He pointed at a round hole in the road containing an upturned cooking pot and a mess of smelly porridge.

'Ruined!' said a small elf by the side of the road. 'Why don't you watch where you're going, you big oaf!'

'And why don't you watch where you're cooking!' squawked Veronica.

'What better place for a pot than a pothole!' the elf countered indignantly.

'Calm down everybody,' said Randalf, tucking his staff back under his arm. 'There's no harm done.'

The elf shrugged and, picking up the pot, strode off down the road. 'Wizards!' it snorted in a contemptuous voice.

The ogre leaned forwards, pulled Randalf up and began dusting him down vigorously.

'Easy, Norbert,' said Randalf. 'I don't know –

soaked, dropped and now pummelled. This isn't what I'd call first-class travel.'

'No, sir. Sorry, sir,' said Norbert.

Randalf looked ahead. He called Joe to his side, and pointed. 'Over there,' he said. 'Just beyond that hill, you can see the spires of Goblintown peeking up. We are almost at our destination. You will be soon kitted out with the finest warrior-hero costume that money can buy.'

'Or rather, that you can *afford*,' Veronica muttered under her breath.

As they approached the high wall that surrounded Goblintown, Norbert placed Randalf and Joe gently down on the ground. The noise from inside became louder and louder. There was shouting, hammering, wailing, whinnying, sawing, singing, ringing, bellowing, buzzing . . . all mixed up together in one tumultuous roar. And the smells!

Burnt tar, sour milk, wet fur, rotting meat – each one fighting to be noticed above the nose-wrinkling odour of unwashed goblins. Joe tried thinking of nice smells – chocolate, biscuits, strawberry ice cream . . .

'And I thought your socks were bad!' Veronica commented.

'Shut up, Veronica,' said Randalf. 'We don't want to hurt their feelings. Goblins can be very touchy.'

'*Humph!*' said Veronica. 'So far as I'm concerned, no one that smelly has the right to be touchy!'

'That's as may be,' said Randalf. 'Just remember, we're here on important business. So, button your beak!'

'Pardon me for breathing,' said Veronica huffily.

'By the way, my fine young friend,' Randalf added. 'I think Henry here is finding this pungent metropolis a little too exciting. Perhaps you'd better put your faithful battle-hound on the lead.'

Sure enough, Henry's tail was wagging excitedly as his wet nose sniffed eagerly at the air. Joe clipped the lead into place.

They were now at the top of a tall flight of stairs before a set of huge wooden doors. Randalf seized the great knocker and hammered firmly against the wood.

Ding-dong!

Randalf turned to Joe. 'The goblins will have their little joke,' he said.

'Yeah,' Veronica chirped up. 'Like not letting us in.'

'Patience, Veronica!' said Randalf sharply. He looked at the door expectantly. Nothing happened. Randalf shuffled about, scratched his head, stroked his beard, rubbed his eyes. 'That famous goblin welcome,' he said at last. 'It's renowned throughout Muddle Earth.'

He knocked again, louder this time. *Ding-dong! Ding-dong! Ding-dong!*

The door flew open.

'I heard you the first time!' shouted a small, grubby, cross-eyed individual with gappy teeth and pointy ears.

'I'm not deaf!'

'A thousand, nay a million apologies, my goblin friend,' said Randalf, bowing low. 'Far be it for me to bring your hearing faculties into doubt. I merely . . .'

'What do you want?' the goblin scowled.

Randalf forced himself to smile. 'We wish to avail ourselves of your finest outfitting-emporium,' he said, 'with the express intention of purchasing your most—'

'You what?' the goblin said.

'We need to buy a warrior-hero outfit for the boy,' said Veronica, flapping her wing towards Joe.

'Leave this to me, V—' Randalf started to say. He was interrupted by the goblin.

'Well, why didn't you say so in the first place?' he snapped, opening the door for them all to enter.

'Shut that door!' shouted a voice. 'There's a terrible draught.'

'Take a deep breath everyone,' Randalf whispered over his shoulder.

'Come in, come in,' said the goblin impatiently. He slammed the door shut behind them. 'Welcome to Goblintown,' he intoned in a bored voice. 'The city that never sleeps.'

'Or washes,' muttered Veronica.

'Enjoy its many sights and sounds . . .'

'And smells,' said Veronica.

'And unique atmosphere.'

'You can say that again!'

'Veronica, I warned you!' Randalf hissed. 'Will you *shut* up!'

'Have a nice day,' the goblin concluded, and yawned.

Joe screwed up his nose. 'Veronica's got a point, though,' he whispered. 'It really does stink here!'

'You'll soon get used to it,' Randalf told him. He turned to the goblin. 'Thank you, my good fellow. I'd just like to say what an honour, not to say, pleasure it is to . . .'

'Whatever,' said the goblin, and walked away.

Joe looked about him. Apart from the smell, Goblintown was amazing. Buildings had been built on other buildings, storey by storey, reaching up higher and higher. Teeming with life, the tall structures lined the maze of narrow alleyways on both sides. Joe looked up nervously as the great towering constructions swayed precariously back and forth. They looked for all the world as if they might topple over at any moment. What was more, since the buildings *were* so high, almost no sunlight penetrated to the alleys at the bottom.

Not that it was completely dark. Oil lamps hung from every building, bathing the bustling streets in a sickly, yellow light and filling the air with greasy smoke. The rank, burning fat joined the other disgusting smells of Goblintown: the foul odour of baking snotbread, the stale pong of unwashed bodies and the stench bubbling up from the drains.

'Follow me!' said Randalf. He pulled a baggy yellow item of clothing from his robes and raised it up high on the end of his staff.

'Are they what I think they are?' said Veronica.

'You never know when a pair of ogre's underpants will come in useful,' said Randalf, striding off. 'Keep your eyes on the pants everybody, and you won't get lost.'

Norbert sighed. 'I wondered where they'd got to,' he said.

'Now, Joe, pay attention,' said Randalf, 'You really must see the sights of Goblintown. On our right,' he announced, 'we have a typical goblin apartment. On our left, the Museum of Moderate Achievements – while that,' he said, pointing up ahead to a particularly rundown building, 'is the Temple of the Great Verucca.'

'The Temple of the Great *Verucca*?' said Joe incredulously.

Randalf nodded. 'It is the site where Wilfred the Swimmer, that ancient goblin explorer, laid the first stone of what was to become Goblintown. Legend has it that he had been looking for a suitable place to build for seven long years when the pain from his great verucca finally forced him to abandon his search. He decided it was a sign. The rest, as they say, is history.'

'Spare us the guided tour!' squawked Veronica, fluttering overhead.

This way and that they tramped. Randalf was in the lead, with the yellow underpants held high, followed by

Norbert, Henry – sniffing every street corner and straining at his lead – and finally, Joe. Goblins thronged the streets, shoving and jostling, arguing, shouting – and completely ignoring the strangers in their midst.

'Which is why,' Randalf concluded, pausing to let the others catch up, 'we call Goblintown the Friendly City. It— *Ooof!*'

One goblin barged into Randalf. Another grabbed the underpants from the end of the staff and raced away through the crowd.

'My word!' shouted Randalf.

'My pants!' cried Norbert.

'Forget them,' said Veronica. 'We're here.'

As one, they all turned – and there, behind the windows of a particularly tall and ramshackle building, was a selection of shop-dummies, all dressed up in ornate warrior-hero costumes. Norbert stared at the gold letters on the sign swinging back and forth above the door.

'*Unc . . . Unc . . . Unc . . .*' he said.

'*Unction's Upmarket Outfitters,*' Randalf read for him. 'Well spotted, Veronica. Come on then, Joe. Let's get you kitted out.'

To Joe's surprise, they did not stay long in *Unction's Upmarket Outfitters.* Randalf led them up the aisle of the magnificent store – ignoring the tuts and sighs of the smartly dressed assistants as he went – to the very back. There, they climbed a broad curving staircase.

They emerged, not on the second floor of the outfitter's as Joe had expected, but in a different shop altogether. A brightly painted sign on the wall announced it as *Mingletrips Middle-of-the-Road Emporium*. The assistants, all of whom wore slightly plainer outfits, watched them suspiciously.

'I was looking for . . .' Randalf began.

'Yes?' said one of the assistants, his left eyebrow arched high.

'For the way up,' said Randalf.

The assistant nodded towards the far window. Joe frowned, puzzled. What were they meant to do there? Randalf, however, seemed unfazed.

'Ah, yes,' he said, and set off. The others followed him again.

Across the shop floor they went, out of the window and up a rusting circular staircase bolted to the outside wall.

They were greeted at the top with a third sign: *Drool's Downmarket Depot*.

'Keep up, we're nearly there,' said Randalf bossily. He began climbing an old wooden ladder propped up against the wall. 'And mind the eighth rung,' he called down. 'It wobbles a bi—'

'*Aaargh!*' Norbert cried out as the rung beneath his feet

splintered and fell. He clung on tightly to the sides of the ladder, too frightened to continue.

'On second thoughts, perhaps it would be better if you went back and waited for us there,' said Randalf. 'And look after Joe's battle-hound,' he added.

Joe watched the quivering ogre slowly lowering himself back to the balcony. Then, somewhat relieved that he wouldn't have to carry Henry up the rickety ladder, he passed Norbert the lead.

'Be good, now,' he told the dog. 'All right?'

'All right,' Norbert replied meekly.

Taking extra care at the missing eighth rung, Joe scampered up the ladder. As he neared the top, he glanced down – and gasped.

Far, far below him, he could see the crowds of goblins streaming this way and that along the narrow alleys. Veronica fluttered down and hovered near his left shoulder.

'Come on,' she said encouragingly. 'Mustn't keep our know-it-all guide waiting.'

With his heart in his mouth, Joe completed the last few steps of the ladder. Randalf was there to meet him.

'Well done, lad,' he said. 'And welcome to the finest outfitter's in all of Muddle Earth.'

'The cheapest, more like,' muttered Veronica.

There was a faded banner above the door. '*Grubley's Discount Garment Store*,' Joe read out – unable to keep the disappointment from his voice.

Just then, a gangly goblin with a large nose and filthy frilly apron appeared from behind them. 'Welcome,' he said.

'Thank you, *errm* . . . Stink,' said Randalf, addressing the goblin by the name on his lapel.

'Actually, it's Smink,' the goblin replied.

'But—'

'Mr Grubley's handwriting,' the assistant said wearily. 'It's almost as dreadful as his dress sense.'

'Yes, where *is* old Grubbers?' said Randalf, looking round.

Smink shrugged. 'He said he had *business to attend to.*' He winced as if smelling something unpleasant.

'Did he now?' said Randalf. He turned to the others, smiling. 'I think everything is going to work out even better than I expected,' he whispered.

Smink had turned away and opened the door from the balcony into the store. Ducking down, he went in. Randalf did the same.

'Just as well Norbert did stay behind,' Joe muttered to himself as he stooped low. 'He'd never have got through this doorway.'

He straightened up to find himself in a room so messy, dark and grubby, it made the wizard's houseboat seem like a showroom.

There were boxes and bundles, bursting with materials, piled up against the walls, next to stacked shelving, stuffed with every conceivable type of boot and shoe. Huge, circular racks – some, three tiers high – creaked under the weight of countless garments, all sorted into different categories. Jackets and jerkins. Capes, cloaks and coats. Leggings and breeches. Jodhpurs and knickerbockers. Bodices, bustles and bibs. While high overhead, still more – in differing colours, sizes and styles – were suspended from large ceiling hooks.

'Oh, yes, sir, I can see the problem,' said Smink, fingering Randalf's cloak with obvious distaste. 'This one's totally threadbare. Shoddy workmanship, completely out of fashion and a hideous colour, if you don't mind my saying so.' He looked up. 'Wizard's cloaks are over here,' he said. 'Walk this way,' and he bustled through the shop with tiny, pigeon-toed steps.

'I couldn't walk that way if you paid me,' Veronica commented.

Smink turned. 'I'm sorry, did sir say something?' he asked.

'Actually, it's the lad we're here for today,' said Randalf. 'He needs kitting out as a warrior-hero. The full works.'

'I see,' said Smink, looking Joe up and down and giving a sniff. 'That would be *battledress*, sir, which is right this way.'

As they all trooped across the floor to the far end of the room, pushing their way through the hanging mounds of garments, Joe felt the whole building swaying gently backwards and forwards. A pair of metal gauntlets fell to the ground with an ominous clatter.

'Well, they'll do for a start,' said Randalf. 'Next, a cloak.'

'The full works, you say, sir,' said Smink. 'Might I recommend the leather Cloak of Impermeability. Fashioned by magic, it will deflect the blow of the mightiest sword.'

'Excellent,' said Randalf. 'Try it on, Joe.' Joe did so and inspected himself in a standing-mirror at the back of the shop. Randalf turned to Smink. 'And headgear?'

'We have everything,' said Smink with a wide sweep of his arm. 'Helmets – horned, winged, spiked or plumed; bonnets – war, jousting and . . . Ah, yes! A skull-faced shriek cap with matching ear pompoms – a bit of a speciality item, that one, sir.'

'I was thinking more of a standard sort of helmet,' said Randalf.

'Of course, of course,' said Smink rubbing his hands together. 'Silly of me. What about this Helmet of Heroism. Very popular, sir. Very hard-wearing feathers.'

He removed a heavy bronze helmet with five purple

plumes, and placed it on Joe's head. It fitted him like a glove.

'Sir will notice the tiny speakers concealed in the ear-rim. They play invigorating marching music as the warrior-hero strides boldly into battle.'

'Just the job,' said Randalf eagerly.

'And there are other matching accessories,' said Smink. 'The Shield of Chivalry, the Breastplate of . . . of . . . of Bravery and Perseverance, the Gaiters of Gallantry – to go with the gauntlets you have already so wisely chosen. And last, but not least, the Sword of Superiority,' he announced as he handed the final item to Joe.

'The Sword of Superiority,' said Randalf, sounding impressed. 'I'll take it. I'll take the whole lot,' he said.

'An excellent choice, if I might say so,' said Smink.

Joe looked at himself in the long mirror, and raised the sword high in the air. It looked quite convincing. He grinned. 'Not bad,' he thought. 'Not bad at all.'

'Sir looks fabulous, if I might be so bold,' said Smink. 'And not only that. These items all come with the Grubley Heroic Quest Success Guarantee – or your money back.' He returned his attention to Randalf and smiled an oily smile. 'Which brings us to the delicate matter of payment.'

'Ah, yes,' said Randalf. 'Payment.' He smiled back

confidently. 'Old Grubbers knows how good my credit is,' he said. 'He told me to stick it all on the slate.'

'He most certainly did not,' came a gruff voice behind him. '*Never ask for credit, 'cause a refusal sometimes offends,*' it continued, getting louder with every word. 'So what cheeky so-'n'-so is pretending I did?'

A stocky, bandy-legged individual with hairy ears and one thick, dark eyebrow, burst out of a rack of petticoats and pantaloons. 'You!' he said, fixing Randalf with a penetrating glare. 'I might have known!'

'Grubbers!' Randalf exclaimed, and went to shake hands.

'It's Mister Grubley to you, *Randy,*' he said, striding past the wizard's outstretched hand and tapping Joe on the shoulder. 'You can get that lot off for a start.'

Reluctantly, Joe removed the armour. Grubley turned to Randalf. 'Let me see. You still owe me for the last one. Quentin the Golden, wasn't it? One sparkly cloak, a pair of patent-leather bootees and the golden swan helmet with pink fur lining. It's cash or nothing from now on! Let's see what you've got.'

Hiding his irritation, Randalf reached into his cape pocket and pulled out a small leather pouch. He opened the top and poured a collection of coins into his palm. 'Eight muckles, five groats and a silver pipsqueak,' he said.

Grubley seized the tiny silver coin and bit into it. 'Hmm,' he said. 'Seems like we *can* do business after all.'

'The bargain-basement's upstairs,' he said, pointing to a rope ladder which led up to a hole in the ceiling.

Perched precariously on the roof of the discount store, the so-called basement was like a huge box on stilts. It was cold and draughty, and swayed alarmingly as the wind howled round its flimsy walls. Like the store they had just left, however, it was crammed full of items of clothing.

'That's the trouble with you wizards,' Grubley was saying. 'You come in here demanding my best stuff for your so-called warrior-heroes and then they go out and ruin it all by getting squashed by an ogre. I mean, this is quality merchandise.'

Veronica snorted dismissively.

'What does he mean, "squashed"?' said Joe nervously.

'Goblins will have their little jokes,' whispered Randalf.

'Here.' Grubley pulled out a cloak made of sacking and decorated with a fake-fur trim, and handed it to Joe.

'Love the fur,' said Veronica sarcastically. 'It's really fetching.'

'And is it protected perhaps by the power of imperme-ability?' asked Randalf. 'Or the hex of deflection?'

'Not exactly,' said Grubley. 'Though I daresay it would make a wound sting a bit less. Probably.'

'We'll take it,' said Randalf.

Other items followed. The Woolly Gloves of Determination. The Cardigan of Optimism. The Wellies of Power. Joe tried them all on. It was when they came to the helmet that he finally spoke up.

'I'm not wearing *that*,' he said.

'Not wear the War-bonnet of . . . umm . . . Sarcasm?' said Randalf. He took Joe's arm. 'Notice how the helmet's round shape has been made to deflect blows from cudgels, truncheons, swords – and how here, at the front, an extra safety-feature has been attached. What's more, not only will the War-bonnet of Sarcasm protect your head, but it will also give the wearer the heroic ability to make rude comments about their opponents' dress sense and physical appearance.' Randalf took the helmet and placed it on Joe's head. 'Both in its workmanship and design,' he announced, 'it's a triumph!'

'It's a saucepan,' said Joe flatly.

'How astute you are,' Randalf said brightly. 'Indeed the helmet can also double as a cooking utensil – for those long expeditions, far away from home . . .'

'But . . .' Joe protested.

'Trust me, Joe,' Randalf interrupted. 'I know you are valiant and brave, but I could not in all conscience allow any warrior-hero to set forth on a quest without an enchanted helmet of such unique power.' He turned to Grubley. 'We'll take it,' he said. 'We'll take the lot.'

Grubley nodded, and began totting up the cost of the armour under his breath.

Randalf glanced through the window at the sun. 'It's getting late,' he said. 'We'll have to get our skates on.'

'Skates?' said Veronica. 'Don't you think the lad looks ridiculous enough as it is?'

'Shut up, Veronica,' said Randalf. He turned to Grubley. 'So, what do I owe you?' he said.

Grubley looked up. 'Eight muckles, five groats and a silver pipsqueak, exactly,' he said.

Reunited at the bottom of the rickety ladder once more, Randalf, Veronica, Norbert, Henry and Joe made their way back down through the succession of clothiers and outfitters to the bottom of the tall, creaking building.

On every new level he came to, Joe found himself glancing into the mirrors – and each time he groaned. Dressed in the sacking cloak, the woolly gloves, the saucepan and armed with a dustbin-lid and a toasting fork, he looked a complete idiot.

As they emerged from the front entrance on to the street, several goblins stopped, turned, pointed and sniggered. Joe tugged at Randalf's sleeve.

'You've turned me into a laughing-stock!' he whispered in embarrassment.

'You can say that again,' Veronica laughed.

'Nonsense,' said Randalf. 'You look magnificent, Joe.

Doesn't he, Norbert?'

Norbert nodded. 'I love the fur trim,' he said. 'And those silver buckles on his wellies are so sparkly!'

'He looks even worse than Quentin the Cake-Decorator,' said Veronica. 'And that's something I never thought I'd find myself saying. I mean, a toasting fork!'

Randalf looked up angrily. 'Toasting fork?' he exclaimed. 'Why you foolish bird. The Trident of Trickery is one of the finest weapons a warrior-hero could possess.'

'Oh, yeah!' said Veronica.

'It is!' Randalf insisted. 'How else could he launch a three-pronged attack on his enemy, eh? You tell me that.'

Veronica rolled her eyes.

'Trust me, Joe,' said Randalf. 'You are the best warrior-hero I have ever summoned to Muddle Earth.'

'Which isn't saying much,' Veronica commented.

Norbert wiped a tear from his eye as he remembered the *other* warrior-hero Randalf had summoned.

'I have absolute confidence in you,' Randalf continued. 'And so will the Horned Baron, I'm sure.'

'But what does a warrior-hero actually have to *do* in Muddle Earth?' Joe asked.

For once, not even Veronica had an answer.

By the time they arrived back at the gates of Goblintown, it was already early evening. The cross-eyed guard stood up from his stool.

'Did you find the . . .' He noticed Joe and snorted with amusement. 'Ah, yes,' he said. 'I see you did.'

Back on board the ogre after a fitful night's sleep beneath the stars, Randalf instructed Norbert which way to go to get to the Horned Baron's castle. Turning right out of Goblintown, they followed a road which crossed a broad featureless plain towards the foothills of a vast mountain range. As they did so, the conversation turned to Joe's name.

'I mean, Joe isn't a *bad* name,' Randalf was saying doubtfully, 'but perhaps we should go for something a little more forceful, noble, impressive. In short, a more warrior-like name.'

'How about Joe the Terrible Toaster?' Veronica proposed. 'Or Josephine the Awfully Annoyed? Or what about Jo-Jo the Extremely Sarcastic . . . ?'

'Shut up, Veronica!' Randalf shouted. He turned to Joe. 'What about Joe the Barbarian? Short and to the point – and with just a hint of mystery. After all, with your Helmet of Sarcasm, Shield of Slight Protection and Trident of Trickery, you're a force to be reckoned with and no mistake.

There isn't a dragon, ogre or whifflepook that wouldn't think very seriously before picking a fight.'

Joe stopped in his tracks. 'Dragon? Ogre?' he said. 'Are you seriously suggesting I should do battle with dragons and ogres?'

'And whifflepooks,' Norbert reminded him. 'Vicious, scaly little beasts, they are,' he said, looking round nervously.

'You're a warrior-hero, a barbarian, Joe,' said Randalf cheerfully. 'Savage blood courses through your veins. A stranger from a strange land, eager for adventure and utterly fearless!'

'Yes, well . . .' Joe began, but a disgusting smell assailed his nostrils before he could finish. '*Pfwooar!* What is that horrible pong?'

Norbert pinched his nose closed. 'De Busty Bountains,' he said.

'And mustier than ever,' said Veronica. 'Perhaps you should also have invested in a Clothes Peg of Destiny,' she said to Randalf. 'Our warrior-hero is looking a bit green.'

It was true. Joe was feeling decidedly ill. Although not as pungent as Goblintown, the warm, stale odour drifting in on the breeze from the Musty Mountains was quite disgusting – a stomach-churning mixture of mildew, mouse droppings and mothballs. As they rounded the corner, the mountains loomed up ahead of them. They were tall, jagged, forbidding and very, very musty.

'They stink!' Joe gasped.

'The Musty Mountains are extremely old, Joe,' said Randalf sharply. 'I daresay one day *you'll* be old and smelly yourself.'

'But—' Joe began.

'And how will *you* like it when everyone who passes you by tells you that you stink? Eh?'

Joe shook his head. Sometimes in Muddle Earth, there was simply no point arguing.

'Anyway, Joe,' Norbert added. 'Don't worry. You'll soon get used to it.'

On and on they went. Mile after mile. With Randalf and Veronica on one shoulder, Joe on the other and Henry trotting along by his side, Norbert strode unwaveringly onwards.

After several hours of going in a straight line, the road was becoming increasingly full of bends. It snaked its way through the valleys between the tall, jagged mountains. To Joe's surprise, Norbert was right; he did get used to the unpleasant smell. Or rather, what with everything else about him, he forgot all about it.

There were hairy squeak-moths that fluttered off as they approached, squeaking loudly. There were flightless scruff-birds which flapped about on the ground, chattering indignantly. There were odd thuds and spooky whooshing noises as rocks fell and the wind blew, and far in the distance Joe thought he heard an odd tinkly-tinkly sound.

When they came to a fork in the road, Norbert

stopped. 'Which way, sir?' he said.

Randalf, who had dropped off for a few minutes, opened his eyes and looked round.

'The Horned Baron's castle, sir,' said Norbert. 'Should I turn right or left?'

'Left,' said Randalf.

'Where does the other road lead to?' asked Joe.

'Nowhere,' said Randalf. He tapped the ogre softly on the head with his staff. 'Proceed, Norbert,' he said.

Further on, as they rounded a sharp corner, Joe stared in awe at a chimney-stack-shaped mountain that loomed into view. Tall and imposing, it towered high above all the other mountains. From the crater at its top came little wisps of smoke which coiled up into the musty air and disappeared.

'What's that?' he asked.

The mountain let out a gentle, rumbling *boom* and a wispy smoke ring. Randalf, who had dozed off once more, grunted in his sleep.

'It's called Mount Boom,' said Veronica.

''Cause that's what it does,' added Norbert helpfully. 'It goes boom!'

Boom.

The feeble noise sounded again. It was accompanied by a second smoke ring. The musty smell grew slightly mustier. This time, Randalf's eyes opened.

'Did I hear something?' he said.

'It was Mount Boom, sir,' said Norbert. 'Booming.'

'Excellent,' said Randalf. He rubbed his eyes. 'Then we are nearly there. The Horned Baron's castle should be just around the next corner. Charming location . . .'

'Apart from the smell,' added Veronica.

The road curved round to the left. Randalf pointed down through the musty, dusty air to a series of tall spires and turrets which peeked up above the line of jagged mountain-tops. 'There it is,' he announced. 'The castle of the Horned Baron.'

Norbert shuddered. 'The place gives me the creeps,' he said. 'It always has.'

'And as for the Horned Baron himself,' added Veronica. 'He can be so . . .'

Just then, the budgie's voice was drowned out by a loud rumbling sound which came from Elfwood. Joe turned to look. The tinkly-tinkly sound grew louder. The next moment, something curious emerged from the distant trees in a flurry of thick dust and sped towards them.

'Stampede!' Veronica squawked. 'Cattle stampede!'

At least that was what Joe *thought* she said. He squinted into the distance. 'Cattle?' he said. 'Are you sure?'

'Not *cattle*, cloth-ears,' said Veronica. '*Cutlery!*'

'Take cover!' Randalf cried as the stampede drew close.

Joe ducked down behind a rock and watched in amazement as the great herd of kitchen utensils pounded past. Knives, forks and spoons, ladles and tongs, scissors

and skewers, peelers, sharpeners, crushers and mashers –
all hurtling on in a wild and frenetic dash towards the
Musty Mountains.

'There's definitely something afoot in Elfwood,' said
Veronica darkly. 'Some strange, potent magic is brewing,
you mark my words. And you know who's at the bottom of
it. Doctor Cuddles . . .'

'Shut *up*, Veronica!' Randalf shouted crossly. 'How
many more times must I tell you? That name is not to be
mentioned in my presence under any circumstances.'

Joe frowned and turned to Veronica. 'But you said—'

'Shut up, Joe!' Veronica hissed. She turned back to
Randalf. 'Don't you think we ought to get going?' she
asked him.

'Quite so,' said Randalf. He cautiously stood up and
looked round. The cutlery had gone. 'Come on, then,' he
said. 'It's safe to proceed.'

Inside the Horned Baron's castle at last, Randalf (with Veronica back on his head) led Norbert, Joe and Henry up a wide and winding staircase to the first floor. Randalf stopped at an imposing oak door.

'Wait here,' he instructed Joe, his voice echoing round the high vaulted ceiling. 'I'll introduce you to the baron when the moment is right. Timing is everything. Trust me, I'm a wizard.'

He turned and knocked.

'Enter!' came a loud, booming voice.

Randalf opened the door and went in. 'My Lord Horned Baron,' he said, and bowed low. Veronica hopped down on to his shoulder. Norbert curtsied. 'And how good it is to see his Lordship looking so well.'

A short, fussily dressed little man stopped his pacing and turned to Randalf. 'Oh, it's you again,' he said.

'Indeed it is,' said Randalf cheerfully.

The Horned Baron scowled. 'You're late!' he snapped. 'I sent for a wizard last Tuesday.'

'A thousand apologies for that, my Lord,' said Randalf, 'but you know how it is. One spell leads to another, and before you know it . . .'

'Indeed I do *not* know "how it is",' said the Horned Baron, his voice just a little too shrill and high-pitched. 'When I summon a wizard to the castle I expect him to drop whatever he's doing and come at once. Is that understood?'

'Absolutely, my Lord . . . Yes, my Lord . . . Sorry, my Lord . . .' Randalf babbled. 'I've been so busy. What with all the other wizards going . . . *umm* . . . on holiday . . .'

'Yes, well, I suppose you'll have to do,' the Horned Baron sighed. 'I've been at my wits' end! Apparently, there's a rogue ogre running amok. Great big brute of a thing it is. It's the last thing I need. What with all the rumours that something is not quite right in Elfwood.'

'Told you,' muttered Veronica smugly.

The mention of Elfwood turned Randalf a deep shade of red. 'An ogre, you say. What you need,' he went on hurriedly, 'is a warrior-hero.'

The Horned Baron groaned. 'That's what you said the last time, when I had that problem with the plumbing. What was his name? Quentin the Cake-Decorator? I'm still clearing up the mess he made.' He shook his head. 'The trouble is, the quality of the warrior-hero depends on the quality of the wizard who summons him, and quite frankly . . .'

His voice trailed away as he looked Randalf up and down, eyebrows raised and top lip curling. Randalf pulled himself up to his full height and puffed out his chest.

'The summoning of a warrior-hero involves hard work, prolonged study and utter dedication to the task,' he said. 'Only the most gifted wizards are able to carry out so demanding a spell. A wizard, I humbly suggest, such as myself.'

'*Humph*,' said the Horned Baron sceptically. 'We'll need more than a cake-decorator this time, Randalf. There's an angry ogre on the loose and his temper is getting worse by the day. According to my sources he goes by the name of Engelbert the Enormous. It's been absolute murder, I tell you. He's been ripping the thatch off cottages, trampling fields and orchards, *and* squeezing sheep . . .'

'Doesn't sound good,' said Randalf, and tutted sympathetically.

'He squeezed a whole flock only last night!' the Horned Baron went on. 'Something must be done!'

'And something *shall* be done!' Randalf announced. 'For I bear news that, after long and painstaking experimentation, I have managed to summon to Muddle Earth a great warrior-hero from afar. He is bold. He is brave. Sharp in intellect and valiant in battle. A warrior-hero whose reputation goes before him. A legend in his own lunchtime . . .'

'Get on with it!' said the Horned Baron irritably.

'Allow me to introduce, Joe the Barbarian!' Randalf said, and turned to the doorway expectantly.

No one appeared.

'Well?' said the Horned Baron. 'Where is he?'

'One moment, my Lord,' said Randalf, and cleared his throat. 'I give you . . .' He turned back to the door and bellowed at the top of his voice, 'JOE THE BARBARIAN!'

Before the echo had even died away, there came the

sound of excited barking and scurrying claws, and Henry dashed into the chamber, ears flapping, tongue lolling and lead dragging along behind him.

The Horned Baron's eyes nearly popped out of his head. 'What in Muddle Earth is that?' he exclaimed. He turned on the wizard. 'Barbarian is right, Randalf!' he said sarcastically. 'Don't they believe in haircuts where he comes from?'

Randalf smiled. 'His Lordship has misunderstood,' he said. 'This is not the warrior-hero of whom I spoke, but rather his faithful battle-hound.'

'Henry the Hairy,' Veronica murmured, and chuckled to herself.

'The real warrior-hero is about to enter,' said Randalf. 'Joe the Barbarian,' he announced again. His face creased up with irritation. 'JOE! Will you get in here. Now!'

Joe's pale face appeared nervously round the edge of the door. 'Did you call?' he said.

'He's not deaf, is he?' asked the Horned Baron. 'I don't give much for his chances if he is.'

'Of course he's not deaf,' said Randalf. 'That said, all the senses of this particular warrior-hero are so acute, so sensitive, so finely tuned that he could lose two or three and still remain completely invincible.'

Joe clattered into the chamber and stood next to the others. The Horned Baron glanced his way and sniffed dismissively. 'He doesn't look up to much,' he said. He nodded towards Henry. 'Are you quite sure *he's* not the warrior-hero after all?'

'Appearances can be deceptive,' said Randalf. 'Take yourself, for instance. *We* know you're a great and noble Horned Baron, yet look at you . . .'

'What . . . what . . . what are you suggesting?' blustered the affronted Baron. 'I'm sure I don't know what you mean!'

Joe smiled nervously. For all his grand title and stately surroundings, the Horned Baron was, it had to be said, rather short. He was also weasel-faced, skinny and with scrawny arms and legs. Even his name was a bit misleading. Joe had assumed that the Horned Baron would have huge curling horns sprouting from the top of his head. Instead, he had to admit he was a little disappointed to see that the baron's name came from the oversized horns on his helmet, which kept slipping down over his eyes.

In short, the Horned Baron was a big let-down.

'What I meant, your Lordship, is this,' Randalf was saying. 'Your greatness and nobility are all the more impressive for being so . . . *well concealed.*'

'*Humph!*' snorted the Horned Baron, unsure how to take the wizard's words. He returned his attention to Joe and sighed wearily. 'I suppose that if this is all that's on offer, he'll have to do.'

Randalf smiled again. 'You know what they say,' he said. 'A barbarian in the hand is worth two cake-decorators in anyone's money.' He rubbed his hands together. 'And talking of money, if we could perhaps move on to the delicate matter of my fee.'

'Your fee?' asked the Horned Baron, his eyebrows arching alarmingly.

'Yes, two golden big'uns, wasn't it?' Randalf ventured.

'Three silver pipsqueaks,' said the Horned Baron, jingling some coins in his pocket. 'And I'm being robbed blind!'

Randalf groaned. So little money to go such a long way. The trouble was, with his recent record, he was in no position to bargain. 'Three silver pipsqueaks it is,' he said and reached out for the money.

The Horned Baron abruptly withdrew his hand. 'But then, there was that incident with the exploding elf, wasn't there?' he said. 'I shall have to make a slight deduction. Oh, and then there's the matter of the melting silver goblet. And that terrible infestation of galloping green mould in the castle bathrooms . . . very nasty . . . In fact, after all the deductions, I calculate that *you* owe *me*.'

'But that's not fair . . .' Randalf began.

'Life isn't fair,' came the reply. 'Yet, for all that, I am a generous Horned Baron,' he said. 'Here, take this brass muckle.'

'You've got to stand up to him,' said Veronica.

'Shut up, Veronica,' Randalf hissed as, swallowing both his words and his pride, he pocketed the single coin. Who knows, perhaps his luck was about to change. Maybe Joe the Barbarian – warrior-hero *extraordinaire* – might just surprise him. He wouldn't count on it, but he'd just have to

do what he always did in
these situations and make
the best of it.

'Go, then!' said the Horned
Baron addressing Joe directly.
'Journey south, seek out Engelbert
the Enormous and put a stop to his
destructive behaviour once and for
all. And when you have slain the
fiend, I want you to bring me
his head. There's a pouch of
silver pipsqueaks for you when
you do.'

'His head?' said Joe, horrified. '*Ugh!*'

'Just a figure of speech,' said Randalf hurriedly, as he
seized Joe by the arm and steered him towards the door.
'Any proof will do.' He turned back to the Horned Baron.
'Consider it done, my Lord.'

Just then, the relative calm was destroyed by a heart-
stopping screech. '*WALTER!*'

Paling slightly, the Horned Baron smiled weakly.

'*Walter!* Where are my new singing curtains? The ones
I showed you in that catalogue. You promised me them ages
ago. You're all talk, you are!' she shouted. 'I don't know, call
yourself a Horned Baron!'

'It's all in hand, my little songbird,' he called back. 'I'm
having them sent over. Made of the finest material, they are,

and with the voice of an angel guaranteed. They're costing me the earth.'

'WAL-ter!' Ingrid screeched indignantly.

'But worth every last brass muckle, of course,' he hastily added.

Before the Horned Baron had a chance to remember precisely where his last brass muckle had actually gone, Randalf bustled the others out of the door, down the stairs and across the courtyard. He paused on the steps of the castle by the outer gate.

'All things considered,' he said, 'I think that went very well.'

'If being humiliated and swindled counts as doing well, then you're right,' said Veronica drily.

'Shut up, Veronica!' said Randalf. He turned to Joe and clapped him on the shoulder. 'And so, Joe the Barbarian, the time is almost upon us,' he announced, trying to sound as cheerful as possible. 'We'll rest up here for the night. Then, as the sun rises over Muddle Earth tomorrow morning, so shall the quest begin!'

The following day dawned bright and early – unlike the day before, when it had been an hour late, and the previous Wednesday when it hadn't dawned until one-twenty in the afternoon. There were unconfirmed rumours flying about that Dr Cuddles was responsible. Whatever, on this particular morning the sun rose when it should – which was just as well, because if it hadn't, Randalf and the rest would have stood no chance of travelling to the Ogrehills in one day.

'Look lively,' Randalf said, several times, as he scuttled about getting everyone ready. Finally, they were off.

Swaying to and fro on Norbert's left shoulder, Joe was far from happy. Quite apart from the ogre-sickness which had returned with a vengeance the moment they'd set off, he was decidedly uneasy about the forthcoming quest.

'All this talk of ogres and squeezed sheep,' he was saying. 'I don't like the sound of it one little bit. I'm not a warrior-hero, I'm just an ordinary schoolboy – and I want to go home.'

Randalf leaned across from Norbert's right shoulder and patted Joe reassuringly. 'Don't worry,' he said. 'Everything's going to be just fine! Trust me, I'm a wizard.'

'That's easy for you to say,' said Joe. 'But look at the size of Norbert – and he's Norbert the Not-Very-Big! What on earth is this . . . this Engelbert the *Enormous* going to be like?'

'Enormous,' said Veronica. 'I think you'll find the clue's in his name.'

'Oh, I'm sure he is,' said Norbert. 'Absolutely massive! Twice as tall as me probably and three times as broad. In fact, Engelbert's bound to be even bigger than my grandfather Umberto the Unfeasibly Large – not to mention Uncle Malcolm Nine-Bellies . . .'

'Yes, yes, Norbert,' said Randalf. 'That's fascinating.' He turned back to Joe. 'The thing is, I don't expect you to actually fight Engelbert.'

'You don't?' said Joe.

'Of course not,' said Randalf. 'That would be ridiculous.'

'So what *do* you want me to do?' asked Joe.

'Psychology,' said Randalf, tapping the side of his head meaningfully. 'It's all about psychology.'

'It is?' said Joe.

'You see,' Randalf continued, stifling a yawn, 'as everyone knows, ogres are just great big softies. Isn't that right, Norbert?'

Joe clung on tightly as Norbert nodded in agreement. 'Really?' said Joe.

'Really,' Randalf confirmed sleepily. 'All you have to do is stride right up to him in your Wellies of Power, wave your three-pronged Trident of Trickery in his face, fix him with a stare from beneath your Helmet of Sarcasm and tell him to stop being so naughty, or else!'

'Or else, what?' said Joe.

'Or else you'll smack his bottom. Then you can make a really sarcastic remark about his appearance and he'll start blubbing like a baby. Simple.'

'If it's so simple,' said Joe, 'then why do you need me?'

'Psychology,' yawned Randalf. 'You're a warrior-hero. Ogres are terrified of warrior-heroes. They're giant-killers, dragon-slayers, troll-bashers – nobody stands a chance against a warrior-hero. It's a well-known fact!'

'But I'm not a warrior-hero,' said Joe. 'I keep telling you, I've never killed a giant or bashed a troll in my life. Honest!'

'In that costume, my lad,' said Randalf, shifting into a more comfortable position propped up against Norbert's right ear, 'Engelbert the whatever-his-name-is will take one look at you, burst into tears and promise to be a good ogre – especially if you say his eyes are too close together and he smells like a pink stinky hog. Trust me, I'm a . . .'

'Wizard?' said Joe. But Randalf was fast asleep. A soft, rasping snore fluttered through the air.

'That's him off again,' said Veronica. 'I've never known

anyone sleep as much. Still, at least it shuts him up.'

'Shut up, Veronica,' mumbled Randalf in his sleep.

'Typical!' said Veronica.

They were returning the way they had come, back along the winding track through the Musty Mountains. Morning drifted slowly past, and soon it was early afternoon.

Boom.

Far far behind them, Mount Boom exploded softly. The hairy squeak-moths huffed to and fro looking for lost socks to eat, the scruff-birds rolled around in the musty dust by the roadside, while a swarm of rotund, antlered beetles buzzed slowly past, in search of killer daisies to pollinate.

'They look like miniature Horned Barons,' Joe laughed.

Veronica nodded, crunched her beak and swallowed. 'Only they taste better,' she said.

Joe winced and turned away. As he did so, he caught sight of something glinting out of the corner of his eye.

'What was that?' he said, looking down.

'What was what, sir?' said Norbert.

'That,' said Joe, pointing down at Norbert's left foot. 'Careful, don't tread on it.'

Sure enough, down by Norbert's left foot, glinting in the half-light, a small silver teaspoon was doing what looked like a forlorn little dance in the dust. Round and round it was going, in ever-decreasing circles. Finally, the circles became so small that the teaspoon stopped in one place, did a last twinkling pirouette, and fell to the ground with a soft tinkly sound.

Joe jumped down and picked it up gingerly. As he held it, the teaspoon gave a little sigh.

'Did you hear that?' said Joe, holding it up. 'I think it gave a little sigh.'

'It's lonely,' said Norbert. 'It must have got separated from the herd in that cutlery stampede.'

'An enchanted teaspoon,' said Veronica darkly.

'Can I keep it?' said Joe.

'Finders keepers,' said Veronica. 'It'll go well with your saucepan and toasting fork.' She ruffled up her neck feathers and raised her beak. 'You can call it the Teaspoon of Terror – and terrify ogres with it!'

'Why have we stopped?' came Randalf's voice. 'And did somebody mention tea?'

'I almost trod on a teaspoon, sir,' said Norbert. 'It could have been very nasty. My Auntie Bertha the Big-Footed was always treading on things. Or *in* things, more like. Why, that time she stepped in a great big dollop of—'

'Yes, yes,' said Randalf. 'Thank you, Norbert. Now, if you're quite ready, Joe, perhaps we should proceed. Our quest awaits us and we've still got a long way to go.'

Joe nodded and slipped the spoon into his back pocket. Norbert bent down, pulled him up on to his shoulder and set off once more. Randalf slumped forwards and drifted back to sleep.

It wasn't long before the road emerged from the highest peaks of the Musty Mountains and began winding its way through the foothills. These were as barren and musty as the mountains, and smelt strongly of old socks. To his right, Joe saw a tall, rounded hill he hadn't noticed at first. Unlike the other foothills, it was covered with thick grass and giant yellow and white daisies, their sweet scent perfuming the air. Stiltmice scampered through the verdant undergrowth; butterflies fluttered overhead. Joe breathed in the beautiful fresh air. He tapped Norbert on the shoulder.

'Not so fast, Norbert. Let's enjoy the view,' he said. 'What a lovely place! What's it called?'

Norbert shuddered anxiously, causing Joe almost to lose his balance.

'Careful!' he exclaimed. 'I nearly fell off just then! Oh, look, Norbert. Over there! How cute!'

A particularly appealing stiltmouse with big blue eyes was stepping daintily through the gently swaying grass, the aromatic breeze ruffling its white fur.

'That's Harmless Hill,' said Norbert.

'Harmless Hill!' Randalf woke up with a start. 'Norbert, my good fellow,' said the wizard. 'Why is it that whenever I wake up I find you standing still, gawping?'

'It's Joe, sir,' said Norbert apologetically. 'He wanted to enjoy the view.'

Just then, the stiltmouse gave a little cry as a daisy opened its gaping jaws and swallowed it whole. It gave an ugly belch.

'I thought it was called *Harmless* Hill!' said Joe, horrified.

'Oh, the hill's harmless enough,' said Veronica. 'It's the killer daisies you have to watch out for.'

Joe shook his head. 'This place is crazy,' he muttered. He looked down to check that Henry was still nearby.

'Here, boy,' he called. 'Come up here with me, just in case there's a "perfectly safe" mountain up ahead, or a "don't worry, you'll be fine" meadow just round the corner.'

'I've never heard of those places,' said Norbert. 'But they sound terrifying!'

'Can we *please* get on,' said Randalf irritably. 'Wake me up when we get to Trollbridge.'

Norbert set off once again, this time at a brisk trot. Joe was getting used to ogre-riding by now, and with Henry safely in his lap, he relaxed. Slowly, his eyes grew heavy and his head began to nod.

The next thing he knew, Joe woke up with a mouth full of mud and Henry licking his face. He looked up. Randalf was on his feet, with Norbert fussing about him trying to brush down his robes.

'No, don't tell me,' Randalf was saying. 'Another pothole! You really should learn to look where you're going, Norbert.'

'It wasn't a pothole,' said Norbert tearfully.

'No,' came an angry little voice. 'It was a kettle hole actually – and my kettle is a complete write-off!'

An elf, who was standing in a small hole in the road, threw a flattened disc of metal, with what appeared to be a spout, down to the ground and marched off in a huff. Joe got to his feet, looked round and gasped. There in front of them was Trollbridge.

Built upon four great arches which crossed the river, the bridge was a solid, yet ornate, stone structure complete with tall pointy-domed turrets and magnificent gate-towers. Only when he looked more closely did Joe see just how neglected Trollbridge actually was.

'It's a bit grimy,' he said. 'And that tower looks as if it's about to collapse,' he added, pointing upwards.

Randalf shrugged. 'Trollbridge has a certain "lived-in" charm,' he said. 'Trolls have many fine qualities, but neatness is not one of them. Now stubbornness is another matter. Trolls can be very stubborn, as you'd know if you'd ever tried to get a troll to tidy its bedroom . . .'

'And they never throw anything away,' said Veronica, flapping her wing at the pile of junk at the foot of the gate-towers. 'I mean, look at all that mess!'

'Good day,' came a gruff, yet cheery, voice from the centre of the pile. 'Can I help you?'

There were bicycle wheels, taps, lengths of wood, screws and nails, nuts and bolts, coils of wire, a mangle, a bird cage, a washing-up bowl . . . and there, perched on a three-legged stool, a squat, bow-legged individual with tufty hair and rather ferocious-looking teeth sticking up from a protruding jaw.

'You certainly can,' said Randalf, stepping forwards. 'We wish to cross your magnificent bridge.'

'That'll be one mangel-wurzel,' said the troll.

'A mangel-wurzel?' said Randalf, and made a great show of searching through his robes. 'I'm afraid I'm fresh out of mangel-wurzels.'

'A turnip, then,' said the troll. 'You must have a turnip.'

'Not as such,' said Randalf.

'Then a carrot,' said the troll. 'Any root vegetable will do.'

'Sorry,' said Randalf.

'A potato?' he suggested. 'It doesn't matter if it's a bit mouldy.'

''Fraid not,' said Randalf.

The troll sighed. 'An onion? A courgette? A baby sweet-corn? All right then, I'll settle for a small dried pea.'

Randalf shook his head sadly.

'What sort of travellers are you?' said the troll. 'I mean, you haven't got a mangetout between you. I don't know,' he tutted. 'So what *have* you got?'

Randalf turned to Joe. 'I find myself in a somewhat embarrassing situation,' he said. 'I mean I've got my warrior-hero-summoning spell and a belligerent budgie, but that's about it . . .'

'You're *not* trading me!' squawked Veronica indignantly.

'Who'd have you?' snapped Randalf. 'Now, Joe. I don't suppose you . . .'

Joe rummaged round in the pockets of his jeans and pulled out an old bus ticket and a lolly stick. He held them out for Randalf's inspection.

'A chariot voucher from a far-off land,' said Randalf holding up the bus ticket.

The troll looked thoughtful. 'It's tempting,' he said. 'A far-off land, you say? Trouble is, I don't get out that much . . .'

'You surprise me,' said Veronica.

'Shut up, Veronica,' said Randalf, and he turned back to the troll. 'No? All right. Then how about this? A miniature paddle?'

'Miniature paddle,' said the troll, eyeing the lolly stick. 'Very nice, very nice. Lovely workmanship, but a bit – how can I put this? A bit on the small side.'

Randalf turned to Joe questioningly.

Joe pulled his front pockets inside out. 'Empty,' he whispered. 'I haven't got anything else . . .' As he spoke, he tried his back pockets, and there, nestling into the corner and stifling a sob, was the small silver teaspoon.

'There's this,' he said uncertainly as he held it up. 'The Teaspoon of . . . of . . . Terror!'

'The Teaspoon of Terror!' said Randalf, taking the spoon with a flourish. The spoon let out a timid little squeak.

Randalf ignored it. 'Forged by elves. Imbued with magic . . .'

'The Teaspoon of Terror,' said the troll, impressed, as Randalf laid it in his large, grubby hand. The teaspoon gave a sigh. 'Of course, a mangel-wurzel is the generally accepted fee, or a turnip. But you seem like an honest fellow . . . Oh, go on, then. A Teaspoon of Terror it is! Welcome to Trollbridge.'

'At last,' Randalf muttered. 'And thank you, once again,' he said as the troll opened the gate and waved them

through. 'It's been a pleasure doing business with you.'

'As long as you remember, next time it's a mangel-wurzel or nothing,' said the troll as he strolled back to his stool.

Joe put Henry on his lead and followed Randalf and the others. It was market day in Trollbridge and the place was buzzing with feverish activity, for though the trolls lived under the bridge, their noisy bargaining, bartering and haggling was conducted up on top. A series of trapdoors sprang open and slammed shut constantly as the trolls hurried between the two. The balustrades on both sides of the bridge were lined with covered stalls and trestle tables, all laden with complete and utter junk, and run by enthusiastic trolls who were politely shouting out what wares they were selling.

'Old string! Do come and get your old string here! All lengths available.'

'I've the finest odd socks in Trollbridge if you'd care to take a look! Specially unwashed and aged by squeak-moths!'

'Mangel-wurzels! Please come and inspect my lovely mangel-wurzels!'

Boxes and sacks stood everywhere, each one filled with junk of all shapes and sizes, and the odd root vegetable.

'The trolls are renowned throughout Muddle Earth for their root vegetables,' Randalf explained. 'Especially their mangel-wurzels. They're passionate about their mangel-wurzels.'

'You don't say,' said Joe, as they passed by a rickety stall weighed down with a great pyramid of the things.

Slowly, they made their way across the great Trollbridge, the sound of the haggling and bartering ringing in their ears.

'I'll give you a jam jar of toe-nail clippings and a broken bucket.'

'Throw in the dried-pea rusk, and it's a deal.'

'Who will buy my sweet red gobstoppers? Sucked three times and dropped on the carpet . . .'

'Bottle tops! Bottle tops!'

'Bottle bottoms! Bottle bottoms!'

Joe stood, completely bewildered. There was so much to take in.

'Keep up, everybody!' Randalf shouted back impatiently from the end of the bridge. 'Norbert, put down that turnip. This is no time for eating. Come *on*, Joe. We haven't got all day.'

'Sorry,' Joe called back and, tugging Henry away from a display of amusingly shaped carrots, hurried to catch up.

'What kept you so long?' said Randalf.

'I was just interested,' said Joe. 'And everyone here seems so friendly and polite.' He frowned. 'But what do they do with all this rubbish?'

'The ways of the trolls,' Randalf said, 'are as mysterious as they are bizarre . . .'

'In short,' Veronica butted in, 'he doesn't know. But you should see the state of their bedrooms!'

'Keep your voice down,' said Randalf, as they passed a second toll keeper at this end of the bridge. 'Trolls' feelings are easily hurt.'

The troll was identical in every way to the toll keeper at the other end – apart from his voice, which was high and shrill.

'Missing you already,' he squeaked.

With Randalf and Joe back on Norbert's shoulders, Veronica on Randalf's head and Henry trotting along behind, they continued on their way. Joe looked round and sighed as Trollbridge disappeared behind him. To his left was a broad and barren plain; to his right, a swampy bog.

All at once, Veronica let out a cry. 'Ogrehills ahead!' she shouted, her wing shielding her eyes from the low sun.

'Excellent news!' said Randalf with a yawn. 'We'll be there before we know it.' He turned to Joe. 'And you, Joe the Barbarian, will be able to prove your warrior-hero prowess once and for all.'

'Fantastic,' Joe mumbled. 'I can hardly wait. In fact . . .' His face suddenly screwed up. '*Pfwoooar!*' he groaned. 'What is *that* horrible pong?'

'Sorry,' said Norbert. 'It must have been something I ate in Trollbridge.'

'Not you,' said Joe. 'I'm talking about that sweet, sickly smell.' It was like a pungent mixture of his dad's aftershave, his mum's aromatherapy oils, and his sister's cheap perfume, all mixed up with rotting vegetation. He held his nose. 'It's worse than the Musty Mountains!'

Veronica flapped her wings in front of her face. Henry whined miserably and rubbed his nose in the dirt.

'It's the Perfumed Bog,' said Randalf. 'I quite like the smell myself.'

'You would,' said Veronica.

'It reminds me of my beloved Morwenna,' he said dreamily. 'Morwenna the Fair, they called her . . .'

'Not behind her back, they didn't,' Veronica muttered. 'At least, not when she grew that beard.'

'That was an accident,' said Randalf defensively. 'I was practising. Morwenna understood, even if her father didn't.'

'Morwenna! Morwenna! Let down your golden beard!' sniggered Veronica.

'SHUT UP, VERONICA!' shouted Randalf, very red in the face.

The further they went, the closer the road came to the Perfumed Bog, until the two were running along side by side, with only a thin line of stones separating them. Joe looked out across the swamp. Shrouded in pink mist, it was vast and flat, with giant lily pads and grassy tussocks, and dark pools of glistening purple mud which plopped and hissed as the perfumed gases bubbled up from below.

'Come here, Henry,' he called, waving the lead, as the dog stopped by the side of the road. Head down and tail up, he began sniffing eagerly all round the ground. 'Henry!' Joe shouted. 'Henry come here!'

At that moment, Joe spotted what Henry had smelled. It was a small, pink warthog-like creature with floppy ears and a curly tail, standing motionless on top of a tussock surrounded by lily-pads and bubbling mud. It was staring, unblinkingly, at the dog.

'HENRY!' Joe yelled.

With a loud yelp of excitement, Henry suddenly bounded forwards and took a flying leap at the tussock. 'Oh, no! He thinks it's a squirrel,' shouted Joe, jumping off Norbert's shoulder and chasing after him.

'Come back!' shouted Randalf. 'Never chase a pink stinky hog!'

'Why not?' asked Norbert.

'In case you catch it, stupid!' said Veronica.

'Henry!' shouted Joe as, leaping from tussock to tussock, he tried to catch up. The more puffed out he became, the more difficult it was to keep his balance. 'Henry, come . . . *Aaargh!*'

SPLASH!

Joe fell face down in the purple mud. Ahead, Henry caught up with the pink stinky hog and lunged for its tail. With a high-pitched squeal, the hog raised its rump and broke wind with astonishing force. The sound – like a small cannon exploding – echoed round the Perfumed Bog. And the smell . . . !

'Someone's caught a pink stinky hog,' said Randalf.

In the Perfumed Bog, Joe picked himself up. The

smell was eye-wateringly horrendous. Henry seemed to be in shock. The pink stinky hog stood on its little tussock triumphantly, tail in the air. From behind it, a small hill rose up from the purple mud.

It had two piggy pink eyes that regarded Henry and Joe unblinkingly. It had a piggy pink snout that wrinkled as it sniffed the air and let out deep piggy snorts of anger. Its two huge tusks glinted in the pink light of the Perfumed Bog.

'Henry,' said Joe softly. 'Time to go, Henry.'

With a whimper, Henry backed away.

The huge pink stinky hog climbed on to the tussock beside the pink stinky hog piglet, slowly turned its back on Joe and Henry and raised its great rump high in the air.

'Henry!' shouted Joe. 'Run for it!'

A sound like a huge cannon exploding echoed round the Perfumed Bog. *And the smell . . . !*

'Someone's caught a pink stinky hog's mother,' said Randalf.

Just then, Henry shot out of the swirling pink mist and

on to the path. Moments later, Joe scrambled after him.

'All aboard,' shouted Norbert, picking them both up.

'To the Ogrehills, Norbert!' shouted Randalf. 'And remember, until we get there, breathe through your mouths!'

The sun was setting as they approached the Ogrehills. Randalf's snores and the gentle thud of Norbert's footfalls were the only sounds in the still air – at least they were until they were joined by another sound, equally tuneless.

'*La, la, la . . .*'

The sound floated across the evening sky. Joe looked up, and there, marching along the road towards them from Elfwood was a stooped, shadowy figure in a cloak and raised hood. Under his arm was a roll of what looked like cloth or carpet.

The tuneless song became louder.

'*La, la, la, la-la.*'

Joe shivered, and the hairs at the back of his neck stood on end.

As the lone figure came closer he lowered his hood, and Joe was surprised to see a familiar face.

'Grubbers!' Randalf exclaimed. 'How good to see you again.'

Grubley looked up. '*Randy*,' he said. 'Out and about, eh? And I see you've got your warrior-hero with you, all kitted out for battle.'

'*La, la, la . . .*'

'You bet,' said Randalf. 'We're on important business for the Horned Baron, aren't we Joe?'

But Joe did not reply. He was listening to the singing.

'*La, la, la . . .*'

Joe frowned. The noise seemed to be coming from the roll of material under Grubley's arm.

'Yes, we're heading for the Ogrehills,' Randalf was saying.

'Rather you than me,' said Grubley, pulling a face.

'Oh, I have absolute faith that your warrior outfit will

do its job,' said Randalf.

'You get what you pay for,' said Grubley.

'Precisely,' said Randalf. 'But I am being rude. Norbert,' he said, 'help me down.'

'Oh, don't get down on my account,' said Grubley. 'I'm already running late as it is.'

'*La, la, la. La, la, la.*' The tuneless song was louder than ever. Had no one else noticed? Joe wondered.

'Running late?' said Randalf, tutting sympathetically. 'But what are you doing so far from Goblintown in the first place?'

'*La, la, la.*'

'I'm on important business for the Horned Baron, too,' said Grubley, raising the frayed, faded and somewhat grubby roll of musical cloth. 'Oh, I've been given the runaround, I can tell you,' he said crossly. 'Been looking all over, I have.' He sighed. 'It's all down to that Horned Baron's wife . . .'

'Ingrid?' said Randalf.

'The Horned Baron only had one wife the last time I looked,' said Grubley. 'She wants a set of singing curtains. Never heard of them myself, but she swears blind she saw them in my catalogue. And what Ingrid wants, Ingrid gets!'

Randalf nodded knowingly.

'So, I've been traipsing around,' he said. 'Here, there and everywhere. Luckily, I've got my contacts,' he added, and tapped his nose. 'I managed to lay my hands on this. Enchanted material. Very rare, I can tell you. I'm heading back to Goblintown to have it made into singing curtains.'

'*La, la, la . . .*'

'Call that singing?' said Veronica. 'More like mournful mooing . . .'

'Shut up, Veronica,' said Randalf. 'I'm sure Ingrid will love them.'

'I hope so,' muttered Grubley, as he turned and hurried off towards Goblintown. 'I do hope so.'

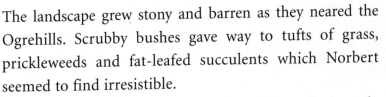

The landscape grew stony and barren as they neared the Ogrehills. Scrubby bushes gave way to tufts of grass, prickleweeds and fat-leafed succulents which Norbert seemed to find irresistible.

'Yum, there's another one,' he said, and abruptly stooped down, broke off a leaf and pushed it into his mouth. Cries of alarm and distress came from his shoulders as Randalf clung on desperately, Veronica flapped about and Joe tried his best to keep Henry from slipping off his lap. 'Be-lish-ush!' he muttered slurpily.

'Norbert, will you *stop* doing that!' said Randalf sharply. 'You nearly sent us *all* flying that time!'

'Sorry, sir,' said Norbert. 'It's just, I haven't had squish-weeds for ages. I'd forgotten how much I like them.'

'Yes, well, I think you've had enough now,' said Randalf. 'I know you. You see something you like and you don't know when to stop. Don't make a pink stinky hog of yourself.'

'No, sir,' said Norbert. 'Sorry, sir.'

'Now get a move on, Norbert,' said Randalf. 'There's a good fellow.'

On they went. The rolling Ogrehills stretched off into the distance.

'That ogre must be around here somewhere. Keep your eyes peeled for squeezed sheep,' said Randalf.

Joe scanned the area all around him. 'What on earth does a squeezed sheep look like, anyway?' Joe wondered out loud.

'Exactly as you'd imagine,' said Veronica.

'Hmmph,' said Joe. 'Well I can't see *any* sheep, squeezed or otherwise. In fact, I can't see much of anything,' he added. 'Apart from rocks.'

'Keep looking,' Randalf said. 'You too, Veronica.'

'If you insist,' said Veronica. 'It's so horrible here. Dry, dusty, desolate. Why would anyone want to live in a place like this?'

'This is where *I* lived,' said Norbert, with a smile. 'I think it's kind of homely.'

'You're right, Norbert,' said Veronica. 'If your idea of home is a rock for a pillow and a sandpit for a bed.'

'A sandpit bed?' said Norbert. Pure luxury. I and my twenty brothers had to sleep on pebbles. And we'd have given anything for a rock pillow. Prickleweed, that's what we had. And if we wanted to go to the loo in the middle of the night, we had to—'

'Yes, yes, Norbert,' said Randalf. 'That'll do. Just keep looking for a sheep.'

'There's one!' Joe shouted excitedly, and pointed ahead. 'Over there! Look!'

'Are you sure it's not a rock?' said Randalf.

'It's moving,' said Joe.

'So it is,' said Randalf. 'Proceed, Norbert.'

As they approached, it was clear that it was indeed a sheep, and not a happy one at that. It was wandering around in circles, looking dazed and bewildered. Its wool was bunched up around its shoulders and hindquarters, and squeezed flat in the middle. It looked like a walking, woolly dumb-bell. When it noticed the ogre stomping resolutely towards it, it let out an odd squeaky bleat, turned on its heels and disappeared over the ridge in a cloud of dust.

'That sheep has definitely been squeezed!' said Randalf. 'After it!'

Norbert tried his best, but the terrified sheep had given them the slip. It wasn't long, however, before Veronica spotted two more.

'Over there!' she said, flapping her wing at the pair of cowering, shivering sheep with wild eyes and dumb-bell wool. 'Freshly squeezed sheep!'

'Good work, Veronica,' said Randalf. 'And if we follow their trail, it'll lead straight to the culprit – none other than

Engelbert the Enormous, I'll be bound!'

Joe swallowed hard. 'I'm feeling a bit nervous,' he admitted quietly.

'Joe, Joe, Joe,' said Randalf, as if talking to a very young child. 'We aren't nervous, are we? Of course we remember we've got our Trident of Trickery. Ooh, scary trident! We've got our Helmet of Sarcasm. Nasty, nasty helmet! All we've got to do is show this Engelbert character who's boss. Who's the boss, Joe? Who's the boss?'

'I'm the boss,' said Joe uncertainly. 'I'm the boss.'

Norbert trudged on, following the sheep's trail. Up and down the undulating rockscape, he went; deeper and deeper into the Ogrehills. Occasionally, they passed the mouths of caves, from which came the sleepy sounds of snoozing ogres.

'Mummy, mummy,' growled some.

'My snuggly-wuggly,' murmured others in deep, gruff voices.

And the air was filled with the slurps of thumbs being sucked and mighty rumbling snores.

'D . . . do you think we're getting close?' Joe asked in a trembling voice.

Randalf nodded. 'Judging by that unfortunate mess over there,' he said. 'That is where our sheep were squeezed. Quiet, everyone!'

The wind abruptly dropped and the air became oddly still. Norbert put Randalf and Joe down, and Joe clipped Henry on the lead. Veronica sat on Randalf's head, feathers ruffled. They all listened intently.

'It's quiet,' she said in a hushed voice. 'Too quiet. I don't like it.'

'Shut up, Veronica,' whispered Randalf, who was thinking exactly the same thing.

'What exactly are we listening for?' whispered Joe.

Just then, an anguished bleat echoed loudly round the hills, and a sheep – with bulging eyes and squeezed wool – came hurtling over the ridge and dashed away across the stony ground.

'What the . . . ?' Randalf began.

'NO!' boomed a loud and angry voice. 'IT'S NOT THE SAME! IT'S NOT THE SAME AT ALL!'

Joe stared in horror in the direction the voice had come from, and as he stared, he heard banging and crashing and a series of loud thuds. A thick cloud of dust rose up.

'OH, WHERE IS IT?' the great voice demanded.

'WHERE, OH, WHERE HAS IT GONE?'

'D . . . do you think *th . . . that's* Engelbert?' whispered Joe.

'Unless I'm very much mistaken,' Randalf whispered back.

'He *sounds* enormous.'

'Oh, I'm sure he won't be *that* enormous,' said Randalf reassuringly. 'Come on, now, Joe the Barbarian. Raise high your Trident of Trickery, adjust your Helmet of Sarcasm and let your Wellies of Power lead you to victory.'

'SOMEONE'S DEFINITELY *STOLEN* IT!' the voice raged. 'AND WHEN I FIND OUT WHO IT IS, I'LL . . . I'LL . . .'

'The time has come, Joe the Barbarian,' said Randalf, pushing Joe forwards. 'Go forth and confront him. You can do it!'

With his trident in one hand and his dog-lead in the other, Joe walked ahead on rubbery legs. Henry cowered by his side.

All at once a truly massive ogre head – more than twice the size of Norbert's – appeared above a ridge. Joe froze. The head was swiftly followed by colossal shoulders, a barrel chest, a bulging gut, legs like tree trunks and feet like boats, until an entire monstrous ogre stood before him. Joe couldn't move.

The ogre roared furiously and advanced, picking up great boulders and looking underneath them, before tossing them aside.

'WHERE ARE YOU?' he bellowed, his face purple and

contorted with rage, his bloodshot eyes bulging in their sockets. 'WHERE *ARE* YOU?' The light glinted on the drool that dripped from his gnashing tusks. Then his three eyes fell on Joe. The ogre paused for what seemed to the reluctant warrior-hero an eternity.

'Oh, my goodness,' Randalf gasped. 'He does seem rather upset doesn't he?'

'I do hope Joe will be all right,' said Norbert anxiously.

Joe raised his trident bravely. 'It's all a matter of psychology,' he reminded himself. He met the ogre's fearsome gaze. 'I . . . I'm a warrior-hero, from afar,' he said. 'Joe the Barbarian! And . . . *um* . . . unless you stop all this nonsense right now I'll have to smack your bottom!'

The ogre blinked.

Joe turned to the others. 'Shall I use the Helmet of Sarcasm?' he hissed. He adjusted his helmet. 'And by the way, I'm sure no one has *ever* told you that your face looks just like the rear end of a pink stinky hog . . .'

The ogre threw back his head and the Ogrehills trembled with his mighty roar.

'What do we do now?' squeaked Joe.

'There's only one thing we can do!' said Randalf. '*RUN!*'

With their hearts in their mouths and dust in their hair, they made a desperate dash for it. Their panicked cries broke the silence. Randalf ran blindly on till he could run no more. Stopping abruptly, he bent double and gulped for air.

'That was close,' said Veronica, landing daintily on the wizard's rump.

'You can say that again,' said Norbert, stomping up behind them.

'That was clo—'

'Shut up, Veronica!' Randalf panted impatiently. He straightened up and shook his head. 'Most unusual,' he said. 'I've never known an ogre that angry before. He should have been terrified of our warrior-hero here . . .'

'Where?' said Veronica.

'Here,' said Randalf. 'Joe . . . Oh, no. Where is he?'

'Joe?' cried Norbert. 'Joe, where are you? Joe! Joe!'

'For crying out loud, Randalf!' said Veronica irritably. 'First sign of trouble and you turn tail and leave him to it.'

'But he was right behind me,' said Randalf, looking all around him. 'And I distinctly gave the order to run. It's not my fault he didn't hear me. That Helmet of Sarcasm must have slipped down over his ears . . .'

'He's gone!' Norbert wailed. 'And so is Henry!'

'Typical!' said Veronica. 'It's Quentin all over again.'

'We've got to go back for them,' Norbert sobbed tearfully.

'Now, let's not be hasty,' said Randalf nervously. 'You saw the mood that ogre was in. Perhaps we should allow the dust to settle a bit first, then, in a week or so, we can . . .'

'*You* brought the lad here to the Ogrehills,' interrupted Veronica accusingly. 'You can't abandon him now. You'd never be able to live with yourself.'

Randalf examined his fingernails closely. 'Of course, I feel bad. Don't get me wrong, Veronica. We *all* do! But be realistic . . .'

'Poor Joe! Poor Henry!' Norbert wailed. 'And poor, dear Quentin. *Boo-hoo!*'

'"Trust me, I'm a wizard", that's what you said,' Veronica continued. 'And he *did* trust you. Joe the Barbarian trusted you. And now, how are you repaying that trust? Eh? By abandoning him.' She clacked her beak reproachfully. 'You're a disgrace! If we don't go back right now, then I'm leaving you!'

'Please sir, please,' said Norbert, sobbing even louder. 'If we could just go and check. Maybe there's a chance . . .'

Randalf sighed. 'All right, all right,' he said. 'You win! I'm just too soft-hearted, that's my trouble! A fool to myself sometimes. Come, let's get this over with. Follow me.' He turned and gathered up his robes. 'But keep close.'

Huddled together for safety, Randalf and Norbert retraced their footsteps, creeping back silently, with Veronica keeping a watchful look out from the top of Randalf's head.

'I think we're getting close,' she announced after a while and flapped her wing up ahead. 'Look at those giant foot-prints, and how the dust has all been stirred up.'

Randalf nodded. Norbert began whimpering.

'Sssssh!' hissed Randalf, placing a finger to his lips. 'We don't want to . . .'

'*OH, NO!*' wailed Norbert, and pointed at a bent piece of three-pronged metal. '*LOOK!*'

It was the Trident of Trickery, twisted out of shape and lying discarded in the dust. Randalf picked it up and shuddered.

'And there!' Veronica cried. She flew down and landed on an abandoned Welly of Power.

Norbert howled with grief. 'Oh, Joe,' he blubbed. He picked up the lone rubber boot and hugged it desperately. 'It must have come off,' he sobbed, 'when he . . . when he . . . he . . .' He straightened up and scanned the horizon for any

sign of his latest warrior-hero friend. Apart from one set of
massive footprints in the dust which marched up and
over the ridge, there was nothing. 'JOE!' he cried.
'JOE!'

The desperate sound echoed round the
barren hills and faded
away unanswered.

'JOE!!'

Veronica flapped up
and landed on his shoulder. 'I
don't think Joe can hear you,'
she said softly.

'You never know,' said Norbert, his
pleading voice willing it to be true. 'If there's one
thing my great-uncle Larry the Unlucky taught me it
was that you should never give up hope. "Something will
turn up." That's what he used to say, before the dragon ate
him. "Something will turn up . . ."'

'I'm afraid *this* has turned up,' said Randalf gently. He
held out a flattened disc of dull silver.

'Wh . . . what's that?' Norbert trembled.

Randalf showed him the bent black handle sticking out
from one side. 'The Helmet of Sarcasm,' he said.

'No,' Norbert gasped. 'It can't be . . . You don't mean . . .'

'As you so rightly said,' Veronica muttered bitterly to

Randalf, 'you get what you pay for.' She tutted. 'Skinflint!'

'But it *can't* be his helmet,' said Norbert, fingering the flat piece of metal. 'Please say it isn't.'

'I'm afraid it is,' said Randalf. He shook his head. 'Completely flattened. Pulverized. Spifflicated. Flatter than a burst gas frog, you might even say . . .'

'Stop it!' Norbert howled, and clamped his hands over his ears. 'Stop it! Stop it! Stop it!'

'There, there,' said Randalf, and patted Norbert on the arm. 'It's all right, Norbert.'

'But it's *not* all right, sir!' Norbert bawled. 'It's not all right at all. First Quentin. Now Joe!' He pulled a grubby hankie from his pocket and blew his nose loudly. 'I just can't bear it!'

Veronica rounded on Randalf. 'You're to blame for all this!' she squawked. 'I never thought Joe was up to it. Warrior-hero, indeed!'

'But he *was*,' Randalf protested. 'I summoned him myself . . .'

'You summoned *Quentin*!' said Veronica. 'And look at him!'

'*Oh-woh-woh!*' wailed Norbert.

'Norbert, calm yourself,' said Randalf. 'We can summon more warrior-heroes. Even better ones . . .'

'*OH-OH-WOH!*'

'Third time lucky, eh?' said Veronica. 'My goodness, Randalf, you can be unfeeling at times. Why don't you bring the twisted toasting fork and squashed saucepan with you?' she suggested scornfully. 'Maybe you can get a refund!'

'Now, there's an idea,' said Randalf thoughtfully.

'*OH-WOH-WOH!*'

'A *bad* idea,' Randalf added hastily. 'Of course, I wouldn't dream of . . .'

'You're right,' said Veronica. 'Grubley would never agree to it.'

'Veronica!' said Randalf sharply. 'I'm surprised at you. Don't take any notice of her, Norbert.'

'So, what *are* we going to do, sir?' Norbert asked tearfully.

'Well, we can't stay here,' said Randalf. 'And I don't fancy going back to the Horned Baron. If we tell him that the rogue ogre is still at large – and that we've lost our warrior-hero into the bargain,' he continued as Norbert sniffled into his hanky, 'he won't be a happy Horned Baron.'

'I'm not happy,' said the Horned Baron, pacing up and down the great reception hall. 'I'm not happy at all!' He was working himself up into a right state.

For a start, Ingrid had been on at him all day about her precious singing curtains – and he hadn't heard a word from Grubley ever since he'd handed over the pouchful of silver pipsqueaks. Worse still, the castle had been plagued by a constant stream of goblins, elves and trolls all complaining that their crops had been flattened, their thatched-roofs torn off, their sheep squeezed – and what was he, as Horned Baron of Muddle Earth, going to do about it? That's what they all wanted to know.

'It's all in hand,' he'd kept telling them. 'Even now, a famous wizard and a highly trained warrior-hero are on their way to deal with the rogue ogre.' Yet, even to himself, the words hadn't quite rung true.

The Horned Baron grunted. 'Randalf the *Wise*, indeed! I've worn wiser pairs of underpants!'

He glanced at the clock for the tenth time in as many minutes and strode over to the window.

'All this intolerable waiting!' he groaned as he stared out. 'That's the trouble with being so powerful and important. You spend half your life waiting for others to carry out your commands!'

'WAL-TER!'

Ingrid's strident voice cut through the air like a rusty knife, sending the dust flying and setting the Horned Baron's teeth on edge. He closed his eyes and slowly counted to ten. For a moment there, he'd quite forgotten about his wife. This was never a sensible thing to do.

'*WALTER!*' she screeched. The crystal chandelier tinkled softly. 'Can you hear me?'

'Nine . . . ten.' The Horned Baron opened his eyes. 'Loud and clear, my little snuggle-muffin,' he called back.

'Don't you "snuggle-muffin" me,' Ingrid shouted. 'Where are my singing curtains? That's what I want to know. Where *are* they, Walter?'

'Everything's in hand,' the Horned Baron replied. 'I'm expecting them at any moment.'

'That's what you said an hour ago,' Ingrid countered. 'But every time there's a knock on the door, it's someone else complaining about their wretched sheep!'

'Any moment now,' the Horned Baron assured her.

'You'd better not be lying to me, Walter,' said Ingrid, her voice becoming more threatening as it grew quieter. 'You remember what happened last time I caught you lying, don't you?'

'All too well,' the Horned Baron called back, and smoothed his straggly moustache tenderly. The green dye had almost grown out.

'Next time, I'll use the whole bottle!' she shouted.

The Horned Baron winced and looked out miserably at the empty road. 'Where are you, Grubley?' he muttered. 'Don't let me down . . .'

'*And* a wire brush!' Ingrid added.

The Horned Baron's eyes grew steely. 'If you *do* let me down, Grubley, there'll be a place waiting for you beside Randalf down in the dungeons.'

'Walter!'

'The smallest dungeon with no window.'

'*Walter!*'

'And twenty hand-picked stinky hogs for company . . .'

'There's someone at the door, Walter!' Ingrid shrieked. 'Do I have to do *everything* myself?'

'And regular visits from the Baroness,' muttered the Horned Baron, trotting towards the door. 'I'm on my way, my sweet!'

'Well done!' shouted Ingrid sarcastically. 'And for your sake, Walter, I hope it's those singing curtains turned up at last. I'm sick to death of hearing about squeezed sheep. I want to be lulled, Walter. I want to be soothed . . .'

'And so you shall, my honeyed sugarplum,' the Horned Baron called back.

He opened the door. A short, slight individual with a striped tunic and a feather in his cap stood on the top step. 'Greetings-elf!' he announced. 'I bring greetings from Mr Grubley of Goblintown.'

'Is there a package to go with the greetings?' the Horned Baron asked hopefully.

'No, just a message,' said the elf, lowering his head and shaking it regretfully.

The Horned Baron rolled his eyes. 'So, what is the message?' he asked.

The elf took a deep breath and cleared his throat. 'Having travelled to the four corners of Muddle Earth, Grubley of Goblintown has procured a length of enchanted material which, even now, is being transformed into singing curtains, the like of which have never before been seen or heard.'

'Thank goodness for that,' the Horned Baron muttered.

'However . . .' the elf continued.

The Horned Baron raised his hand. '*However?*' he said. 'I don't like the sound of that.'

'I could skip to the "best wishes" if you like,' said the elf.

'Is there nothing about when the curtains will be ready?' asked the Horned Baron.

'That's part of the "however",' said the elf.

The Horned Baron tutted. Above his head, he could hear Ingrid stomping backwards and forwards with growing impatience. 'All right, then,' he sighed. 'Get on with it.'

'However,' the elf resumed, 'due to unforeseen circumstances, the curtains are taking somewhat longer to make than expected. They will be delivered to you tomorrow teatime at the very latest, probably . . .'

'Tomorrow teatime!' gasped the Horned Baron. '*Probably!*'

'*Grubley's Discount Store* would like to take this opportunity to apologize for any inconvenience . . .'

The Horned Baron snorted. 'You don't know the half of it,' he muttered. 'I don't know how I'm going to explain all this to her upstairs.' He shook his head. 'Is that it, then?' he asked the greetings-elf.

The elf nodded. 'Just about,' he said. He held out his hand. 'That'll be three brass muckles.'

'What?' said the Horned Baron. 'You mean Grubley sent a greetings-elf without paying for the stamp?'

'Ah, yes,' said the elf. 'I forgot. There's a PS. Sorry about the stamp. It can come off my final bill when we settle up.'

'Final bill!' the Horned Baron shouted. 'Settle up! I'll settle up all right. One dungeon, twenty pink stinky hogs and a no-good wizard should just about do it!'

'Is that the message you wish to send back?' asked the greetings-elf.

'Yes, I . . .' The Horned Baron frowned and stroked his chin. 'That is, *no*,' he said.

'No?'

'No,' the Horned Baron confirmed. 'Simply thank Grubley for his message and tell him I look forward to his arrival . . .'

'WALTER!'

'His *speedy* arrival,' he corrected himself.

'OK,' said the greetings-elf, 'though personally, I liked the stinky hogs message better myself.' He stuck out his open palm a second time.

The Horned Baron sighed and dropped three muckles into the outstretched hand. The greetings-elf pulled a stamp from a pocket, licked it and stuck it on to his forehead. Then he turned and skipped off down the stairs and away. For a fleeting

~ 118 ~

instant, the Horned Baron imagined that *he* was a greetings-elf, setting off without a care in the world.

'*WAL*-TER!!'

The carefree daydream popped. He closed the door. 'Yes, my sweetness,' he called up the stairs.

'Was that my curtains?' she shouted back.

'Not as such,' the Horned Baron confessed.

'What's that supposed to mean?' demanded Ingrid.

'It was *news* of your curtains, my sweet,' he explained. 'There was been a slight hitch . . .'

'*Hitch*, Walter?' said Ingrid. 'I don't like the word *hitch*. You know that. I don't like it at all.'

'I know, my turtle dove,' said the Horned Baron soothingly. 'There have been unforeseen circumstances. You know how it is! Grubley's promised me they'll be here tomorrow,' he added.

'*Tomorrow!*' screeched Ingrid. 'But what am I supposed to do tonight? I shan't be able to sleep a wink, I just know I shan't. And you know what I can be like when I'm over-tired.'

'Indeed, I do,' said the Horned Baron wearily.

'Grumpy, Walter. I shall be very grumpy. You won't recognize me!'

'Oh, I think I might,' he muttered beneath his breath. 'Believe me, Ingrid,' he called upstairs, 'you just can't rush these things. I mean, singing curtains, Ingrid, fashioned from only the finest enchanted cloth, tasselled and sequinned, and hand-stitched by a master sewing-elf. It'll be well worth the wait when they do arrive, you have my word . . .'

'*If* they arrive,' Ingrid shouted, and the entire castle shook as she slammed the door of her bedchamber hard shut. The sound of loud thuds and muffled sobs echoed above as Ingrid threw herself around the room.

The Horned Baron shook his head. 'This is all your fault, Grubley,' he said. 'I mean, why put a blasted advertisement for blasted singing curtains in that blasted catalogue of yours if you don't actually have any blasted singing curtains in stock and have to go chasing round Muddle Earth searching for some? Blasted funny way to run a business!' His eyes narrowed. 'You've upset my beloved Ingrid, that's what you've done – and when Ingrid's upset, *I'm* upset! And when I'm upset . . .'

'The Horned Baron's going to be so pleased with me,' said Grubley.

'So you already said,' the goblin muttered as he rethreaded his sewing-elf. 'Twice.'

'But he is!' said Grubley. 'I can't wait to see his face . . .'

'*La, la, la,*' sang the material.

The goblin picked up a large, shiny pair of scissors, laid the material out across the workbench and began to cut it in half.

'*La, la . . . Ouch! Ouch! Ouch!*'

'Will you stop doing that!' shouted the goblin, and slammed the scissors down. He turned to Grubley. 'You see the trouble I'm having! Every time I try and cut the cloth in two, it makes a racket. And it's *very* off-putting,' he said. 'Are you absolutely sure you want curtains? I could do you a very nice roller blind.'

Grubley shook his head. 'Apparently, the catalogue specified singing *curtains*,' he said, 'and the Horned Baroness has set her heart on them.'

The goblin picked up the scissors again. 'I don't know why you advertised something you don't keep in stock in the first place,' he grumbled.

'That's the strangest thing,' said Grubley. 'I don't remember putting them in the catalogue.'

'Well, someone must have,' said the goblin.

'I know,' said Grubley, frowning. 'I just don't under-stand it.' He looked up. 'Still, I've got the cloth now. That's the most important thing. And as soon as you've made it up as curtains, I'll get them over to the Horned Baron's castle. So if you wouldn't mind . . .'

'It's all right for you,' said the goblin. 'You don't have to work with material that won't keep quiet.' He fingered the frayed cloth, which gave a high-pitched squeak. 'Giving me the heebie-jeebies, it is.'

'Here,' said Grubley, reaching into his pocket and

pulling out a pair of large furry earmuffs. 'Try these.'

The goblin stared at them. 'What am I supposed to do with them?' he said.

'They're earmuffs, stupid,' said Grubley irritably. 'You put them over your ears.'

The goblin did as he was told, flattened out the material and raised his thumbs. He hadn't heard a thing.

'Excellent,' said Grubley. 'Now get on with the curtains.'

The goblin looked at him blankly.

'*Get on with the curtains!*' shouted Grubley.

The goblin frowned and mouthed the word, *what?*

Irritated, Grubley lifted one of the earmuffs and leaned forwards. 'GET ON WITH THE CURTAINS!' he bellowed into the goblin's ear.

'All right, all right,' the goblin said, pushing the earmuffs back into place. 'I'm not deaf!'

'Give me strength!' Grubley muttered.

The goblin sat down on the stool, picked up his scissors again and this time – despite the singing, wailing and frequent cries of '*Ouch!*' – cut the cloth and set the sewing-elf off stitching at a furious pace.

'Very nice,' said Grubley, holding the curtains up at last. 'Very homely. A genuine pair of singing curtains.'

'*La, la, la. La, la, la,*' sang the curtains, in a discordant duet.

'Call that singing!' said the goblin. 'More like . . .'

'Oh, don't *you* start,' said Grubley. 'The Horned

Baroness is tone deaf. She'll love them, and that's all that matters.' He frowned. 'Randalf the Wise,' he said. '*Wise*, indeed! Heading for the Ogrehills, he was. Not very wise at all, if you ask me!'

'We came, we saw, we ran away,' said Veronica from the top of Randalf's head as Norbert trudged back down the mountain road. 'Joe the Barbarian, mighty warrior-hero and Henry the Hairy, faithful battle-hound – missing, presumed pulverized . . .'

'Yes, all right, Veronica,' said Randalf. 'You've made your point.'

'Engelbert the Enormous,' she continued, 'missing, presumed sheep squeezing . . .'

'Shut *up*, Veronica!' said Randalf.

Norbert wiped away a tear. 'Have you decided where we're going yet, sir?' he asked.

Randalf sighed and nodded. 'Home,' he said.

'Home, sir?' said Norbert.

'Yes, Norbert,' said Randalf. 'Let's go home.'

Two of Muddle Earth's three moons were high in the sky. They shone down brightly on a gathering of twenty or so ogres who were all sitting in front of their caves, around a huge, roaring fire. The air echoed with the sound of soft, satisfied slurping as the ogres sucked their thumbs.

One ogre – the biggest of them all – was rubbing a dog slowly up and down his cheek, and smiling happily. The dog was wagging his tail and emitting a curious yodelling bark of utter contentment.

One of the ogres removed his thumb from his mouth and turned to the boy next to him. 'Old Engelbert's just his old self again,' he said.

'Yeah, you *have* calmed him down, Joe,' said another.

'He just needed a bit of understanding,' said the first ogre.

'It's all any of us need,' chipped in a third.

'After all,' said the first, 'how would *you* like it if you'd lost your special snuggly-wuggly?' He held up a tatty teddy with one eye, one ear, one arm and no legs. 'I don't know what I'd do if Trumpet ever went missing!'

Joe nodded. He couldn't quite believe what he was seeing or hearing. The other ogres held up their own snuggly-wugglies one after the other – a grubby fluffy bunny, a fuzzy blanket, a tattered scrap of towel . . .

'Course, Engelbert was always particularly proud of his snuggly-wuggly,' said the first ogre. 'Bit niffy, it was. And threadbare. But Engelbert loved it. And do you know why?'

'Why?' said Joe.

''Cause it was enchanted,' said the ogre. 'It sang.'

'Did it now?' said Joe thoughtfully.

'His mother got it for him when he was a baby,' the ogre went on. 'From one of the wizards on the Enchanted Lake. Roger the Wrinkled, his name was . . .'

'Course, that was back before the wizards disappeared,' the second ogre interrupted. 'You can't get anything enchanted these days. That snuggly-wuggly was unique. Irreplaceable.'

'Which is why Engelbert took it so badly when it went missing. It used to lull him to sleep every night.'

'Engelbert loved his snuggly-wuggly,' said the second ogre. 'He said it smelled of warm hugs. Took it everywhere, he did . . .'

Engelbert, who had clearly been listening in, suddenly sat forwards. 'Until somebody took it!' he exclaimed. 'I woke up last week and there it was, gone.' His face clouded over. 'Stolen, it was! Someone had stolen my snuggly-wuggly. My lovely singing snuggly-wuggly . . .'

'Steady on, big fellow,' the other ogres told him. 'Stay calm.'

'It made Engelbert angry,' Engelbert continued, his voice trembling and his face all blotchy and red. 'And sheep are no good. They might be soft, but they make such a horrible sound – even when you hardly squeeze them at all.'

Henry barked excitedly, and licked Engelbert's bulbous nose. A broad smile spread over the ogre's features.

'Not like Henry here,' he said. 'He has a lovely singing voice.'

'This snuggly-wuggly,' said Joe. 'Did it go *la, la, la . . . ?*' he crooned, singing in his deepest, groaniest voice.

'Yes,' said the ogres excitedly. 'How did you know?'

'I think I may have seen it,' he said, as he remembered his encounter with Grubley on the road from Elfwood.

'Anyway, it doesn't matter now,' Engelbert said. 'I don't need my old snuggly-wuggly back. Not now I've got Henry.' He rubbed him affectionately up and down his cheek again.

Henry wagged his tail with pleasure and barked his strange yodelling bark. Engelbert chuckled.

'Just listen to that,' he said, and tickled him under his tummy. 'He's perfect.'

Joe nodded sadly. '*I* think so,' he said. 'The thing is, Engelbert, he belongs to me. And I would miss him, too. I've had him ever since he was a little puppy.'

Engelbert looked up. His jaw dropped. 'You're . . . you're not going to take him away, are you?' he said. 'You wouldn't leave Engelbert without a snuggly-wuggly again? I couldn't bear it.'

'And you know what happened last time,' the other ogres warned him.

'I know,' said Joe. He turned to Engelbert. 'But, supposing I could get your real snuggly-wuggly back,' he said. 'You'd let me have Henry back then, wouldn't you?'

The ogre pouted. 'I don't know about that,' he said reluctantly.

'Engelbert, I'm talking about your *old* snuggly-wuggly,'

said Joe softly. 'Your *best* snuggly-wuggly. The snuggly-wuggly you've had since you were a baby ogre, that sings you to sleep and smells of warm hugs.' He smiled. 'The snuggly-wuggly you love as much as I love Henry.'

Engelbert looked at Joe, then at Henry – then back at Joe.

'All right, then,' he said at last. 'It's a deal.'

Shortly after teatime the following day there was a loud knock at the castle door. The Horned Baron ran to answer it. Grubley was standing there.

'At last!' the Horned Baron exclaimed. 'You took for ever!'

'Singing curtains can't be rushed,' Grubley explained. Having passed the greetings-elf halfway between Goblintown and the castle, he already knew how desperate the Horned Baron was to receive them. 'Besides,' he added, 'what's all this stuff about dungeons and wizards and pink stinky hogs?'

'Never mind!' the Horned Baron humphed. 'You've got them, that's the important thing.' He frowned. 'Where are they?'

Grubley took off his backpack and opened it up. The sound of two muffled voices singing in discordant harmony filled the hallway. Grubley pulled out the pair of curtains and displayed them over a crooked elbow.

'They look a bit tatty,' said the Horned Baron. He wrinkled his nose. 'And they niff a bit,' he added. 'Perhaps you'd see your way to knocking a little bit off the final price . . .'

'You must be joking,' said Grubley, outraged. 'These singing curtains are unique. You wouldn't believe the lengths I had to go to to find them.'

The droning song grew louder. It echoed round the vaulted ceiling and floated up the stairs.

'Walter!' came a strident, yet hopeful, voice. 'Is that *singing* I can hear? Have my singing curtains finally arrived?'

'Y . . . yes, they have,' the Horned Baron called up. 'If you can call that tuneless cacophony *singing*,' he muttered under his breath.

'Course, you don't have to have them,' said Grubley, folding the curtains up. 'If you don't want them, I know plenty who do . . .'

'Oh, Walter,' Ingrid replied. 'You wonderful Horned Baron, you! I knew you wouldn't let me down. I never doubted you for a moment.'

'But if you *do* want them,' Grubley continued, as he opened his backpack, 'then, as you well know, you owe me a pouch of silver pipsqueaks.'

'Daylight robbery,' the Horned Baron complained. 'One pouch is more than enough . . .'

'WALTER!' Ingrid shrieked. 'I am a patient woman. But

you are trying that patience, Walter. You are pushing it to the very limit.' She paused. 'I WANT MY SINGING CURTAINS NOW!'

'Right away,' the Horned Baron said. He turned to Grubley and thrust the pouch of silver pipsqueaks into his hand. 'I take it hanging the curtains up is included in the fee.'

'Not normally,' said Grubley. The Horned Baron's eyebrows drew together menacingly. 'But for such a valued customer,' he added in an oily voice, 'I'd be only too happy to oblige.'

Just then, there was a furious hammering at the door. Grubley jumped. The Horned Baron spun round.

'What now?' he said.

'WALTER!'

'Coming . . . I mean, going . . .' the Horned Baron called back, as he headed first for the staircase, then back for the door, not knowing for a moment whether he was coming or going.

The hammering resumed, louder than ever, and accompanied by a loud voice shouting, 'Open up! Open up! It's a matter of life and death!'

The Horned Baron raised his eyebrows to the ceiling. 'If it isn't one thing, it's another!' he said.

'WAL-TER!!'

'You take the curtains up,' the Horned Baron told Grubley. 'I'll see who's at the door. It's probably another case of badly squeezed shcep.' He shook his head. 'When I get my hands on that Randalf character . . .'

As Grubley disappeared upstairs, the Horned Baron crossed the hallway. Before he arrived at the door, however, it burst open and slammed back against the wall behind. Silhouetted in the doorway, the Horned Baron saw a wiry, dishevelled youth with matted hair, dusty clothes and one wellington boot.

'Don't tell me,' he said. 'You're here to complain that your sheep have been squeezed. Look, for the hundred-and-first time . . .'

'Horned Baron,' said Joe, as he strode into the hallway. 'Just the person I wanted to see.' He held out his hand. 'It's Joe. Remember? Joe the Barbarian? Warrior-hero?'

'Barbarian? Warrior-hero?' said the Horned Baron distractedly as he glanced past Joe and up the stairs. 'Joe . . . Ah, yes. I didn't recognize you without the saucepan on your head. How are you and how did you get on? And where's that wizard?'

From upstairs, there came the enthusiastic sound of *oohing* and *aahing*. 'Oh, Walter, they're divine!' Ingrid called. 'No one else has got anything like them. Wonderful!

The very height of fashion!' There was a pause. 'They *are* the very height of fashion, aren't they, Walter?'

'Yes, dear,' he replied wearily. 'And the pinnacle of good taste.'

Joe smiled.

'New curtains,' the Horned Baron explained.

'*La, la, la. La, la, la . . .*'

'*Singing* curtains,' he explained. 'Ingrid's set her heart on them. Apparently, they're all the rage.'

'Yes,' said Joe. 'That's what Grubley said, when I saw him.'

'Singing curtains!' Ingrid trilled. 'My very own singing curtains!'

'Very rare,' said Joe. 'Very hard to come by – you don't find enchanted material every day.'

'And what if they are?' said the Horned Baron, suddenly defensive. 'I dare say a Horned Baron's entitled to buy his beloved wife a little gift now and then. More to the point, what are *you* doing here?'

Joe breathed in and pulled himself up to his full height. This was the part he'd been practising. 'I, Joe the Barbarian, have performed the task you bade me carry out.'

'You, what?' said the Horned Baron.

'I have brought you the head of Engelbert the Enormous.'

The Horned Baron's jaw dropped. 'You have?' he said, then frowned suspiciously. 'Where is it, then?'

'*WAAAARGH!!*'

The screeching shriek of terror was quite the loudest noise Ingrid had emitted all day. It was deafening. It made the windows rattle and the staircase shake.

'*WAAAAAARGGHH!!!*'

Even the Horned Baron, who was used to Ingrid's hysterical response to spiders, bugs and not getting her own way, realized that this time, something was definitely not right. The poor woman sounded terrified out of her wits. *Something* was up there and, for the first time since Joe had burst in, the Horned Baron was pleased to have a warrior-hero in the castle.

'Follow me,' he said, turning and heading up the stairs.

As they burst into Ingrid's bedchamber, the door to her *en-suite* bathroom slammed shut.

'Get rid of it!' shrieked Ingrid from behind the door. 'It's hideous!'

The Horned Baron looked round to see the great, knobbly, three-eyed head of Engelbert the Enormous sticking in through the window. 'What's the meaning of this?' he demanded.

'The head of Engelbert the Enormous,' said Joe. 'As you requested.'

'But it's still attached to his body!' thundered the Horned Baron. 'This is an outrage! What kind of a warrior-hero *are* you?'

'And what kind of a Horned Baron are *you*?' Joe retorted.

'Stooping so low as to buy curtains made out of an ogre's snuggly-wuggly!'

'An ogre's snuggly-wuggly?' said the Horned Baron with surprise.

'*La, la, la . . .*' sang one curtain tunelessly.

'*La, la, la . . .*' its neighbour droned back.

The Horned Baron's eyes widened. 'Are you telling me that these singing curtains have been fashioned from an ogre's snuggly-wuggly?'

Joe nodded. At that moment, a huge hairy hand thrust its way through the window and seized first one, then the other curtain, and whisked them away.

'Grubley!' roared the Horned Baron. 'Grubley, I demand my money back.'

But Grubley was not there. As his name echoed round the castle walls, Grubley was already on the road and hurrying back to Goblintown as fast as his legs would take him.

'One snuggly-wuggly,' Engelbert was saying as he rubbed it up and down his left cheek. 'Another snuggly-wuggly.' He rubbed the second one up and down his right cheek. 'It's even better than before.'

'Twice as good,' said Joe, relieved that the ogre didn't seem to be upset that his snuggly-wuggly had been cut in two. 'But remember what you promised, Engelbert,' he said. 'It's time for you to keep your side of the bargain.'

'What do you mean?' said Engelbert, then winked

(with his middle eye) just to show that he was joking. 'Here we are then, Joe the Barbarian,' he said and, reaching into the bed chamber again, placed Henry gently down on the rug. 'Look after him,' said Engelbert. 'He's one in a million!'

'I know he is,' said Joe, as Henry raced across the room and jumped up at him, tongue lolling and tail wagging. He looked up at the window to see Engelbert smiling back at him. 'Goodbye, Engelbert,' he said. 'And thank you.'

'Goodbye, Joe,' boomed the ogre as he stomped away. 'Goodbye, Henry,' his voice floated back.

Henry barked.

'Walter!' screeched Ingrid from the bathroom. 'That lumpy great ogre is stealing my singing curtains! Walter!'

'*La, la, la . . . La, la, la . . .*' sang the curtains – softer and softer as they were carried off, until the sound of their tuneless discord faded away completely.

'There,' said Joe to the Horned Baron. 'He's gone. And now he's got his snuggly-wuggly back, there won't be any more sheep squeezing. I can guarantee it.' He smiled. 'And now to the matter of my fee.'

'What?' exclaimed the Horned Baron.

Henry growled. The Horned Baron eyed him warily.

'Ah yes, your fee,' he said. 'A handful of brass muckles, wasn't it?'

'A pouch of silver pipsqueaks,' said Joe. 'That was what we agreed.'

'I most certainly . . .'

Henry growled again, not loudly, but just enough to remind the Horned Baron he was still there.

' . . . did,' the Horned Baron said. 'A pouch of silver pipsqueaks it is.' He reached into the folds of his jerkin, pulled out a jangling leather pouch and, with a long, miserable sigh, reluctantly handed it over.

'Thank you,' said Joe. 'And now, if you'll excuse me, I've got to see a wizard about a journey home.'

He turned, whistled for Henry and strode back to the entrance to the bedchamber. As he reached the door, Ingrid let out a tremendous screech of rage, followed by an even louder, 'WALTER!'

The Horned Baron blanched. 'I'll see you out,' he said, as he trotted after Joe.

'*WALTER!*'

'That is, if I can't tempt you to stay,' he said. 'How would you like to be my personal bodyguard?'

'*Errm* . . . No thanks,' said Joe. He quickened his pace, taking the stairs two at a time and hurrying across the hallway. Henry kept close to heel.

'Wait a moment,' puffed the Horned Baron. 'I'll make you an offer you can't refuse . . .'

'By-eee!' Joe called back. He slammed the door shut and dashed off.

Behind him, Ingrid's voice rang out. 'Call yourself a Horned Baron!' she shrieked. 'You're pathetic! A disgrace! I'm opening the cupboard, Walter. I'm getting the green dye out, Walter – *and* the wire brush . . .'

Joe smiled to himself. What with Engelbert getting his snuggly-wuggly back and the Horned Baron getting his comeuppance, things were going rather well. Now, all he had to do was persuade Randalf to send him back home, and then *everything* would have reached a satisfactory ending.

And as for the story he had to get done when he arrived back, after his time in Muddle Earth, 'My Amazing Adventure,' would be the easiest essay he had ever had to write.

'Come on, Henry,' he said. 'Let's see if we can't make it back to the Enchanted Lake before daybreak.'

The sun had already risen by the time Joe and Henry arrived at the Enchanted Lake. As the low, bright rays of light cut through the early-morning mist, a broad, shimmering fish flopped down through the air and into the gaping beak of a waiting lazybird.

'Another day in Muddle Earth,' Joe murmured and shook his head. 'I'm almost getting used to it.' He turned to Henry. 'Almost,' he said, staring up at the great lake of water hovering high above his head. 'How on earth do we get up there?'

Henry barked and wagged his tail.

'Clever boy,' said Joe, for there, beside Henry, was a small bird-box on top of a pole, with a bell hanging from it on a hook. A notice said, *Ring for attention.* Joe rang the bell.

A lazybird flew out of the box, a small elf clinging to its back, and flapped upwards.

'*Ding-dong,*' droned the elf, disappearing over the lip of

the lake. '*Ding-dong. Ding-dong . . .*'

Joe and Henry waited, and waited. Then a loud voice came from above. 'Grab on to the rope!'

Joe scrambled to his feet and looked up. 'Norbert!' he exclaimed.

The ogre was far up above his head and leaning precariously over the side of the water's edge. A long rope, with a basket secured to its end, was dangling down from his great fists. Joe reached out and grabbed a hold.

'That's it!' came Norbert's voice, encouragingly. 'Now climb in, both of you, and I'll pull you up.'

Trembling with unease, Joe climbed into the basket, sat cross-legged and pulled Henry on to his lap. He wound the lead around his arm, and gripped the sides of the basket tightly with both hands.

'Ready?' shouted Norbert.

'Yes,' Joe shouted back. 'As ready as I'll ever b— *Whooah!*' he cried out, as the rope jerked, the bowl wobbled and he found himself rising up, up, up into the air. He'd forgotten just how high the Enchanted Lake was.

'This is terrifying!' he shouted.

'Be thankful you're not

getting up here the way the others had to,' Veronica's voice floated back. 'It took several flocks of lazybirds to lift Norbert off the ground – and you should have seen the state of his shirt when they'd finished!'

Henry whimpered. Joe hugged him and whispered that everything was going to be all right.

With a last grunt of effort, Norbert pulled the basket up over the edge of the lake and held it next to a small flotilla of kitchen sinks. Randalf and Veronica were in one, Norbert was squashed into the second, while the third was empty. All three were roped together.

Randalf leaned forwards. 'Joe!' he said.

'Randalf!' Joe replied.

'Am I glad to see you,' said Randalf.

'Not half as glad as I am to see you,' said Joe.

'Indeed, I am *twice* as glad,' Randalf insisted.

'Whatever,' said Veronica. 'Let's just get back to the houseboat before someone – mentioning no names, of course,' she said, eyeing Norbert accusingly. 'Before *someone* pulls out another plug.'

'I didn't *mean* to,' Norbert protested.

'Never mind all that, Norbert,' said Randalf. 'You're getting the basket wet. Joe, you and Henry climb into that spare kitchen sink, and Norbert will paddle us all back. Won't you, Norbert? There's a good fellow.'

Everyone took their places. Norbert began paddling furiously.

'And then you must tell me everything that happened,' Randalf shouted across the foamy water. 'Every single detail.'

'He did *what*?' Randalf exclaimed.

'He tickled Henry's tummy,' Joe repeated. 'And I could tell at once that Henry liked it. I looked round for you lot, but you'd all run off.'

Randalf coughed with embarrassment and turned a florid shade of pink. 'A tactical retreat, my lad,' he said. 'Withdrawing. Regrouping . . .'

'Running for dear life,' added Veronica.

'Shut up, Veronica,' said Randalf. 'Go on, Joe.'

'It was just like you said,' said Joe, and tapped the side of his head. 'Psychology!'

'You see,' said Randalf triumphantly. 'Didn't I tell you?

With your Trident of Trickery and Helmet of Sarcasm . . .'

'Oh, no,' Joe interrupted. 'It had nothing to do with *them*. In fact, they just got in the way, so I took them off.' He looked up guiltily. 'I'm afraid they got a bit squashed when Engelbert accidentally trod on them.'

'Never mind that now,' said Randalf. 'What exactly did you mean by psychology?'

'Well, it was clear that Engelbert liked Henry,' Joe explained. 'From the moment he picked him up and rubbed him up and down his cheek, he was a changed ogre. A real softy . . .'

Randalf frowned. 'He'd lost his snuggly-wuggly, hadn't he?' he said. 'That's what he was so angry about. And when he found Henry he calmed down again.'

Joe nodded.

'It's all falling into place,' said Randalf. 'The fits of rage. The squeezed sheep. Norbert, you should have realized.'

'Sorry, sir,' said Norbert.

'Yet Henry is with you now,' said Randalf eyeing the dog thoughtfully. 'How did you manage to get the ogre to give him back?'

'Simple,' said Joe. 'I found the snuggly-wuggly he'd lost.'

'Where?' asked Randalf, intrigued.

'At the Horned Baron's castle,' said Joe, and smiled at Randalf's obvious confusion. 'I'll give you a clue,' he said. 'We all saw the ogre's snuggly-wuggly earlier on,' he said, 'when we were heading for the Ogrehills. 'Saw it, *and* heard it . . .'

'Grubbers!' Randalf exclaimed. 'Why, he had a roll of singing material under his arm, didn't he? I remember now, he was on his way to Goblintown to have it turned into curtains for the Horned Baron's wife.' He frowned. 'Norbert, you're an ogre. I would have expected you to recognize another ogre's snuggly-wuggly.'

'Sorry, sir,' said Norbert once again. 'I don't seem to have had a very good day, do I?' he added sadly.

'Grubley, Grubley,' said Randalf, sucking air through his teeth and shaking his head. 'I never trusted him. What a rogue! What a scoundrel. Stealing an ogre's snuggly-wuggly! Because of him, the whole of Muddle Earth was thrown into turmoil.' He clapped Joe on the shoulders. 'And so it would have remained, my lad, if you hadn't come along.'

'It . . . it was nothing,' said Joe.

'Nothing?' Randalf cried. 'Why, Joe the Barbarian, warrior-hero from afar, Muddle Earth will be for ever in your debt.'

'That's great,' said Joe, 'and now, if it's all the same with you, I really *really* would like to be getting home. I've done my bit . . .'

'But, Joe,' said Randalf. 'Joe the Barbarian. There is one small matter . . .'

'Oh, yes, I was forgetting,' said Joe as he pulled the pouch of silver pipsqueaks from his pocket. 'The Horned

Baron gave me this. It's my fee.' He held it out. 'You may as well have it. I won't be needing it where I'm going.'

'Oh, Joe,' said Randalf. 'Your bravery is unsurpassed, your ingenuity unequalled and now I find your generosity is also unmatched – and yet that was not the little matter to which I was referring.'

'Then, what is it?' said Joe. His heartbeat was beginning to race. 'I've kept my side of the bargain. Now it's time to keep yours. You *must* send me home.'

'I can't,' he said.

'Can't?' said Joe. 'What do you mean, *can't*?'

Randalf looked down. 'I mean, I can't,' he said.

'He's right, you know,' said Veronica. 'He wouldn't know where to start, I can vouch for that.'

Joe's stomach churned. His head spun. 'But . . . but you brought me here,' he said.

'I know,' said Randalf. 'I used my warrior-hero-summoning spell,' he said. 'Unfortunately, it is the only spell I have to hand.'

'Yeah,' said Veronica scornfully, 'that's because all the other spells – including the warrior-hero-returning spell are . . .'

'Are elsewhere,' Randalf interrupted hurriedly.

'Can't you fetch it?' said Joe.

'I'm afraid not,' said Randalf.

'You mean to say, I'm stuck here!' said Joe indignantly.

'For the time being,' Randalf confirmed.

'No, no, I've got to get back . . .' said Joe. 'Why can't you *fetch* it?' he demanded. 'Why?'

'Because . . . because . . .' Randalf faltered.

'Go on, tell him,' said Veronica. 'You know where it is. After all, there's only one place it could be!'

'Where?' said Joe.

Randalf grimaced. 'Giggle Glade,' he said.

'Giggle Glade?' said Joe.

'It's in the middle of Elfwood,' said Randalf.

'Elfwood?' said Joe. Veronica had mentioned Elfwood before.

'It's the residence of . . .' He shuddered violently. 'Dr Cuddles.'

'Dr Cuddles . . .' said Joe slowly.

'Blimey,' said Veronica. 'He's more of a parrot than I am, and that's saying something for a budgie!'

'Dr Cuddles is . . . is the one who stole Roger the Wrinkled's *Great Book of Spells*,' Randalf confessed. 'He's been using it ever since. You remember the flying cupboards?'

'And the stampeding cutlery?' said Norbert.

Joe nodded. Randalf shuddered again.

'That was no doubt the work of Dr Cuddles,' he said. 'If anything goes wrong in Muddle Earth, you can bet your last pipsqueak, somewhere at the bottom of it all, you'll find Dr Cuddles of Giggle Glade!'

'That's it!' Veronica exclaimed.

'He's power mad!' said Randalf. 'He'll stop at nothing to take control of Muddle Earth and become its absolute ruler. And if that should ever happen,' he went on, 'then all the denizens of Muddle Earth would be forced to dance to his evil tune . . .'

'*That's it!*' squawked Veronica a second time.

'*What's* it?' said Randalf irritably.

'It wasn't Grubley who stole the ogre's snuggly-wuggly,' said Veronica. 'He was telling the truth when he said he obtained it from one of his contacts. The question is, who was that contact?'

Randalf shook his head. 'You don't mean . . .' he said.

Veronica tutted impatiently. 'Just think about it. Who stood to gain from Engelbert destroying the Horned Baron's castle in his rage?' she asked. 'Who would have welcomed a bit of argy-bargy between the goblins and the ogres? And where was Grubley coming from with that roll of singing material? Elfwood! And who lives in Elfwood?'

'Dr Cuddles,' said Randalf, Norbert and Veronica in hushed unison. 'Stealing an ogre's snuggly-wuggly! What will he think of next!' They all shook their heads.

It was Joe who broke the long silence that followed. 'That's handy,' he said.

Randalf looked at him quizzically. 'Handy?' he said.

'You'll be able to find out when we pay him a visit to

ask him to return the *Great Book of Spells*,' he said.

Randalf laughed nervously. 'Joe, my dear boy, nobody pays a visit to Giggle Glade. You can't just ask Dr Cuddles to return the spell book. That's what Roger the Wrinkled and the other wizards thought. "We'll discuss it over a nice pot of tea, Randalf," they said – and look what happened to them!'

'What?' said Joe.

'Well, I don't actually know,' admitted Randalf. 'But they didn't come back!'

Joe shrugged. 'If going to see Dr Cuddles of Giggle Glade is my only chance of returning home, then it's a risk I'm prepared to take. Besides,' he said, before Randalf – or Veronica – could speak, 'you're forgetting something very important.'

'And what might that be?' asked Randalf.

Joe smiled. 'I am JOE THE BARBARIAN!' he proclaimed in his biggest voice.

'I . . . I know that,' said Randalf uncertainly. 'But . . .'

'Trust me,' said Joe. 'I'm a warrior-hero.'

A chill wind whistled through the trees of Elfwood. The leaves rustled, the boughs creaked. At its very centre, the dappled light illuminating Giggle Glade was fading fast.

'We failed, master,' came the nasal voice of Dr Cuddles's assistant.

'Yes,' came the squeaky reply, followed by high-pitched giggles. 'We failed.'

'And we planned the singing curtains scam so well! The fake advertisement in the catalogue. The theft of Engelbert the Enormous's snuggly-wuggly – ooh, those ogres can be *so* stupid! The haggling with that odious little goblin, Grubley . . . It was all going so well.'

'Yes,' Dr Cuddles giggled unpleasantly, 'by now, Muddle Earth should have been in chaos! And I would have been its ruler. I didn't think my old friend, Randalf the Apprentice, had it in him to use that spell a second time.' The sinister giggles grew louder. 'Curse that warrior-hero!'

'My thoughts entirely,' his assistant agreed.

'But our work shall continue. I shall devise an even better plan! One that cannot fail! I shall destroy the warrior-hero once and for all!' he shouted, each word interspersed with the hideous giggling. 'I shall conquer the Horned Baron!'

All round the clearing, the woodland creatures were troubled by the sound of the raised voice. As it reached its terrifying crescendo, stiltmice tottered, tree rabbits fell out of their trees, while the roosting batbirds – already wary after an attacking flock of cupboards had left them battered and uneasy – deserted their perches and flapped off across the sky.

'That all sounds absolutely super,' said his assistant.

'Now, how about a nice cup of tea and a snuggle-muffin. I've decorated one specially with your face . . .'

'What would I do without you, Quentin?' said Dr Cuddles. 'Now, I need to get down to my plan.' He stroked his chin. 'I must cover every angle. Allow for every possibility.' He looked up. 'I'm thinking dragons. I'm thinking mangel-wurzel marmalade. I'm thinking small, tinkly teaspoons . . .' He giggled and rubbed his hands together gleefully. 'It's going to be perfect, Quentin.'

'Ooh, you're so evil, master,' Quentin purred.

The giggles grew menacing. 'You haven't seen anything yet, believe me, Quentin,' he said. His voice (and giggles) became louder. 'And there is not a thing that Randalf, or anyone else, can do to stop me! I, DOCTOR CUDDLES OF GIGGLE GLADE, SHALL BECOME LORD AND MASTER OF MUDDLE EARTH!!!' he roared, and he threw back his head in crazed triumph.

'*Tee-hee-hee-hee-hee-hee-hee-hee . . . !*'

Book 2

HERE BE
DRAGONS

Prologue

I t was night-time in Muddle Earth and the air was still. High up in the sky, its three moons – one purple, one yellow and one green – were dotted about the dark, cloudless sky. They shone down brightly, like three spotlights, casting multicoloured light and shadow on buildings, trees and the Enchanted Lake, which floated at the top of a waterfall. They glinted on the massed ranks of shiny cutlery which stood in a broad semicircle at the entrance to a vast mountain cave.

To the left was the knife section. Several neat rows of knives – some smooth, some serrated, some straight, some curved – ascended in size, from modest butter knives at the front, through steak knives, bread knives and carving knives, to a line of hefty meat cleavers at the back.

To the right were the spoons, also standing in neat rows; first egg spoons, then teaspoons, then dessertspoons and tablespoons, and finally a somewhat rowdy collection of tall ladles, all jockeying for a good position.

Between these sections were the rest. Everything from forks, whisks, skewers and spatulas, to grinders and graters, egg slicers, nutcrackers and garlic crushers.

They all seemed to be waiting. But waiting for what? Nobody seemed to know. There was a rumour that a small teaspoon had gone missing and that they shouldn't begin until it showed up. The hanging around, however, was taking its toll. Tempers were fraying. The forks were fidgeting, the spoons were pushing and shoving among themselves, while the steak knives – never ones to be messed with – were beginning to throw their weight about, jostling the ladles and trying to pick fights with everyone apart from the meat cleavers. At the front of the central section – primly keeping itself to itself – the egg slicer pinged and twanged impatiently.

When *was* it all going to begin?

Just then, there was a movement from the front. A pair of sugar tongs strode pompously across the dusty ground and climbed on to a small boulder. The coloured moons glinted on its highly polished whorls and curlicues. It raised a single tong and tapped sharply on the rock.

Apart from the egg slicer, which had instantly fallen into expectant silence, none of the cutlery had noticed the newcomer at the front. It tapped again, more insistently this time.

A couple of spoons near the front nudged each other and shushed the others. A group of cheese knives cut their communication short, cocked their curved blades to one side and turned to face the front.

One by one, the individual pieces of cutlery fell still, until it was so quiet that you could have heard a toothpick drop.

There was a dull thud at the front of the central section as a silver toothpick dropped to the ground, followed by an apologetic murmur when it picked itself up again.

The sugar tongs tapped on the rock a third time, and raised one tong high into the air. Then, having satisfied itself that everyone was paying attention, it waved its tong with a flourish.

As one, the cutlery began playing and the air filled with a strange and haunting percussion. Jingling and jangling, clinking and clanking, the cutlery followed the commands of the conducting sugar tongs – now playing softly, melodically; now rising up, little by little, towards a glorious clashing crescendo.

Just as it was about to reach its loudest, the music was suddenly joined by another sound. It was deep and gravelly. It made the ground tremble. It was coming from the entrance to the cave.

The sugar tongs nodded approvingly, and urged the cutlery to play louder still. The cutlery obliged.

The next moment, a tendril of smoke – glittering in the coloured light of the moons – came coiling out from the inky darkness of the entrance to the cave. It looped and spiralled, and floated away. It was replaced by another, as the deep, rumbling roar grew louder.

Something was stirring.

The sky lightened, the moons set and the sun rose on another day in Muddle Earth. At the Horned Baron's castle, there was the sound of heavy footsteps and angry muttering as the Horned Baron himself ran down the castle steps and out into the garden.

'Where are they?' he grumbled. 'Where can they possibly be? I— *Ooof!* Who's that?'

'It's me, sir,' came a small voice. 'Benson.'

The Horned Baron looked down at the ground by his feet, where a small goblin with a big nose – one of the castle gardeners – lay sprawling in the dust. 'Well, watch where you're going, Benson.'

'I will, sir. I'm sorry, sir,' he said as he climbed to his feet and brushed himself down. 'I was just putting the final touches to the garden,' he explained, and swept his arm round in a wide arc.

The Horned Baron looked round. With the trestle tables standing bare, the tents and stalls lying on the ground waiting to be erected, and a small army of goblins rushing this way and that, arms full and constantly bumping into each other, the scene was one of absolute chaos. From the look of things, they'd hardly even *started* to get the garden party ready.

'Never mind all that,' he said, grabbing Benson by the sleeve. 'Have you seen them?'

'Seen who?' said Benson.

'Not *who*, you imbecile,' bellowed the Horned Baron. '*What!* The Baroness's sugar tongs! Have you seen them?'

The gardener shook his head slowly. 'I'm afraid I

haven't, sir,' he said. The Horned Baron sighed with irritation. 'They must have disappeared like the others,' Benson went on.

'The others?' the Horned Baron roared. 'What do you mean, the others?'

'All the other cutlery. Cook can't find any of it anywhere. Disappeared, it has. All of it. There isn't so much as a silver toothpick left in the whole of the castle.'

The Horned Baron blanched. 'Are you telling me . . . ? Do you mean to say . . . ?' He swallowed. 'Are there at least some butter knives? Tell me there are some butter knives.'

'No.'

'Teaspoons?'

'Not a single one.'

'And what about . . . ?'

'All gone, sir. From the carving knives to the ladles for the mulled punch. They've all vanished without a trace.'

'But this is an outrage!' the Horned Baron thundered. He turned pale. 'What's Ingrid going to say? She's already in a state over the sugar tongs. *"I can't possibly hold a garden party without any sugar tongs!"* – her very words. What on earth is she going to say when she discovers that the rest of the cutlery has disappeared as well?'

Just then, there was a loud *crash* behind them. Benson and the Horned Baron turned to see two goblins sprawling on the ground. 'I'm so sorry,' said one apologetically as he rubbed his head.

'My fault entirely,' said the other. 'I wasn't looking where I was going.'

The two of them were surrounded by pencils, sticks and playing cards. The Horned Baron bent down and picked up a pencil.

'What is this?' he said.

'It's a pencil, sir,' said the goblin.

'I can see that!' the Horned Baron snapped. 'But what's it doing here? What are all of them doing here?'

'It's cook's idea,' said the first goblin.

'She's using a sword to slice the bread and a ruler to spread the butter,' the second goblin chipped in.

'The pencils are for stirring the tea,' the first goblin explained.

The Horned Baron groaned wearily.

Benson picked up a pointed twig. He held it out for the Horned Baron to see. 'It's my own invention,' he said proudly.

The Horned Baron did not look impressed. 'A pointed twig?'

'Not just a pointed twig,' said Benson. 'It's a sugar lump

stabber. Sugar tongs are a thing of the past. They're history. Why, with a sugar lump stabber like this you can—'

Abruptly, the Horned Baron bent over double and clutched his head in his arms. 'This is a catastrophe,' he wailed. 'A calamity! Ingrid's going to go berserk. She'll never speak to me again!' He frowned thoughtfully. 'Then again, every cloud has its silver lining.'

He noticed a playing card at his feet. Benson and the two kitchen goblins watched him as he picked it up and turned it over. He took a deep breath.

'So, what is this and what's it to be used for?' he asked.

'It's a playing card,' said the first goblin.

'It's for . . .' The second goblin faltered. 'For . . .' Suddenly his face brightened. 'Playing *cards*.'

The Horned Baron's face turned from pink to red to purple. Benson butted in, fearing his employer was about to explode. 'They're to go in the games tent over there,' he said, pointing to a round, green tent sandwiched between a trestle table and a *Test Your Strength* booth. 'For our younger guests,' he explained. 'I've organized all sorts of entertaining pastimes. *Pin the Tail on the Pink Stinky Hog, Hunt the Exploding Gas Frog, Musical Worms, Pass the Pancake . . .*'

'Yes, yes,' the Horned Baron interrupted. 'Carry on.' He turned to go. 'I must go and tell Ingrid,' he said. 'She won't like it, though. She won't like it one little bit . . . *OOOOF!* Not again!' he bellowed as a second scurrying figure walked slap bang into him. 'Can't *anyone* in this place watch where they're going?'

'I'm so, so sorry,' lisped a soft, slightly muffled voice. The Horned Baron turned to see a tall, stooped individual dressed in a hooded cape. 'I didn't see you there, your Baron-ness. Careful with that stick, you could have someone's eye out with that . . .' His voice faded away. He shifted the heavy bundle from under his right arm, to under his left. 'So, where do you want it?'

'I beg your pardon,' spluttered the Horned Baron.

'This,' said the stranger, holding up the bundle. There were poles and hooks and a roll of lilac and shocking pink canvas.

'What is it?' asked the Baron. 'Tell me it's a set of cutlery. Please, I'm begging you.'

'Oh, you are a one,' came the voice from inside the hood. 'It's the Rose-Petalled Pavilion of Loveliness, of course.'

'Of course,' said the Horned Baron flatly. 'How silly of me. I need sugar tongs, not to mention knives, forks and spoons – and you bring me a Rose-Petalled Pavilion of Loveliness.'

'That's right, sir,' the voice confirmed. 'No garden party should be without one. Trust me. The Baroness will love it.'

'I do hope so,' said the Horned Baron. 'Put it up over there,' he said, pointing to an empty corner.

'WALTER!'

As his name echoed round the garden, the Horned Baron blanched. He looked up at the Baroness's bedroom window. 'Coming, my turtle dove,' he called back. 'I've got something here that's going to make you very, very happy.' He clutched the pointed twig tightly.

'It had better!' Ingrid's voice floated back, low and loaded with menace. 'Remember what happened last time you failed to make me very, very happy, Walter.'

The Horned Baron rubbed his ears gently, and winced at the memory. 'How could I forget?' he murmured. 'How could I ever forget?'

The air around Trollbridge was still, quiet – and decidedly niffy. The trolls' love of mangel-wurzels had one unfortunate side effect which afflicted them while they were asleep. A rasping sound, like a brass band tuning up, floated up from the sleeping town.

Batbirds roosting close by found their eyes beginning to water as the odour hit them. And as a gentle breeze got up, an unfortunate tree rabbit took the full blast, and tumbled from its high branch in a dead faint.

Perched on a stool at the centre of a great pile of rubbish – elbows on his knees and head in his hands – was the toll-keeper of Trollbridge's main gateway. A stocky character with tufty hair and protruding teeth, he had – like the whole of Trollbridge – overslept. His helmet was on crooked and there was a half-eaten mangel-wurzel in his lap. His snoring was slow and regular. His tummy gurgled and his trousers rumbled.

'*Pfeeeeeep!*'

From the back of his patched, baggy trousers came a movement. There was something in his back pocket, and it was trying to escape.

The troll held his breath for a moment as, still sound asleep, he reached round and scratched his backside. As he did so, the movement in his pocket grew increasingly agitated. The next moment, something shiny and silver popped up from the pocket. It was the head of a spoon.

'*Pfeeeeeeeep!*' went the troll, and a passing batbird fell from the sky.

The spoon wriggled, squirmed and tumbled out of the pocket and on to the ground with a soft tinkling clatter.

It gave a little sigh, picked itself up – and sighed again.

The early-morning sun glinted on the tiny spoon as it tripped daintily through the rubbish. Past a rusty watering can and a chipped plate it went, over heaps of nuts and bolts, and out on to the wide, dusty road.

Something was calling it. Something that could not be ignored.

Joe Jefferson was rudely awakened from a deep sleep by a loud *crash*. He rolled over, but kept his eyes clamped tightly shut. He listened intently.

There were various sounds to be heard. A clock ticking. Plates clattering. Someone in another room humming tunelessly . . .

Joe's heartbeat quickened. Could that be his bedroom clock ticking? Was it his mum preparing breakfast he could hear? Was that his dad humming in the shower?

Dare he open his eyes to see?

Slowly, he opened his left eye a fraction. The room was dark, its contents indistinct. So far so good. Was he back in his own bedroom once more, after what must have been the weirdest dream of his life?

His eyes snapped open.

No, he was not! He was in a hammock on a houseboat on a floating lake. What was left of his so-called warrior-hero outfit – saucepan lid, welly and a sackcloth cloak with a fake-fur trim – was lying about him, waiting for him to get dressed.

'Damn and blast!' he exclaimed, sitting bolt upright. 'I'm still here in Muddle Earth.'

'And good morning to you, too, I'm sure,' said Veronica huffily.

Joe turned to the budgie perched on the knotted cords at the foot of his hammock. He noticed her feathers were looking damp and dishevelled.

'I . . . I'm sorry,' he said. 'I just thought . . . hoped . . .' His eyes misted over. 'Dreamed . . .'

'Ah, dreams,' said Veronica understandingly. 'I dream of

a nice little cage. Nothing fancy. A little mirror, some bird-seed, perhaps a little bell to tinkle if I get bored. But I have to make do with this houseboat and Randalf the so-called Wise. Randalf the *Mean*, more like it. A little mirror. I mean, is that too much to ask? Well, is it?'

Just then the door opened, and a short, portly individual with thick white hair and a pointy wizard's hat walked in. It was Randalf the Wise. Joe's dog, Henry, was by his side, dripping wet. The moment he saw Joe, he bounded across the room, jumped up at the hammock and began licking Joe all over his face.

'Morning, Joe,' said Randalf. 'I've just taken Henry for his early morning swim.' He patted his round stomach. 'Nothing like an early morning swim to set you up for the day.'

'Next time, wake me up before you dive in,' said Veronica peevishly, shaking water from her feathers.

'Ah, there you are, Veronica,' said Randalf brightly. 'Forgot you were on my head. Sorry about that.'

'This wouldn't happen if I had a nice cage, like a normal budgie,' said Veronica. 'And a little mirror, perhaps a bell if I got bored . . .'

'You're not still going on about that, are you?' said Randalf. 'I've told you before, cages are for canaries. You're my familiar. Your place is here, where I can keep an eye on you.' He patted the top of his head. Veronica fluttered over and landed on it.

'Dreams,' she said, with a sigh.

CRASH!

It was the noise that had first woken Joe, only louder. And it was followed immediately by the sound of the door at the far end of the room slamming back against the wall. A massive, knobbly ogre hurtled in, a heavy frying pan clutched in one great fist.

'Norbert!' Randalf shouted. 'What *do* you think you're doing?'

'That elf, sir!' Norbert blustered. 'It's been at the snuggle-muffins.'

As Joe turned, he caught sight of something small and plump scurrying across the floor. The next instant, the frying pan crashed down heavily behind it, missing the elf by a fraction. The houseboat rocked and swayed.

'And stay out of my kitchen!' Norbert cried.

The elf skidded to a halt, and darted back between Norbert's legs. Norbert watched it going, his head getting lower and lower – until he collapsed in a heap.

The houseboat pitched about violently.

'Be careful, Norbert!' said Randalf. 'You don't want to capsize the boat.'

'*Again*,' added Veronica tartly.

'Sorry, sir,' said Norbert, as he climbed to his feet.

The elf made a dash for the clock on the wall. 'Half-past morning!' it shouted cheerily as it shimmied up the pendulum and disappeared through a small door above the clock face.

'Time for some breakfast,' said Randalf.

'Squashed tadpoles! My favourite,' said Norbert, examining the contents of Randalf's dripping hat. 'They're delicious frittered.'

'Ugh,' Joe shuddered.

'An acquired taste,' said Randalf nodding. 'And stiltmice are pretty tasty, too . . .'

'Tadpoles, stiltmice,' said Joe, shaking his head with disgust. 'When my mum makes fritters she uses pineapples, or bananas . . .' His face dropped. His lower lip quivered.

'Joe,' said Randalf, looking concerned. 'If these fritters mean so much to you, then perhaps . . . this evening . . .'

'It's not the fritters!' Joe shouted. 'It's my mum. And my dad. And the twins – and even Ella. I miss all of them.' He took a deep breath. 'I want to go home.'

Randalf clapped his hand on to Joe's shoulder. 'Believe me, my boy, there's nothing I'd like better than to send you home. I've been racking brains for a solution, but . . .'

He shrugged. 'Don't give up hope, Joe. I'll give the matter my full attention later. Something will turn up. I just know it will.'

Joe hung his head. He had no idea how long he'd been in Muddle Earth. Since the length of the days and nights never seemed to be the same from one day to the next, it was impossible to tell. All he knew was that Randalf had said the same thing on a dozen occasions before. *Something will turn up.* But would it? Why should this time be any different from all the others? He was about to say as much when he heard a weak knock at the door.

Randalf sat down at the small table. 'Bring on the fritters, Norbert, old fellow,' he said. 'I'm so hungry, I could eat a pink stinky hog!'

'Wasn't that the door?' said Joe.

Norbert frowned and scratched his head. 'It still is,' he said. 'Isn't it?'

'I didn't hear anything,' said Randalf.

'Neither did I,' said Veronica.

There was a second knock, even feebler than the one before – followed by a squeaky little sneeze.

'*Atish-ii!*'

'You're right,' said Randalf. 'Wonderful hearing my boy – *warrior-hero* hearing, one might say. Get the door, there's a good chap, Norbert,' said Randalf.

Norbert hesitated. 'You mean it *is* a door,' he said. 'For a moment, I wasn't sure . . .'

'Of course it's a door,' said Randalf.

The third knock was followed by a second sneeze and a long, weary groan.

'Just, open it, Norbert!' said Randalf. 'Now.'

Norbert strode back across the room and pulled the door open. And there – silhouetted against the low sun – was a short, bony creature, dripping with water from head to foot and standing in a pool of his own making. The peaked cap he was wearing bore the insignia E.M.

He pulled a soggy envelope from the inside of his saturated mailbag and held it up.

'Imp . . . *atish-ii.* Import . . . *atish-ii.* Important . . . *atish-ii! atish-ii! atish-ii!*' He pulled a handkerchief from his pocket, wrung it as dry as he could, and blew his nose upon it. 'Of all the stupid places to live,' he complained, 'you lot had to choose the middle of a floating lake. Have you any idea how long it's taken me to swim up that waterfall? I mean, I'm not one to complain—'

'Glad to hear it,' said Randalf sharply. 'Now hand over the envelope.'

'Not to you,' said elf.

'And why not, pray?' said Randalf, affronted.

'Because you're not the person named on this envelope,' the post-elf told him. 'The directors of Elf Mail take a very dim view of letters, cards, parcels or packages being handed over to the wrong person.'

'But if you've come to the right address, it *must* be for

me,' said Randalf. 'Unless it's for Norbert here. Or Veronica.'

The post-elf looked from one to the other, before shaking his head. And for a foolish moment, Joe wondered whether it might be for *him*.

'Who *is* it for, then?' Randalf demanded.

The elf looked down. 'Grand Wizard . . .'

'Well, that certainly rules *you* out, Randalf,' Veronica muttered.

'Shut up, Veronica,' said Randalf.

'Grand Wizard, Roger the Wrinkled,' the elf announced. 'And you,' he said, pointing accusingly at Randalf, 'are not wrinkled. Roger the *Fat*, maybe, but not Roger the Wrinkled. Besides,' he added, 'the canary called you Randalf.'

'The *canary*!' Veronica squawked. 'How dare you!'

Randalf drew himself up to his full height. 'I am Randalf the Wise,' he announced, 'personal assistant to Grand Wizard, Roger the Wrinkled who, while away on . . . on vacation, has left me in charge.' He plucked the envelope from

the elf's hand. 'I am authorized to deal with *all* his corre-
spondence.'

The elf made a grab for the letter, but Randalf was
quicker and hid it behind his back. The elf looked close to
tears.

'I'll get into trouble,' he said. 'They'll take away my
peaked cap and badge.'

'*I* won't tell if *you* won't,' Randalf reassured him. 'It will
be our little secret.'

'What about the canary?' asked the elf suspiciously.
'Can it be trusted?'

'You've just delivered your last letter, postie,' Veronica
muttered.

'Her beak shall remain sealed,' said Randalf. 'Trust me,
I'm a wizard. Now, off you go.' He turned to the ogre.
'Norbert, show the elf the door.'

Norbert pointed to the door. 'That's the door,' he said.

With the post-elf gone, Randalf scanned the envelope.
'An elegant, noble hand,' he said of the writing. He raised it
to his nose and breathed in deeply. 'And with, if I'm not very
much mistaken, the faintest scent of rose petals . . . I wonder
who it could be from? A sorceress, perhaps? Or a princess?'

'Why don't you open it and see?' said Veronica.

'Because, my impatient feathered friend, half the
pleasure of receiving an envelope is wondering what it
might contain,' said Randalf. 'At the moment, it could be
anything.' He pushed his finger into the fold of the envelope

and tore along the top. 'A love letter, a cheque, notification of some great success . . .'

'Or a final demand for payment,' Veronica noted.

'We shall see,' said Randalf. He reached inside the envelope. His finger and thumb closed around a large pink and white card. 'Ah, the thrill of anticipation!'

He pulled the card out and scanned it quickly. His eyebrows shot up.

'Well?' said Veronica. 'Good news or bad news?'

'It is an invitation,' said Randalf.

'Good news, then,' said Veronica.

'From the Horned Baron and his lady wife . . .'

Veronica groaned. 'Spoke too soon.'

'Read it out, sir,' said Norbert.

Randalf nodded and cleared his throat. '*Dear Roger the Wrinkled* . . .'

'I don't know,' Veronica grumbled. 'Reading other people's letters. It's disgraceful.'

'Shut up, Veronica,' said Randalf. 'Where was I? Ah, yes. *The Horned Baron, Lord of Muddle Earth, Emperor of the Far Reaches and Monarch of the Glen; beloved, munificent, bountiful, much-loved, fair-minded ruler of* . . .'

'Get on with it,' said Veronica.

Randalf frowned, and continued reading. '. . . *and his beautiful wife, Ingrid* . . . blah blah blah . . . Ah, here we go,' he said. '. . . *do cordially invite Roger the Wrinkled and his fellow wizards to a Garden Party, to be held in the well-maintained,*

~ 174 ~

spacious, luxuriant grounds of their beautiful ancestral castle. (Turn left at the Musty Mountains and follow your nose) . . .'

'Yes, yes,' said Veronica impatiently. 'We all know where his castle is. But when is this garden party?'

'Ah, yes, of course,' said Randalf. He returned his attention to the invitation. 'I . . . errm . . . Oh, Great Moons of Muddle Earth! It's today! At two o'clock this afternoon! And they want a wizard, preferably Roger the Wrinkled, to open it.'

'They'll be disappointed, then,' said Veronica. She snorted. 'Garden party, indeed! Have you seen the state of the Horned Baron's garden? Why anyone in their right mind would want to have a party in it beats me . . .'

'You're missing the point, Veronica,' said Randalf. 'The fee for a wizard cutting the ribbon and saying a few words at the opening of a regal garden party is three gold pieces and as much blancmange as you can eat. I'm down to my last brass muckle,' he added woefully. 'I can't afford to miss such an opportunity . . .'

'But how will we get there?' Veronica persisted. 'You said it starts at two o'clock.'

'Quarter to afternoon!' chimed the clock-elf, putting his head out of the door.

'We do what we always do when we need to get somewhere really, really quickly,' Randalf replied.

Norbert paled. 'Not the winged boots . . .'

'There's no other choice,' said Randalf firmly.

Joe turned to Norbert. 'The *what?*' he said.

'Remember what happened last time,' said Veronica with a shudder. 'Some wizards never learn.'

Randalf clapped his hands together urgently. 'Chop-chop, everyone,' he said. 'Let's get this show on the road.'

'But what about me?' said Joe.

Randalf smiled. 'There's always room on Norbert's shoulders for a warrior-hero, my lad,' he said. Henry barked and wagged his tail. 'Yes, and for his faithful battle-hound.'

'That's not what I meant,' said Joe. 'You promised to help me get home. *I'll give the matter my full attention,* you said.'

'*Later,*' said Randalf. 'I said I'd do it later. And I shall.'

'But when?' said Joe.

'We'll find a way,' he said, cheerily. 'But for now . . .' He shrugged. 'Duty calls. My hands are tied.'

The elf leaped out of the clock. 'You'll never make it,' it laughed. 'You'll be late, late, late!' it said, and collapsed in a fit of hysterical giggles.

'Too cheerful by half, that clock,' muttered Veronica. 'It needs to be wound up.'

'You're right,' said Randalf. 'I'll do it now.' He turned to the clock. 'You're a pathetic, miserable excuse for a time-piece, what are you?'

The furious elf grimaced. 'Are you talking to me?' it demanded in its most threatening voice. 'Are you talking to *me?*'

'There,' said Randalf, 'I've wound it up. Now let's get going. There isn't a moment to lose.'

As the sun rose in the sky, the tiny teaspoon picked its way, slowly and carefully, from tussock to scented tussock, sighing as it went. Drawn on by a strange force, the teaspoon had left Trollbridge and travelled down the dusty Ogrehill road, before turning off into the Perfumed Bog.

Pausing for a moment on top of a particularly highly perfumed tussock, the tiny teaspoon turned its bowl, as if to listen. From somewhere to its left there came a wheezing, squelchy-squelchy noise.

It was closer than before. The teaspoon sighed, trembled and leaped to the next tussock.

And the next.

And the next.

In front of it, something glinted and twinkled in the long grass. The spoon kept on, picking itself up when it fell, refusing to give up. The glinting and twinkling grew brighter.

All at once the grass parted and there, crouching down in the perfumed sludge, was an exploding gas frog – and an enormous one at that. It winked one bulbous eye, then the other. It shifted forwards on its massive forelegs, ready to strike. The warts all over its purple skin throbbed ominously.

The teaspoon slipped as it landed, then picked itself up once again. 'Ah,' it sighed.

The exploding gas frog reared up. Its warty lips parted and a long, thick, sticky tongue flashed through the air and wrapped itself around the tiny teaspoon.

As it disappeared inside the dark, fetid moistness of the gas frog's greedily waiting mouth, the teaspoon let out a last, lingering sigh.

'Aaaaa . . .'

The gas frog snapped its jaws shut, swallowed and grinned contentedly. It turned lazily around, and was just about to hop off back to the ooziest part of the bog where it could digest its meal undisturbed, when something started to happen.

First, a low gurgling noise came from the pit of the gas frog's stomach. Then its warty skin began changing colour – from purple to red to green to orange. Its grin became a grimace.

'*Gribbit*,' it croaked in alarm. '*Gribbit. Gribbit . . .*'

It tried jumping up and down on the spot, it tried beating itself on the back, it tried falling heavily to the ground – but all to no avail. The teaspoon was stuck fast.

The gas frog rolled about helplessly. Its eyes bulged, its tongue lolled, its limbs stuck out rigid and useless. It shuddered and juddered, unable even to croak, and swelled to an immense size. The skin was stretched so taut and so thin that at any moment . . .

BANG!

The sound of the gas frog exploding echoed all round the Perfumed Bog, causing slimy bog demons to dive for cover and pink stinky hogs to break wind. It was deafening. And, when the remains of the hapless gas frog finally fluttered back to earth, also rather messy.

Flying high above the Perfumed Bog in a great, wide arc, the tiny spoon sighed.

At the entrance to the cave, the orchestra was in full swing. To the enthusiastic conducting of the sugar tongs, the spoons were clinking, the knives were clanging; ladles clashed, cake forks clicked – and the egg slicer attempted a rather ambitious solo, which ended in a nasty tangle with a carving knife.

From within the cave, the wispy coils of smoke grew thicker, denser. The orchestra played louder than ever.

Clatter! Clatter! Clink! Clonk!

All at once, cutting across the strange metallic music, came a loud hissing whistle, like a great locomotive letting off steam. Thick grey and white clouds of smoke and steam billowed from the cave and swallowed up the ranks of the cutlery orchestra. Yet still they played on.

Clatter! Clatter! Clink! Clonk!

Then, as the air cleared, a snout with two smoking nostrils could be seen protruding from the entrance to the cave. It sniffed at the air, it trembled – and came a little further forward.

Slowly, slowly, the rest of the great, scaly head appeared. A pair of heavy lids rose, one after the other, to reveal two yellow eyes which looked around in bemusement before focusing in on the wide array of shiny cutlery spread out before it. Its scales rattled as it quivered with obvious delight.

At the sugar tongs' command – and without missing a beat in the music – the orchestra took a step backwards. The creature emerged a little further. A long, scaly neck came into view.

Again, the sugar tongs directed the orchestra to fall back; again, the creature advanced.

An armoured body appeared, and four long, scaly limbs, each one ending in calloused knuckles and taloned toes.

Clatter! Clatter! Clink! Clonk! Clatter! Clatter! Clink! Clonk! The orchestra played on, taking another step back with every *clonk*.

Inch by inch, the creature slowly emerged from the safety of its dark, shadowy cave and out into the bright morning sunlight. It noted the shape and size of each knife, it sniffed at the skewers and spoons – but the further out it came, the further back the orchestra retreated.

Growling menacingly, the creature reared up on its hind legs, flapped its pair of broad, leathery wings and lashed its long serpentine tail. Then, looking up at the sky, it snorted wildly. Two plumes of thick, black smoke emerged from its nostrils and, when it opened its jaws, a searing flame of orange and red accompanied its loud, resounding roar.

The huge, magnificent and fearsome beast had, for many long years, been coiled up around its treasure, sleeping. Now, the cutlery had woken it up. There they were, before it, sparkling brightly in the sun and making such sweet music. The dragon wanted them.

If only they would keep still!

For a second time, the dragon tilted its head back and roared. The tongues of flame licked at a passing squadron of flying wardrobes, scorching their doors – and sending one into a fatal tailspin. It came to earth in the foothills of the

Musty Mountains with a loud, splintering crash.

The cutlery trembled.

Clatter! Clatter! Clink! Clonk!

They fell back another step.

The dragon lowered its head and eyed the orchestra greedily. The sight and sound of the enticing silver cutlery had left it so excited it could barely control itself.

It wanted to add the gleaming silverware to its great glittering hoard. It wanted to possess it; to count it, to sort it, to polish and caress it. It wanted to feel the smoothness of the spoons, the prick of the forks; it wanted to wrap its coils around the cutlery and guard and protect it until the end of time.

The dragon's eyes narrowed as the cutlery backed away. What were they all playing at? Why were they teasing so dreadfully?

The dragon's muscles quivered. Its tail switched this way and that, stirring up the dust. Its nostrils smoked. It was all the creature could do to hold itself back from making a roaring dash at the orchestra – but if it did that, the cutlery might scatter and it would end up with nothing but a few soup spoons.

No, the dragon would have to be cleverer than that. It crouched down, its low-slung body close to the ground and its great, muscular haunches quivering. Then, with one eye fixed on the orchestra, it turned its head, as if about to leave.

The music faltered as the cutlery wondered what to do next. The sugar tongs raised one arm and beckoned.

The orchestra advanced a step.

In an instant, quick as a flash, the dragon twisted round and pounced. The great, scaly beast landed before the orchestra in a cloud of dust and whisked its tail round in a large circle that penned them all in. They were trapped, each and every shiny one of them.

At least, that was what the dragon thought. The cutlery, however, had other ideas. Already, at various points, pieces were breaching the tail-wall and breaking free.

A posse of egg spoons was scaling the long, arrow-shaped tip to the dragon's tail; half a dozen ladles were helping each other over the upper-section, while on the ground in the middle, the egg slicer was jumping down on the curved prongs of a large fork, catapulting knives perched at the other end to freedom.

The dragon bellowed with rage so loudly that the mountains shook. It clacked its talons and flicked its tail up into the air, sending those hapless spoons and forks still clutching on to its scales hurtling up into the sky and away. At the same time, the rest of the cutlery orchestra took the opportunity to make a run for it.

They dashed off across the dusty mountain plateau with remarkable speed and agility. The dragon was left standing. Thrusting forwards, it opened its jaws and sent a blazing torch of fire roaring after them. The flames scorched the ground – and burnished the backsides of a couple of slow dessertspoons. But the cutlery did not stop.

One by one, the stragglers and strays were returning to the main group. Together, they all darted off down a narrow track between two huge boulders.

The dragon stood, perplexed. One moment, it had captured the most wonderful collection of gleaming silverware to add to its hoard; the next, it had lost them all!

In a flurry of dust, smoke, flashing talons and flapping wings, the dragon hurtled across the plain after the fleeing silverware. It would not give up; it *could* not.

The chase was on.

The Horned Baron stood at the top of the castle staircase looking out across the mountains. He glanced at his large, gold pocket watch for the fifth time in as many minutes and shook his head.

'Ten past two, and still no sign,' he muttered. 'What on earth can have happened to them?' First the cutlery, and now this. A garden party without wizards? It simply wouldn't do! Ingrid would never forgive him. 'Where are they?' he groaned. 'Where *are* they?'

'They're here,' said Benson.

'The wizards?' said the Baron excitedly.

'No,' said Benson amiably. 'The sugar-stabbers you

dropped just now. Luckily I picked them up.' The goblin held out a sharpened twig.

'Oh, that,' said the Horned Baron.

'Was the Baroness pleased with them? Was she?' asked Benson, excitedly.

'Not exactly,' said the Horned Baron, rubbing his arm and wincing.

'WALTER!' Ingrid's voice sliced through the hazy afternoon sunshine like a blast of icy air. The Horned Baron shivered.

'Sugar tongs are the least of my worries. Right now I need a wizard. *Any* wizard,' he said nervously. 'Yes, my angel,' he called back.

'Don't you *angel* me,' Ingrid's strident voice rang out. 'You're nothing but a great, big, useless, good-for-nothing lump!'

'I am?' called the Horned Baron.

'Yes, you are, Walter! My corset's burst! Stupid, cheap, flimsy thing!' she complained. 'I don't know where you got it from.'

'The mega-turbo girdle?' the Horned Baron muttered in disbelief. 'The heavyweight, super-reinforced model? Flimsy?' He groaned softly. 'It cost me a fortune . . .'

'Did you hear me, Walter?' Ingrid shrieked. 'I don't know, call yourself a Horned Baron! You can't even do the simplest things right.'

'A thousand apologies, light of my life,' the Horned

Baron called back wearily. 'I shall be up at once.'

'And bring twenty-five metres of tent-cloth with you,' she demanded. 'We'll have to alter the dress. And don't forget your needle and thread this time!'

'As your gorgeousness desires.' The Horned Baron groaned.

'If there's anything I could do to help,' said Benson.

'I think you've done enough,' said the Horned Baron, snapping the sharpened twig and dropping it on the step. He turned away and was about to stride off when a thought occurred to him.

He looked Benson up and down – at his stooped, angular body, at his little beard. With the right clothes, he would make an excellent wizard.

'Actually, on second thoughts, Benson, there *is* something you could do,' he said. 'Get yourself kitted out in a gown and a pointy hat, and meet me back here in . . .' He glanced at his watch. It was eight minutes past. 'In twenty-two minutes.'

'WALTER!' Ingrid shrieked, piercingly loud. 'I'M WAITING!'

'Slow down, Norbert!' Joe cried out, as he lurched this way and that on top of the ogre's left shoulder. He gripped Norbert's collar as tightly as he could with one hand, and held

Henry, who was sitting on his lap, with the other. 'Slow *down*!'

'Can't, sir,' said Norbert breathlessly. 'It's these dratted winged boots.'

'Please try!' Joe pleaded. 'I almost fell off just now!'

They seemed to be taking a short cut down a very steep Musty Mountain track.

'*Whooooah!*' Norbert cried, his arms windmilling wildly as he struggled to maintain his balance.

'This is all Randalf's fault,' said Veronica, who was clinging on to the rim of the wizard's pointy hat. She bent over and bellowed in his ear. 'Wake up, you ridiculous little man! Wake up!'

But Randalf merely snored a little louder. He always fell asleep when riding on Norbert's shoulder – and the bumpier the ride, the deeper the sleep.

There was a violent jolt and, for a moment, Joe was falling backwards into the blurred beige and khaki landscape, while Henry was sliding forwards. Then Norbert stumbled a second time. Joe grabbed at Henry, and clutched a crease of material in the ogre's jacket.

'NORBERT! SLOW DOWN!' roared Joe and Veronica together, with Henry barking his agreement.

'Can't … slow … down …' Norbert gasped, every word an effort, as he careered down a dry gully and bump-bump-bumped his way over a section of large, round pebbles. 'Boots … won't … let … me …'

Joe looked down. Norbert was wearing a pair of

winged boots with four wheels beneath the soles and a spoked wheel sticking out of the heels at the back – just like Joe's Rollerblades back home. The ogre had seemed fine with them, at first . . .

'The Winged Boots of Colossal Speed,' gasped Norbert. 'I'm OK going uphill. It's coming down the other side I need a little practice at.'

Just then, the ground in front of them fell away completely. Norbert's legs pedalled furiously in thin air. Veronica screeched. Henry whimpered. Joe gritted his teeth and waited for the inevitable jolt.

'*Ooof!*' he gasped a moment later as Norbert landed. They were back on the road again – and travelling as fast as before.

'I warned him!' Veronica shrieked. 'I *pleaded* with him not to put Norbert in the Winged Boots of Colossal Speed.'

'You did?' said Joe.

'And would he listen?'

'Obviously not,' said Joe.

'Watch out!' squawked Veronica.

'Oh, help!' Norbert cried out. 'I think I'm about to take another short cut . . . *Whooooooooaah!!!*'

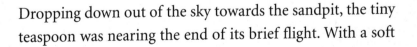

Dropping down out of the sky towards the sandpit, the tiny teaspoon was nearing the end of its brief flight. With a soft swooshing noise – and the hint of a little sigh – the teaspoon landed in soft sand and buried itself up to its handle.

Some way to its right, a family of goblins was seated round a blanket.

'There's not enough sand in this!' said the youngster.

'Shut up and eat your snotbread sandwich, Gob,' his dad told him. 'Your mother spent ages preparing a lovely picnic, and all you've done since we arrived here is complain.'

'Don't go on,' said Gob sullenly. He took a bite of the sandwich. 'What's that?' His eyes lit up with excitement.

'What?' said his mother, her mouth full of cold bad-breath porridge.

'That,' said Gob, jumping up and running over to where the tiny teaspoon had landed. 'Mum! Dad! I've found something!' he called.

'Hog poo?' said his mum.

'Stiltmouse dribble?' said his dad.

'No, it's not something to eat,' said Gob. He crouched down, took hold of the piece of silver sticking out of the sand and pulled. 'It's a . . . a teaspoon,' he said, holding it up. 'A tiny silver teaspoon. Can I keep it?'

'If you like, dear,' said his mother. 'Pop it in your pocket so it doesn't get lost, and let's be on our way. If we set off now, we should be back at Goblintown by teatime.' She smiled. 'You can use your new spoon to stir your spittle tea.'

As it dropped down into the pocket, the teaspoon let out a little sigh. It was warm and moist and smelly in the goblin's trousers, and – the teaspoon trembled – very, very dark.

As they approached the bottom of the Musty Mountains, the road levelled out. In the distance, Joe glimpsed the high turrets and castellations of the Horned Baron's castle and heard garden-party-like sounds floating in on the breeze – a low murmur of voices, a chinking of teacups on saucers and, every now and then, names being announced over a megaphone.

Norbert stopped skating and came to a halt. His heart was thumping; his legs trembled with fear and exertion.

'You know,' he panted, 'I think I'm really getting the hang of these winged boots. Why, with a little more practice . . .'

'. . . You might succeed in breaking our necks,' said Veronica coldly.

Randalf's eyes snapped open. 'Are we there yet?' he said, looking round at the bleak, rocky landscape.

'Almost,' said Norbert, still panting.

Randalf cocked his head to one side. He listened

dreamily to the babble of the guests, the chinking of the cups and saucers – and the band, which consisted of a drum, cymbals, a wheezing set of bagpipes and something that sounded like a pink stinky hog having its tail pulled.

'The garden party must have already started!' he exclaimed. He glanced at his watch. 'Three o'clock! Oh no, we're late! What *is* the Horned Baron going to say?'

'How about, *You're late, you useless, good-for-nothing, miserable excuse for a wizard . . .*'

'Shut *up*, Veronica!' said Randalf. He leaned down and tapped the ogre's head with his staff. 'Proceed, Norbert,' he said. 'To the Horned Baron's castle as fast as you . . . Joe! What do you think you're doing?'

Joe jumped to the ground. He put Henry down beside him. 'If it's all the same to you, we're going to walk the rest of the way,' he said.

Veronica launched herself off from the brim of Randalf's hat, flew down and landed on Joe's head. 'Good idea,' she said.

Norbert lurched forward unsteadily.

'Whooah!' cried Randalf. 'On second thoughts, put me

down, Norbert, and take off those boots. They're quite unsuitable for a garden party.'

'But I was just getting the hang of them,' said Norbert, promptly falling over.

'No arguments,' said Randalf, picking himself up. 'Follow me, everyone!'

They continued in silence. The sounds of merry-making grew louder. Various smells began to permeate the mustiness of the mountains – newly baked cakes, hot toffee, candyfloss. And as they rounded the corner, an imposing grey fortress rose up before them.

'The Horned Baron's castle!' Randalf announced and, leaving the others to catch up, he strode ahead to the main gate.

A seated guard looked up from a tattered scroll with a list of names.

'I am Randalf the Wise,' Randalf announced impor-tantly. He waved Roger the Wrinkled's invitation under his nose briefly, then stuffed it back into his pocket. 'But I may be on your guest list as Roger the Wrinkled. And these,' he said, pointing to the others, 'are . . .'

'Yeah, yeah,' said the guard, stifling a yawn. 'Whatever.' And without even referring to the scroll, he waved them all through.

Somewhat peeved, Randalf stepped through the archway and into a courtyard. A goblin in a grubby costume approached, with a megaphone in one hand. 'I'm the herald,' he said. 'How would you like to be announced?'

'Randalf the Wise,' Randalf told him. 'Grand wizard.'

'Could have fooled me,' muttered Veronica.

'Eh?' the guard shouted. 'Speak up. I said, speak up.'

'My name,' he bellowed, 'is Randalf the Wise! And these,' he continued, introducing the others in his loudest voice, 'are Norbert the Not-Very-Big, Joe the Barbarian and his battle-hound, Henry, and Veronica, my familiar.'

The guard turned and raised the megaphone to his lips. 'Dandruff the Wide,' he announced. 'Halfwit the Non-Furry Pig . . .'

'Give me that!' said Randalf impatiently. He seized the megaphone from the guard and announced himself.

'Stop that!' said the herald, grabbing the megaphone back and hiding it behind his back. 'Announcing the guests is *my* job.' He turned to Joe and Henry. 'What did you say your names were again?'

'Hurry up and get on with it,' said Randalf irritably.

'Hurry-Up! and Getonwithit!' announced the herald through the megaphone.

'Come on,' said Randalf, ushering the others through the gate. 'Let's find the Horned Baron. Maybe there's still time.'

Veronica snorted. 'Time for what? In case you hadn't noticed, they've started without us.'

A waiter approached them, a wooden tray balanced on his upraised hand. 'Cup of spittle tea?' he said, gruffly. 'Cough sandwich?'

'No, thanks,' said Joe, feeling slightly queasy.

'Did I hear someone mention spittle tea?' said a tooth-less goblin who was passing by.

'That's right,' said the waiter. He poured some of the frothy liquid from the pot into a grimy looking cup, added some brown sugar lumps and a pencil, and handed it over.

'Ooh, lovely,' said the goblin. 'But what's the pencil for?'

'Sorry,' the waiter said. 'I'm afraid we haven't got any spoons.'

'Never mind,' said the goblin, tossing the pencil over his shoulder. He spat into the teacup and stirred it up with a dirty finger.

'Ugh,' Joe groaned, and turned away.

In front of him were stalls, booths, tents, trestle tables and marquees all crammed together, higgledy-piggledy, inside the castle garden – though garden was hardly the right word for the courtyard, with its high surrounding walls and single dead tree.

In one corner was a pot filled with limp pansies. In the one opposite, was a lawn the size of a tablecloth – cast in shadow by a large sign warning visitors to *Keep off the Grass.* And in the middle – in the shadow of the dead tree – was a small birdbath, with several lazybirds asleep beneath it.

If the *garden* bit of the garden party was a disappoint-ment to Joe, however, the *party* bit was not. Everyone was eating cake with pointy twigs and stirring their tea with pencils. On a tatty bandstand, a tatty band played an assortment of tatty instruments. Joe smiled. The instrument that had sounded like a pink stinky hog having its tail pulled, was in fact a pink stinky hog having its tail pulled. Next to it, a small goblin hit himself on the head with a cymbal, and a large troll played a wheezing solo on a battered set of bagpipes.

'Roll up! Roll up!' came a voice from his left, shouting above the music. '*Smells in a Jar*. Come and try my *Smells in a Jar*.'

Joe joined a small crowd of trolls, goblins and assorted others clustered in front of a big trestle table. He saw the stallholder at the front select one of the tall jars from the table and hold it up.

'You sir,' he said. 'You look like a goblin of discernment.'

He held the jar out towards a lanky goblin, who nodded. The glass stopper was removed. The goblin leaned forwards, closed his eyes and sniffed.

'*Mmmmmm!*' the goblin rolled his eyes. A huge smile spread across his face. 'Don't tell me, don't tell me . . .'

'Well?'

'I'm getting smelly sock – left foot, I'd say. And just the faintest hint of ogre's underpants.'

'Very good,' said the stallholder. 'I call it *Gym-Kit*. It's one of my most popular smells, after *Spilt-Potty*.'

Chuckling to himself, Joe continued through the jumbled maze of amusements and refreshments, exhibitions and competitions. He paused by a big striped tent with a handwritten sign tied up above the open door-flaps.

Mangel-wurzel Judging in Progress.

Curious, Joe went to the entrance and peered inside. The tent was heaving with trolls, standing about in twos and threes and discussing the mangel-wurzels laid out on the table before them.

'This one's really big,' he heard one saying.

His neighbour nodded. 'And so's this one.'

'Yeah. This one's big too, ain't it?' said another.

'Very big. That one there's big as well.'

'And that one, that's big. The one over there, that's big an' all. And the one next to it, and the one next to that, and . . .'

Joe walked on, past a toffee-nose stall, where you could dip your nose in a bucket of warm toffee, and a candyfloss stall where you could floss your teeth with candy. He was looking at an interesting display on a stall marked *Broken, Missing or Useless*, when he realized that neither Randalf, Veronica nor Norbert were anywhere to be seen. Even Henry had disappeared.

He decided he'd better retrace his steps. It was only when he arrived back at the stage – where the band had been replaced by three rows of tap-dancing stiltmice – that Joe spotted Randalf.

'Randalf!' he cried. 'Randalf!'

The wizard turned and greeted him. 'There you are, my boy. I was just about to ask the herald to call you. Now

where have the others got to?'

'I thought they were with you,' said Joe.

Randalf frowned. 'What do you suppose that is?' he said.

Joe followed his gaze. He was staring at a flamboyant marquee – lilac and pink, with a floral pattern and silver trimmings – which stood in the corner by the wall.

'The Rose-Petalled Pavilion of Loveliness,' said Joe, reading the florid sign outside the marquee.

'Sounds delightful,' said Randalf. 'Remind me to check it out later. But first, we've got business to attend to!'

Just then a mysterious figure in a long, hooded cape pushed a pink tent-flap open and slipped out of the pavilion. He looked round furtively and scuttled into the crowd.

'Randalf the Wise and Joe the Barbarian, if I'm not mistaken,' came a petulant voice behind them. Randalf and Joe spun round to see the Horned Baron glaring back at them. 'Where's Roger the Wrinkled?' he demanded. 'He was meant to be here at two o'clock to open the garden party.'

'He's . . . *errm* . . . otherwise engaged. Top secret,' Randalf added, and tapped his nose conspiratorially. 'He sent me in his place.'

The Horned Baron rolled his eyes. 'I might have known,' he said. 'You're late! And Ingrid's furious!'

Randalf tutted sympathetically. 'That's Elf Mail for you!' he said. 'The invitation only arrived this morning. We got here as quickly as we could.'

'*Hmmph*,' said the Horned Baron. 'It was most inconvenient. I tried dressing up Benson as a wizard, but Ingrid wasn't fooled for a moment. And then there was nothing to cut the ribbon with. All the cutlery's disappeared!' He sighed. 'Had to get an elf to chew through it! Absolute catastrophe, it was.'

'Tragic,' said Randalf. 'Still I'm here now. If there's anything I can do, for a small fee . . .'

The Horned Baron's expression darkened.

'I don't know,' Randalf went on, 'any awards to be presented, cups or medals to be given out, then I'm your wizard.'

'You're no Roger the Wrinkled, that's for sure,' said the Horned Baron. 'But you'll just have to do . . .'

'*WALTER!*'

The Horned Baron trembled from head to foot. 'Oh, good grief,' he muttered. 'What *now*?'

'*WALTER! WHERE ARE YOU?*'

'Coming, my precious!' he called back. He turned to Randalf. 'Must go!'

'Indeed, Horned Baron,' said Randalf. 'And as I say, if there's *anything* I can do. Anything at all . . .'

At that moment, the megaphone burst into life. 'Would the Horned Baron go immediately to the Rose-Petalled Pavilion of Loveliness. Horned Baron to the Rose-Petalled Pavilion of Loveliness. Horned Baron. Calling the Horned Baron . . .'

The Horned Baron turned, then hesitated. 'If you want to make yourself useful, Randalf,' he said, 'go to the marquee and find out what they want. It's that one,' he said, pointing rather unnecessarily at the lilac marquee with the shocking pink rose petals.

Randalf nodded. 'Of course, sir,' he said, 'and . . .'

'*WAL-TER!!*' Ingrid's voice cut through the air like a rusty axe.

'Go, Randalf!' said the Horned Baron sternly. He tugged at his sleeves, straightened his helmet and turned to leave. 'And whatever it is, sort it out. There's a good wizard.'

Randalf turned to Joe. 'Duty calls,' he said. 'Go and find the others. Henry's with Norbert in the Snuggly-Wuggly Corner I expect.'

'Snuggly-Wuggly Corner?' said Joe.

'Next to to the Face-Smudging.'

'Don't you mean Face-*Painting*?' said Joe.

'You haven't seen the troll who's running it,' said Randalf. 'Oh, and Veronica said she wanted to check out the birdbath. Can't think why . . .' He glanced at his watch. 'We'll all meet back here in half an hour. All right?'

Joe nodded. 'Half an hour,' he said.

Randalf watched Joe disappearing into the crowd. He was a good lad. It was such a shame he wasn't able to send him home. He looked round at the lilac-and-pink Pavilion of Loveliness and sighed.

Joe reached the Snuggly-Wuggly Corner just in time to

prise Henry away from an over-exuberant ogre. Norbert was sitting beside them on the floor, sucking his thumb and hugging a frayed toy rabbit. When Joe found Veronica, she was on the birdbath discussing bird cages and small mirrors with several lazybirds.

Back at the Rose-Petalled Pavilion of Loveliness, Randalf lifted the tent-flap and disappeared inside.

Randalf looked round. The marquee was large, carpeted, bathed in a soft lilac-and-pink light, and seemed empty. Randalf let the tent-flap fall back behind him and stepped forward. Immediately, a fiendish booby trap twanged and whirred into action.

A rope tightened, a cork popped, a weight dropped and a noose tightened around Randalf's ankles. With a loud *whoosh*, it whisked him up into the air, where he dangled helplessly from the central pole, his head a metre from the ground.

'Well I never!' Randalf chuckled. 'A most extraordinary fairground attraction.' He wriggled about, sending all the blood to his head. 'I must say, I rather like the way it makes my nose tickle.' He craned his head up a little. 'Most enjoyable, thank you. You can let me down now.'

As if in response, there came a *clink, clink, clink* from outside. It was coming closer, and getting louder and louder.

'Whatever's that?' he wondered.

Outside, all heads turned towards the gates of the castle.

'It's the cutlery! It's returned,' shouted an under-gardener.

'Typical!' muttered Benson. He dropped the handful of pointy twigs he was carrying as the sugar tongs rushed past. 'And there was me thinking sugar tongs were history.'

Cutting a swathe through the crowds, the cutlery charged across the garden. To the front were the spoons, clinking and clanging, behind them the forks and the knives, with the great meat cleavers clanking hot on their heels. Bringing up the rear was the egg slicer, plinking and twanging in an out-of-breath sort of way.

Joe spun round. Norbert laid aside the fluffy toy rabbit he was snuggling and craned his neck. Veronica fluttered above the birdbath as the cutlery clattered past.

'They're all aiming for that marquee,' someone shouted. 'Look.'

Sure enough, with the sugar tongs leading the way, the cutlery was heading noisily towards the lilac-and-pink Rose-Petalled Pavilion of Loveliness. The sugar tongs swept back the tent-flap and hurried in. The others followed.

'My goodness,' said Randalf, his heart beginning to pound furiously. 'Powerful magic is at work here. I don't like this. I don't like this one tiny bit . . .'

Just then, as the final items of cutlery – the egg slicer and a tiny silver toothpick, engraved with the name *Simon* – went inside the marquee, there came a roar so mighty that the ground trembled.

'*ROOOAAARRRGGGHHH!!!*'

The egg slicer twanged with terror as a great talon scraped across its backside.

'Eek!' squeaked the toothpick in dismay.

Outside, someone shrieked: 'It's a dragon!' as a great, winged creature swooped down on the lilac-and-pink tent.

Horrified shouts and cries exploded all around, as everyone tried to get as far away from the Rose-Petalled Pavilion of Loveliness as possible. With their backs to the castle walls, or cowering under trestle tables, or simply crouched down and clutching at one another for safety, they watched as the dragon landed.

It raised its head and let out a triumphant blast of flame. At last, after the long and mighty chase, the treasure was trapped!

The dragon leaned forwards and grasped the tent in its great scaly arms, its savage talons interlocking at the back. Then, with a grunt of effort, it tugged as hard as it could. The guy ropes snapped and the tent pegs scattered as the dragon gathered up the cutlery inside the canvas, turned it upside down so nothing could escape, and slung the whole lot over its shoulder. With a powerful leap, the dragon launched itself up into the sky and soared away.

For a moment, there was silence in the castle garden. Then, from over by the stage, came a lone voice.

'Now *that's* what I call a fairground attraction,' it said.

'Hear! Hear!' said someone else, and some elves burst into polite applause.

Having watched it all, the tall, stooped individual in the hooded cape standing by the gate groaned. 'It's got the wrong person. Master's going to be *so* disappointed,' he muttered as he slipped away.

The herald was running around the birdbath in the middle of the garden, megaphone to his lips. 'The Horned Baron's been stolen! The Horned Baron's been stolen.'

From all round, came a gasp, followed by concerned

muttering and murmuring (and the occasional snigger). Then came a distinctive voice: 'No, I haven't.'

The goblin spun round and found himself face to face with an all-too-familiar helmet and moustache. 'Your Horned Baron-ness!' he exclaimed. 'Can it really be you?'

'Of course, you fool! Who did you think it was?'

The herald raised the megaphone. 'The Horned Baron's safe! The Horned Baron's safe!'

There was some more polite applause (and a few scattered boos). The Horned Baron glared at the crowd.

'Now, what's all this I hear about cutlery? Have the sugar tongs been found?'

'Have the sugar tongs been found?' blasted the herald through the megaphone.

'Do you have to repeat everything I say?' stormed the Horned Baron.

'Do you have to repeat everything the Horned Baron says?' thundered the herald at the crowd.

'Not them. You!' shouted the Horned Baron.

'Not them . . .'

'Give me that!' interrupted the baron, grabbing the megaphone and turning back to the crowd. 'Now, will someone please tell me what is going on!'

'Randalf went into the lilac-and-pink Pavilion of Loveliness,' said Joe, stepping forwards. 'And then all the cutlery came crashing through the garden, led by some sugar tongs, and disappeared inside the pavilion as well.'

'Did you say sugar tongs?' said the Baron excitedly.

'And then a dragon swooped out of the sky and gathered up the pavilion, Randalf *and* all the cutlery, and flew away.'

'But this is terrible!' said the Horned Baron.

'I know,' said Joe, tearfully. 'Poor Randalf.'

'No, I meant the sugar tongs,' said the Horned Baron. 'I mean, what's Ingrid going to say?'

'But what about Randalf?' Joe persisted. With the wizard gone, so too was his only hope of ever leaving Muddle Earth.

'WALTER!'

'I've got enough on my plate without having to deal with some second-rate wizard who's got himself into a scrape,' said the Horned Baron. 'Besides, *you're* the warrior-hero. I'd have thought battling with dragons was right up your street.'

'*WAL-TER!*'

'Now, if you'll excuse me, duty calls,' said the Horned Baron, turning away. 'Coming, my gooey cupcake!' he called.

As the Horned Baron strode off, Joe noticed Norbert pushing his way through the crowd from the opposite direction. Henry was trotting beside him; Veronica was on his head.

'Cheer up,' she said chirpily. 'It might never happen.'

'It already has,' said Joe glumly. 'Randalf was carried off by that dragon.'

'You what?' Veronica exclaimed. 'Oh, the silly old fool!'

'Dragon!' said Norbert. 'Nooooo!!' he wailed, and burst into tears.

'Trust Randalf,' said Veronica, 'to end up as a dragon's dinner.'

'Dinner!' howled Norbert.

'We've got to rescue him,' said Joe. 'Now, did anyone see which way the dragon went?'

'I've got a pretty good idea,' said Veronica. She launched herself off Norbert's head and fluttered off. 'Follow me,' she said, 'to the Broken, Missing or Useless stall!'

As soon as they reached the stall, Veronica found what she was looking for. There, sandwiched between a moth-eaten cardigan and a rusty mangel-wurzel slicer, was a tatty scroll. Joe picked it up.

'*Three turnips, half a cup of grass, one bottle of stilt-mouse milk . . .*' he read. 'It looks like some sort of shopping list.'

'No!' said Veronica. 'On the other side, stupid!'

Joe turned the scroll over. It was a map of Muddle Earth. There was the *Enchanted Lake* where he had first arrived. And *Goblintown*, where Randalf had kitted him out as a warrior-hero. And the *Ogrehills . . .*

Veronica tapped the top left-hand corner of the scroll with her beak. 'Here,' she said impatiently. 'Look!'

Joe looked across the map and gasped. For there,

written across a vast bleak landscape in flamboyant curly-wurly writing, were three words:

Here Be Dragons.

'Here be dragons?' said Norbert, with a shudder. 'I don't like the sound of that!'

'We must go there!' said Joe firmly. 'It's our only chance of finding the dragon.'

'And when we find the dragon?' said Norbert. 'What do we do then?'

'We'll work something out,' said Joe uncertainly. 'Besides, we have no choice.'

'Joe's right,' said Veronica. 'Oh, I know Randalf and I have had our differences. He can be cranky, incompetent . . . miserly . . . pompous, vain and intolerably smug . . . moody, clumsy, lazy, greedy . . . and absolutely impossible to live with . . .' She took a deep breath. 'But he's all I've got.'

'It's decided then,' said Joe. 'We'll set off at once.'

'And you will think of something, won't you?' said Norbert tearfully. 'Before dinnertime.'

'Trust me,' said Joe, grimly. 'I'm a warrior-hero.'

Before the goblin child who found it had managed to use it even once to stir his spittle tea, the tiny teaspoon had dropped down from his pocket to the pavement unnoticed, and disappeared. Over cobbled streets it went, through a crack in the great gates and down the city steps – tinkling and sighing as it went – out of Goblintown and away.

On, on, on, it journeyed. This way, that way – following the force that drew it ever onwards.

Tripping and falling, and sighing as it picked itself up. Then on again. Clinking over rocks, squelching through mud and leaving a fine, broken line through the sand and dust.

At a junction, it jumped a troll cart spilling over with a great mound of straw. *Clink, clunk.* It hopped on to the wheel, up the side and – *pluff* – down in the soft, yellow mattress of straw.

As it lay there, warm and content, the sun glinted down on its polished bowl and elegantly curved handle. It caught the eye of a passing batbird, returning early to its roost.

With a flapping of wings – like a burst of applause – the

batbird swooped round in the sky, and dived.

Down, down it came, legs extended and claws open. Then, with a delicate twist – and a loud squawk – it plucked the glittering object from the top of the hayrick and soared off.

The tiny teaspoon sighed.

Far below, Muddle Earth was spread out like a tatty scroll. The Perfumed Bog. The Enchanted Lake. The Musty Mountains . . .

As the wind blew back against it, the teaspoon shivered – softly at first, then more forcefully. The batbird tightened its grip too late. The tiny teaspoon had already slipped out of its grasp and was falling, falling, falling . . .

Tinkle, clink!

It landed. With a little sigh, it picked itself up. It was standing directly in front of the gates to the Horned Baron's castle. Trembling with anticipation, it hopped on. Through the gate it went, across the gravel and . . .

Gone! They were gone! The teaspoon sighed sadly, wearily. But they *had* been there. All of them. That much was certain. It turned and listened. Yes, there. Over there . . .

The tiny teaspoon turned, sighed, and left the place where the cutlery had been such a short while before. Keeping to the shadows, it hopped back through the castle gates and on into the dusty highlands beyond.

The sounds of the garden party gradually faded away. A wind got up, the sun went down, Mount Boom came nearer. It puffed and wheezed and sometimes exploded weakly – *boom.*

Up ahead were four other travellers. An ogre, with a budgerigar on its head and a young warrior-hero and a dog on its shoulder. The tiny spoon trembled as something stirred in its memory. The touch of warm fingers, the snugness of a dark pocket. It was the young warrior-hero who had found him when he got separated from the others.

With a quivering sigh and a soft *tinkle, tinkle*, the tiny teaspoon picked itself up and quickly followed them.

Silhouetted against the low, setting sun, the dragon swooped down out of the sky and landed at the entrance to its mountain cave. It swung the heavy marquee full of cutlery to the ground with a *clunk*, sat back and wiped its brow.

A batbird circled overhead. The dragon raised its scaly head and blasted it with a searing jet of flames. The batbird flew off, backside and tail-feathers singed, screeching with indignation. The dragon scoured the sky and scanned the scorched, barren land for a sign of any other unwelcome intruders.

There was none.

Then again, you couldn't be too careful. The dragon seized the great clanking bundle in its claws and lugged it into the cave. Down on its belly, it slipped and slithered its way along a low, narrow tunnel and on into a large, domed cavern deep inside the mountain.

The cavern was warm, smoky, sulphurous. The dull red glow of molten rock glimmered from cracks in its towering walls. Gleaming dimly in the faint light was a tall pile of treasure. The dragon purred as it got closer and nuzzled it softly.

There were golden helmets, rusty tap fittings, jewel-encrusted crowns, swords, saucepans, shields with ancient designs, medals and trophies, bracelets and bedsteads, tiaras and tin cans – all heaped together in the centre of the stone floor. And, over by the wall, standing by itself, was a magic golden harp, softly weeping.

The muffled clinking and clanking of the cutlery grew louder as it was plonked down on the pile. With a slash of one long talon, the dragon ripped a large hole in the fabric of the former Pavilion of Loveliness. The cutlery came tumbling out.

The dragon's eyes widened with delight as the wonderful hoard spilled out in front of it. Fine knives, gorgeous forks, dear little teaspoons – and the most adorable silver egg slicer. Cleavers and skewers. Waffle irons and sugar tongs. And – with toothpicks in its beard and forks in the most unlikely places – what appeared to be . . .

A wizard!

The dragon's eyes narrowed. It patted its grumbling stomach and threw back its great scaly head.

'ROOOAAARRRGGGHHH!!!'

'You never know,' said Joe. 'Perhaps it'll just play with him. Like Henry plays with his favourite rubber ball . . .'

'It'll eat him,' said Veronica matter-of-factly.

'You don't know that for certain,' said Joe.

'Bound to,' she said. 'It will be ravenous after that long flight. Toasted wizard would make the perfect dinner . . .'

'Don't say that, Veronica,' said Joe weakly.

'Unless it's so hungry it just eats him raw.'

'Veronica! Shut up!'

Veronica shrugged. 'You did ask,' she said sulkily.

'Yes, but . . . Whooooah!'

'Sorry!' came Norbert's breathless voice as he suddenly lurched to one side. 'There was a pothole.'

'Don't you apologize, Norbert,' said Joe. 'You're doing a fantastic job on those Winged Boots of yours. We're going to be there in no time.' He turned and glared at the budgerigar on Norbert's head. 'We haven't given up on him, even if you have, Veronica.'

'I just think we should be prepared for the worst,' she said.

Norbert let out a stifled sob.

'Well, you're upsetting Norbert,' said Joe, trying to sound brave. 'Now, if you can just stop talking about how hopeless this all is, perhaps I can work out a plan.'

'You're right, of course. Forgive me,' said Veronica. 'So, how exactly *do* you plan to slay this dragon?'

'*Slay?*' said Joe. He scratched his head. 'I thought we

could talk. Bargain. Barter. I thought I'd be able to *reason* with it . . .'

'Reason with a dragon?' said Veronica. 'Don't make me laugh. I'm telling you, unless Randalf's extremely quick on his pins – which would be a first – he's a goner. That dragon will burn him to a crisp with one blast of his fiery breath!'

Just then, above the noise of the clattering wheels, there came the faint sound of a distant roar.

'Hear that?' said Veronica.

'Hear what?' said Norbert.

Joe stared grimly ahead. 'Just go faster, Norbert!' he told the ogre. '*Faster!*'

The tiny teaspoon sighed as it tripped and slipped down into one of the deep imprints left by the ogre's Winged Boots of Colossal Speed. The dust fell in about it, taking the edge off its shine and making it difficult to scrabble out of the narrow trench.

Back on solid ground, it cocked its bowl to one side, and listened. Far, far ahead, it heard a deep, ominous roar that echoed around the rugged landscape and that left it trembling along the length of its handle.

Not so far away – but getting further with every passing minute – were the others. The ogre, the budgerigar, the warrior-hero and his battle-hound.

With a soft sigh, the teaspoon set off once again, tinkling along the stony track as fast as it possibly could.

Inside the cave, the sounds echoing around the great, domed cavern were getting louder. The cutlery was in its orchestra formation, attempting to tune up. It swayed on the mound of treasure – clinking and clanking – while the dragon lumbered noisily about.

The spoons clattered. The knives clashed. Once, an entire set of cake forks was almost destroyed as the dragon's great bulk came crashing down towards them. It was only the quick thinking of the sugar tongs – and a handily placed saucepan lid – that prevented them being crushed and twisted out of shape.

Petrified, Randalf watched it all. He was crouched down behind a jagged boulder over by the wall, trembling at the sight of the dragon which seemed to be whipping itself up into a frenzy of rage. How he had escaped, he would never know.

One moment he'd been tied up inside the Pavilion of Loveliness, with sharp, pointy cutlery prodding and jabbing every inch of his body; the next, a great claw was slashing through the material, the rope – and very nearly his neck.

Randalf shuddered at the thought.

Of course, from the sound of roaring, the smell of

burning and the gut-churning sensation of flight – not to mention the crowd shouting, 'It's a dragon! It's a dragon! Run for your lives!' – Randalf had suspected that he'd been seized by some sort of dragon. But nothing could have prepared him for the sight of the terrifying creature which reared up in front of him as he had tumbled from the tent on a wave of cutlery.

It was gigantic. Monstrous! Every glinting scale was the size of a dinner plate; every claw, a long, curved rapier. Its smoking nostrils alone were big enough to accommodate the wizard's head, pointy hat and all.

As the dragon had spotted the cowering wizard, its eyes had opened wide and its snout had come to within an inch of Randalf's nose. Its nostrils had sniffed. Its stomach had rumbled. Wisps of smoke had coiled into the air . . .

'*Eeek!*' Randalf had yelped and made a dash for it.

With a *clink-clank-clatter-crash* he'd scrambled desperately over the pile of treasure as the dragon had made a grab for him, missed, and snorted with frustration.

Randalf trembled from the tip of his beard to the toes of his boots. He *had* escaped – but for how long? Sending out short bursts of flame, the dragon was clambering all over the pile of treasure, looking under shields and dustbin lids, rooting around in the forks and spoons, and tossing object after precious object aside.

Then – sniffing at something suspicious – it inadvertantly sucked a plumed gold helmet right up inside one of its vast nostrils. It coughed, it snorted, it sneezed – and the helmet shot out at enormous speed, smashing against the side wall with a loud *clang*.

Randalf shrank down behind the rock.

'Why me?' he groaned softly. 'Why do these things always happen to me? Oh, what wouldn't I give to be back on my lovely houseboat, with my feet up, a cup of tea in one hand and a snuggle-muffin in the other.'

The dragon continued searching the heap of treasure, tearing into the metal objects with a horrible vigour and determination. With his heart in his mouth, Randalf risked a peek from behind the rock.

The bad news was that the way out was on the other side of the cavern. The good news was that, by sticking to the shadows, he might just be able to skirt round the walls unseen.

Head down and heart beating fit to burst, Randalf set off. He scurried from rock to boulder, crevice to crack, in short hurried bursts. The last stretch was the most difficult. Between the ridge he was crouching behind and the stone stack by the entrance, there was a broad expanse of bare rock.

'Just stay calm,' he told himself. 'Wait till the dragon's turning the other way and . . . *Now*.'

Setting off like a sprinter from the starting blocks, Randalf dashed across the empty stretch. The dragon snorted.

'Almost there,' Randalf whispered, urging himself on. 'Almost . . .'

Just then, a shrill voice cried out, 'Mistress! Mistress!' It was the magic harp. 'He's over here!' it shrieked. 'The fat wizard's over here!'

The dragon spun round, eyes blazing, talons glinting. Randalf tripped and sprawled on the floor of the cave like a stranded stiltmouse. The dragon's eyes were fixed on him. Too terrified to move, he watched as the monstrous creature flapped its leathery wings, flexed its talons and lunged forwards, its great jaws gaping.

'*ROOOAAARRRGGGHHH!!!*'

'Ooh, I heard it *that* time,' said Norbert, as the noise echoed all around them.

'We must be getting close,' said Joe.

Norbert shuddered. 'It sounds really cross.'

'Either that,' said Veronica, 'or it's *hungry*. Maybe we're not too late, after all.'

'That's the spirit, Veronica,' said Joe.

'Good old Randalf,' the budgerigar chuckled. 'Giving that dragon a run for his money . . .'

Abruptly Norbert sat back and skidded along on the seat of his pants. Veronica squawked. Joe cried out. Henry barked and leaped down on to the safety of solid ground.

'Sorry,' said Norbert breathlessly. 'It's the only way I know how to stop.'

'But why *have* we stopped?' Veronica demanded, smoothing down her ruffled feathers.

'Because of *that*,' said Norbert, and pointed.

Joe and Veronica turned and followed the line of his grubby outstretched finger. It was the entrance to a cave.

'Smoke,' said Veronica softly.

'Footprints,' said Joe.

Henry wagged his tail and barked, first at the cave, then up at Joe.

'Is he in there, boy?' said Joe. 'Is Randalf there?' He swallowed nervously. 'With the dragon?'

A roaring sound echoed through the air, and fresh smoke billowed from the cave entrance. Henry barked excitedly.

'Angry or hungry, it still sounds dangerous,' said Norbert in a quavery voice.

'Are you sure you want to do this, Joe?' said Veronica.

'No one would think any the worse of you if you didn't.'

Joe shook his head. '*I* would,' he said. 'Besides, without Randalf, I'll never get home. I'll be stuck here for ever.'

'There are worse places to be stuck,' said Veronica. 'Like the inside of a dragon's belly, for instance.' She noticed the expression in Joe's eyes. 'Still, if you must, you must,' she added. 'I'll come with you.'

'So will I,' said Norbert, 'if you undo my boots first.'

'Thank you,' said Joe. Henry barked. 'Thank you all.'

'Victory or death!' Veronica squawked.

Joe groaned.

'It'll be all right,' he told himself, muttering under his breath. 'I've taken on a giant ogre before now. And that wasn't so bad. It's what Randalf's always saying, *You just have to bluff, lad. Show them who's boss.*' He wiped the beads of sweat from his brow. 'But a dragon,' he gasped. 'A monstrous, great, fire-breathing dragon!'

He looked ahead at the dark smoke billowing from the cave entrance. It was getting thicker and more pungent by the second. Eyes streaming and heart pounding, he marched bravely on. And as the entrance came closer, he could hear strange noises echoing down the tunnel – snorts and snuffles, gurgles and growls, and a small, high-pitched voice pleading for its life . . .

'Please, please, *pretty*-please, put me down, there's a nice dragon,' Randalf was babbling.

Upside down again, he was dangling from the dragon's claws – his head inches away from the beast's vast and odorous beaked mouth. A forked tongue shot out and flickered round his face. The eyes widened. The jaws cracked open . . .

'No, no, no,' Randalf started up again. 'You don't want to eat me. *Ugh! Ugh!*' he said, screwing up his face. 'Nasty! Chewy! Tough!' He spat. 'Horrible!'

Staring at him curiously, the dragon opened its great mouth wider. Randalf found himself staring down into a long, blood-red tunnel. The stench was incredible; the heat, intolerable.

'For pity's sake,' he gasped. 'You can't eat me, I'm a wizard!'

Behind them, the cutlery started up a low, mournful, clanking funeral march. The dragon narrowed its large yellow eyes.

Suddenly, from outside, a clear, if slightly nervous voice could be heard.

'It is I, Joe the Barbarian! Subduer of ogres, friend of wizards and champion to the Horned Baron himself! And I think you should know – eating people is wrong!'

As soon as his brave words left his mouth, Joe regretted them. What had he been thinking? After all, a dragon was a dragon – and this one, he already knew, was a monster!

From the cave came the sound of scratching, and the dragon's huge, scaly head popped out. It looked around with blazing yellow eyes. Its gaze fell on a boy, a budgie, a not-very-big ogre and a rather scruffy looking dog.

It snorted. A ring of black smoke coiled into the air and sailed away.

Joe desperately tried to stop his teeth chattering. This was no time for his nerve to go.

'Behold, mighty dragon!' he cried. 'I, Joe the Barbarian, stand before you with my fearless battle-hound, Henry . . . the Ferocious. And Norbert the Not-Very . . . *errm* . . . Easily-Calmed-Down-Once-You've-Got-Him-Started. You certainly wouldn't want to make him angry, believe me.' Joe nudged Norbert.

'Grrrrr!' said Norbert feebly.

The dragon raised an eyebrow.

'And he's not alone!' said Joe, urgently. 'For he has come with a great big army of . . . really, *really* angry ogres.'

The dragon frowned and inched forwards for a closer look. It peered round.

'Of course, you can't see them . . . they're masters of camouflage!' said Joe. 'But they are there. Hiding behind rocks. Hundreds of them. And armed – armed to the teeth. Just waiting for my word to throw themselves into battle.'

The dragon began drumming rhythmically on the ground with its talons.

'And that's not all,' said Joe desperately. 'I've got budgies.'

'*Unnh?*' grunted the dragon.

'Yes, budgies,' said Joe. '*Attack* budgies! This is my Wing Commodore. In charge of two dozen budgie squadrons.'

'All trained in unarmed combat and at the peak of their physical condition,' added Veronica quickly. 'Vicious, ruthless and under strict instructions to take no prisoners.' Her voice dropped to a low and, she hoped, menacing whisper. 'You mess with one of my squadrons and . . . and . . . and they'll mess on you!'

'You have been warned,' said Joe. 'I and my mighty army have come,' he said, sweeping his arm around in a circle, 'to set the wizard free. Release him now, and no one will get hurt.'

The dragon looked puzzled. 'Get hurt?' it said. 'Why, darling, of course no one's going to get hurt – unless *I* decide otherwise!'

Joe gasped. 'It can talk,' he hissed.

Veronica nodded. 'Dragons are very good mimics, just like parrots – or lazybirds when they can be bothered. Who's a pretty dragon? Who's a pretty dragon?'

'Shut up, Veronica,' Joe hissed, and turned to the gigantic beast. 'Where is Randalf?' he asked in his biggest, deepest voice. He frowned. 'We're not too late, are we? I mean . . .' He faltered. 'You haven't eaten him, have you?'

The dragon threw back its head and trilled with laughter. 'Randalf! So that's his name, is it? No, darling, I wouldn't dream of eating anyone called Randalf. I mean, what a perfectly dreadful name!'

Joe breathed a sigh of relief.

'Since you're here, you'd better come inside,' the dragon said. 'I won't have it said that Margot Dragonbreath kept guests standing outside in the cold. Come on! Come on!' And with that, the head disappeared back inside.

Joe looked at Veronica, who looked at Norbert, who looked at Henry – who dashed off into the cave, barking and wagging his tail. The others followed him in.

'It's so typical of you dragon-slayer types,' the dragon was saying. 'You see a magnificent creature like me and you just jump to conclusions.'

Behind her, the cutlery was clinking and clanking. Her voice rose above it.

'You assume that I can't wait to devour you whole. I mean, it's so vulgar . . .'

Clatter! Clatter! Clink! Clonk!

'Whereas nine times out of ten . . .' She was shouting now. 'What I really fancy is a toasted teacake and a sponge finger . . .'

Behind her, the cutlery had worked itself up into a frenzy of noise and activity. The dragon spun round furiously.

'Oh, do settle down!' she shouted. She tossed her head. 'I feel one of my migraines coming on.'

The cutlery obliged, bringing the noise down to a more soothing pianissimo. Joe stood open-mouthed, scarcely able to believe what he was seeing.

He was in a huge cavern – hot, dark and incredibly messy. There was junk strewn all over the floor and rising up in the middle into a great unstable heap. Most of the objects were silent and still, but some – the knives, forks, spoons and other assorted bits of cutlery he had seen earlier at the garden party – were anything but.

What *is* going on? Joe wondered.

They were clinking and clanking. They were hopping and jumping about. A collection of knives to his left were clashing their blades and clacking their handles. To his right, a group of forks were twanging and banging. There was a trio of soup spoons; a ladle quartet. And all of them dancing to the same insistent beat which, once again, was building up . . .

Clatter! Clatter! CLINK! CLONK!

What a racket! Joe thought, and winced. What on earth was it up to?

The dragon put a claw to her thin lips. '*Sssshhh!*' she hissed. 'I won't tell you again.'

For a second time, the cutlery became quieter. Not silent. But quiet enough for Joe to hear another noise – a curious muffled grunting and groaning which was coming from somewhere near the wall.

'*Grrrmmbll flammell-flan,*' the voice complained. '*Pfleeem . . .*'

Joe peered into the shadows. There – not ten metres away from the entrance to the cave – was a portly figure, seated on the floor, struggling to remove a large metal bucket which was wedged firmly on to his head. Joe stared . . .

'Randalf?' he said. 'Is that you?'

'*Omm kmomf miff!*' the voice bellowed back.

Joe strode across and seized the bucket. 'Take hold of his legs, Norbert,' he said. 'And when I give the word, pull.'

Norbert did as he was told. Veronica sat on his head, watching. Henry wagged his tail slowly.

'All set?' said Joe.

The cutlery clanged and clattered behind them.

Norbert tightened his grip on the wizard's ankles. 'All set,' he said.

'Pull!' yelled Joe.

At first – apart from a loud echoing scream from the bucket – nothing happened. Joe altered his grip.

'Again!' he cried.

This time, as Norbert tugged the legs, Joe twisted the bucket. There was a loud *pop!* Norbert let go of the ankles and fell down. Joe staggered backwards, the bucket in his hand. And there between them – still seated on the ground with his legs stuck out in front of him – was Randalf. He blinked twice.

'*Waargh!*' he screamed as he saw the dragon. 'She tried to eat me!'

The dragon groaned. 'Typical,' she said. 'Here we go again.'

'She *did!*' Randalf insisted indignantly. 'She had hold of

me and was getting ready to swallow me whole. If you hadn't come along when you did . . .'

'I was simply curious,' the dragon told Joe. 'He came with that lot,' she added, pointing towards the noisy cutlery. 'I thought he was a free gift.'

'A free gift?' Randalf spluttered, outraged.

'The trouble was, he would wriggle so!' the dragon went on. 'He slipped out of my grip and dropped down, headfirst, and got wedged in that,' she said, nodding at the bucket. 'It was entirely his own fault.' She leaned down and pulled Randalf to his feet. 'Now, if you'll just keep still, you funny little man, and allow me to introduce myself. I am Margot . . .'

'A *free gift*!' Randalf bellowed. 'How dare you!'

The cutlery was getting louder again, with one group of meat cleavers particularly rowdy. The dragon clasped her head.

'I am,' she moaned. 'I'm getting one of my migraines.'

Clatter! Clatter! Clink! Clonk!

'A free gift indeed.' Randalf shook his head. 'I'll have you know, madam, that I am a wizard. Randalf the Wise is my name; wizardry, my game. Indeed, I am the finest wizard currently in residence upon the Enchanted Lake.'

'The *only* wizard, more like,' Veronica cut in.

'Shut up, Veronica!' said Randalf.

'Wizard, eh?' said Margot, looking up. She nodded back at the cutlery wearily. 'In that case, perhaps you could get that lot to quieten down a bit.'

Randalf took a sharp intake of breath and shook his head. 'It's not as easy as that, madam,' he said. 'This cutlery is clearly enchanted. Dark forces are at work here, I'll be bound.'

'Yes, and I bet I know *whose* dark forces!' chirped Veronica.

'Shut up, Veronica!' Randalf snapped. 'As I was saying, tricky thing, enchantment. Takes a lot of skill and know-how and years of training. But luckily for you, madam, enchantment is a bit of a speciality of mine.'

'Lucky you!' Veronica muttered sarcastically.

'Veronica, I'm warning you!' Randalf hissed. He turned to Margot. 'Tell me everything you know about this cutlery.'

'Well, they just showed up outside my cave,' she said. 'Wakened me, they did, with their enchanting music – and then led me a fine song and dance until I finally caught up with them. I wanted them for my hoard, you see. What dragon wouldn't?' She shook her head. 'But now I'm beginning to wish I'd left well alone.'

'You're not the only one,' Randalf murmured as he rubbed his bruised and battered body.

The cavern throbbed with noise. The dragon rolled her eyes. 'They're so *loud*,' she said. 'I don't know how I'm ever going to get back to sleep.'

'Sleep?' said Joe. 'I thought you'd only just woken up.'

'That's dragons for you,' said Veronica. 'They spend ninety-nine per cent of their lives asleep and the rest of the time drooling over treasure . . .' She sniffed. 'If you can call this heap of junk *treasure.*'

'I beg your pardon,' said Margot, affronted.

'Well, just look at this place,' said Veronica, with a sweep of her wing. 'I've never seen such a tip.'

Margot's nostrils began smoking. 'How dare you!' she roared. 'That's my hoard you're talking about. Precious heirlooms. Priceless treasures . . .'

'Like the bucket, eh?' said Veronica.

'Bucket? Bucket!' said Margot fiercely. She picked it up from the floor, pulled herself up as high as the cavern would allow and glared at them furiously. 'This is no bucket! Have you no taste? No eye for beauty?' she roared. 'Why, this is the sacred Potty of Thrynn, emptied only once every thousand years.'

'Ugh!' Randalf cried, spitting, snorting and checking his beard for bits.

'Ugh?' said Margot. 'It's a work of art.'

'It's a potty!' said Randalf. 'And it was on my head!'

'And not quite empty, from the look of it,' said Veronica.

'It's very beautiful,' said Joe, trying to smooth things over. He looked round the cavern. 'You have so many lovely things.'

The dragon's eyes softened. 'I do, don't I?' she cooed. 'And you clearly have an eye for such things, young man. I can tell.' She beamed. 'It's taken me years to build up my collection. A silver shield here, a jewel-encrusted coronet there . . .' She looked round, smiling proudly – until her gaze fell on the loud and disobedient cutlery. 'Leave that breast-plate alone!' she shouted at a set of skewers. 'And you ladles, there. Stop that at once!'

Clatter! Clatter! Clink! Clonk!

She turned back to Joe and rolled her eyes. 'Honestly, darling,' she said. 'I don't know how much more of this I can take.'

Joe nodded sympathetically. 'Do you have any more priceless treasures in your hoard?' he asked.

'Of course, darling!' said Margot. 'Enchanted mirrors, magic swords, impregnable warrior armour – you know, all the usual.' She scanned the great hoard of treasure. 'But they're nothing compared with my most precious items . . .' She broke off, and began rooting through the great pile of valuables. 'They're here somewhere,' she muttered, and sighed. 'I must admit, it is all just a teensy bit disorganized.'

'What are they?' asked Joe, joining in the search.

'Oh, they're special. You need a real collector's eye to appreciate them,' said Margot. 'They're absolutely to die for.'

Randalf tutted impatiently. 'Yes, yes,' he said. 'I'm sure they're very nice, but we really should be going . . .'

'Are *these* them?' said Norbert. He picked up two rather battered tin cans.

Margot spun round. 'Yes, yes, they are!' She beamed at Norbert. 'Well done, you! I can see that you have a real collector's eye!' she said, and laughed. 'Three of them, in fact!'

Norbert beamed happily.

Clatter! Clatter! Clink! Clonk!

'Look at the workmanship,' Margot shouted above the sound of the rowdy cutlery. 'So subtle, so expressive. And to think these were created to hold . . . baked beans! It takes one's breath away!'

'They're really beautiful,' said Joe uncertainly.

'They are,' Norbert agreed. 'Far too beautiful to be left lying around. You need to display them to their maximum advantage,' he told the dragon. 'On a plinth, maybe. Or in a showcase.' He turned and frowned. 'In fact, if you ask me, the whole place could do with a really good tidy-up!'

'You think so?' said Margot.

'Oh, definitely,' said Norbert. 'It always works in my kitchen at home. You see, you have to have a system. I keep all my saucepans on hooks and my frying pans above the pantry door. They're handy for hitting elves over the head,' said Norbert. 'But here, I'd suggest piles.'

'Oh, I like the sound of that,' said Margot.

'Yes,' said Norbert, waving his arms about theatrically. 'Over here we could have the rusty pile. And over here, the sharp, pointy thing pile. And here . . .' He eyed the sugar tongs tap-dancing on a saucepan. 'We could have a noisy pile.'

'Not *too* noisy, I hope,' said Margot, flicking her tail at the passing choir of spoons.

'And here,' said Norbert, standing in the centre of the cavern, 'you could have a great big stupendous pile of sparkly things!'

'Darling!' cooed Margot. 'You're an artist.'

Back at the Horned Baron's castle, the garden party had

come to an abrupt end. After all the excitement – and chaos – of the dragon's sudden arrival and departure, no one felt much like partying any more.

'What a day!' Benson sighed.

'You can say that again,' said an under-gardener, pulling splinters of wood from his hair.

'Goodness knows what got into the cutlery!' said Benson. 'And as for that dragon!'

'The last dragon I saw was Gretchen,' said the under-gardener. 'And that was at least ten years ago . . .'

'And look at the state of the place!' said Benson.

The toffee stall was in ruins, the jars of smells lay broken on the ground beside pools of spilled face-paints, while the mangel-wurzels that hadn't been trampled underfoot had all disappeared – pocketed by the trolls as they had set off back to Trollbridge. Over at Snuggly-Wuggly Corner numerous small furry animals were climbing through the broken fence and scampering away. And in the midst of it all, the pink stinky hog ran this way and that, squealing indignantly as it searched for its missing tail.

The Horned Baron stomped through the trail of destruction, muttering under his breath.

'Absolute fiasco!' he said. 'Disaster! Everything's in ruins! The guests have all gone home! Ingrid's in hysterics!' He patted the beads of sweat from his forehead. 'At least things can't get any worse!'

'Norbert!' said Randalf impatiently, as the ogre busied himself around the dragon's cavern. 'We really *must* be going.'

'Not so fast, Fatso! I thought you were going to do something about that cutlery,' said Margot, raising herself up and fixing the wizard with a yellow-eyed stare.

'Yes, of course,' said Randalf, trembling and stepping inadvertantly into the Potty of Thrynn. 'Blast!'

'*Blast?* Is that a new spell?' said Veronica.

'Shut up, Veronica!' said Randalf angrily, and clanked off to sulk in the corner.

'That's close enough, potty-breath,' said the harp fiercely.

'Now,' said Margot brightly. 'Let's get tidying! You, Joe, are in charge of the sharp, pointy things pile.'

'You mean swords and spears and enchanted warrior armour?' said Joe excitedly.

'Yes, yes, whatever,' said Margot. 'And you, attack-budgie, can be in charge of the rusty pile.'

'Thanks a lot,' said Veronica, flying off.

'And you and me, Norbert, we'll make a lovely big pile of sparkly stuff!'

'Lovely,' said Norbert, clapping his hands together. 'I adore sparkly stuff.'

Just then, a conga-line of all the knives – from dainty

butter knives to hefty meat cleavers – went dancing past, clanking out the jerky rhythm as they went. The dragon's furious voice rang out.

'Randalf! Darling! They're still at it! Margot's getting a teensy-weensy bit angry!' she bellowed.

Over in the corner, Randalf snorted as he tried to prise the potty off his foot. 'Madam, a little bit of patience, please. The enchantment is obviously powerful and needs careful . . . *Blast!*' The potty was stuck fast.

'Still trying that *Blast* spell?' trilled Veronica from somewhere above his head.

'Shut up, Ver . . .' Randalf's jaw dropped.

There above him, perched on a cave ledge, was an old, rusty and decidedly battered bird cage. Veronica was hopping about inside it.

'Lovely, isn't it?' said Veronica in a gooey voice. 'A cage!' She sighed. 'It's got a perch that swings. And a little bell. And look, just what I always dreamed of – a mirror!' She smiled at her reflection. 'For when I want to see a friendly face . . .'

'Veronica!' said Randalf sharply. 'Cages are for canaries. Remember who you are! You're a wizard's familiar, and your

place is down here on the brim of my pointy hat.'

'Your hat hasn't got a mirror,' Veronica protested. 'Or a bell.'

'Veronica!' Randalf shouted. 'Pointy hat! Now!'

'Or a perch that swings,' said Veronica defiantly.

'*Veronica!*'

'Is that *you* causing a disturbance again, wizard?' roared Margot. 'Margot's getting angry! You won't like Margot when she's angry!'

'I was just working on a spell,' said Randalf sheepishly.

'Well, get on with it,' said the dragon fiercely. 'Now, Norbert, darling, where were we? Oh, how clever! The watering cans of Poot – yes, they do sparkle delightfully, don't they?'

Casting a furious glance at Veronica, Randalf clanked across the cavern to where a collection of butter knives was doing a noisy samba. He started waving his arms about, and muttered under his breath.

Meanwhile, Joe was collecting marvellous swords, magical helmets and spears of fantastical design, and making a neat pile at the far side of the cavern. Henry barked happily by his side.

'Can I try some of this armour on?' Joe asked, holding out a silver helmet with elaborate wings and curving horns.

'My dear boy,' said Margot, 'help yourself. That warrior-hero stuff really is quite a bore. Not nearly sparkly enough for me. Take anything you fancy.'

'Thanks,' said Joe, beaming. If he had to stay in Muddle Earth for a while longer, he might as well look like a convincing warrior-hero.

'I'd forgotten I had such wonderful treasures after my little nap,' cooed Margot. 'It's easily done.'

Joe tried on a bronze breastplate. 'How long *have* you been asleep?' he asked.

'Oh, no time at all,' said Margot. 'Twenty years or so, I think.'

'Twenty years!' Joe exclaimed.

'Give or take the odd year,' said Margot. 'We dragons need our beauty sleep, you know. Besides, twenty years is nothing. Matilda, over there,' she said, waving vaguely towards the entrance to the cave, 'has been asleep for twice as long. And as for Agnes, well, no one's seen her for centuries. Normally, I'd have slept for longer – but that cutlery woke me up.'

Clatter! Clatter! Clink! Clonk!

Margot sighed. 'Delightfully sparkly – but they do go on rather.'

'You can say that again,' said the harp grumpily from a corner.

Joe picked up a particularly ornate sword. 'Do all dragons have hoards of treasure?' he asked.

'Of course, dear boy,' said Margot. 'We all simply adore beautiful trinkets. That's all we want. That and the occasional sheep or two.' She sighed. 'Oh, but the tales they tell about us! Burning down castles. Battling with knights on horseback. Devouring princesses and damsels-in-distress – whatever *they* might be. I mean, there just aren't enough hours in a day for all that nonsense.'

Joe nodded.

'And as for warrior-heroes coming along thinking they can just slay you,' Margot went on, huffily. 'It's a damn cheek, if you ask me!'

'How dare you! Stop that!' an angry voice cried out. 'Leave me alone!'

It was the harp. A dozen butter knives and a set of soup spoons were taking it in turns to pluck at its strings.

The dragon turned irritably, and sent a warning blast of hot smoke in their direction. The harp swooned. The knives and spoons scurried away, but regrouped by the candlesticks and chandeliers, where they jumped about furiously, clashing and clattering.

'Darling, perhaps you could try out your warrior-hero skills on that lot,' she said.

'Actually,' said Joe, 'I'm not really a warrior-hero.'

'You'd never have guessed to look at him!' Veronica, who was swinging happily to and fro in her cage, shouted back.

'I was summoned to Muddle Earth by Randalf, here,' said Joe, nodding towards the wizard. 'He's promised to send me back home when he can. That's why I'm here. I couldn't let him get eaten by a dragon – not that you would have,' he added hastily.

'No, well one wouldn't, naturally,' said Margot. 'Oh, but poor you, Joe. All lost and alone in a strange world . . .'

Clatter! Clatter! Clink! Clonk!

The dragon groaned and turned to Randalf. 'Oh, please hurry up,' she said weakly. 'My head's splitting!'

Randalf shook his head. 'I'm afraid bewitched cutlery can be very tricky, madam. Very tricky indeed.'

'Honestly! Call yourself a wizard,' said Margot scornfully. She turned to Joe. 'I must say, I don't fancy your chances of leaving Muddle Earth.'

'Joe will be fine,' said Randalf, shaking his head. 'But I'm afraid this cutlery has been bewitched by an expert. I'll have to return to my houseboat and consult my spell book. To that end, we shall be taking our leave. I bid you good day, madam.'

'Oh, no you don't,' said Margot. She twisted herself round, blocking Randalf's escape with her tail.

'What . . . what is the meaning of this?' Randalf blustered.

'Norbert here has been a poppet. Joe has been a perfect gentleman – and that attack-budgie seems very nice . . .'

Clatter! Clatter! Clink! Clonk!

'But none of you are going anywhere until every last

piece of that confounded cutlery has been made to lie down and be quiet,' she bellowed. 'I don't care what you do. I don't care how long it takes. But I want them silenced, once and for all!'

Clatter! Clatter! Clink! Clonk!

A strong, chill wind whistled through Elfwood. Tree rabbits, perching in the lower branches of the oaks and pines, snored restlessly in their sleep and huddled together for warmth, while roosting batbirds, high up at the top of the jub-jub trees, cried out as they were swung to and fro.

'*Ouch!*'

Trudging through the trees came a stooped figure, his bony fingers clasping at his flapping cape and keeping the hood raised. With each step, his boots sank deep into the squidgy mulch of mud and fallen leaves, slowing him down and making him sweat with effort despite the cold.

At the centre of the woods was a clearing – Giggle Glade, its name – and in the centre of the clearing was a modest dwelling, built of wood and ornately decorated. The caped figure fought his way to the door.

The wind was howling round the house, setting the

powder-blue shutters rattling and the wooden roof tiles clacking. Inside the house, seated in shadow upon a high-backed and intricately carved throne, Dr Cuddles waited.

'Soon,' he giggled. 'Very soon.'

As if on cue, the front door burst open. Dr Cuddles smiled.

'Is that you, Quentin?'

'Y . . . yes, Master,' panted Quentin as he forced the door shut against the buffeting wind. 'Goodness me,' he said. 'It's blowing a gale out there. I had to battle with it every step of the way.' He shook his head wearily. 'I'm utterly pooped.'

'Pooped?' Dr Cuddles giggled. 'How delightful. I trust you bring good news.'

Quentin lowered his hood, smoothed down his slightly ruffled golden curls and twirled the ends of his magnificent moustache. He looked up. The throne was set in deep shadow. Only Dr Cuddles's startlingly blue eyes were visible. Glinting and unblinking, they bored into him from the darkness. Quentin felt his knees begin to tremble.

'Well?' said Dr Cuddles. 'I take it that the Horned Baron has been taken care of at last.' He giggled unpleasantly. 'I'm sure our scaly friend enjoyed her little snack.' The high-pitched, somewhat sinister giggling grew louder. 'Did she crunch his bones?' he said. 'Did she tear him limb from limb?'

'Actually, sir,' said Quentin, hanging his head. 'There's something I've got to tell you.'

The eyes narrowed to slits. 'Well?' he demanded.

Quentin swallowed nervously and took a deep breath. 'Things didn't go quite according to plan,' he said in a rush.

Dr Cuddles sighed. 'Explain yourself,' he said coldly.

'There was a bit of a mix-up,' he said. 'At the garden party. It seems that the dragon might have chewed up the wrong person.'

'The wrong person?' said Dr Cuddles testily.

'He just turned up at the last minute and spoiled everything,' said Quentin. 'There was nothing I could do.'

'*Who?*' He sounded furious now.

'That wizard c . . . c . . . character,' Quentin stammered. 'Randalf. Randalf the Wise . . .'

'I might have known,' Dr Cuddles muttered, drumming his stubby fingers on the arms of the throne. 'Why can't he keep his big nose out of my affairs?'

Quentin permitted himself a little smile. 'If I know my dragons,' he said, 'it probably saved his big nose till last.'

Dr Cuddles giggled. 'Oh, I do hope so,' he said. 'But that still leaves the small matter of the uneaten Horned Baron.'

'Plan B, Master?' said Quentin.

'Plan B,' Dr Cuddles confirmed. He clapped his paws together and a dozen elves appeared as if from nowhere. 'Unlock Roger the Wrinkled and bring him to me,' he commanded. 'Go!'

'At once, Master,' the elves twittered, and scurried off to do as they had been told.

Quentin, relieved that Dr Cuddles hadn't taken his news too badly, removed his cape and hung it on a hook on the door. 'How about a nice snuggle-muffin?' he said. 'I decorated some specially for you earlier and . . .'

'Quentin,' said Dr Cuddles. 'This is no time for snuggle-muffins.'

'No, sir,' said Quentin. 'Silly of me.'

Just then, there came a scuffling from the corridor and the sound of raised voices. A door flew open and the elves bustled into the room tugging on a long, heavy lead, at the end of which was a decidedly bedraggled, not to say wrinkled, wizard. From the top of his high-domed forehead to the tip of his long, pointed chin, spread an intricate network of wrinkles. His ears were wrinkled, his cheeks were wrinkled, his nose was wrinkled – even his wrinkles were wrinkled.

'How dare you treat me like this?' he blustered. 'I can't possibly be expected to work under these conditions!'

'My word, you *are* wrinkled, aren't you?' giggled Dr Cuddles. 'I always forget.'

'Well, is it any wonder?' snapped Roger. 'Chained up in that poky little room, working every hour under the sun. I'm telling you, I can't take much more of it.

And then *this!*' He tugged at the lead. 'The indignity of it all.'

'It's your own fault,' said Quentin sharply. 'You shouldn't keep trying to escape.'

'I've already explained all that,' said Roger loftily. 'I was just stretching my legs.'

'You were running,' Quentin reminded him.

'Just answering a call of nature,' said Roger.

'You were disguised as a washerwoman,' said Quentin.

'I explained that as well,' Roger began uncertainly. 'It all started when I was a child and used to try my mother's dresses on . . .'

'Never mind all that,' Dr Cuddles cut in. 'I summoned you here to discuss a matter of great importance to me . . .'

'The Horned Baron,' said Roger the Wrinkled.

'You read my mind,' giggled Dr Cuddles.

The wizard nodded. 'I trust the cutlery performed to your satisfaction,' he said.

'Yes, it did,' said Dr Cuddles. 'Unfortunately, there was a slight hitch.'

'A hitch?' said Roger.

'Quite amusing, really,' said Dr Cuddles, giggling rather

hysterically. 'It seems the cutlery lured the dragon to Quentin's pink pavilion just as we planned but, unfortunately, the pavilion contained the wrong person.'

'The wrong person?' said Roger.

'Why, Roger!' Dr Cuddles giggled. 'You're beginning to sound like an echo.'

'An echo?' said Roger.

Dr Cuddles's giggle turned decidedly nasty. 'I have decided to put Plan B into action,' he said.

The wizard's wrinkled face collapsed. 'Not the . . .'

'Yes, Roger,' said Dr Cuddles, giggling wildly. 'The flying wardrobes.'

'But Dr Cuddles,' said Roger. 'I really can't advise that. Not yet. They're not ready.'

'My dear Roger,' said Dr Cuddles, 'I hope I don't need to heat up the metal underpants again.'

Roger the Wrinkled took a step backwards. 'Not the underpants, I beg you!' he pleaded. 'It's just that . . .'

'Just *what?*' The sound of his drumming fingers grew louder.

'Well, the flying bit is easy,' Roger the Wrinkled explained, 'but putting the wardrobes together is an absolute nightmare! I mean, the instructions never make sense, and there's always an extra screw left over . . .'

'Enough of all these excuses!' roared Dr Cuddles. He clapped. The elves jumped to attention. 'Fetch me the *Great Book of Spells.*'

'At once, Master,' the elves trilled, and scuttled off through a different door.

'. . . and as for the splinters!'

'Be silent, Roger!' said Dr Cuddles sharply. 'Under my close supervision, I shall allow you to consult the *Great Book of Spells*,' he announced. 'We launch the wardrobes tonight!'

'But . . .'

Dr Cuddles giggled. 'I have absolute confidence in your skills, Roger. You and your fellow wizards had better not fail me – or else.'

Roger shuffled about uncomfortably. 'The under-pants?' he said nervously. Dr Cuddles nodded.

Puffing and panting, the elves returned with a heavy wooden box; the spell book locked up inside it. They scuttled over to the throne.

'The *Great Book of Spells*, Master,' the elves said in unison.

'Put it on my lectern,' Dr Cuddles told them. 'Then, when Roger has finished reading the appropriate spell, put him on his lead and take him back.' He turned to the wizard. 'And no tricks,' he giggled. 'Do you understand?'

'Tricks, Dr Cuddles?' said Roger. 'I don't know what you mean.'

The steely eyes glared out of the shadows. 'Take care, Roger the Wrinkled,' Dr Cuddles said with a giggle. 'I shall be watching your every move.'

The tiny teaspoon was almost at the end of its epic journey. As the mountain cave came into view it sighed, tripped and fell, picked itself up and sighed again. The end was literally in sight.

With a soft *tinkle-tinkle*, the teaspoon hopped into the cave entrance.

Even though it was getting dark outside, with the sun down on the horizon, it was far darker inside the cave. The teaspoon paused and cocked its bowl to one side.

Noise. There was lots of noise echoing down a tunnel that led deep into the mountain. Clinking and clanking. Clashing and clattering.

And raised voices . . .

'I'll do anything,' shouted one, clearly at the end of its tether. 'Just make them be still!'

'I'm doing everything I can!' cried another.

'Which isn't much!' taunted a third.

The tiny teaspoon continued. *Chink, chink, chink.* Over stones and gravel, and the occasional small bone, it continued along the tunnel, heading for the dull red glow at the end. Closer and closer it got; louder and louder the echoing noises became.

All at once, the tunnel opened up and the tiny teaspoon found itself at the edge of a vast underground cavern. There were the individuals it had followed from the castle, their backs turned. Behind them was a dragon. And behind the dragon . . .

The tiny teaspoon let out a little sigh and hopped up and down on the dusty floor.

It was the sugar tongs who first noticed the newcomer. Its raised tong clunked insistently on the side of a golden goblet. The knives rustled, the spoons clinked, the forks clanged as, one by one, the cutlery all became aware of the tiny teaspoon in their midst.

From every corner of the cavern, they appeared. The meat cleavers and skewers, the forks, whisks and ladles, the egg spoons and soup spoons, cake forks and butter knives – and even the dumpy egg slicer – all began hurrying to the spot where the tiny teaspoon was performing its strange, bouncing little dance.

'Oh, good grief!' the dragon groaned. 'What's happening now?'

'I'm attempting a reverse enchantment,' said Randalf importantly, waving his arms about, 'with a triple bypass and a double switchback. Very tricky, it is. I need absolute silence.'

'Fat chance,' said Margot, above the din. 'It's getting worse than ever!'

'Yes, but listen,' said Joe. 'It's different.'

Instead of the cacophony of noise the cutlery had been making since their arrival, one by one, they were all beginning to strike up the same pounding beat – CRASH! CRASH! CRASH! CRASH! – until the whole great mass of them were pounding together.

'It's the teaspoon,' said Joe. 'Look. They're following its lead.'

Randalf nodded wisely. Sure enough, the great clash of noise rang out every time the tip of the bouncing teaspoon's handle hit the ground.

'Well spotted, my boy,' he said. 'That's my double switch-back taking effect.'

'I'll tell you something else,' said Joe. 'I've seen that teaspoon before.'

'Oh, one teaspoon looks very much like another in my experience,' said Randalf, performing a strange little jig on one leg and puffing heavily.

'Hurry up!' urged Margot. She

clutched her head and rocked slowly back and forwards as the deafening noise continued. 'I really, really don't think I can stand any more of this.'

'Reverse enchantment can't be hurried, madam,' Randalf replied. He stopped hopping, raised his arms and began whispering urgently under his breath.

'You really have no idea what you're doing, do you?' said Veronica.

'Shut up, Veronica,' hissed Randalf.

All at once, the tiny teaspoon hopped up on to a boulder and tapped insistently. At the sound, all the other cutlery fell still. Every knife, every fork, every spoon. The cavern was silent, at last – silent, except for a faint *squeak, squeak, squeak* as Veronica swung backwards and forwards in her cage.

'I don't believe it!' she said. 'What did you do, you old fraud?'

'I've absolutely no idea,' said Randalf, who looked as surprised as everyone else.

Just then, the tiny teaspoon turned and began hopping back the way it had come.

Everyone held their breath.

The sugar tongs moved first. With a shudder and a creak, they tripped after the teaspoon. The rest of the cutlery, calm now and in well-ordered ranks, followed close behind. As the last of them – the small toothpick with *Simon* engraved on it – disappeared into the tunnel, Margot let out a long, happy sigh of relief.

'They've gone,' she said. 'Thank goodness for that. I don't know how to thank you.'

Randalf lowered his arms at last and turned to the dragon. '*I* do,' he said.

'This is brilliant!' Joe called out above the noise of the rushing wind. 'Absolutely *fantastic*!'

He'd been on aeroplanes before, roller-coasters and the tops of open-air buses – but none of these came even close to the thrill and excitement of riding on a dragon's back.

Resplendent in the new warrior-hero outfit that Margot had allowed him to select from her treasure, he was sitting on a comfy, padded seat between Margot's great leathery wings. To his right was Norbert, with Veronica perched on his shoulder; in his lap was Henry.

'A-*maz*-ing,' he murmured as he looked all round him, trying to take everything in.

Above him was the inky star-studded sky, cloudless and crystal clear, with its three moons shining brightly. Below him was Muddle Earth, spread out like a great map and bathed in the purple, yellow and green moon-light. A batbird, flying too near, was scorched and sent packing by a warning blast of the dragon's fiery breath.

Looming up before them was Mount Boom, tall, dark and imposing. *Boom*, it went, the sound barely audible above the throb of the slowly beating wings. And beyond the volcano, spreading on as far as the eye could see, were the Musty Mountains.

'Hold on to your hats,' Margot cried out as, with a twitch of her wings and a flick of her tail, she banked sharply and soared down towards Mount Boom.

Boom, went the volcano, exploding weakly and sending out a little puff of grey and yellow smoke.

'*Wheee!*' cried Joe.

Once, twice, three times the dragon flew around Mount Boom, before soaring back up, up into the sky. 'It's been such a long time since I last stretched my wings properly,' said Margot excitedly. 'I'd forgotten quite how exhilarating it could be!' And with that, she folded her wings and dived into a long, swooping loop-the-loop.

'*Whoooah!*' Joe shouted, stomach in his mouth. As they levelled out, he threw back his head and laughed. 'Again!' he roared. '*Again!*'

'*Wurrgh!*' Randalf groaned. Unlike the others, he did not have a seat, comfy or otherwise. Instead, he was at the back of the dragon, lodged between a couple of jagged tail-fins and clinging on for dear life as the long, serpentine tail swished this way and that. 'Why do I have to sit back here?' he shouted.

'Because you're too fat to sit up front,' Margot called back firmly.

'But what about *him*?' shouted Randalf, pointing at Norbert – and almost falling off.

'That's different,' said Margot. 'Norbert's my friend, aren't you, darling?'

Norbert beamed happily.

'This is an outrage!' protested the wizard. The rushing wind drowned out his words.

Joe turned. 'Did you say something, Randalf?' he called.

Randalf shouted back. Joe could see the wizard's mouth move, but what with the noise of the rushing wind and the dragon's beating wings, he could barely make out a thing.

'What?' he bellowed.

Randalf's face contorted with effort as he shouted back. Again his words were whipped away on the wind.

'Can *you* hear what he's saying?' Joe asked the others.

'Probably just telling us how much he's enjoying the ride,' said Norbert, grinning and waving at Randalf.

'Which makes a nice change,' Veronica added. 'After all, normally by now he'd be fast asleep.'

Far in front of them, beyond the Musty Mountains, the Enchanted Lake came into view and glistened in the coloured moonlight. Joe felt a pang of disappointment. 'We'll soon be there,' he said.

Norbert turned to him and grinned. 'It's lovely to be

carried for a change instead of doing the carrying,' he said. 'How about one more circuit of Mount Boom?'

'Oh, yes!' Joe exclaimed.

'Is that all right, Margot?' Norbert called out.

'For you, dear heart, anything,' said Margot, as she dipped her wings and soared round in a great circle, back towards the mountain.

Randalf gripped on desperately as the tail lashed fiercely. 'What's going on now?' he roared. But nobody heard.

This time, as Margot approached Mount Boom, she came in low and steep, clipping the summit and swooping around the smoking crater. Joe looked down into the blood-red chasm. It glowed like the embers of a dying fire, and a warm, slightly sickly mist swirled around his face, making his throat tickle and his eyes water.

Boom.

The dragon tipped her wings and glided away safely as the solitary puff of smoke popped out of the top of the crater. Then, with a hard beat of her wings, she soared off around the volcano. Faster and faster she flew, circling it over and over again. The vertical rock sped past in a blur to their right. The moons seemed to spin in the sky.

'*Wheeee!*' shouted Norbert and Joe, and whooped for joy.

'*Woof!*' barked Henry.

'*Wurrgh!*' Randalf groaned.

'*WATCH OUT!*' screeched Veronica. There in front of

them – and coming towards them at great speed – was something big, brown and rectangular. '*DUCK!*'

'That's no duck,' Margot shouted back. 'It looks more like a wardrobe!'

'Just get out of its way!' Veronica screamed.

Margot swerved just in time. The wardrobe – doors flapping like wings – clattered over her head, grazing the top of her crested crown as it passed.

'There's another one!' Veronica shouted, as a second wardrobe came flying noisily towards them, its flapping doors clattering loudly.

'Leave it to me,' Margot replied grimly. This time, she made no effort to dodge out of the way. Instead, she opened her mouth as wide as it would go and sent a broad, blazing tongue of fire roaring out ahead of her.

The wardrobe was promptly swallowed up in the jet of flames and incinerated in an instant. As the dragon beat her wings triumphantly and flew on, a sprinkling of ash drifted down to the ground below her.

'That was awesome!' gasped Joe.

'Good to know that I haven't lost it,' said Margot proudly.

'Just as well,' said Veronica. 'Look!'

Everyone turned and gasped. A dozen or more wardrobes were flapping in low from Elfwood in a long straight line. This was getting stranger and stranger, even for Muddle Earth, thought Joe.

'They're heading for the Horned Baron's castle!' he shouted, and turned. 'Randalf, what's going on?'

Randalf shouted something back.

'What?' called Joe above the roaring wind. 'Margot, slow down a minute.'

The dragon slowed to a lazy hover. More wardrobes flapped into view. A huge armada was filling the sky.

'I said,' Randalf shouted back, 'first singing curtains, then enchanted cutlery and now flying wardrobes – which, by the look of them, are up to no good.' Just then, a particularly solid-looking wardrobe struck the top of a castle tower with a loud *crash*. Randalf shook his head. 'There's powerful magic at work here!' he said. 'And, as I always say, where there's magic . . .'

'. . . there's money!' finished Veronica. 'Typical!'

'I don't know what you mean,' shouted Randalf huffily. 'The Horned Baron's castle is clearly under attack. It's my solemn duty as a wizard to render what support I can in this, his hour of need.'

'It's amazing how brave you can be with a dragon in tow,' said Veronica scathingly.

'Shut up, Veronica! Now, follow that furniture!' shouted Randalf.

'Oh, I see. Just like that!' said Margot hotly. 'Don't the others get a say?' She craned her neck round. 'Norbert, dearest, what would *you* like to do?'

'I . . . I . . . I . . .' he stammered, glancing back and forth between Randalf and the dragon. 'I think . . .'

'Yes, Norbert?' said Margot.

The ogre nodded. 'Yes,' he said. 'I think we should go and help the Horned Baron.'

'For you, Norbert, anything,' said Margot sweetly.

'Thank goodness for that,' Randalf snapped. '*Whoooooah!*' he cried out, as the dragon suddenly lurched forwards.

'We're going in!' Margot's voice floated back. She beat her wings. She lashed her tail. 'And woe betide any item of furniture that gets in my way!'

Out of the sky she flew like a speeding bullet, hurtling down towards the Horned Baron's castle. Joe clung to Henry (whose ears were flapping back in his face) with one hand and clutched his helmet to his head with the other. Veronica tucked her head under her wing and dug her claws into Norbert's shoulder.

'Ouch,' Norbert yelped.

'Norbert, what is it?' Margot cried. She swung her wings round and flicked her tail. It had the same effect as slamming the brakes on. Joe kept a tight grip on Henry as he and Norbert were flung forwards. Randalf sailed past them, his arms waving, his mouth open.

'*HELP!*' he screamed. '*Help.*' His voice was rapidly fading away. 'Hel . . .'

'Catch him!' Norbert bellowed. 'Margot, catch him!'

'Are you sure?' said Margot.

'*Yes!*' Norbert howled.

'Oh, all right, if you insist,' she said and, with no further ado, she flapped her wings and spiralled down out of the sky.

Joe held his breath.

The sound of Randalf's cries echoed upwards as he tumbled downwards.

'Hel . . .'

'. . . el . . .'

'. . . elp . . .'

Down in the courtyard of the Horned Baron's castle, the wardrobes were coming in to land. Benson and the herald – who were crouched down together behind the birdbath – watched a particularly large piece, with ornately carved doors and ball and claw feet, flap down noisily and strike the ground with a loud *crash*.

It landed on its side, wobbled, toppled and keeled over on to its back. A thick cloud of dust and sand flew up into the air.

'Well I never,' said the herald. 'Raining wardrobes. That's a first.'

Benson shook his head. 'It can't be good for the flowers,' he said.

Another wardrobe crashed down to their right, flattening a pot of pansies as it landed.

'Terrible waste,' muttered Benson.

'*Sshhh.*' The herald raised a finger to his lips and pointed into the clearing cloud of dust. 'I thought I heard something.'

There was a long, low creak and one of the wardrobe doors opened slowly.

The herald huddled up closer to Benson behind the birdbath. 'There's something inside it,' he said. 'Listen.'

There was a faint jangling sound, getting louder by the second.

'I'm frightened,' said the herald, squeezing Benson's hand rather too tightly.

'Perhaps I should go and have a look,' said Benson, making a move to pull himself to his feet.

'No, don't!' said the herald, clutching hold of Benson's arm and pulling him back down. 'You can't leave me here alone!'

All at once, with a loud bang, both wardrobe doors flew open. Benson jumped. The herald grabbed hold of him and clung on tightly.

'I can't look,' he whimpered. 'What is it?'

Benson shook his head. 'Well, it makes sense, I suppose . . .'

'What?' said the herald, dread in his voice. 'Bendy bugs? Horned wangtubbers. Wide-mouthed fribblesnooks . . . ?'

'Hangers,' said Benson. He stared open-mouthed as hanger after small wooden hanger fluttered out from the shadowy depths of the wardrobe and up into the night sky.

'Hangers?' said the herald.

'Coat hangers,' said Benson. 'A flock of them . . .'

'A flock?' said the herald. He pulled away from Benson and opened his eyes cautiously. His jaw fell open. 'You're right,' he murmured weakly. 'It's a flock of coat hangers.'

'And there's more coming from that wardrobe over there,' he said.

The herald laughed. 'They had you pretty worried there for a moment, didn't they?' he said.

'They still do,' said Benson, darkly. 'Look.' He pointed up to the top of the East Tower, where the hangers were already flying through an open window. 'The Baroness isn't going to like this,' he said. 'She isn't going to like this one little bit.'

Randalf watched the ground hurtling towards him and desperately racked his brain for a not-breaking-every-single-bone-in-your-body spell.

Just then, there was the sound of ripping material – and he was no longer falling. In fact, with the ground now seemingly speeding away from him, it was clear that he was flying – soaring back away from the rocks and dust and up into the purple, yellow and green moonlit sky.

'Yes!' Joe yelled, and punched the air in triumph.

'Hooray! Hooray!' shouted Norbert.

Below them, suspended by the seat of his pants in Margot's talons, swung a rather red-faced Randalf.

'I was about to weave a spell of feather-lightness,' he said with as much dignity as he could muster. 'But thank you anyway.'

'Oh, don't thank me, Fatso,' said Margot, gaining height with every flap of her wings. 'Thank dear, sweet Norbert, here.'

'*Hmmph!*' said Randalf.

'Sorry, I didn't quite catch that,' said Margot, swinging Randalf lazily. There was an ominous sound of ripping.

'Thank you, Norbert,' said Randalf.

'You're welcome,' smiled Norbert, and nodded at the torn pants. 'You should get those mended when we get to the castle, before you catch your death of cold . . .'

'Yes, *thank* you, Norbert,' said Randalf, darkly.

As the dragon approached the castle walls, Joe saw the full extent of the chaos within. There were wardrobes – and bits of wardrobe – everywhere.

Some had crashed down on the tents and stalls, some had smashed to smithereens on the paving stones, losing their doors and splintering their sides, while others were still airborne, waiting to land. They were darting this way and that, banging into walls and each other. Most of them seemed remarkably poorly put together, with missing hinges, odd-length legs and, in some cases, doors that didn't match.

'Coo-ee!' shouted Norbert, and waved.

Randalf, who was back in his place on the dragon's tail, called to him. 'What is it, Norbert?'

'The Horned Baron,' said Joe, pointing. 'Look.'

Below, the Horned Baron was running about like a headless chicken and shouting at the top of his voice.

'Run for your lives! We're under attack! Take cover!'

'What an inspiration to us all the Horned Baron is,' muttered Veronica.

CRASH!

'Blimey,' Joe gasped. 'That was close!'

One of the wardrobes had smashed down on to the ground, snapping the *Keep off the Grass* sign and missing the Horned Baron by a hair's breadth. The Horned Baron, now down on his knees and trembling, held his head in his hands as scores of hangers exploded from the broken wardrobe and swooped down on him like a flock of angry batbirds. Their hooks rained blows down on his horned helmet.

Plink! Plink! Plink!

'*Ouch! Ouch! Ouch!*' cried the Horned Baron.

Just then, an under-gardener with a bucket on his head dashed past. 'The flowers!' he shouted. 'Mind the flowers!'

To a hanger, the flock wheeled away from the Horned Baron and gave chase.

'Get off!' he shouted, as the hangers hammered down against the bucket.

'And keep off the grass!'

The same scene was being repeated everywhere Joe looked. Gardeners and under-gardeners, footmen in livery, butlers, servants and kitchen hands were all under attack – and it seemed there was nothing any of them could do to repel the fearsome invasion.

'Oh, woe is me!' the Horned Baron howled miserably. 'We're doomed. We're all doomed. Will no one help me in my hour of need?'

'For the right price,' came a voice from above his head.

The Horned Baron looked up and gasped. Not only were they being bombarded by wardrobes and attacked by coat hangers, but now the dragon had returned. Frozen to the spot, he stared, horrified, at the vast hovering creature with its leathery wings, its slinky tail, its ferocious crested head and – he rubbed his eyes in disbelief – its passengers . . .

'Randalf?' he shouted up to the figure clutching on to the dragon's tail. 'Is that you?'

'It certainly is,' Randalf shouted back. 'Wizard for hire, at your service. 'Now about my terms . . .'

'Anything,' said the Horned Baron. 'Anything at all! Just *do* something! Now!'

'A hundred gold big 'uns,' Randalf called.

The Horned Baron sucked in air noisily through his teeth. 'Fifty,' he said.

'Ninety,' Randalf responded.

'Seventy-five, and that's my final offer,' said the Horned Baron.

'*WALTER!*' came a loud, piercing scream. It was Ingrid, and she was not happy.

'Eighty,' said Randalf.

'Eighty, it is,' said the Horned Baron. 'But not a big 'un more. *Watch out!*' he bellowed, as a decidedly lopsided wardrobe appeared out of nowhere, doors clapping and hangers jangling, and hurtled towards the hovering dragon.

'Furniture on the starboard side!' Veronica squawked.

Margot nodded. With a flick of her tail, she ducked behind the tall gate towers.

The wardrobe smashed into the heavy studded doors and broke into a thousand pieces which tumbled down to the ground. From inside, another flock of coat hangers emerged. They soared up into the air and closed in on the dragon.

Margot smiled and sent out a roaring tongue of flame. The hangers were turned instantly to ash.

Down in the courtyard, the Horned Baron burst into applause. 'Bravo!' he shouted. 'Now come and deal with the rest of them.'

'For eighty gold big 'uns,' said Randalf.

'Yes, yes,' said the Horned Baron impatiently, ducking down to avoid a wardrobe hurtling across the courtyard, totally out of control. 'Just get on with it!'

Randalf nodded. 'Land over by that wall, Margot,' he

said, pointing. 'If that's all right with you, Norbert,' he added archly.

'Oh, yes, perfectly all right, sir,' said Norbert. 'Excellent idea, sir.'

'Thank you,' said Randalf. 'I . . . *Whoooah!*' he gasped as the dragon swooped down over the courtyard, knocking wardrobes and hangers aside as she flew and – with a graceful twist – landed at the base of the high wall.

She turned and roared menacingly.

Joe leaped to the ground followed by Henry, wagging his tail and barking furiously. He drew his sword. Norbert jumped down beside him and, seizing a length of broken tent pole, swung it round his head. Randalf joined them, Veronica perched on his shoulder. He raised his arms.

'Let battle commence!' he roared, and turned. 'Norbert, you'd better go first, there's a good fellow.'

Norbert stepped forward as a rickety looking wardrobe with mismatched door handles lurched past. With a blow from the tent pole, the wardrobe fell apart.

'Shoddy workmanship,' said Randalf, picking up a loose screw and examining it.

Margot took to the air and hovered protectively over Norbert, who wielded his makeshift club and lumbered to the aid of two footmen trapped beneath the birdbath. He beat off several waves of attacking coat hangers.

The footmen emerged from their hiding place and shook their fists at the retreating wardrobes. 'And don't come back, or you'll get more of the same!' the smaller of the two shouted defiantly.

Just then, Veronica squawked with alarm. 'Watch out! More enemy furniture approaching – and not just wardrobes!' she screeched.

'Help!' shrieked the footmen and scurried back beneath the birdbath.

'Cowards!' said Randalf from behind Norbert.

Norbert strode off towards the approaching furniture – a couple of badly constructed cupboards and a large dresser with wonky shelves.

'Norbert!' cried Randalf. 'Come back!'

'Three wardrobes and a chest of drawers incoming!' Veronica's voice rang out.

Randalf ran after Norbert. Joe followed close behind, waving his sword at a couple of singed coat hangers.

'Let Margot take care of them,' said Randalf as the dragon swooped overhead in hot pursuit of a fleeing battalion of bookends. 'Norbert! Norbert! Come back here and protect me . . . Please!'

Above them, Margot's voice resounded loudly. 'Take that, you overgrown bundle of firewood!'

Her tail swished through the air, and dealt a shattering blow to a fat chest with crude teddy bear carvings. The chest split and spilled its contents of garish teddy bear-patterned quilts, which promptly flapped at the dragon.

'Get off me!' Margot's muffled voice cried out as she

clawed desperately at the vast quilt with orange and red
teddy bears which had wrapped itself around her neck.

'*Aaaargh!*' she cried.

The quilt clung on all the
more tenaciously.

'Mothballs,' she
groaned.

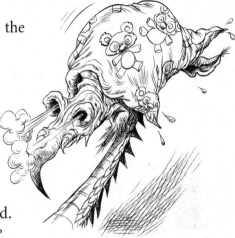

A second teddy bear
quilt fluttered in damply
and tangled itself around
the dragon's head.

'*Ugh!*'   she   roared.
'Someone still wets the bed!'

'Three more wardrobes, twin bedside cupboards and a
set of occasional tables!' Veronica announced urgently from
Randalf's shoulder.

Just then, the air whistled as the first of the wardrobes
sliced down through the air at a steep angle.

CRASH!!!

The doors flew open and out leaped a crowd of pugna-
cious pillows, spoiling for a fight.

'*Aargh! Oof! Ouch!*' Randalf shouted as the pillows
attacked him, thudding into his stomach and thumping
him around the head. 'Help! *Help!* Norbert!'

'*Mffll blffll,*' Margot thudded to the ground next to Joe.
She tried desperately to disentangle herself from the quilts.
'*Helmmpff!*'

Joe's head spun with it all. There were cries of pain and terror coming from every corner of the courtyard as more badly constructed wardrobes and flimsy cupboards came crashing down. A chest of drawers fell particularly awkwardly, smashing to bits and spilling its contents. Knickers, corsets and balled-up socks tumbled out and joined the battle.

'Two wardrobes and a piano stool to your left!' Veronica announced.

With his heart in his mouth, Joe gripped his sword and, with a swish and a swoosh, sliced through the quilt around Margot's head.

The dragon looked round. 'Thank you, my dear boy,' she said gratefully. 'Those dreadful quilts smelt worse than the Potty of Thrynn!'

'Warrior-hero at your service,' smiled Joe.

'You're an angel!' Margot shouted as she launched herself up off the ground and soared back into the air. The incoming piano stool never stood a chance.

'Four more wardrobes and . . . *Aaargh!*' Veronica squawked as a volley of cups, saucers and plates whistled past her and smashed on the paving stones below. 'Margot!' she screeched. 'See to that Welsh dresser at once!'

Joe turned and joined Norbert, who was hurrying to help Randalf. The wizard was losing a fight with a pair of pink satin pillows shaped like love-hearts.

'Help me!' he cried as the pillows boxed his ears.

'Take that!' Joe roared as he raised his sword and lunged at the first pillow. There was an explosion of feathers. 'And that! And that! And that!' he cried as he stabbed and slashed at the second.

A snowstorm of feathers filled the air, so thick he could barely see his hands before his face. Suddenly, a huge bolster swung round and landed a crunching blow on Joe's helmet, jamming it down hard over his eyes.

He was blind!

All around him, the noise was building up to a mighty crescendo. Banging and crashing, splintering and smashing. Roars of triumph and howls of defeat. Clattering, shattering, screaming and shouting. And above it all, the sound of the dragon's mighty roar as she swooped this way and that.

Which way is the battle going? Joe wondered as he fought to prise the helmet off his head.

He couldn't see a thing. His arms were aching, his head was throbbing – and the swirling feathers were making him sneeze. Lunging and parrying as best he could, he stumbled blindly over the thick mattress of fluffy down, scraps of quilt and splinters of shattered hangers which covered the ground.

'Randalf!' he called out. 'Norbert! Veronica! Where are you?'

He paused and listened, but no one replied. He lowered his sword thoughtfully. Unless it was his imagination, the noise finally seemed to be abating. From his right, there came a grinding *crunch*; from his left, a muffled *thud*.

Then nothing. Nothing at all.

Joe trembled. It was quiet now. Almost too quiet. With a final despairing effort, Joe seized his helmet by its ornate wings and tugged with all his might.

Pop!

The battered helmet finally came off. Blinking through the slowly settling blizzard of feathers, Joe looked round.

'*Woof!*'

'Henry!' shouted Joe. 'Over here, boy.' The next second, Henry came bounding out of the storm of feathers, tongue lolling and tail wagging. Joe crouched down and ruffled his fur. 'Good dog,' he said. 'I'm glad you're safe. But where's everyone else? Eh? Where are they all?'

'Well, I can't speak for the others,' came Randalf's voice. 'But I'm here.'

'And I'm here, sir,' said Norbert.

'Where?' said Randalf.

'I don't know,' said Norbert thoughtfully. 'But I am. And Veronica's here with me to prove it.'

'For my sins,' the budgie muttered.

Soon, the whole courtyard was buzzing with conversation. Joe turned his head, first this way, then that, following the different voices. And as the feathers settled, he began to make out the bodies that went with those voices.

There was Norbert, sitting on a pile of splintered timber, with Veronica perched on his shoulder.

There were Benson and the under-gardener, who'd had the bucket stuck on his head, emerging from behind an upturned table, looking at some broken flower pots and tutting loudly.

And there was Randalf. He was holding up what looked to be a pair of frilly lace pantaloons and examining them closely. When he caught Joe staring at him, his face turned bright crimson.

'I . . . I need a new pair,' he stammered. 'Margot ruined mine.'

'You're worse than Roger the Wrinkled,' Veronica commented darkly.

Joe looked round. Splintered smouldering wood lay everywhere. There were doors off their hinges, drawers in pieces, broken hangers, bookends, crockery and everything shrouded in the blanket of feathers from the pillows and quilts.

'We did it,' he said proudly. 'We won the battle!'

'Indeed we did,' said Randalf, hurriedly screwing the silk underwear up into a ball and thrusting it into his pocket. 'Thanks to my inspired generalship.'

'Yes, inspired by terror,' said Veronica. '"Norbert! Help! Help!"' she mimicked.

'Shut up, Veronica,' said Randalf.

'Margot?' said Norbert. 'Has anyone seen Margot?'

'I'm up here, dear,' came a voice from the top of the castle gates.

They looked up to see the dragon perched comfortably, examining her talons.

'Margot, you were magnificent!' said Norbert. 'We'd never have managed without you.'

'One good turn deserves another, Norbert, dear heart,' said Margot. 'Without you, my cave would still look like a Broken, Missing or Useless stall. Speaking of which,' she said, 'I really should be getting back.' She sighed. 'A hoard of treasure can be such a burden.'

'Speaking of treasure,' Randalf muttered. 'Eighty gold

big 'uns is not to be sniffed at.' He looked round the court-yard for the Horned Baron.

The dragon reared up on her hind legs, flapped her wings and launched herself off into the first pink blush of morning.

'Farewell!' she cried. 'It has been charming getting to know you all. Joe, Henry, Veronica and particularly you, Norbert, of course. You know, I think I'll even miss old Fatso! Remember, Norbert, darling – keep in touch!'

'I will,' Norbert called back.

The dragon flapped off into the night. 'See you all in twenty years or so,' she called, her voice getting fainter.

Norbert wiped a tear from the corner of each of his three eyes. 'Bye-bye, Margot,' he whispered.

Joe waved.

Randalf chuckled. 'Did you all hear that? She said she'd

miss me!' he said softly. He stared after the departing dragon. 'Randalf the Wise. Dragon-tamer . . .'

'I think her words were, *old Fatso*,' said Veronica.

'Shut *up*, Veronica!' said Randalf. 'Oh, look, *there* he is!' He cupped his hand to his mouth. 'Oh, Horned Baron!' he called. 'Horned *Baron*!'

Joe turned to see a short, stooped figure scuttling along the castle wall. His helmet was even more dented than Joe's own, with the horns sticking out at crazy angles.

'*HORNED BARON!*' Randalf bellowed. '*SIR!*'

The Horned Baron stopped and looked round innocently. 'Did somebody call me?' he said.

Randalf strode towards him, cutting a swathe through the piles of feathers and splinters of wood. 'It is I, sir,' he said. 'Randalf the Wise. Supplier of warrior-heroes and dragons in emergencies.' He smiled broadly. 'Eighty gold big 'uns, I believe we agreed.'

'Quite, quite,' said the Horned Baron. 'Send me a bill. You'll take a cheque, won't you?'

'I'm strictly a cash wizard,' said Randalf firmly. He held out his hand. 'Eighty gold big 'uns, if you please.'

'I don't carry that much on me,' said the Horned Baron, patting his pockets and shrugging. 'Sorry.'

'But . . . but . . .' Randalf blustered.

The Horned Baron smiled and laid a hand on the wizard's shoulder. 'But enough of this. After all, we shouldn't be talking about money now. This is a time for celebration! Three cheers for Randalf the Wise!'

Benson and a couple of footmen cheered weakly.

'Well done!' said the baron. 'Now, what's everyone waiting for?'

Several under-gardeners and the herald looked at each other, then back at the baron.

'Well?' he said. He paused and threw an angry look round the courtyard. 'Start clearing up this mess!' he snapped. 'What on earth is Ingrid going to say?'

Just then, a loud clapping noise erupted from the other side of the castle. Everyone looked up to see one single, solitary wardrobe flying over the towers and castellations back in the direction of Elfwood.

As the wardrobe flapped away into the distance, glinting in the low, early morning sunlight, a muffled voice was heard crying out.

'Walter! *Walter!*'

'An IOU!' Randalf stormed. 'Not worth the pair of frilly lace pantaloons it's written on!'

It was later that day and he and the others were back on the houseboat.

'Of all the low-down, two-timing, back-stabbing, sneaky tricks to play!' He turned to Joe. 'Let this be a warning to you. Never, *ever* trust the word of a baron, no matter how pointy his horns.'

'Still, it is an IOU,' said Joe. 'Even if you couldn't find anything else to write on, you did get his signature. That must be worth something.'

Randalf blushed.

'Show him your knickers,' said Veronica. 'Go on!'

Randalf handed the pantaloons to Joe. 'IOU eighty big 'uns,' read Joe, 'signed *The Grand Old Duke of York* . . .'

'What?' said Randalf. He snatched back the pantaloons and stared miserably at the fake signature. 'I'm just too trusting,' he said and sighed. 'Typical of the Horned Baron to pull a fast one. And after everything I did for him!'

'Everything *Margot* did, more like,' said Veronica. 'What a fine dragon she turned out to be. A real lady. And generous too,' she added. 'She gave us some lovely presents. Norbert's baking trays, Joe's warrior-hero outfit, not to mention my gorgeous little cage.' She

tinkled her little bell and preened in front of the mirror. 'My own little home,' she sighed. 'Remind me, Randalf,' she said, turning to the wizard. 'What did she give you?'

Randalf gave the Potty of Thrynn a vicious kick. '*Ouch!*' he cried.

'It goes with your knickers!' said Veronica smugly.

'Shut up, Veronica!' said Randalf.

From inside the kitchen came the sounds of whistling, whisking and the clattering of pots and pans.

'Still, could be worse, I suppose,' said Randalf. 'Norbert's cooking has certainly improved. And Joe, my boy, you certainly look the part in that outfit. Shame about the dented helmet. Are those wings meant to stick out like that?'

Joe smiled. 'It'll make a nice souvenir,' he said, 'when I go back home. When will that be again?'

'I'll see to it as soon as I can,' said Randalf, suddenly finding the details on the side of the Potty of Thrynn extremely fascinating.

'But when?' said Joe. 'Haven't I done enough yet?'

Randalf traced the outline of what appeared to be a large bottom engraved into the silver. 'Wonderful work-manship,' he murmured.

'*When?*' said Joe.

Randalf took a tentative sniff at the potty. 'I must wash my beard again,' he muttered.

'Randalf!' said Joe sharply. 'When are you going to send me home?'

The wizard turned. 'You know how it is,' he said. 'Waiting for an auspicious moment and all that. The align-ment of the stars. The configuration of the moons . . .'

'No! No!' Joe shouted. 'You know that's not true. The moment could come and go, and you *still* wouldn't be able to do anything because you don't know the spell! We've got to go to Elfwood and recover Roger the Wrinkled's *Great Book of Spells*. It's the only way.'

'The lad's right,' said Veronica. 'Even if it does mean meeting up with Dr Cuddl—'

'Veronica!' Randalf shouted. 'I forbid you to use that name in my presence.'

'Besides,' said Veronica, swinging gaily to and fro on her perch, 'if you stand any chance of ever seeing those eighty gold big 'uns, you're going to have to go there.'

'I am?' said Randalf.

'Where else do you think that wardrobe took Ingrid?' she replied.

Randalf groaned. 'You don't mean . . .'

'He – who shall remain nameless – has got the *Great Book of Spells*,' said Veronica. 'He's got Roger the Wrinkled and the other wizards – and now he's added Ingrid to his collection. It's all part of his master plan.'

'Then, there's no choice,' said Joe firmly. 'We must go to Giggle Glade.'

'Better hang on to that potty, Randalf!' said Veronica. 'From the look on your face, you're going to need it.'

A solitary wardrobe lay on the ground beside the front door of the little house at the centre of Giggle Glade. It was still. One door was open and one closed. A pile of hangers lay in a corner. Dr Cuddles looked at it through the window.

'You have done well,' he giggled. 'My self-assembled pine-clad beauty!'

He turned away and slipped into the shadows.

Quentin nodded his head vigorously. 'That was one of mine, master,' he said. 'The instructions were ever so tricky, and I had three screws left over.'

'Excellent,' Dr Cuddles went on, giggling unpleasantly. 'Even though our losses were high!'

'I told you we needed more time,' said Roger the Wrinkled. 'The Welsh dresser was only half done, and someone sent off the teddy bear linen chest with all your quilts by mistake.'

'We all have to make sacrifices,' said Dr Cuddles, a slight choke in his voice. 'I might not have the Horned Baron, but I have the next best thing!' He giggled.

'Ooh, Dr Cuddles, you're *so* wicked,' said Quentin.

'He'll be like putty in my hand,' Dr Cuddles giggled. 'What won't he do to get his beloved Ingrid back? He'll be knocking on my door, *begging* me to return her. And when he does . . .'

The room resounded with his sinister, high-pitched giggling.

'Cuddles?' screeched an imperious voice. 'Cuddles!'

The giggling stopped. 'What can that infernal woman want now?' Dr Cuddles muttered. 'Surely she can't have broken free of the restraints already.' He turned and clapped his paws together.

Nothing happened.

'Where are those confounded elves?' he shouted.

'*Cuddles!*' Ingrid's voice sliced through the air like a knife.

Dr Cuddles shuddered. 'Roger!' he shouted. 'Quentin! Come back here!'

'*CUDDLES!*'

'Aah, this is the life,' sighed the Horned Baron.

He was reclining on a mountain of well-stuffed, if heavily patched, cushions in front of a roaring fire, his toes covered by a quilt with teddy bears on it. The curtains were drawn. The candles were lit.

The Horned Baron sipped from a large mug of spittle

tea and plucked a hairy toffee from the box on his lap. Many hours had passed since Ingrid's unfortunate disappearance. He popped a second toffee into his mouth. Poor, dear Ingrid . . .

Knock, knock.

The rapping at the door shattered the silence of the cavernous room and reminded the Horned Baron just how quiet it was.

'Enter,' he called.

The door opened and Benson approached. 'Bad news, sir,' he said. 'There's still no sign of the Baroness.'

'Oh dear, what a terrible shame,' said the Horned Baron. 'Still, mustn't grumble.' He raised the mug to his lips and sipped the spittle tea. 'Delicious,' he murmured. 'Throw another piece of wardrobe on the fire on your way out, Benson. There's a good chap.'

As the gardener shut the door behind him, the Horned Baron leaned back into the plump cushions and closed his eyes.

'Really must rescue Ingrid.' He yawned. 'One of these days.'

The weary pieces of cutlery huddled together round a large sign which read *Nowhere* as the sun set on another day.

They'd come so far. So very far. A soft wind blew and,

as the moons of Muddle Earth rose in the sky, the cutlery glinted in the purple, yellow and green light.

The tiny teaspoon stood apart from the rest. It seemed to be listening to something that only it could hear. Something far off. Something calling to it . . .

With a little sigh, the teaspoon turned. The journey ahead was long, but it had to be done.

Tinkle, tinkle, it went as it tripped back across the stony ground. *Clink, chink, clatter, clang,* went the knives, forks, spoons and all the rest of the cutlery as they followed on behind.

Through the mountains they journeyed, across the plains. By dawn the following morning, the tall trees of Elfwood could be seen on the distant horizon.

The tiny teaspoon trembled with excitement. The calling was closer. It sighed softly.

Soon. Very soon . . .

'Cuddles!' A raucous voice shattered the silence of Giggle Glade. 'I shan't tell you again. I want my hot-water bottle refilling and I want it now!'

Dr Cuddles managed a weary giggle.

'*Cuddles!*'

'Is that you, my little caged song thrush?' replied Dr Cuddles. He glanced out of the window for any sign of visitors. There was none. He giggled anxiously. 'How the Horned Baron must be missing you?' he said.

'He can't live without me!' Ingrid screeched. 'And when he finds out how I've been treated, he'll knock your block off! Now, see to my hot-water bottle. Immediately!'

Dr Cuddles shook his head. His piercing blue eyes narrowed. 'Oh, Horned Baron,' he muttered, giggling menacingly. 'You're going to pay for this. You mark my words! You're going to pay for this dearly!'

Book 3

DOCTOR CUDDLES
~ OF ~
GIGGLE GLADE

Prologue

A new day was dawning in Muddle Earth. Stiltmice were stirring, batbirds were coming in to roost, and tree rabbits were rubbing their big blue eyes with their little pink paws.

At one end of the sky the horizon was tinged a muddy brown colour as two of the three moons of Muddle Earth – the purple and the yellow ones – set. (The green moon, despite high expectations and the most expert of forecasts, hadn't bothered to make an appearance at all that night.) At the other end of the sky, the sun was rising. Its dazzling rays glinted on the uppermost peaks of Mount Boom and the Musty Mountains.

Boom, went Mount Boom weakly, and a ring of pinky grey smoke rose slowly into the air.

Far below, padding silently on broad paws along the dusty mountain road, a great, pink, striped cat emerged from the swirling mist. It paused, threw back its head and let out a loud, rumbling roar. Its sabre teeth gleamed. Every creature within earshot fell silent: the hillfish froze, a passing batbird wheeled noiselessly away, while the tree rabbits hid their eyes behind their long, floppy ears. The great pink cat scratched at the ground and roared a second time.

'I know, I know,' said its rider from astride the ornate, jewel-encrusted leather saddle secured round the creature's broad chest. 'It *is* good to be back.'

She dismounted, surveyed the scene, and gave a smile of satisfaction. The low sunlight shone on her flame-red plaits and golden skin, accentuating the curves of her firm muscles.

Her powerful physique was set off magnificently by a split-leg, tooled-leather tunic with a bear-fur trim and matching reversible chiffon and organza cloak, all topped off with a winged helmet of burnished bronze with silver inlay detailing. Her shapely ankles were emphasized by the lizard-gut thongs of her sling-back sandals, rising criss-cross fashion right up to her knees. At her dragon-skin belt, she was wearing a gold, limited-edition armoury sword and accessorized catapult. The entire ensemble was completed with a precious little goat-ear shoulder bag.

'We've been away too long,' she said, thoughtfully fingering the notches and dents of battle which scarred the blade of her sword. 'Orc wrestling, giant tickling, hag worrying. I've had enough, old friend. It's time we settled down.' She surveyed the horizon. 'What we need is a nice, old-fashioned wizard to work for. No more smelly slime-demons and boring old sorcerors to sort out. Just a few goblins to boss around, and all the milk you can drink! I don't know about you, but I can't wait to put my feet up. These sandals are killing me!'

She ruffled the creature's soft, furry, pink ears. The battle-cat purred loudly. Brenda the Warrior-Princess seized the reins and leaped back into the saddle. The cat's shoulder muscles rippled. It snarled fiercely and tossed its head.

'Onwards, Sniffy!' she cried, her voice echoing around the barren landscape, and tugged at the reins. 'To the Enchanted Lake.'

The sun shone down bright and warm on Muddle Earth; its mountains and forests; its roads, bridges and towns – and on the Enchanted Lake, which rose up into the air like a vast, watery toadstool.

Sunlight shone through the transparent column of water, casting a rainbow-coloured shadow across the bubbling Perfumed Bog. Dazzled and confused by the bright light, a large silver fish swam too near to the bottom of the hovering lake, fell out of the water and down into the gaping beak of a waiting lazybird crouched beneath.

Flop, plop . . . Gulp!

Far up above the lazybird, the sun sparkled on the rippling surface of the lake and the ornately decorated houseboats, which were bobbing about in the fresh gathering breeze. It shone on the twisting chimneys, on the varnished prows and polished brass fittings, and through the glinting windows, sending beams of sunlight slicing through the dusty shadows inside.

A boy was standing at the entrance to the master cabin of the only occupied houseboat on the Enchanted Lake, banging on the door with his fist. His name was Joe Jefferson. Beside him sat Henry, his dog.

'Wake up, Randalf!' Joe was shouting. 'Wake up!'

Henry barked.

The snoring from inside the cabin paused for a moment – before continuing with renewed vigour. A small budgie fluttered down and landed on the boy's shoulder.

'It's not locked, you know,' it said.

Joe seized the brass handle and pushed the door open. The sunlight flooded in, revealing the snorer – a rotund, bearded wizard sprawled across a tiny four-poster bed. His arms stuck out, his neck was cricked, while his feet hung over the bottom of the bed, the big toes protruding through the large frayed holes of a pair of woollen socks.

As the bright light hit his face, he snorted, grunted and smacked his lips. The eyelids fluttered for a moment, but remained shut.

'Randalf!' said Joe, his voice loud and thick with irritation. He strode forwards, Henry by his side, and shook the wizard by the shoulders. 'Randalf, you promised!'

'And you *believed* him?' said Veronica the budgie, flapping up on to the top of the four-poster bed.

'Ran-*dalf*!' Joe shook him more vigorously. '*Ran-dalf!*'

The wizard turned over and continued to snore.

'Leave this to me,' said Veronica. The budgie hopped on to the pillow and put her beak next to Randalf's ear. 'Oh, Randy,' she trilled. 'Randy, wake up. There's a stiltmouse in the bed.'

The wizard's eyes snapped open. 'Stiltmouse!' he cried. 'Where? Where?' He sat bolt upright in bed, banging his head hard on the curtain frame above him. '*OUCH!*' he bellowed.

Joe struggled not to laugh as Randalf looked round fearfully, eyes wild and pointy hat quivering.

'Stiltmice!' yelled Randalf. 'Nasty, horrible, twitching little things. *Urgghh!*'

He noticed the faces grinning at him. His eyes narrowed. 'There is no stiltmouse, is there?' he said.

Veronica and Joe laughed. Henry barked.

'I see,' said Randalf, pulling himself up with as much dignity as he could muster. He rubbed his throbbing head and winced.

'You need a new bed, by the way,' said Joe, chuckling softly. 'This one's far too small.'

Randalf glared at him indignantly. 'I'll have you know that this is a king-sized bed.'

'Yes, it belonged to King Alf the Elf,' Veronica butted in. 'And even *he* traded it in for something bigger. Boy, they really saw you coming at *Krump's Discount Furniture Store* . . .'

'Shut up, Veronica!' said Randalf sleepily, yawning, stretching – and losing his balance. He keeled over, grabbing hold of one of the bed curtains (which came away in his hands) as he fell, and landed on the floor with a loud bang. The houseboat swayed.

'*Ouch!*' he roared – even more loudly than before. He turned to Veronica. 'This is all your fault for waking me so fraudulently!' he said. 'Stiltmouse, indeed!'

'It's your own fault for oversleeping, Fatso!' said Veronica calmly.

'Yes!' Joe broke in, with feeling. 'You said we'd leave by the first light of dawn, and it's almost midday! You promised!'

'But—' Randalf began.

'You know full well,' Joe continued without taking a breath, 'that if I'm ever to leave Muddle Earth, we must go to Giggle Glade in Elfwood and retrieve the *Great Book of Spells* from Dr—'

'And so we shall, my lad!' Randalf interrupted before the dreaded name could be spoken. 'So we shall! After all, given everything you've done for Muddle Earth, it's the least I can do.'

'Actually,' interrupted Veronica, 'doing *nothing* is the least you can do, and that's something you're an expert at.'

'Shut *up*, Veronica!' said Randalf. 'Believe me, my boy, we shall go to Elfwood . . .'

'But when?' Joe demanded. '*When?* No matter how often you promise we'll go, whenever the time comes you've always got an excuse for *not* going,' he said crossly. 'What was it yesterday? Oh, yes, you had to stay in to wash your beard. And the day before? Mangel-wurzel shopping in Trollbridge. And the day before that, tree rabbit racing in Goblintown. And last week it was the wrong kind of rain, and the week before that . . .'

'I know, I know,' said Randalf sympathetically. 'Several important matters and unfortunate, unforeseen difficulties have come up recently. But I have cleared my desk, I have wiped the slate clean . . .'

'You? Cleaning?' Veronica sneered. 'That'd be a first!'

Randalf ignored her. 'I said we would set off today and I meant it.' He frowned. 'It's odd,' he murmured thoughtfully. 'I distinctly remember setting the clock.' He left the bed cabin and strode across the living room. 'I do hope it's not being difficult again.'

The hands of the clock were both pointing downwards,

indicating that the time was half past six in the morning –
or the evening. With the sun high in the sky, it was clearly
neither. Grumbling ominously under his breath, Randalf
seized hold of both sides of the clock and gave it a violent
shake. The clock rattled and clunked, and something went
boing!

'Clock repairer, too, eh?' said Veronica sarcastically. 'Is
there no end to your talents?'

Randalf huffed and puffed. 'Ridiculous contraption!'
he muttered. 'It's never worked properly.'

'Nor did the spell you paid for it with,' Veronica
reminded him.

'That's neither here nor there!' said Randalf dismissively.

'Tell that to the goblin maiden whose hair all dropped
out,' muttered Veronica.

'It's that blasted clock-elf, that's what it is,' said
Randalf. He hammered on the door of the clock. 'Come on!
Show your face, you incompetent numbskull!' he shouted.
'Open up!'

The door remained shut. Randalf reached forward and
pulled it open. A cluster of cogs and flywheels clattered to
the floor; a length of spring uncoiled. Randalf's lips pursed,
his beard trembled. There was no sign of the clock-elf.

'What the . . . !' he exploded. 'Where's that ridiculous
creature got to now?'

Veronica fluttered down and landed on Randalf's
shoulder. 'There's a note,' she said, pointing with her wing.

Randalf peered inside the clock. Sure enough, pinned to the wall just above a small hammock, was a piece of card. Randalf reached in and tore it away.

'*Gone to unwind,*' he read out. '*Back in a fortnight of Thursdays.* Well, of all the cheek. Just taking off without so much a word of explanation . . .'

Just then, there was a *plop* followed by a *splash*. Randalf turned to Veronica. 'What was that?'

Veronica shrugged her shoulders. 'Just a fish, probably,' she said. 'After all, apart from the wizards, they're the only things daft enough to live up here – and the wizards have all disappeared. Whose fault is that, I wonder?' She said, tapping the side of Randalf's head with her beak.

Pretending not to notice, Randalf returned his attention to the broken clock. 'Probably a blessing in disguise the clock-elf's gone,' he said. 'Remind me to go to Grubleys and see about a replacement. Apparently he's got some new ones in stock. The Horned Baron's got one. It sings the time, tap-dances and tells jokes . . .'

'Never mind all that!' said Joe, exasperated. 'What about our quest?'

Randalf sucked in air noisily between his teeth. 'It's getting a little bit late for that, don't you think?'

'Randalf!' snapped Joe.

'All right, all right,' said Randalf. 'But if I could just—'

From outside, there came a second *plop-splash*. It was louder this time. Closer . . .

The next moment, the door burst open and the ogre, Norbert the Not-Very-Big, ambled in, yawning and rubbing his eyes.

'Was that you, Norbert?' said Randalf.

Puzzled, Norbert blinked his three eyes one after the other. 'It still *is* me!' he said. 'Isn't it?' He slapped his forehead with the palm of his hand. The houseboat swayed from side to side. 'Don't tell me I've changed into someone else in my sleep again,' he said agitatedly. 'Do you remember the time I turned into that short goblin seamstress called Truffles?'

'That was a *dream*, Norbert,' said Randalf patiently. 'I explained all that. And of course you're still you! I was simply asking whether you had caused the loud *plop* and *splash* we heard.'

'Can't say I noticed,' said Norbert. 'But then, what with dodging all those flying rocks, I wasn't really paying attention.'

'Flying rocks?' said Randalf.

'One of them missed my head by a hair's breadth,' he said.

'Thus missing your brain by at least three metres,' muttered Veronica.

Randalf shook his head. 'I can't say I like the sound of these flying rocks,' he said. 'They could be a bad omen, worse even than last Wednesday's light drizzle. Perhaps we ought to postpone our departure . . .'

'NO!' shouted Joe. He could bear it no longer. 'It's always something! Light drizzle, falling leaves – now flying rocks. You promised that we'd set off today, and a promise is a promise.'

'And it is a promise I fully intend to keep,' said Randalf reassuringly. 'I was merely going to propose that we set ourselves up with a good, hearty breakfast first.'

'Snuggle-muffins, sir?' suggested Norbert.

'Just the job,' said Randalf. 'And some porridge, Norbert. And a tankard of foaming stiltmouse milk. Ooh, and some jub-jub fruits – but make sure you peel them first . . .'

Henry barked.

'And some bone fritters for our valiant battle-hound, here,' Randalf added.

'Can't we just go?' Joe complained.

'We could,' said Randalf slowly. 'But I think it would be unwise to set out on a perilous quest such as ours on an empty stomach.'

'You tell him, Fatso,' chirped Veronica.

Again, Randalf chose to ignore her. 'And while you're about it,' he said to Norbert, 'get the picnic hamper packed up with some goodies, there's a good fellow. We'd better stop off for lunch on the way.'

Joe groaned. This was going to take ages. Everything had to be just so. The crusts had to be cut off the sandwiches, the stiltmouse milk had to be at exactly the right temperature (a tad cooler than tepid), there had to be twists of salt for the the hard-boiled eggs – and as for the snuggle-muffins: Randalf insisted that Norbert decorated each one with coloured icing and sprinkles, and wrapped them individually in paper doilies.

Finally, after seconds and – in Randalf's case – thirds, breakfast was over and the picnic hamper was ready and waiting by the door. Joe sat on the basket, all dressed up in his warrior-hero costume, twiddling his thumbs impatiently. With his burnished copper shield and razor-sharp sword, his helmet, breastplate and boots – all courtesy of his old friend, Margot the dragon – he certainly looked the part of a great questing warrior-hero. All he needed now was for the quest to get started.

'*Now* can we go?' he said wearily.

'Of course,' said Randalf. He looked out of the window. The sky was getting cloudy. 'I'll just go and change into my waterproof pointy hat,' he said. 'Just in case.'

Joe groaned.

'All dressed up and nowhere to go, eh?' said Veronica, fluttering down beside him.

'Why does he always do this?' said Joe grumpily. 'He knows how important this quest is for me.'

Just then, Randalf's voice floated back from the master cabin. 'Check the portholes are shut securely,' he shouted. 'And that the lamps are all out. And Norbert, if you could just run a mop over the kitchen floor . . .'

'You see!' said Joe, exasperated. He began pacing up and down the living room.

Finally, Randalf emerged in a pointy hat with a small umbrella attached to its tip. 'I've been thinking,' he said. 'Maybe it *would* be best to set off tomorrow. We can make a nice early start.'

'No!' said Joe. 'No, no, no . . .'

Veronica nodded sympathetically. 'You know the reason he keeps putting off this quest,' she said. 'He's frightened of going to Giggle Glade. Frightened of what he's going to find there . . .'

'Frightened?' said Randalf indignantly. 'Me? I'm a wizard. I take danger in my stride . . .'

Just then, a boulder the size of a large loaf of snotbread came crashing through the window. Randalf let out a little squeak of alarm and leaped up into Norbert's arms.

'Aargh!' he screamed. 'It's an omen! It's an omen!'

Veronica stared at the quivering wizard. 'Taking danger in your stride, I see,' she said.

Crash!

The roof splintered and the ceiling cracked. From outside came the sound of furious roaring.

'*Aaaaargh!*' screamed Randalf, even louder. 'Batten down the hatches! Man the lifeboats . . . !'

'Lifeboats?' said Veronica. 'What lifeboats? Norbert's sunk them all!'

'Just *do* something! Randalf shouted desperately. '*Any*thing! We're under attack!'

Meanwhile, in Goblintown, the shops were opening up for business. Built one upon the other – most exclusive at the bottom and tackiest at the top – the shops formed tall, swaying towers. One housed milliners; another, ironmongers; another, bakers . . . In the centre of the town was a stack of clothing shops, at the very top of which was *Grubley's Discount Garment Store* – a fusty, musty, rundown establishment selling a wide selection of the cheapest, nastiest outfits to be found anywhere in Muddle Earth.

The shop itself, with its rows and rows of sparkly clothes, was deserted. But from the little workshop at the back came the sound of voices. Raised voices . . .

'Get back to work this instant!' shouted Grubley the owner, a stocky character with bandy legs, hairy ears and one thick, dark eyebrow that looked stuck to his forehead like a length of bear-fur trim.

'Can't!' snapped the goblin at the workbench.

'Can't?' said Grubley. 'If I don't get that order out by lunchtime, Boris the Big-Nosed is going to have my guts for garters. You know what ogres can be like!' His eyebrow furrowed. 'This instant, Snitch,' he bellowed. 'Do you hear me?'

The goblin winced. 'Only too well,' muttered the goblin. 'Be that as it may, I can't get back to work. The sewing-elf is doing a bunk,' he explained and nodded over to the corner.

Grubley turned and peered into the shadows, where a short, slight elf was busy tying a small bundle in a spotted handkerchief on to the end of a stick.

'What in Muddle Earth is going on?' Grubley demanded. 'Where do you think you're going?'

'On holiday,' said the elf happily.

'Holiday? Holiday?' Grubley spluttered. 'But elves love their work. They don't have holidays!'

'We do now!' said the elf, a happy smile spreading out across his bony features. He swung the stick up on to his shoulder and, striking up a cheerful whistle, marched out of the door.

Grubley was left standing there; outraged, red-faced, speechless.

'That's the trouble these days,' muttered Snitch. 'You just can't get reliable elves.'

All over Goblintown, the same scene was being repeated as elves of every description poured out on to the dark, narrow streets and headed off towards the gates of the walled city. As well as the sewing-elves, there were clock-elves and cake-mixer-elves; lamplighter-elves and greetings-elves – and even the somewhat giddy spin-dryer-elves bringing up the rear. They were all talking excitedly, the air filled with their squeaky voices as they joined in the mass exodus.

Behind them, the goblins stood in their doorways and hung out of their windows, staring forlornly as their little helpers departed. How ever would they cope without them?

The elves – growing more excited with each passing minute – headed off along the road to Elfwood in a gathering cloud of dust, their knotted, striped and spotted handkerchiefs bobbing about in the hazy early morning sunshine. As they continued, so their band grew larger and larger as others joined their number.

From Goblintown, Trollbridge and the Enchanted Lake they came; together with greetings-elves, already out with their sacks of letters, and those elves who had set up residence in potholes, who now gathered up their pots, swung them on to their backs and got caught up in the happy, chattering throng.

'I've never been on holiday before!' cried one.

'Me neither!' cried another.

'Ooh! This is *so* exciting!' cried a third as the front of the mighty crowd reached the edges of the forest. A cry went up.

'Elfwood! Elfwood! Elfwood!'

Meanwhile, in the sumptuous Grand Bedchamber of the Horned Baron's castle, its lord and master – the Horned Baron himself – was sitting up in his huge four-poster bed. There was a tray on his lap, upon it a single rose in a long-stemmed glass and a silver napkin ring, engraved with *HB*. A grubby napkin, monogrammed with the same floral letters, was tucked in at the neck of his silk pyjamas.

He had a piece of half-eaten rot fudge in one hand and was sipping from a cup of spittle tea in the other. As he wiped the pearly froth from his moustache, the horned helmet wobbled on his head.

Benson – newly promoted from head gardener to the Horned Baron's personal manservant – was on the other side of the room, drawing the curtains. 'I trust sir slept well,' he said.

'Very well,' the Horned Baron replied brightly, and chewed at the piece of rot fudge. 'Very, mffvery mffwell,' he mumbled.

Ever since his wife Ingrid had gone missing, the Horned Baron had been sleeping like a log. Every night he would drop off the moment his helmeted head hit the pillow, waking ten hours later when Benson brought him his breakfast, feeling fit and refreshed.

He swallowed the lump of fudge. 'I was having the most wonderful dream,' he said thoughtfully, and smiled to himself. In it, a bald Ingrid was being lowered slowly into a huge vat of stinky hog milk. Just as her enormous feet were disappearing from view, he'd woken up.

'. . . the ransom note?' he heard Benson saying.

'What's that?' asked the Horned Baron.

'I was wondering whether sir had replied to the ransom note,' Benson explained.

'Ransom note . . .' the Horned Baron repeated absent-mindedly as he stirred an extra sugar lump into his spittle tea.

'Yes, sir, the ransom note,' said Benson. 'For the Baroness.'

'Ah, yes, I've *mffllmmf*,' he mumbled as he stuffed another large piece of fudge into his mouth. He swallowed noisily. 'I've tried, but I can't seem to find a greetings-elf. But never mind.' He sighed, and leaned back against the plump satin pillows. 'I'll get round to it soon enough.'

Benson paused and looked round. 'If I might be so bold, sir, you know what the ransom letter said. If you don't reply by nightfall, they'll shave off all her hair.'

'*Mffllmmff*,' he muttered and tutted softly. 'Absolutely terrible.'

'And after that,' Benson continued, 'they'll immerse her in a vat of stinky hog milk.'

The Horned Baron smiled dreamily. 'Stinky hog milk,' he murmured. 'Mortifying. Poor, dear Ingrid. It really doesn't bear thinking about . . . Now, fetch me a fresh pot of spittle tea, there's a good chap. This one's getting cold. And while you're there, rustle me up a couple of slices of mouldy toast.'

Meanwhile, in Elfwood, more and more elves were arriving. The air was filled with their giggling, singing and endless happy chatter – for although the elves of Muddle Earth did indeed love their work, they seemed to be overcome with excitement at the prospect of a holiday.

But this was no ordinary holiday. This was the sort of holiday that would appeal to any self-respecting elf. This was a *working* holiday, with lots and lots of back-breaking, hard physical labour. That was what was being offered. That was what the mysterious call they all answered had promised them; a working holiday in Elfwood. Giddy with joy, the elves skipped and danced and sang out at the tops of their lungs.

'*We're all going on an Elfwood holiday!*' they chirruped, over and over. '*We're all going on an Elfwood holiday! We're all going on an Elfwood . . .*'

'Oh, do give it a rest!' complained a tall, crabby old tree, its gnarled branches trembling.

'Those squeaky little voices go right through you,' muttered a slender willow in a copse nearby.

'I know!' 'Yes, they do!' 'You can say that again!' her companions agreed, their leaves quivering with distaste as the elves swarmed round their trunks and over their roots.

'They cut through you like a chainsaw!' said a tall, spreading beech darkly.

'Ooh, Brett, don't!' gasped its neighbours.

Ever since Dr Cuddles had taken up residence in Giggle Glade, hundreds of their friends and relations had been cut down and turned into boards, planks and beams, wardrobes and cupboards, tables and chairs. Now, or so it was rumoured on the grapevine (the grapevine which wound its way round the entire forest was a terrible gossip), Dr Cuddles had ordered the construction of something enormous, something monumental – and (it was whispered) made entirely of wood.

'That Dr Cuddles has got a lot to answer for,' the beech muttered, its coppery leaves flapping menacingly. 'I'll— Get *off* me!' it shouted and flicked a branch, sending the half dozen elves who had been swinging from it flying off into the air.

They landed on soft mattresses of leaves, rolled over, leaped to their feet as if nothing had happened and scampered off to join the others. There were hundreds of them by now. *Thousands!*

'The whole place is crawling!' screeched an elegant silver birch.

'I'll shed a bough and brain the little squeakers!' bellowed an old elm, anchored to the bank of a babbling brook.

'Frilly knickers, chocolate drops, roast bananas, atishoo-atishoo, all fall down,' the brook babbled.

'And as for you!' stormed the old elm. 'Babble, babble –
morning, noon and night!' It rustled threateningly. 'I swear,
one of these days, I'm going to dam you up!'

Meanwhile, at the very centre of the wood, in a clearing that
was getting larger by the day, other noises could be heard.
There was a bang and a clatter. A piercingly shrill voice. A
sigh of resignation.

Inside the house, with his ear pressed up against a
closed door, was Quentin the Cake-Decorator. His hair was
damp, his legs were shaking. He didn't know how much
more of this his nerves could take.

'A little bit more off the fringe! And keep it straight!
Straight, you moron!' Ingrid screeched.

Quentin trembled. That voice! It cut through him like
a knife. He crossed and uncrossed his legs nervously.

'Imbecile!' she roared. 'Call yourself a hairdresser! I've
blown my nose on more talented handkerchiefs! I've slept
on mattresses that could use a pair of scissors better than
you! I've . . .'

Quentin clamped his hands over his ears. 'Poor Dr
Cuddles,' he found himself thinking. 'Then again,' he
thought, 'as long as she's giving *him* a hard time, she's
leaving *me* alone.'

An hour earlier, Dr Cuddles had entered her chamber

with scissors, razor and a bowl of warm soapy water balanced in his stubby arms. He was intending to carry out the first of the ransom-note threats by shaving Ingrid's head. Things, however, had obviously not gone as Dr Cuddles planned.

Quentin tentatively removed his hands from his ears and listened.

'You see, you really are a good hairdresser when you make the effort,' Ingrid was purring. 'Much better. I look beautiful.' She giggled. 'Don't you think I look beautiful, Dr Cuddles? You want me to look beautiful, don't you?'

Quentin blanched. She was being nice! That was when she was at her most dangerous. Beads of sweat broke out across his forehead. Any moment now, she would want something, and with the house-elves all having been assigned to other duties, it was he, Quentin, who would have to get or do whatever that something might be. He shuddered miserably as he remembered the night before. All that wobbly strawberry jelly! All that wire wool!

'Stinky hog *cleansing* milk, you mean, you silly thing,' Quentin heard Ingrid saying. She was giggling coquettishly. Quentin shivered with foreboding. 'Oh, I shall look forward to that. Then you can give me a back-rub, Cuddles. And a foot-massage . . .'

All at once, the door burst open. Quentin let out a little scream and jumped back. Dr Cuddles stood in the doorway, his piercing blue eyes glaring out of the shadows.

'You startled me, M . . . Master,' Quentin stammered. 'I was just . . . just about to enquire whether you'd like a . . . a . . . a nice snuggle-muffin for your mid-morning snack?'

'This is no time for snuggle-muffins,' said Dr Cuddles coldly.

'Cuddles!' Ingrid cooed from inside the room. 'Hurry back with that stinky hog cleansing milk.' Her voice hardened. 'Ingrid doesn't like to be kept waiting, remember.'

'How could I forget?' said Dr Cuddles, rolling his eyes. 'You did send that ransom note, didn't you, Quentin?' he said, giggling nervously. 'You did say that we'd shave off her hair, immerse her in a vat of stinky hog milk . . .'

'*And* tickle her feet with a lazybird feather! *And* prod her repeatedly with a wet fish!' Quentin interrupted, flapping his hands about agitatedly. 'I told them *everything*!'

Dr Cuddles shook his head slowly from side to side.

'That Horned Baron,' he growled. 'I'm going to make him pay for this if it's the last thing I do!'

'Cuddles!' screeched Ingrid. 'I'm waiting!'

'Coming, my back-combed beauty,' Dr Cuddles called back. He turned to Quentin, eyes blazing. 'Fetch the stinky-hog milk. Open the gates ready for our visitors. And tell Roger the Wrinkled I want to see those plans at once. Good grief, do I have to do *everything* around here?'

Meanwhile, in the northern fringes of Elfwood, a vast set of cutlery was busy getting prepared for the next stage in its epic journey. The knives whetted their blades on stones, the forks sharpened their prongs, while the ladles and spoons polished and buffed themselves up, until the entire cutlery set could be seen reflected in each of their gleaming bowls.

A tiny teaspoon, with glinting curlicues on its handle, stood on top of a boulder. The back of its silver bowl glinted in the early morning sun as it cocked it to one side.

It was listening.

Meanwhile, in the far off Ogrehills, a gruff yet plaintive voice cried out.

'Has anyone seen Fluffy? He was here a minute ago. Fluffy! *Flu-uffy!*'

But the ogre's snuggly-wuggly comforter – a particularly soft and hairy elf – was gone. Off down the dusty mountain track he was skipping, a tune on his lips and a knotted handkerchief on a stick over one shoulder.

Meanwhile, under Trollbridge, a lumpen troll reached out for a turnip-slicer-elf that wasn't there.

Meanwhile . . .

'Do you think it's safe yet?' said Randalf.

A good five minutes had passed since the last flying rock struck the houseboat, and Randalf had just poked his head out of the picnic hamper in which he'd been hiding – a pink snuggle-muffin stuck to his forehead. There was no reply.

'Where's everybody gone?' he called.

'Out here, Fatso,' came Veronica's voice.

Tentatively, Randalf ventured out on to the deck, where he found the others at the balustrade. They were all looking over the side, peering down through the clear water beneath them. Veronica, perched on Joe's left shoulder, flapped a wing at something far below.

'I've never noticed *that* before,' she said.

Joe frowned. Despite the distortion from the rippling water he, too, could see something. He squinted. Not some-*thing*, he realized with a shock, but some*one*...

'Look,' he said. 'You can make out the shoulders and legs. And red hair.' The figure below the hovering lake raised an arm in unmistakable greeting. Joe gasped. 'He's seen us!'

Just then, a voice called up, loud and clear. 'At last! I've been chucking pebbles at every houseboat for the last hour trying to get someone's attention. I was beginning to think all the wizards had left the Enchanted Lake.'

'You're not wrong there,' muttered Veronica.

Joe glanced down at a boulder the size of a large pillow, lying on the deck to his right. That was some pebble!

Randalf cupped his hands to his mouth. 'I am a wizard,' he called out. 'And who might you be?'

'It is I, Brenda, Warrior-Princess,' came the booming reply. 'Weave a spell of levitation, mighty wizard, that I may join you on the Enchanted Lake.'

Joe blushed. Despite the broad shoulders and stout legs – not to mention the deep and powerful voice – *he* was evidently a *she*.

Randalf also blushed. 'Spell of levitation,' he murmured. 'Spell of levitation ... *er* ...'

'I think she means Norbert and the rope ladder,' Veronica sniffed.

Randalf leaned over the balustrade. 'I seem to have mislaid my spell book, your highness,' he shouted down. 'But I do have a rope ladder and an ogre,' he added. He turned and snapped at Norbert, 'Come on, Norbert! Don't keep our guest waiting!'

Having sunk
every rowing boat
on the Enchanted
Lake, followed by
every bath tub and then
every kitchen sink from every
houseboat, Norbert was forced to
become increasingly resourceful.
Joe watched as the great ogre –
squashed inside a huge baking tray and
using spatulas as oars – paddled slowly across the
lake, a wooden washing-up bowl on a piece of string
bobbing along beside him.

At the edge of the hovering lake, Norbert pulled the
coiled rope ladder from his shoulders and, having wrapped
one end around his ham of a hand, tossed the other end
down over the side. Joe saw the rope
ladder go taut, the ogre's arms
and neck strain – and the baking
tray begin to take on water.

Brenda must have climbed up
at incredible speed, for the next
moment her flame-red plaits
appeared, and the warrior-princess
pulled herself up over the lip of water
and into the waiting washing-up bowl.
She seized the ladles Norbert was

holding out and, in a blur of hands and spray, sped towards the houseboat.

Randalf was there to greet her. 'Enchanted to make your acquaintance,' he said giddily as Brenda leaped up on to the deck and fell to one knee before him.

'Enchanted,' sneered Veronica. 'You couldn't do "enchanted" if your life depended on it!'

'Ignore her,' said Randalf, unable to tear his eyes away from the magnificent warrior-princess. 'And . . . and please stand up.' He wiped his right hand on his robes and stuck it out. 'Randalf the Wise,' he announced. 'Would you care for some refreshments? Some spittle tea?'

Brenda got to her feet, seized Randalf's hand and shook it vigorously. 'Pleased to meet you,' she said, and as she followed him inside the houseboat, added, 'You seem to have something stuck to your forehead, Rudolf.'

'A snuggle-muffin,' said Veronica. She fluttered across the room to her cage, where she perched on the little bar and swung indignantly backwards and forwards.

Randalf wiped a tear from his eye – brought about by Brenda's bone-crushing grip – and plucked the snuggle-muffin from his head. 'This needs some more icing, Norbert,' he said. He turned to the warrior-princess. 'Now tell me, Brenda, what can I do for you?'

'What can you do for me?' said Brenda, and chuckled throatily. 'It is more a case of what *I* can do for *you*. I stand before you, a warrior-princess, veteran of a thousand battles.

I have wrestled with mud hags and clashed swords with orc lords. Now I offer my services to you, oh mighty sorcerer.'

Randalf swooned. Veronica tutted. Norbert took a bite of the snuggle-muffin.

'No heroic deed too small to be considered,' she added, and reached round for her sword, which she held up. Joe noticed the light glint on eight notches carved into the handle. 'Each one of these represents a mighty quest,' she said and smiled. 'There's room for plenty more.'

Joe stepped forwards bashfully. 'You're . . . you're a real warrior-hero,' he said. 'We were just about to set off on a quest of our own.'

Brenda's eyes narrowed. 'And who might you be?' she asked.

'Joe Jefferson,' said Joe. 'I'm . . .'

'He's Joe the Barbarian, a warrior-hero,' squawked Veronica. 'See? We've already got one.' The swinging perch itself seemed to squeak with indignation. 'The position's taken, thank you very much. So, buzz off! Go on, sling your hook!'

Brenda frowned. 'Warrior-hero?' she said.

Joe shrank back. He felt her piercing gaze boring into his own. 'Actually,' he began, 'I . . .'

'You tell her!' Veronica called out encouragingly. 'Conqueror of ogres. Defeater of dragons. Slayer of wardrobes.'

'Really?' said Brenda, sounding impressed.

'Yes, and that's his battle-hound . . .' said Veronica, with a wave of her wing. 'Fang. Fang the Ferocious. You don't want to mess about with Fang.'

'His real name's Henry,' said Joe.

Brenda reached forwards and stroked Henry on the head. Henry rolled over and waited for her to tickle his tummy.

'Traitor,' muttered Veronica.

Brenda straightened up and proffered her hand. 'Put it there, Joe the Barbarian!' she said. 'Always glad to meet a fellow warrior-hero. So what is this quest of which you speak?'

'Our quest?' Randalf broke in. 'Oh, just a little bit of business to clear up in Giggle Glade. You're welcome to join us,' he added as casually as his thumping heart would allow. 'Usual rates; a quarter of any treasure found, plus all the snuggle-muffins you can eat . . .'

A smile spread across the warrior-princess's face. 'A little bit of business?' she said. 'Sounds perfect. But I wouldn't want to tread on the mighty Joe's toes . . .'

'You're right!' squawked Veronica. 'You'd be treading all over Joe's toes with your nasty big feet.'

'No you wouldn't,' said Joe quickly. 'Honestly, you

wouldn't! After all, we'll need all the help we can get on this quest. We have to travel to Giggle Glade to recover the Grand Wizards' *Great Book of Spells*, a sacred text which has fallen into the clutches of the most malevolent fiend ever to have breathed the air of Muddle Earth!'

Brenda turned on Randalf. 'Is this your "little bit of business", Rupert?' she demanded.

Randalf blushed and threw a filthy look at Joe for being such a blabbermouth. The last thing he wanted was to scare her off. 'Yes,' he admitted quietly. 'Yes, it is.'

'Great stuff!' said Brenda. She clapped her large hands together gleefully. 'Count me in!'

'You mean you would accompany us on this noble yet perilous expedition?' said Randalf, scarcely able to believe his own ears.

'No problem,' said Brenda. 'When do we depart?'

Randalf smiled. 'You know what they say; there's no time like the present.' He shook his head. 'As I keep trying to impress upon young Joe, here.'

'But . . .' spluttered Joe.

'Young people today,' said Randalf, winking at Brenda conspiratorially. 'You know what they're like. Always procrastinating. Always putting off till tomorrow what should be done today . . . But now you've turned up, we can finally set off. We'd be honoured if you would accompany us.'

'But, Randalf . . .' said Joe indignantly.

'Do come along, Joe,' said Randalf fussily. 'There really is no time to lose.'

With that, the wizard turned on his heels and followed Brenda out on to the deck. Norbert went after them, a peevish Veronica perched on his head.

At last, thought Joe. A real warrior-hero! Now they stood a real chance! He wouldn't have to bluff and bluster any more, not with Brenda to back him up. Now he could wrest the *Great Book of Spells* from the evil Dr Cuddles, he could release the grand wizards, free Ingrid – whatever it took – and finally return home to the real world; the place where he belonged.

'*Uh-oh*,' Randalf's voice floated back from the deck.

Joe groaned. His hopes and dreams melted away like snowflakes in a fire. What now?

Quentin was standing outside Ingrid's bedchamber, his ear pressed to the door.

'Ooh, Dr Cuddles!' came Ingrid's shrill voice. 'That tickles!'

'I can't do this if you keep moving!' Dr Cuddles's muffled voice was sounding increasingly desperate. Quentin consulted his note book. *12.30: Tickle feet with lazybird feather*, he read.

Dr Cuddles's voice rose to a high-pitched wail. 'Careful.

No, don't sit down. No . . .'

Ingrid squealed with delight. 'You silly thing!' she chided. 'Why ever not?'

'Ouch!' Dr Cuddles cried out. 'Helpmmff! *Hffmmpppfff!'*

Quentin shivered with foreboding. It sounded as though the master was being smothered. He raised his fist and hammered on the door. 'Dr Cuddles, sir?' he called.

'Come on in!' Ingrid trilled. 'The more the merrier!'

'No, don't come in*fffmm,*' shouted Dr Cuddles. 'I'll . . . come . . . out . . .' he said, every word an effort.

All at once, the door flew open and Dr Cuddles rushed from the room, his robes crumpled and askew. He slammed the door behind him, locked it, and slipped into the shadows.

Quentin shuddered. He could hear Ingrid cooing from behind the locked door. 'Don't be long, Cuddles,' she was saying – and a hard edge crept into her voice as she added, 'I'm sure I don't have to remind you what happened last time you kept Ingrid waiting!'

'She's mad,' Dr Cuddles muttered and giggled nervously. 'Quite, quite mad!' He fell still; his piercing blue eyes blazed. 'I'll have that Horned Baron,' he snarled. 'I'll make him wish he'd never been born!'

Quentin nodded. 'It is in connection with the Horned Baron that I bring news,' he said. 'The first of the elves are arriving.'

'Excellent, Quentin,' Dr Cuddles said, giggling happily. 'Have them assemble in rows outside in Giggle Glade, and show the new arrivals where to go. I shall address them all at moonrise.'

'Cuddles!' It was Ingrid. She sounded far from happy. 'Cuddles, you haven't massaged my other foot!'

Dr Cuddles groaned miserably. 'In the meantime, Quentin, you know where to find me.'

'CUDDLES! *NOW!*'

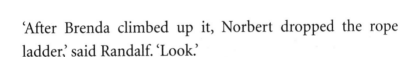

'After Brenda climbed up it, Norbert dropped the rope ladder,' said Randalf. 'Look.'

Joe looked. There, beneath the rippling lake, curled up on the ground beside a sleeping lazybird, was the rope ladder.

'Well, at least we tried,' said Randalf with a sigh. 'We'll just have to wait for him to make another one. Shouldn't take long. Couple of months, maybe. Brenda,' he said, turning to the warrior-princess, 'how about that cup of spittle tea?'

'A couple of months!' Joe exploded. 'I can't wait a couple of months!'

'And nor shall you,' said Brenda.

The warrior-princess immediately took control of the situation. 'Norbert,' she said, 'bring me the longest piece of rope you have. Rudyard, fetch four coat hangers.'

The pair of them jumped to her command. When

Norbert returned with the rope, she instructed Joe to tie one end to the houseboat's chimney. The other, she secured round the pillow-sized boulder. Then, having barked commands to some character by the name of Sniffy who seemed to be waiting for her at the bottom, Brenda hurled the boulder with tremendous strength.

Clutching hold of the balustrade as the boat wildly dipped and swayed, Joe had watched, puzzled, as the boulder sailed off through the air. What on earth – or rather *Muddle* Earth – was she up to? he wondered. Over the edge of the lake it went and down to the ground below. The rope flew with it. There was a thud and a distant *yowl*, and the rope abruptly went taut.

Suddenly, Joe realized exactly what was going on. Brenda had rigged up a makeshift cableway they could use to descend to the ground.

'Great idea,' he said enthusiastically.

'Absolutely ingenious method of getting down!' Randalf agreed. 'Now, why didn't *I* think of that?'

'Do you really want me to tell you?' said Veronica.

Brenda went down the cable first, with Henry – tail wagging furiously – around her neck. 'Just to show how easy it is,' she added, glancing pointedly at Randalf, who was beginning to make excuses and wanting to change his hat. Joe watched her glide down the rope, over the edge of the lake and out of sight.

'It's fun,' she called back a moment later. 'Next!'

Norbert was
the second to leave the
houseboat, with Randalf clinging
to his back, eyes tightly shut and screaming
hysterically. Veronica flapped beside him (reminding
the wizard that he took danger in his stride) as they
swooped down. Now it was Joe's turn.

'GO!' Brenda's booming voice echoed up.

Jaw set in grim concentration, Joe gripped the two
sides of the hanger. His heart was racing. His knees were
trembling.

'Here goes nothing,' he muttered as he kicked off from
the side of the houseboat and launched himself into the air.

Down, down, down, he sped. The slide was far faster
than it had looked and Joe now realized why Randalf had
screamed so hysterically. Not that *he* was going to scream!
Not Joe the Barbarian. For he was a warrior-hero, and
warrior-heroes didn't scream – particularly when there was
a warrior-princess about.

As he neared the edge of the lake, his legs struck the water, sending up a plume of spray and increasing the drag on his arms. It was all he could do to hang on.

'Nearly there,' he told himself. 'Just hold on tight and ... *Wow!*'

The view which opened up below him as he sped past the lake was magnificent.

'*Whee!*' he cried. '*Wheeeeeeeee!*'

Everything rushed below him in a blur of green and brown. The ground came nearer. Ahead of him, he could see Randalf and Norbert, with Veronica back on top of his head, and Brenda beside him – and next to them, what looked like a massive, stripy, pink cat sniffing at a terrified Henry.

Joe landed with a bump, rolled over and looked up to see the others looking down at him. 'That was amazing!' he gasped.

Henry licked his face.

'Well done, sir,' said Norbert, helping him to his feet.

'Glad someone enjoyed it,' said Randalf grumpily, wiping the dust from his crumpled pointy hat and straightening the attached umbrella.

'Unlike some,' said Veronica scornfully. 'Squealing like a pink stinky hoglet, you were. I've never been so ashamed.'

Brenda stepped forward. 'Well done,' she said warmly. 'I must confess that when I first laid eyes upon you I had some doubts. But you tackled that task with the skill and determination of a true warrior-hero!' She clapped a heavy arm round Joe's shoulder. 'We'll make a great team, you and I. That fiend with the spell book doesn't stand a chance.'

Blushing furiously behind his beard, Randalf pushed his way between the two of them and eased Joe out of the way. 'Of course, he was nothing when he first came to me,' he said. 'I taught him everything he knows.' He smiled up at Brenda ingratiatingly. 'And you know what they say, a warrior-hero is only as good as his teacher.'

Brenda frowned. 'There are some things you can't teach, Ronald,' she said. 'Like bravery.' She stepped past him and seized Joe by the arm. 'Come, Joe the Barbarian. You shall ride beside me on Sniffy.'

The great, stripy, pink cat purred as Brenda leaped up into the saddle. She reached down and pulled Joe – who had Henry under one arm – up after her. Then, with a tug on the reins, they were off. Norbert followed, with Randalf on one shoulder and Veronica on the other.

Randalf was not a happy wizard. 'You really have such bony shoulders, Norbert,' he complained testily. 'It's like sitting on a sack of rocks.' He snorted irritably. 'Now, if Joe would just move up a little, I'm sure there's room on Sniffy for one more . . .'

'Shut up, Ronald!' said Veronica.

'Pass me another snuggle-muffin, Norbert,' said Randalf. 'There's a good fellow.'

Norbert, who had Veronica perched on his head, reached forward and rummaged about in the hamper which was resting somewhat precariously on a raised grassy tussock in the middle of the Perfumed Bog. Sickly sweet-smelling bog-mist swirled about them, tingeing the low, late-afternoon sun purple and covering everything in its musty scent. Norbert retrieved a snuggle-muffin and held it out.

'No, not that one,' said Randalf, looking at the small green-and-yellow-iced cake in his hand. 'I wanted the pink one with the glacé cherries and chocolate sprinkles.'

Norbert frowned. 'Someone must have eaten it,' he said. 'This is the last one.'

'Unless there's one stuck to your forehead, Randalf,' added Veronica with a giggle.

'Oh, really!' the wizard exclaimed petulantly. 'I was looking forward to that snuggle-muffin!' His resounding voice caused a huge pink stinky hog to break wind from a nearby tussock and a startled gas frog to explode. 'Who ate it?' Randalf demanded.

Veronica nodded towards the adjacent tussock, where Brenda was deep in conversation with Joe. '*She* did,' said Veronica. 'Half a dozen of them, she's had. Mind you, to be fair, you did promise her all the snuggle-muffins she could eat.'

'Of course, being a warrior-princess and all, she needs to keep her strength up,' said Randalf with a dreamy smile. He turned to Norbert. 'All right, Norbert, give me that . . . *Norbert!*'

Blushing bright crimson, Norbert wiped the telltale crumbs of cake and icing from his mouth. 'You feb you bibn't wamp ip!' he spluttered, showering Randalf with bits of half-chewed snuggle-muffin.

'Oh, Norbert!' Randalf exclaimed.

Norbert swallowed. 'There's lots of snotbread sand-wiches left,' he said helpfully.

Another startled gas frog exploded close by. In the distance, a pair of stinky hogs paused, grunted and passed wind noisily. Only Brenda and Joe seemed unaware of the altercation taking place on the neighbouring tussock.

'And *this* one,' Brenda was saying, lightly fingering one of the many nicks in the blade of her long sword, 'was when

I had that run-in with Hilda the Hairy Hag. Those thunderbolts of hers can really sting, you know.'

'Wow, thunderbolts!' gasped Joe, who was growing more and more impressed with every successive story Brenda recounted. 'That sounds amazing!'

'And this,' she went on, moving down the blade, 'resulted from an incident with Harry-and-Larry – a monstrous two-headed ogre. Terrible creature he was, though he could never make his minds up about anything. I had to knock his heads together.' She chuckled. 'He won't be forgetting Brenda, Warrior-Princess, in a hurry!'

'Incredible,' said Joe quietly. 'You've done all that!'

'Indeed I have,' said Brenda, a faraway look in her eyes. 'Indeed I have. But now I want to settle down; find a nice little home for me and Sniffy,' she said, nodding across to her pink, stripy battle-cat, who was lying on a third tussock some way off, trembling.

On hearing her name, Sniffy whimpered plaintively. She didn't like this wet place with its swampy mud and pongy mist.

Henry, who was sharing the same tussock, licked her face and barked encouragingly.

'I've had my share of adventure,' Brenda went on. 'Now it's time to take life a little more easily, and Rudolf seems a nice enough wizard. I just hope I'm not putting *your* nose out of joint, Joe.'

'No, no,' said Joe. 'Not at all. In fact I'm glad you're here. Although Randalf summoned me and Henry to Muddle Earth, he can't send us back again. If we don't manage to rescue the *Great Book of Spells* and release the other wizards, then I'll have to stay here for ever and . . . and . . .' He sniffed.

'You're homesick,' said Brenda.

Joe nodded. 'I miss my mum and dad,' he said. 'And the twins. And even my sister, Ella.'

'Is she a warrior-princess?' asked Brenda earnestly.

Joe smiled. 'Not exactly,' he said. 'Although if looks really could kill, then she'd be pretty deadly.'

Brenda shuddered. 'Sounds like Sybil the Sorceress,' she said. 'Now, her looks *could* kill.' She touched a jagged notch down near the end of the blade. 'Not to mention her breath!'

'Sybil the Sorceress,' Joe whispered in awe.

'Mind you, she proved no match for Brenda, Warrior-Princess.' Brenda wrapped a great, muscular arm around Joe's shoulders and squeezed tightly – rather *too* tightly. 'Don't worry, Joe. I'll see to it that you get home. Trust me,' she said, 'we'll complete this quest successfully if I've got anything to do with it!'

'But you don't understand,' said Joe, breaking free from her powerful grip. 'Weeks, I've been waiting to set off on this quest. Weeks and weeks. And what happens when we *do* finally get going? Ten minutes in and Randalf wakes up and says we've all got to stop for a picnic!'

'Those snuggle-muffins *were* rather good,' said Brenda, licking her lips appreciatively. 'But you're right, Joe. We should be making tracks. The sun's getting low and we don't want to spend the night in the Perfumed Bog.' She climbed to her feet. 'Ralph! Sniffy!' she called across to the other tussocks. 'We must set off at once.'

'Already?' Randalf's disappointed voice floated back.

'You can ride beside me on Sniffy,' said Brenda.

Randalf beamed. 'I'll be right with you,' he said.

Goblintown was already badly missing its holidaying elves. With none of them around to do the little chores that kept the town ticking over, the whole place was running down. Oil lamps sputtered, went out and stayed out. Letters remained unsent, wet washing went unspun. And with none of the clocks working, it was as though time itself had stopped. Only the mounting piles of rubbish on every corner of every street indicated just how long there had been no elves about to tidy up.

Inside the buildings which lined the rubbish-strewn

streets, the story was the same. There were no sewing-elves, mending-elves, washing-elves . . . No elves at all! And in their absence, nothing was being made. The workrooms of the milliners, ironmongers, furniture makers and dress-makers were all standing idle.

One shop, however was a hive of activity. Goblins become very active when there's money around – and the helmeted figure trying on new robes smelled very strongly of money.

'How do I look?' the Horned Baron asked, looking into the mirror.

'Oh, I say!' the mirror – a tall, free-standing swivel affair set in an ornate mahogany frame – replied. 'You're the fairest Horned Baron of them all.'

'I am?' said the Horned Baron uncertainly.

'No doubt about it,' said the mirror. 'This outfit really suits sir down to the ground. And fits to a T. Could have been made for sir.'

The Horned Baron twisted this way and that, keeping his eyes on his body and checking out his appearance from every angle. 'I'm still not sure,' he said. 'I just don't know if it's me.'

'Sir looks fabulous,' the mirror assured him. 'The lilac complements your sallow complexion and magnificent jet-black moustache so well. And the sparkly bits match that mischievous glint in your eye.' It paused. 'Is sir planning on going somewhere nice this evening?'

'I thought I might take in a nightspot or two while I'm

here in Goblintown,' said the Horned Baron vaguely.

'Well, you're certainly going to impress the ladies in that little get-up,' said the mirror.

The Horned Baron nodded happily.

Situated on the ground floor of a towering stack of clothes shops, *Unction's Upmarket Outfitters* was renowned for its staggering array of outrageously priced outfits – and its talking mirror. Normally, the Horned Baron wouldn't have dreamed of shopping in so expensive a place. Ingrid would never have allowed it.

But then Ingrid – bless her enormous cotton socks – was no longer around. Sadly, tragically and possibly for ever, Ingrid was gone. And with her, the Horned Baron's days of having to shop at *Grubley's Discount Garment Store*. Quite apart from the fact that Grubley had swindled him in that incident with the singing curtains, the goblin had nothing on offer but cheap tat. Whereas these new clothes . . . You could *feel* the quality.

The Horned Baron craned his neck round. 'Are you absolutely sure my bum doesn't look big in these sparkly tights?' he said.

'Quite the opposite,' said the mirror. 'In fact I was just thinking how slimming they are – particularly tucked into those patent-leather bootees. And the sequinned tunic emphasizes both the breadth of your shoulders and neatness of your waist. So very flattering,' it said. 'So very *you*, sir, if I might make so bold!'

'You've talked me into it,' announced the Horned Baron. 'I'll take the whole lot.'

'An excellent choice,' said the mirror. 'And a snip at only two hundred and fifty gold pieces. Sir is going to cause an absolute riot on the dance floor.' It paused. 'Did sir have any particular nightspot in mind?'

The Horned Baron nodded slowly. Two hundred and fifty gold pieces did seem an awful lot for a tunic, tights and bootees. Then again, it would be worth it. '*Mucky Maud's Lumpy Custard Club* is supposed to be rather good,' he said.

'Oh, absolutely!' gushed the mirror. 'I've heard that the custard pies there are to die for.' It chuckled. 'And Mucky Maud herself won't be able to keep her big custard pie-throwing hands off you!'

'I'll have you know I'm a happily married man,' said the Horned Baron blushing furiously. (If Ingrid should ever, *ever* get to hear of this . . .)

'Oh, you can trust me,' said the mirror conspiratorially. 'Now if sir would like to proceed to the till . . .'

Just then, the door at the front of the shop burst open and the Horned Baron looked round to see his manservant – bright pink and panting – dashing in. 'There you are, sir!' he said breathlessly. 'I've been looking all over.'

The Horned Baron sighed impatiently. 'What is it now, Benson?' he said. 'Can't I have a single moment's peace?'

'Please, sir,' said Benson, lowering his head. 'Sorry, sir, but it's really important.' He rummaged in his pocket. 'There's been another letter concerning the baroness.'

'Ingrid?' said the Horned Baron, blushing more furiously than ever. 'A letter?'

'Delivered by batbird,' said Benson. He handed over the sheet of parchment. 'It says they're going to baste her in oil and boil her in a cauldron!'

The Horned Baron tutted and shook his head. 'What appalling luck,' he said.

'But, sir!' said Benson.

'Not now, Benson,' said the Horned Baron. 'I'm already

late for my helmet-polishing, not to mention my horn-sharpening.'

'As I always say,' the mirror enthused, 'it's those little finishing touches that make all the difference.'

'But, sir,' Benson tried again. 'The letter . . . Ingrid . . . What are you going to do?'

'First things first,' said the Horned Baron. 'After all, it wouldn't do to rush these things, now would it?'

The ragtag group continued on their quest along the dusty road. To their right, the Perfumed Bog fizzed and popped in the fading light. To their left, the jagged peaks of the Ogrehills were silhouetted against the sky. Before them – far, far in the distance – a line of pointy tree tops was just appearing above the horizon.

Joe was up on Norbert's right shoulder, with Henry trotting along behind them. Randalf, for once awake while travelling, was sitting in Sniffy's ornate saddle beside Brenda. The huge grin on his face was so fixed, so unmoving, it looked painted into place. Randalf the Wise was in seventh heaven.

'Oh, do tell me that story about when you fought the warty gutguzzler of the Black Lagoon. What rude names did you say you called it?' He swooned giddily. 'Ooh, Brenda, Warrior-Princess, you're so brave and strong and wicked . . .'

Brenda laughed (the sound of peeling bells, Randalf thought) and clapped the wizard on the back.

'*Ooof!*' gasped Randalf, his smile momentarily disappearing.

'Enough about me, Rodney,' said Brenda. 'Tell me, where exactly *is* this Giggle Glade?'

Randalf peered into the distance and nodded. The tree-line was closer now. 'Giggle Glade is right in the middle of that,' he said. 'Elfwood.'

Brenda flinched. 'Elfwood?' she said. '*Elf*wood? As in *elves*?'

*C*lonk!

'Ouch!' cried Randalf, who was back on Norbert's shoulder, as he attempted (and failed) to duck an oncoming branch.

Clonk!

'OUCH!' Randalf howled, gingerly rubbing his forehead. 'Do watch where you're going, Norbert! That really hurt!'

'Sorry, sir,' said Norbert. He stooped down as low as he could get. 'Is that better?'

Clonk!

'Oh, for crying out loud!' Randalf exclaimed, as the tiny umbrella was knocked from the top of his pointy hat. 'Norbert, put me down. There's nothing for it. I'll just have to walk.'

Norbert did as he was told.

'Ah, that's better,' said Randalf as he strode off into the

forest. 'Keep up, you lot,' he called back. 'No dawdling! After all, we *are* on an important quest, you know.'

Veronica fluttered down and landed on the brim of his pointy hat. 'What's the hurry, Fatso?' she said. 'No, don't tell me. It couldn't have anything to do with the fact that you've got a warrior-princess on a battle-cat backing you up, by any chance?'

'Wonderful, isn't she?' said Randalf, a dreamy smile playing on his lips.

Behind them, Joe tugged on Henry's lead. 'Come on, boy,' he said. 'If you stop to sniff round every tree, we'll never get anywhere.'

Joe looked around him. With its tall, burnished trees glowing in the twilight, its tangle of flowering brambles and clumps of feathery ferns, Elfwood was certainly beautiful. But something about it made him feel vaguely uneasy, as if he were being watched. He turned and saw Brenda still lingering at the forest's edge.

'What's the matter, Brenda?' said Joe. He walked back to her and took her gently by the arm. 'Is there something wrong?'

'Well,' Brenda began.

'Yes?' said Joe.

'The thing is . . . I don't quite know how to say this.' Brenda looked down at the ground shamefacedly.

'You can tell me,' said Joe, softly 'What's bothering you?'

'It's Elfwood,' said Brenda. '*Elf*wood.'

'Yes,' said Joe.

'A wood full of *elves*,' said Brenda, tears in her eyes.

'What's that, Brenda?' came a voice. It was Randalf who, finding himself on his own, had marched back to find out what was keeping the others. 'Elfwood? Full of elves?' he said. 'If you're looking forward to seeing elves in Elfwood, I'm afraid you're going to be disappointed. There haven't been any elves in Elfwood for years.'

'There haven't?' said Brenda, the colour returning to her cheeks.

'I was forgetting, you've been away, haven't you?' said Randalf. 'Well, Brenda, such is the demand for the hard-working little fellows that the last place you'll find them now is in Elfwood.'

'It is?' said Brenda, smiling.

'They're all in Trollbridge, and Goblintown and the Horned Baron's castle these days, working their little socks off, bless 'em,' said Randalf. He shrugged. 'I'm sorry to have to disappoint you.'

Brenda laughed. 'I'll cope,' she said, with a toss of her fiery-red plaits. She clapped a great hand on Randalf's shoulders. 'Come then, Raymond, show me the way to Giggle Glade.'

The hairs at the back of Randalf's neck tingled deliciously. 'I'd be delighted,' he said.

For a good ten minutes, they made excellent progress through the woods as the shadows lengthened. Elfwood looked particularly beautiful in the setting sun as the twilight air slipped from yellow to gold, to a deep burnished copper. Birds twittered from the branches. Creatures scratched and scurried in the dappled shadows. A warm, gentle breeze whispered through the trembling leaves.

'Don't the woods look pretty,' Joe said.

'He thinks we look pretty,' said a voice just behind him.

Joe spun round. There was nobody there. It must be my imagination, he thought, or maybe the wind in the branches. He hurried after the others, tugging Henry along behind him.

He caught up with them in a small clearing. Randalf was sitting on an old tree stump, red-faced and short of breath.

'It's no good,' he was saying. 'I can't go any further. I'm absolutely shattered . . . Must rest . . .'

'Oh, honestly!' said Veronica. 'Take more than three steps and Fatso, here, has to lie down.'

'Tell her to shut up, Norbert,' said Randalf weakly. 'I'm just too weary.'

'Shut up, Veronica,' said Norbert meekly.

'It *is* getting dark,' said Brenda, looking round, 'and this seems a nice place for a camp. We'll stop here for the night, and set off again bright and early tomorrow morning.'

'My thoughts entirely,' said Randalf, stretching out on

the tree stump. 'You take charge of setting up camp, Brenda, while I try to regain my strength.'

'That fat one's sitting on poor old Auntie Ethel,' came a whisper from behind Joe.

'Blooming cheek!'

'Just ignore them and they'll soon go away.'

Joe looked round. Was he going mad? 'Hello?' he called. 'Is there anybody there?'

'Stop fooling about, Joe,' said Randalf, his hat down over his eyes, 'and help Brenda. Ooh,' he groaned, 'I can feel my ankles swelling.'

'Lay the blanket out over there,' Brenda was telling Norbert. 'Then go and get some firewood. Veronica, you collect some kindling. And Joe, find some small rocks and lay them in a circle here. This is where we'll make our camp-fire.' She unhooked a great, black cooking pot from Sniffy's back. 'I'll just rustle up a little something for supper.'

'Don't be too long,' said Randalf. 'I can feel myself growing weaker.'

'In the head!' said Veronica.

'Kindling, Veronica,' said Randalf. 'Good quality kindling is the basis of any good fire. Isn't that right, Brenda?'

'That's right, Rudolf,' replied the warrior-princess, dicing up several carrots and onions from Sniffy's saddlebag, and throwing them into the pot.

Muttering under her breath, Veronica fluttered off into the gathering shadows. Norbert followed her, his axe grasped in his great hands. Joe began collecting rocks and making the circle for the fire. From a little way off came the sound of a sing-song voice.

'One potato. Two potato. Yo, ho, ho and a rotten old bum!' it said.

Joe decided he was going to get to the bottom of this. He walked towards the sound of the voice. Just beyond the clearing, he stopped. There in front of him was a woodland stream flowing through the trees and babbling cheerfully.

'Football. Tennis. Elbow. Grease those wheels and trim that sail. Lilacs are a girl's best friend . . .'

Talking streams! thought Joe, with a shake of his head. Only in Muddle Earth!

Suddenly, he realized how terribly thirsty he felt. Kneeling down, Joe cupped a handful of the cool, clear water and was just about to drink when a firm hand clapped him on the shoulder.

'No!' said a voice sternly.

Joe looked up. It was Brenda. 'Never drink from a babbling brook without boiling the water first. Just in case,' she said, filling the cooking pot.

'In case of what?' asked Joe.

At that moment, the air filled with anguished cries. *'Ouch!' 'Ooh!' 'Ow!'*

'He'll pay for that!' came a voice. 'You just wait!'

Brenda and Joe rushed back to the clearing to find Randalf still stretched out on the tree trunk.

'Was that you?' asked Joe.

Randalf frowned. 'I thought it was *you*,' he said.

They looked at each other. 'Norbert?' they both said together.

Just then, the ogre in question burst from the trees, his great arms wrapped tightly round a huge bundle of firewood. He strode over to Joe's circle of rocks and dumped the whole load down beside it.

'Heavy work,' he said as he wiped the sweat from his brow.

'Did you have to make so much noise, Norbert?' said Randalf. 'You had me worried for a moment.'

'*Mffllmm blmmnflck!*' Veronica muttered as she appeared from the trees, her beak stuffed full of twigs, straw and bits of dried bark. She fluttered down, perched on one of the rocks and opened her beak. The kindling fell to the ground. Veronica turned to Brenda. 'So, what did your last slave die of?' she said.

'That's enough, Veronica,' said Randalf.

'Well, honestly!' said Veronica, her neck feathers all ruffled. 'I'm only little. Not like that great, gallumphing redhaired oaf of a—'

'Veronica!' said Randalf sharply. 'That is no way to talk to a warrior-princess.' He turned to Brenda. 'I'm sorry, your highness,' he said. 'She doesn't mean it.'

'I most certainly do!' said Veronica hotly. 'I—'

'Shut up, Veronica!' said Randalf loudly.

'*Hmmph!*' she squawked indignantly, and flew up to an overhanging branch.

With the fire set, lit and blazing, Brenda placed the cooking pot full of water over the flames and it wasn't long before they were all sitting down on Norbert's great, thick blanket, eating Brenda's rather watery carrot and onion stew. The wind dropped. The stars came out. The full moon glinted on the forest canopy, far above their heads.

Veronica pecked at some birdseed in the firelight. Joe was sitting next to Henry, one arm wrapped around the dog's neck. Sniffy lay curled up in front of the fire, purring contentedly. Brenda herself was sitting cross-legged, polishing her sword, the glow from the fire gleaming on her finely chiselled features.

Randalf put down his bowl of stew. Their eyes met. Randalf smiled. 'Tell us more of your adventures, Brenda,' he said, stretching out on the blanket. 'My word, this is comfortable after that king-sized bed,' he sighed happily.

'More adventures,' said Brenda, inspecting the nicks on her blade. 'Now let me see . . .'

'Too late,' said Veronica. 'He's already nodded off.'

A low rasping snore filled the air. Brenda smiled. 'Likes his rest, doesn't he?' she said. 'But then we could all do with a good night's sleep,' she said. 'We've got a big day ahead of us. Sniffy will keep guard, won't you Sniffy?'

The great, pink, stripy cat got up from her place by the fire and stretched luxuriously. Henry barked and trotted over to keep her company.

Joe lay back on the thick blanket, his hands behind his head, and stared up at the moonlit sky. It had been a long day. Finally, they had set out. Finally, he was on his quest.

Beside him, Randalf's low rasping snores were soon accompanied by Norbert's loud rumbling ones and Veronica's muffled whistle. Joe closed his eyes. From far away he could hear a distant babble.

'Shut the door. Open the hamster. Rhubarb, rhubarb. Pardon me, your highness . . .'

Joe smiled to himself. Even the voices had turned out to be nothing more sinister than a babbling brook. Muddle Earth! he thought drowsily. What a place!

Brenda sheathed her sword and, having tossed another log on the fire, settled herself down.

'Now they're burning a piece of Great-aunt Lavinia,' muttered an indignant voice.

'And there are sparks going everywhere!' another whispered.

'Just you wait and see,' said a third darkly. 'We'll show them!'

If Joe had heard these voices, he would have realized that they didn't belong to a babbling brook, a talkative stream or a gossiping river. But he didn't hear them, nor the odd rustling, shuffling noise that began to echo through the air – for Joe was sound asleep.

A full moon shone down over Giggle Glade, brightly illuminating the forest clearing below, where hundreds of small, bony elves were assembled, flittering, twittering and giggling excitedly. They were waiting in rows in front of a raised podium, upon which stood a tall lectern and a row of seven chairs.

'The moon is up,' one was saying. 'I'm so excited!'

'I can't wait,' said another.

'Me, neither,' a third – then a fourth and fifth – chirped up.

Soon the whole great multitude of elves were chattering

to themselves in agreement. If there was hard work to be done, then they wanted to get started.

Just then, a gangly figure in tight leggings and a glittery red coat, jumped up on to the stage and clapped his hands together.

'Welcome!' he said. Instantly, the flittering, twittering and giggling stopped. 'Welcome to Giggle Glade and a holiday that none of you will ever forget!'

'Hooray!' the elves cried out, their squeaky voices echoing through the air.

'Back-breaking work!' he announced.

'Hooray!'

'Endless toil!'

'Hooray!'

'Task after arduous task!'

'*Hooray!*' the elves cheered, louder than ever.

'And who's the one who's made it all possible? The one who's extended this warm invitation? The one you've all been dying to meet. The one . . . the only . . . Dr Cuddles of Giggle Glade!'

A tumultuous roar of approval went up as Dr Cuddles appeared, his dark, hooded robes wrapped tightly about him. He climbed the neatly turned stairs at the edge of the podium, mounted the mahogany and inlaid rosewood lectern and raised his head. Two piercing blue eyes glinted fiercely from the shadowy hood as he surveyed the gathering. The elves fell silent.

'Thank you, Quentin,' said Dr Cuddles nodding towards the glittery figure, who blushed modestly. Dr Cuddles's gaze grew more intense as he glared down at the elves. 'I promised you hard work, and that's exactly what you shall have!' he announced.

The elves found their voices again. 'Hooray!' they cried out in unison.

'You will be engaged in a great enterprise, the like of which has never before been seen in Muddle Earth,' he continued, his voice loud and clear. 'You are to build a towering construction from scratch – chopping down the trees . . .'

'Here we go again,' came a weary voice from the edge of the clearing.

'He needs to be taught a lesson,' muttered another crossly.

' . . . preparing the wood and assembling the structure from top-secret plans.' He paused. 'Top-secret plans,' he repeated. 'Quentin,' he snapped. 'Where are the top-secret plans?'

'Sorry, sir,' said Quentin sibilantly. 'Come on, you lot,' he said. 'Up on the podium with you.'

Grumbling under their breath, a line of seven wizards – each one with long robes, a pointy hat and a rolled scroll of blueprints in their hands – climbed the steps and, with a muffled jangle, filed across the podium. They each took a place on one of the seats. As they sat down, the chain linking them all together glinted in the moonlight.

On the left was Roger the Wrinkled. Beside him, Bertram the Incredibly Hairy and his brother, Boris the Bald. Then Eric the Mottled, Ernie the Shrivelled, Melvyn the Mauve, and last – and also least – Colin the Nondescript.

Dr Cuddles's blue eyes blazed. 'Thank you, Quentin,' he said again, his voice laced with unspoken menace. 'These top-secret plans have been divided into seven parts,' he went on. 'Each of you will be assigned to one wizard who will oversee the construction of your individual section. When all seven sections have been completed, they will come together under my expert guiding hand.' Dr Cuddles pulled himself up to his full height and raised his head. 'We have the tools!' he announced.

The elves cheered.

'We have the expertise!'

The cheering grew louder. All at once, cutting through the echoing roar of the excited elves, came a loud and strident voice. '*Cuddles!*'

The light in Dr Cuddles's bright blue eyes visibly dimmed. 'Ingrid,' he murmured. He turned to Quentin. 'You go,' he said. 'She likes you.'

'But she called for you,' said Quentin. 'I fear I would be a dreadful disappointment.'

The wizards sniggered behind their beards.

'I'm waiting, Cuddles!' Ingrid shouted imperiously, her voice a curious mixture of eagerness and impatience. 'Are the oils ready? Is the water hot enough? I'm so looking forward to my lovely bath!'

Dr Cuddles groaned. His gaze hardened as he turned to the elves. 'To work!' he bellowed. 'To work. *Now!*'

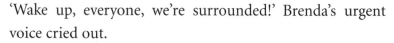

'Wake up, everyone, we're surrounded!' Brenda's urgent voice cried out.

Awakened by Sniffy's piercing yowl and Henry's forlorn barking, she'd opened her eyes to find the campsite had become a prison, surrounded by a wall of trees. During the night, the trees had crowded in around them until they were penned up in a space the size of Norbert's blanket.

Brenda leaped to her feet. Norbert's three eyes snapped open. Veronica sighed and pulled her head out from under

her wing. Joe stirred, sat up and looked round.

'What's going on?' he exclaimed.

'It seems that our battle-creatures were less vigilant than we had hoped,' said Brenda, shaking her head.

Joe stared round at impenetrable wall of rough bark surrounding him. 'The trees!' he gasped. 'They've moved!'

'The small one's woken up now,' came a voice.

Joe started. Norbert looked round in surprise. 'That tree,' he said. 'It spoke!'

'Ooh, and that's that great big bully who hacked my branch off,' said another.

'And mine!' 'And mine!' 'And mine!' came a chorus of indignant voices.

'I don't like the look of this,' said Brenda darkly. 'Perhaps wizard Robert, here, will be able to conjure up a powerful spell to move the trees from our way.'

'I shouldn't count on it,' muttered Veronica, fluttering up into the air. 'What you lot need is wings.'

'Hey, one of them's getting away,' said a tall copper beech.

'It's only the budgie,' his neighbour replied. 'Completely unimportant.'

'Unimportant!' squawked Veronica, twisting in mid-air and swooping down on to Norbert's head. 'I'll have you know I'm the linchpin of this entire operation!'

'It's that fat one that sat on Auntie Ethel who seems to be in charge,' came a voice. 'When he's not asleep, that is.'

'I'll soon see to that,' rumbled a giant horse chestnut, releasing a volley of conkers in their hard, prickly casings. They landed on Randalf's head, causing him to jump up in surprise. '*Ooh! Ouch! Ow!*'

'That'll teach him to throw his weight around in Elfwood,' the tree muttered gleefully.

Randalf climbed to his feet and straightened his pointy hat with dignity. 'There appears to be a misunderstanding,' he began. 'We are on an important quest, and we simply camped here for the night.'

'Camped, he says. Ooh, the nerve of the fellow!' an affronted voice exclaimed. 'How would *he* like it if we barged into his home and set fire to his beard?'

'And sat on *his* Auntie Ethel!' said another.

'He wouldn't like it,' came a voice from the back. 'Not one little bit. Go on, Bert, drop a branch on him!'

'What are you waiting for, Ronald?' said Brenda. 'Cast a spell!'

'If only,' said Veronica.

'Shut up, Veronica,' said Randalf. 'Why don't you do something useful instead of just perching there. Go and get help.'

'What kind of help?' said Veronica. 'Friendly woodcutters? Or perhaps a flock of trained woodpeckers?'

Brenda drew her sword. Norbert fingered his axe gingerly. Joe clutched his own sword and backed into Randalf. The clearing seemed to be getting smaller by the minute.

'And what do they think they're going to do with those?' an ancient elder sneered. 'There's far too many of us and far too few of them, you know.'

'Oh, why did I let you all talk me into going on this insane quest?' wailed Randalf. 'Why did I think we could ever get to Giggle Glade and destroy Dr Cuddles? What a fool I've been!' He sank to his knees with a sob.

'Did he say *destroy* Dr Cuddles?' one of the trees asked in surprise. 'Did he? What did you hear, Enid?'

'Oh, Ashley, you never listen, do you?'

'He did,' came a gruff voice. 'He definitely said *destroy*.'

'But that would be marvellous,' said another. 'Maybe we should let them go after all.'

Randalf stopped rolling on the ground, moaning, and looked up. With a shuffling, rustling, grunting sort of a noise, the trees were moving slowly out of the way. Little by little, a narrow avenue was opening up, along which, when it was wide enough, Randalf and the others could walk. Randalf picked up his hat and staff and puffed out his chest.

'I told you it was just a misunderstanding,' he said to Brenda. Veronica flapped down and landed on his hat. 'I've got to hand it to you, Randalf,' she said, 'you've certainly weaved some sort of spell on these trees.'

'Come on Norbert, Joe,' Randalf called, striding forward. 'Don't dilly-dally. We've got important business to attend to in Giggle Glade!'

'Go on!' yelled a loud voice excitedly. 'Go on!'
Others joined in. 'Throw it!' 'Go on, throw it!' And a
chorus of, '*In his face! In his face!*' broke out, followed by
whoops and cheers and cries of encouragement.

'I'm waiting!' shouted a voice above all the rest. 'Let me
have it!'

There was a brief silence, followed by a loud, squelchy
SPLAT! And, with a huge cheer, the crowd roared its
approval.

The Horned Baron, who was listening from outside,
turned to his manservant. 'Sounds like a lively crowd
tonight, Benson,' he said.

'Indeed, sir,' said Benson, seizing his arm. 'But as I was
saying, the latest ransom note, sir. You really should read it.
Here, look . . . This time, it says they intend doing something utterly dastardly if you don't answer their demands at
once. They're going to start with her toenails, then move up

to her fingernails, and *then . . .*'

'Not now, Benson,' said the Horned Baron distractedly as a second *SPLAT!* and a roar of laughter exploded from the other side of the door. He twirled his moustache, straightened his gleaming horned helmet and adjusted his sparkly tights. '*Mucky Maud's*, here I come!' he announced as he shoved the swing doors open.

The heat, the noise and the heady pungent aroma of sweet, creamy desserts all combined to create an atmosphere that made Goblintown's infamous *Lumpy Custard Club* unique. The Horned Baron went weak at the knees as he looked round the great terraced chamber.

'Marvellous,' he whispered.

There were goblins everywhere – customers seated on stools at innumerable overladen tables; waiters and waitresses with trayfuls of phlegm pies, sneezed-on treacle tarts and bowls of multi-coloured gloop balanced on their upraised hands; a conga-line, dripping with lumpy custard and stinky rice pudding, weaving its way around the club. The place was seething.

At the crowded bar, a scrum of goblins struggled to gain the attention of the barkeeper – a surly looking character wearing a white shirt and black bow tie – bellowing out their orders and jostling for position. In the corner, a lone goblin with a long face and a lugubrious expression cranked the handle of a barrel organ round and round, filling *Mucky Maud's* with the sound of swirling hurdy-gurdy music.

Above their heads, a glitter ball slowly turned, sending darts of light flying through the air.

'Absolutely first rate!' the Horned Baron exclaimed, a huge grin plastered across his face. 'It's all so deliciously . . . *mucky*.' He sighed. 'Ingrid would never approve.'

'Quite so,' Benson shouted above the din and waved the ransom note under his nose. 'And with the Baroness in mind, if we could . . .'

Just then, a slightly stooped gnome wearing a long, stained black jacket and grubby striped trousers appeared before them. 'Good evening!' he said warmly. 'And welcome to *Mucky Maud's Lumpy Custard Club* and a night to remember! I don't believe we've seen sir here before.'

'This is my first time,' the Horned Baron admitted.

'I knew it,' said the goblin. 'As head waiter, I pride myself on never forgetting a face – or so magnificent a helmet. It looks freshly buffed.'

The Horned Baron nodded. 'And I've just had the horns repointed,' he said.

'Splendid,' said the head waiter. 'Perhaps sir would like me to put it away safely in the cloakroom?'

'Absolutely not,' said the Horned Baron, shaking his head. 'I never go anywhere without my helmet,' he said. 'I am, after all, the Horned Baron.'

The gnome gasped with surprise. 'The Horned Baron, I should have known!' he said. 'The *Horned Baron*. My word, sir, but we are honoured.' He extended a sticky hand. 'Smarm at your service, sir.'

The Horned Baron nodded.

Smarm giggled. 'The Horned Baron!' he said. 'I can hardly believe it! And you've got such a treat in store this evening. Now, if sir would like to take a bib and follow me, I shall show you to the best table in the house.' He winked conspiratorially. 'It's right in the firing line.' He turned on his heels. 'Walk this way.'

'If I could walk that way, I'd be seriously worried,' Benson muttered under his breath as he followed Smarm and the Horned Baron down the steps from the doorway and on to the club floor.

The music grew louder; the crowd more uproarious. As Smarm led him past the bar, the Horned Baron – bib secured around his neck – watched with interest as a tall ogre in messy dungarees pushed his way to the front.

'What'll it be?' demanded the barkeeper gruffly.

'Get me a double meringue cream-pie,' said the ogre.

'Coming right up,' said the barkeeper as he ladled a thick, sticky mixture into a large glass, topped it off with two meringues and a cherry, and tossed the whole lot into the waiting ogre's face.

SPLAT!

'Lovely!' said the ogre, his voice slightly muffled. He slammed a gold piece down on the counter. 'And one for yourself!'

'Don't mind if I do,' said the surly barkeeper. He looked up and down the bar. 'Next!' he bellowed.

Voices shouted out insistently. 'Me! Me! Me!' 'I was here first!' 'Stop pushing in!' 'A sneezed-on treacle tart with all the trimmings!'

'Would sir like something from the bar?' asked Smarm.

'Yes,' said the Horned Baron. 'Barman,' he called out imperiously. 'A couple of the finest custard pies known to Goblinkind, if you please.'

'You'll have what you're given and like it,' the barkeeper growled, causing a ripple of laughter to run the length of the bar.

'Send them over to the upper table,' said the head waiter. He turned to the Horned Baron. 'This way, sir.'

He led them up a short flight of stairs to a jutting

platform. The table there was occupied, the six seats taken up with half a dozen brightly made-up goblin matrons in stained ball gowns and dripping tiaras. Smarm quickly ushered them away and wiped a dirty cloth over the table top.

'Take a seat, your Baron-ness,' he said, holding the back of a chair and pushing it in as the Horned Baron sat down. 'The evening's entertainment will soon be getting under way.'

Benson took the chair opposite – just as two rice puddings with yellow toe-jam sailed over his head. In the corner close by, two goblins squealed with delight as they were abruptly splattered with strawberry and garlic blancmange.

'Looks like it's already started,' observed the Horned Baron.

'That's nothing, sir' said the head waiter. 'You just wait till the heavyweight trifles start flying.'

Just then, a waiter – dripping with rice pudding and chocolate sauce – arrived from the bar with the two large custard pies on a tray. He set them down in front of Benson and the Horned Baron.

'Compliments of the house,' said Smarm.

'Thank you,' said the Horned Baron, picking up his pie. He turned to Benson. 'Here's custard in your eye!' he cried, and shoved the custard pie into his manservant's face.

'*Blobberly bloof!*' Benson spluttered, wiping his mouth on his bib. 'You're too kind, sir. Allow me!' He picked up his own pie and pushed it into the Horned Baron's eagerly awaiting face.

'*Yum!*' said the Horned Baron. 'Outstanding! Two more custard pies,' he called out to the departing waiter. 'And keep them coming!'

With the head waiter gone, the Horned Baron turned to Benson, his eyes gleaming excitedly. 'My word, this makes me feel young again!' He leaned back in his chair. 'I'd quite forgotten what it was like on a Saturday night in Goblintown,' he said. 'In the old days, I really used to let my hair down.'

Benson frowned. 'You did, sir?'

'Or course, that was when I still had hair to let down,' said the Horned Baron. 'You wouldn't think it to see me now, Benson, but in the past – when I was young – I was quite the ladies' man.'

'You're right, sir,' said Benson. 'You *wouldn't* think it!'

'Oh, yes, Benson,' the Horned Baron went on, 'there wasn't a goblin maiden in all Goblintown who could resist my charms, I can tell you.'

Benson nodded. 'This would be *before* you met Baroness Ingrid,' he said.

'Obviously, Benson,' said the Horned Baron wistfully, a faraway look in his eye. 'I knew when I met Ingrid that my custard pie throwing days were over.'

Just then, a second waiter appeared. 'Two custard pies,' he announced.

'That's us,' said the Horned Baron.

With the organ-grinder cranking the handle of his barrel organ round faster and faster, the thumping music grew increasingly frantic. All round the vast room, tables of goblins, trolls and ogres bellowed out their orders. 'More stinky-toffee pudding.' 'Stiltmouse milk mousse all round!' 'Gob pie!' And, as the air filled with volley after volley of lumpy custard pies flying across the room, yells of delight and shrieks of pleasure echoed round the walls.

A stray custard pie struck the side of the Horned Baron's helmet and dangled from one of the pointy horns. 'My goodness!' he exclaimed with a chuckle. 'The place really is beginning to jump!' He turned his attention to the lumpy custard pie in front of him. He smacked his lips. 'Would you care to do the honours, Benson?'

Suddenly, all the lights went out, plunging the club into darkness. The Horned Baron drew back from the custard pie and peered round. The next moment, a spotlight came on at the far end of the room and shone down on a set of red satin curtains at the top of a grand, sweeping staircase.

The crowd, as one, held its breath. All at once, the curtains trembled, parted and a portly troll appeared at the top of the staircase. A great cheer went up.

'It's her!' someone shouted.

'It's Mucky Maud!'

Resplendent in a tight, sparkly cocktail dress (with a

particularly magnificent blancmange stain down one side), her thick hair, decorated with lazybird plumes, piled up high on her head, Mucky Maud cut an impressive figure. And as the barrel organ music struck up a tune, she made her way slowly, slinkily, down the flight of stairs.

When she reached the bottom, Mucky Maud turned to the lugubrious goblin at the barrel organ. 'Play it again, Spam!' she whispered.

The organ-grinder pulled a lever and turned the handle. A loud, pounding beat burst forth – *Oom-pah-pah! Oom-pah-pah!* – and the Horned Baron smiled as the strains of a familiar tune started up. Mucky Maud raised her head and started singing.

'*You put the lumps in my custard,*
You put the wobble in my jelly,
You really curdle my caramel, baby,
When you trifle with me!'

Her voice growing louder, Mucky Maud sauntered through the club, in amongst her adoring audience. Every so often, she would pause for a moment at a table – to ruffle goblin hair, tickle goblin chins, and push eager goblin faces down into waiting custard pies. Whatever she did, the crowd cheered. She had them eating out of the palm of her hand – literally!

As the song approached its soaring finale, the organ-grinder cranked up his barrel organ. Mucky Maud's strident voice soared over the deafening accompaniment.

'*And so I say . . .*'

The Horned Baron held his breath. She was coming towards him.

'*And so I say to you . . .*'

She was approaching his table. He turned away, his cheeks burning with embarrassment. It was as though Mucky Maud was singing to him; as if the words of the song were meant for him, and him alone . . .

'*And so I say-i-yaaaaaay . . .*' As she held the note, she came up behind the Horned Baron and trailed her long fingers across his shoulders and over his shiny helmet. All at once, she fell still, took a breath and completed the song in a low, husky whisper. '*Don't you ever trifle with me.*'

'Bravo!' roared the Horned Baron, clapping enthusiastically. 'Bravo!'

Mucky Maud moved round to face him. The Horned Baron looked up. Their eyes met.

'You!' he gasped.

It was gone four in the morning. Already, pink stinky hogs were stirring in the Perfumed Bog as the first batbirds flapped across the sky above their heads. The sky was cloudless. The air was still. It promised to be a beautiful day.

In *Mucky Maud's Lumpy Custard Club*, the night was finally coming to an end. Most of the customers had already gone home, and the waiters and waitresses were busy clearing up the mess they'd left – hosing down the tables and stacking the chairs. An ogre and a couple of goblins were still propping up the bar.

'Sixsh more cushtard piesh,' one of them demanded groggily.

'You've had enough,' said the barkeeper gruffly as he rubbed a filthy cloth over the glasses, making sure they'd be nice and dirty for the evening.

'Oh, go on, me old mate,' pleaded the ogre.

'Bar's shut,' said the barkeeper sharply. 'And I am *not* your "old mate". Go on, push off. Haven't you got homes to go to?'

'Shp'oe sho,' said the ogre and the two goblins in unison, and they turned and shuffled reluctantly away.

'Shtill, it'sh been a good night,' one of them muttered as he fell with a *splat* into a soggy heap of trifle and blancmange. He licked his fingers. 'A *very* good night.'

In the corner, the barrel organ was still pumping out music, but slowly now, and softly, as the lugubrious goblin grew wearier and wearier. He eyed the upper table sleepily, where Mucky Maud was sitting on the Horned Baron's knee. Until she decided to leave, Spam had no option but to keep playing – and judging by the giggles and guffaws of laughter coming from her direction, there was no saying when that might be.

'I still can't get over it,' the Horned Baron sighed, his face turning serious. 'After all this time ...'

'I know,' said Mucky Maud.

'Oh, Fifi!' he said suddenly, and grasped her hand. 'How could I ever have been so stupid?'

Mucky Maud shook her head. 'It was fated never to be, Walter,' she  said. 'After all, you were wealthy, well-to-do, with the whole of Muddle Earth at your feet.' She paused. 'While I ... a young troll from the wrong side of Trollbridge ...'

'But Fifi, you had such dreams back then. Whatever happened to the troll I once knew who said she would never rest until she had made her fortune in the Muddle Earth turnip market? Eh? What happened to those dreams, Fifi?'

'Oh, Walter, I tried, believe me,' said Mucky Maud. 'Gave it my best shot. But in the end, I had to concede that I wasn't good enough. I simply didn't have what it took!'

'But, Fifi . . .'

'You don't know what it's like in the turnip business,' she went on. 'It's a cut-throat, troll-eat-troll world, believe me. The endless contests and shows. The constant pressure . . . Too much rain. Not enough. The blight, the canker, the root rot. Not to mention the purple turnip weevils . . .'

'The purple turnip weevils?' said the Horned Baron.

'I told you not to mention them,' said Mucky Maud. She sighed. 'Anyway, that's all in the past now. When I finally admitted to myself that I'd never make it big in turnips, I came to Goblintown – to start a new life. I got into custard and never looked back.'

From the opposite side of the table there came a low gurgle as Benson – fast asleep and head down in a bowl of custard – burped. The Horned Baron snorted. 'I told him not to have that third rancid butter surprise,' he muttered.

'Of course, I had to change my name,' she continued without a break. 'If it ever got out, it would have caused an absolute scandal. I'd never have been able to show my face in Trollbridge again. And so Mucky Maud was born.'

'You'll always be Fifi to me,' said the Horned Baron, squeezing her hand affectionately. He shook his head sadly at the thought of what could have been; what *should* have been. 'But, Fifi!' he groaned. 'Why didn't you come to me?'

Mucky Maud sniffed. 'Look at it from my point of view. You, the Horned Baron, ruler of Muddle Earth and me, a mere custard-club singer. It would never have worked out.

We both knew that!' Her eyes filled with tears. 'And now it's too late!' she wailed.

'But it doesn't have to be too late,' the Horned Baron said gently. 'I've got a little vegetable garden back at my castle. We can grow turnips! I'll take you away from all this. We can start again . . .'

'Oh, Horny,' said Mucky Maud. 'Could we? Dare we? This is all a dream!'

'A dream that together, we shall make come true,' the Horned Baron told her. He looked round. 'Benson!'

The manservant started, looked up and wiped the custard from his face. 'Sir?' he mumbled sleepily.

'We're leaving, Benson,' said the Horned Baron. 'Take Mucky M . . .' He turned to her. Their eyes met and they smiled at one another. 'I mean, take Miss Fifi's cape,' he said.

Benson looked puzzled. 'But sir . . .' he began.

'No "buts", Benson,' the Horned Baron snapped. 'Just do it!'

'*P*ut *the kettle on, mother, it goes with your eyes. The moon's a baboon . . .*'

Randalf spun round and stared at the ogre, aghast. 'Norbert!' he said. 'You haven't . . . You didn't . . .'

'I think you'll find he did,' Veronica observed.

'*Pieces of eight!*' said Norbert, a look of puzzlement on his face. '*Pieces of eight . . . nine . . . ten green bottles, running down the hall . . .*'

'You did, didn't you?' Randalf said. 'You drank from the babbling brook.'

Norbert nodded sadly.

'After I specifically told you not to,' Randalf sighed. 'That's all we need,' he said. 'A babbling *ogre*.'

'*Mud pies and pointy sticks . . . I . . .* I'm sorry,' said Norbert. 'But I was so thirsty . . . *Friday. Tuesday's child is full of cake . . .*' He grimaced, clamped his hands over his mouth and looked round woefully.

~ 384 ~

'Don't worry,' said Brenda. 'It'll wear off.'

'But when?' Norbert mumbled. '*Where? Wet? Wellington boot?*'

'When Nature calls,' said Brenda cheerfully, slapping the ogre on the back.

Joe giggled.

Norbert removed his hands. He frowned. 'You mean when I have a wee . . . wee . . . *wee Willie Winkie, running through . . .*'

'That's exactly what she means, Norbert,' said Randalf. 'And in the meantime, I'd be grateful if you would do your best to remain quiet. Stealth and silence are the hallmarks of a successful quest. You do *want* our quest to be successful, don't you?'

'*Mm-hmm,*' said Norbert, nodding earnestly, his hands clamped back in place.

'Then let us proceed,' said Randalf. 'Brenda, lead the way!'

Keeping close together, the intrepid travellers continued through Elfwood as fast as they could – which, thanks to Randalf's increasingly frequent stops, wasn't that fast at all. Puffing and panting, he would have sat himself down on every tree stump he came to if Brenda hadn't been there to urge him on.

'Not far now, sir,' she said, seizing his arm and steering him away from a particularly inviting beech stump in front of them. 'Just a little bit furth . . .'

'I can't,' Randalf groaned as he sat down heavily, mopping his brow and gasping for breath. 'Must . . . take . . . rest . . .'

'Well done, Fatso,' said Veronica sarcastically. 'You've broken your own record. That was less than a minute since the last tree stump.'

'Non . . . non . . . nonsense,' Randalf panted. 'We've been walking for miles, haven't we, Brenda?'

'Well, I wouldn't say *miles* exactly,' said Brenda. 'And perhaps you could try not to stop quite so often, Rudolf.'

'Come on, Randalf,' said Joe encouragingly. 'You can do it.'

'It's all right for you,' said Randalf, gathering himself. 'But you don't have my delicate feet. I tell you, my little toe is killing me . . .'

'Not to mention the dodgy excuses!' Veronica butted in.

'Shut up, Veronica!' said Randalf.

'Well, honestly!' said Veronica. 'Who are you trying to kid?'

'This isn't getting us anywhere,' said Joe. He turned to Norbert. 'Can you carry him?'

The ogre nodded, his hands still firmly pressed against his mouth.

'I'm not getting back on Norbert's shoulder,' said Randalf. 'Not with all these low branches.'

Joe sighed. 'Perhaps he could carry you piggyback,' he said.

'Very appropriate,' Veronica sniggered.

'Oh, if you insist,' said Randalf. He heaved himself off the tree stump and stood behind the ogre. Norbert crouched down. Randalf jumped up stiffly on to his back and grabbed on round his neck. '*Eeek!*' he cried out. 'Norbert, I'm slipping!'

Norbert swung his arms round behind his back, jigged Randalf up and supported him under his legs.

'That's better,' said Randalf.

'*Flapjack, pelican, walrus, trumpet,*' said Norbert, blushing furiously. 'S . . . sorry, sir,' he mumbled. 'I'm . . . trying . . .'

'You can say that again,' muttered Veronica.

' . . . not . . . to . . . say . . . anything . . . silly . . . *billy, pudding and pie, Major Minor, Dr Cuddl . . .*'

'That is *enough*, Norbert!' said Randalf, clamping his own hands over the ogre's mouth. 'And don't slobber!'

'Right, well if we're finally all ready, I think we should make a move!' said Brenda in her most warrior-princessy voice. 'Which way, Rupert?'

'Follow me, everyone,' said Randalf confidently. 'I know these woods like the back of my hand. Just keep going to the right . . . To the *right*, Norbert!' he said as the ogre lurched to the left. 'That's it. And do try to keep up. No dawdling at the back!'

Joe followed, close on Norbert's heels, with Henry – still on his lead – trotting beside him and Veronica on his shoulder. Sniffy padded silently behind him. Brenda – sword drawn and eyes peeled – brought up the rear.

And so they continued, on and on. And on and on and on and on and on . . . The sun rose high, crossed the sky, and began to sink back down again. And still they journeyed on. Occasionally, Norbert – who was having difficulty not slobbering, causing Randalf's hands to slip – would start babbling again. For the most part, however, they travelled in silence, until . . .

'Something's wrong,' said Joe.

'You can say that again,' said Randalf. 'I should be back on the houseboat, feet up, sipping a nice lukewarm cup of spittle tea, not trudging through Elfwood on the back of a lumpy, bumpy, dribbling ogre who can't stop babbling.'

Joe shook his head. 'It's not that,' he said.

Brenda caught him up. '*What's* wrong, Joe?' she asked, looking round anxiously. 'Have you seen something? A monster? A dragon? A . . . an . . . elf, maybe?'

Joe shook his head and pointed at a tree stump some metres away. A particularly inviting beech stump . . . Joe had recognized it at once.

'We've been going round in circles!' he exclaimed. 'Oh, Randalf. We're lost!'

Veronica snorted. 'Trust Fatso! "I know Elfwood like the back of my hand," he said. Wild goose chase, more like.'

'It . . . it wasn't me,' Randalf blustered. 'It was Norbert.'

'*Mm hmmm mmm*,' muttered Norbert indignantly

behind Randalf's hands.

'It's true,' said Randalf. 'Never could tell his left from his right.'

Norbert lowered his arms. Randalf fell to the ground.

'*Tennis balls! Washing machine! Cheese on toast!* . . .' His face twisted up with frustration, Norbert turned on his heels and stomped off into the trees.

'Norbert?' Randalf called after him. 'Norbert, come back at once. You can't leave me here.'

'He just has,' said Veronica.

Randalf sighed and sat down on the beech stump.

'If you don't know where it is,' said Joe, 'how are we going to get to Giggle Glade?'

'Did you hear that, Eileen?' came the gruff voice of a nearby elm. 'They *don't* know how to get to Giggle Glade.'

'I know, Stan. I did wonder why they were taking such a roundabout route,' his neighbour replied. 'I just assumed that fat one knew where he was going.'

'Me, too,' said a willowy willow. 'And I didn't like to say anything,' she added. 'It seemed a bit forward.'

'They want to go *that* way, don't they?' said Stan.

'Absolutely,' said Eileen, 'bearing left at Delilah the holly bush – taking care to mind her prickles and down towards the sycamores . . .'

Joe beamed. 'Thank you,' he said.

The trees rustled.

'Ooh, what a nice young man,' said a silver birch, her

leaves trembling. 'So polite!'

'Yes, not like that great big, three-eyed one,' said an outraged oak.

Just then, Norbert emerged from behind the tree, grinning broadly and tightening his belt. 'That's better,' he said. 'I think I'm almost back to normal now, sir. I've just . . .'

'Yes, yes, spare us the details, Norbert,' said Randalf, taking control of the situation. He pulled himself up off the tree stump and, with Veronica up on the brim of his pointy hat, strode off towards the holly bush. 'Hurry up, you lot,' he called back. 'We've wasted enough time already.'

With the trees guiding them through the woods, the small party made good progress.

'They'll be there in no time, Sid,' commented

one of the sycamores.

'That's true, Sam,' said another, with a shudder that sent a shower of whirlygigs spinning down through the air. 'With a bit of luck, they'll be able to do something about that dastardly Dr Cuddles.'

'And not a moment too soon,' said another, 'what with Giggle Glade getting bigger by the day.'

'I'm counting on them,' said another. 'I . . . ooh, they need to bear a little bit further left, don't they? Past Finnbar – is that his name? That great fir tree . . . And taking care not to wake Uncle Cedric . . .'

'No chance of that,' said yet another. 'He's been sleeping like a log for years.'

'That's it. *Now* they're on the right track.'

Joe was feeling much more confident now. Randalf seemed to have found his second wind, Norbert was back to normal and even Veronica was chirpier than usual.

'We must be getting near,' she was saying. 'Listen.'

Joe cocked his head to one side. From far away, he could hear the distant sound of hammering and drilling and sawing . . .'

'Ooh,' shuddered a great pine tree, her needles quivering. 'Can you hear that, Daphne?'

'Dr Cuddles's fiendish plans,' a willow replied in a shaky voice. 'It's enough to make you weep.'

'Don't worry,' said Joe. 'We're going to put an end to Dr Cuddles once and for all.' He turned. 'Aren't we, Brenda?'

The warrior-princess nodded, but Joe couldn't help noticing that her face was pale and drawn, her nose twitched and her eyes darted round constantly into the shadows. Beside her, Sniffy seemed just as uneasy.

'Are you all right, Brenda?' Joe asked.

'I'm not sure,' said Brenda. 'It's just . . .' She was staring at the ground in front of her. 'What *is* that?'

Joe frowned. 'A bit of cloth,' he said, picking up a small scrap of red and white spotted material by Brenda's foot. 'Why?'

'It looks like a handkerchief,' said Brenda, a tremble in her voice. 'An *elf's* handkerchief.'

'How can it be?' said Joe. 'You heard what Randalf said. There aren't any elves in Elfwood.'

Brenda pointed to her left. 'If that's true, then what is *that*?'

Joe retrieved a small silver thimble from the ground.

Even he had to admit that it looked the perfect size for tiny elf fingers.

'And that!' said Brenda, beads of sweat appearing on her brow. 'And that – and *that*!'

Joe looked round at the forest floor. It was littered with tiny objects. There was a tiny bone comb. A miniature fan. A small tasselled cap. A couple of minute wooden buttons . . .

'Elf droppings!' Brenda cried out in horror.

Just then, Randalf's voice floated back. 'Hurry up, you lot! We're here!'

'Did you hear that, Brenda?' said Joe excitedly. 'We've made it to Giggle Glade!'

Brenda nodded dumbly, but she clearly wasn't listening.

Joe took her gently by the arm. 'Come on, Brenda,' he said. 'Don't worry about these things. They've probably been lying here for years.'

Reluctantly, Brenda let Joe lead her on. Even more reluctantly, Sniffy, whose nose was quivering suspiciously, went with them. They rounded a vast, spreading horse chestnut tree. And there was Randalf.

'There you are!' he said, talking in a loud stage whisper.

While Brenda and Sniffy hung back, Joe went over to him, and peered through the leafy branches into the clearing beyond. 'Wow!' he gasped.

In front of him, towering up from the bare ground and supported by rickety scaffolding, was a huge wooden construction which looked for all the world, or so Joe thought, like a giant rabbit's head. From the right came the sound of chopping axes. From the left, the squeal of a circular saw. While from the head itself (if that's what it was), the drum-like beat of a hundred banging hammers echoed through the air.

Around the edge of the clearing, the trees wailed and waved their branches. 'Oh, there goes Arnold,' moaned a tree close by as, with a creak and a thud, a tall pine tree slammed to the ground.

'And now they're starting on Montague,' cried another.

The whole of Giggle Glade was a hive of activity, with trees being felled, stripped and turned into planks and boards which, in turn, were being used to construct the curious structure. Orchestrating the whole process was a wizard with long robes and a particularly wrinkled face,

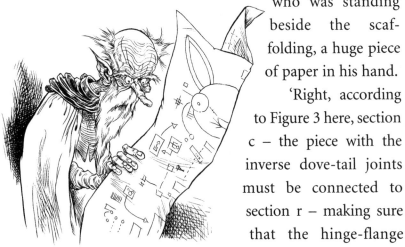

who was standing beside the scaffolding, a huge piece of paper in his hand.

'Right, according to Figure 3 here, section c – the piece with the inverse dove-tail joints must be connected to section r – making sure that the hinge-flange (see Figure 8) is uppermost, and the dowling trim (see additional notes) is on the left . . .' He paused, looked up at the rabbit's head, then back at the plans. 'No, hang on a moment.' He turned the paper right round. 'Section *d* should be attached to section *m*, but not before the floating divet has been secured.' He frowned. 'Floating divet? What on Muddle Earth is a floating divet? Who writes this stuff?'

'*You* did!' a chorus of tiny voices replied.

'That's Roger the Wrinkled,' Randalf whispered to Joe. 'He taught me everything I know.'

'It took him about five minutes,' muttered Veronica.

Randalf shook his head. 'Poor Roger,' he said. 'I knew something awful had happened to him, but I never imagined he'd be reduced to this.'

Joe followed Randalf's gaze to the giant ball and chain attached to Roger the Wrinkled's ankle.

Randalf shuddered. 'Bound and shackled and forced to do the bidding of Dr . . . Dr . . .' He looked away, unable to speak the whole name out loud.

'Just as well we've got Joe the Barbarian and Brenda, Warrior-Princess on our side, isn't it, sir?' said Norbert.

'Yes,' said Randalf, slightly less than certainly. 'Where *is* Brenda.' He looked round. 'Oh, there you are. What are you doing back there?'

Brenda emerged from behind a tree. 'What are those voices?' she asked nervously.

'Come and have a look.' He smiled at her as he parted

the overhanging branches. 'You're in luck, my dear,' he said. 'Giggle Glade is absolutely crawling with elves! Who'd have thought it?'

'*Eeek!*' squeaked Brenda.

Randalf frowned. 'Brenda?' he said. 'Where are you going? Brenda, *why* are you climbing that tree? Brenda, speak to me!'

'*Tee-hee-hee*,' giggled a portly oak tree as Brenda and Sniffy scrambled high up into its branches as quickly as they could. 'Ooh, that tickles. *Ooh! Ah! Ha-ha-ha!*'

'Brenda, whatever's the matter?' Randalf whispered as loudly as he dared. 'Do you sense danger? Is it fire-breathing dragons? Awesome orcs? The warty gutguzzler from the Black Lagoon . . . ?'

'No,' Brenda sobbed. 'It's *elves*.'

'Elves?' Randalf squawked with disbelief. 'You can't be serious! A great big, strapping warrior-princess like you afraid of tiny little elves. I don't believe it!'

Joe sighed. 'I think Brenda's got a bit of a thing about elves,' he said.

'Nonsense,' said Randalf. He peered up at the tree. 'Brenda, tell me it isn't true. Please, Brenda . . .'

'It's t . . . t . . . true,' she stammered. 'Hate them! Hate them! Hate them! Horrible, bony little bodies. Squeaky little voices . . .' The branch she was clinging to juddered violently. 'Make them all go away. Please!'

'But Brenda,' Randalf pleaded. 'I believed in you. Your

huge muscles, your great big battle-cat. What about all your heroic deeds? The hags you've wrestled, the sorcerors you've squashed?'

'Why do you think I've been roaming the Northern Wastes all this time?' sobbed Brenda, burying her face in her hands. 'Because I was hiding away from those nasty little things and trying to conquer my fears. And I thought I had. I really did. I thought I was finally ready to return to Muddle Earth, but no . . . No!' Sobs racked her powerful body. Beside her, Sniffy whimpered miserably at his mistress's distress.

'Ooh, hark at her!' said the oak.

Suddenly overwhelmed with exhaustion, Randalf sat down heavily on the ground.

'I always knew there was something a bit odd about that so called *warrior-princess* of yours,' said Veronica.

'Well, that's it, then,' said Randalf wearily. 'All over. Abandon quest. We may as well go home.'

'Go home?' stormed Joe. 'That's precisely what I intend to do – and I'm not talking about a houseboat on a floating lake!'

'But we can't,' said Randalf. 'Not without our warrior-princess.'

'We can and we shall!' said Joe, his head high, his eyes gleaming. 'I, for one, refuse to give up now. Not when we've come so far. We've battled through the forest. We've found Giggle Glade. Now it's time to do what we came here to do. We're going to free Roger the Wrinkled. We're going to find that *Great Book of Spells*. And we're going to destroy Dr Cuddles!'

'Bravo, I say,' said a towering hazelnut tree nearby. 'That's the kind of fighting talk I like to hear.'

'Same here, Dolores. It's time someone stood up to that starey-eyed little bully!'

Joe drew his sword and raised it high in the air. 'Who's with me?' he cried out.

'I'm with you!' Veronica shouted back.

'*Cauliflower cheese. Wingnuts!*' said Norbert. 'Sorry, hiccups!' He smiled. 'What I meant was, I'm with you, Joe. I'm with you every step of the way.'

They all turned to Randalf. 'And you?' said Joe.

Randalf sat up, his face etched with miserable resignation. He shook his head. 'I'm going to regret this,' he said. 'It's completely against my better judgement, so don't blame me when it all goes wrong . . .'

'Well?' said Joe.

'All right,' said Randalf. He climbed to his feet. 'But you go first.'

'CHARGE!' Joe roared. Waving his sword above his head, Joe burst from the cover of the trees and ran headlong across the stripped clearing, Henry hard on his heels, barking excitedly. Elves squeaked and darted out of their way.

The wizard looked up from the great piece of crumpled paper in his hands, the links of his heavy chain clanking as he moved. 'My goodness!' he exclaimed, his eyes twinkling brightly. 'It's a warrior-hero!'

Joe stopped before him.

'A little on the short side, perhaps – but that's a marvellous shield!' He smiled at Joe. 'What brings you here?'

'Come to rescue you,' said Joe breathlessly. 'To set you free.'

'Oo-ooh!' came a chorus of sing-song squeaky voices, and Joe looked round to see various elf faces peering up at him.

'Don't mind them,' said Roger the Wrinkled. He clapped his hands together. 'Get on with your work!' he said brusquely.

'At once, sir!' they said, returning to their various tasks. 'With pleasure!'

'Eager little creatures, aren't they?' said Roger the Wrinkled. 'A joy to be in charge of.'

Joe frowned. 'You don't exactly *look* in charge,' he said. 'Not with that ball and chain . . .'

'I know,' said Roger, looking down at his shackled feet. 'Frightful bore, isn't it,' he said. 'Still, there's really no need to worry. Everything's under control.'

'It is?' said Joe, surprised.

'Oh, yes,' said Roger the Wrinkled, tapping the side of his nose mysteriously. 'Certainly, I have no need of a rescue – although it was awfully considerate of you to offer. Tell me, where exactly *did* you spring from?'

Joe turned. Norbert was approaching, with Randalf (looking decidedly sheepish) behind him. 'I'm with them,' he said. 'We're on a quest!'

Roger the Wrinkled looked up. His face wrinkled with surprise. 'Norbert?' he said. 'Norbert, is that you?'

'Yes, sir,' said Norbert, striding forwards.

'How lovely to see you again, Norbert,' said Roger the Wrinkled. 'It certainly is. And how terribly clever of you to have come all the way here to rescue me.'

'Oh, it wasn't just me, sir,' said Norbert modestly.

'Who's that behind you? The wizard fell still and screwed up his face in such amazement that his wrinkles got wrinkles. 'That's not young Randalf, is it?' he said.

A red-raced Randalf peered round from behind Norbert. 'Hello, sir,' he said, speaking more meekly than Joe had ever heard him speak before.

'Well, well, well,' said Roger the Wrinkled. 'Who'd have thought it? That *you* could have organized all this!'

'It wasn't that difficult,' said Joe. 'After all, he is a wizard.'

'A wizard?' said Roger the Wrinkled, chuckling loudly. 'Oh, my dear young warrior-hero, Randalf here isn't a wizard.'

'He isn't?' said Joe.

'No, no,' said Roger the Wrinkled. 'Randalf here is a very junior apprentice. He hasn't even passed his preliminary wizardry exams yet, have you Randalf?'

'No, sir,' said Randalf, squirming with bright-red, shamefaced embarrassment.

'I told you so!' said Veronica triumphantly as she fluttered up from the brim of Randalf's hat. 'I told you that you'd be found out one day.'

'Veronica, is that you?' said Roger the Wrinkled. 'How lovely your plumage is looking.'

'Oh sir,' said Veronica giddily. 'Do you really think so?'

'And to think you came all this way to rescue me,' said Roger the Wrinkled. 'I'm touched. I really am.'

Randalf shook his head. 'But how did it happen, sir?' he

said. 'A great big, powerful wizard like yourself getting kidnapped. I don't understand.'

'I don't think we need to go into the details, Randalf,' Roger the Wrinkled said quickly, his wrinkles forming deep creases. 'I should never have stepped into the wardrobe in the first place – but there was a rather fetching evening gown in there which just happened to catch my eye . . .'

Norbert hiccuped nervously. '*Frilly knickers, frilly knickers . . .*'

'How did you know?' said Roger, blushing a deep scarlet. 'Well, before I knew it, the door slammed shut and Dr Cuddles turned the key. Then he had me transported back to Giggle Glade inside the darned thing, blast his big blue eyes!'

Joe trembled. 'Couldn't you have cast a spell?' he asked.

'There wasn't the time,' said Roger the Wrinkled. 'It all happened in an instant.' He sighed. 'I've been under lock and key, along with the other wizards, ever since.'

'So where does the rabbit's head fit in?' asked Randalf, nodding towards the wooden construction.

'On top of the rest of the rabbit,' said Roger the Wrinkled.

Randalf frowned. 'I mean, what is it *for*?' he said.

'It's all part of Dr Cuddles's latest fiendish plan,' said Roger the Wrinkled. 'I'm afraid that's all he told me. He's quite mad, you know.'

All round them, the teams of elves blithely continued

what they were doing, whistling to themselves as they worked. Chopping and planing, screwing and nailing. Fashioning the individual sections of timber which, when they were completed, were passed along a line of elves, across the clearing and up the scaffolding, where they were hammered into place. From the fringes of the growing clearing, the trees muttered to themselves nervously.

'I'm going to be next, I just know I am,' said a weeping willow tearfully.

'Courage, Lucinda,' said a neighbouring hornbeam. 'If we're going to go, we're going to go with dignity.'

'*Ouch!*' cried a nearby oak, as the elves cheerfully attacked the base of its trunk with a volley of axe blows. 'Farewell cruel world!'

'Oh, now they're starting on Oswald,' the willow

sobbed. 'That it should have come to this. If only that fat one would hurry up and *do* something!'

'Him!' snorted the hornbeam. 'He doesn't do *anything* in a hurry!'

'You can say that again, Norris,' said a prickly hawthorn. 'Spends half his time sitting down!'

Even as the trees were grumbling to themselves, Randalf was once again making himself comfortable – on the great iron ball chained to Roger the Wrinkled's ankle. He looked up at the wizard. 'So, now that we're here, what would you like us to do?' he asked.

Roger the Wrinkled frowned, the deep lines corrugating his forehead. 'Do?' he said. 'To be perfectly honest, I'm not sure what you can do. As I was saying to the young warrior-hero, here . . .' He smiled at Joe, the corners of his eyes crinkling alarmingly. 'What did you say your name was?'

'It's Joe,' said Joe.

'Joe the Barbarian,' added Veronica.

'Quite,' said Roger the Wrinkled. 'As I was saying to Joe, grateful though I am that you've come all this way, your journey has been unnecessary. I don't need to be rescued.'

'Oh, dear, what a shame, I was really looking forward to getting stuck in,' said Randalf cheerily. He climbed to his feet. 'Still, if you're quite sure, sir, we'll leave you to it. See you back at the houseboat.' He turned to Joe and Norbert. 'Come on, you two,' he said. 'We're not needed. Come along

Veronica,' he added, patting the brim of his hat.

'Hang on a minute!' said Joe indignantly. 'Aren't you forgetting something?'

'You heard what Roger said,' Randalf told him. 'He doesn't need our help.'

'That's as may be,' said Joe. 'But *I* need *his* help!'

Roger the Wrinkled turned towards him, his face creased up in concern. 'You do?' he said.

'Oh, it's nothing,' said Randalf hurriedly. 'Come on, Joe. You can see that Roger the Wrinkled's got a lot on his plate . . .'

But Joe was having none of it. 'I need a *real* wizard to get me home,' he told Roger, speaking over Randalf, who was tugging at Joe's sleeve and urging him to go. 'Randalf summoned me here to Muddle Earth, but he doesn't seem to know how to send me back. I've been here for ages. Ages and ages! I've battled with fearsome ogres, tussled with fire-breathing dragons . . .'

'Slight exaggeration,' Randalf muttered.

'Be quiet, Randalf,' said Roger the Wrinkled sternly. 'It sounds to me as though you've been dabbling in matters you know nothing about.'

'You can say that again,' said Veronica, fluttering through the air and landing on Roger the Wrinkled's pointy hat.

Randalf hung his head. 'Shut up, Veronica!' he hissed out of the corner of his mouth.

Roger the Wrinkled turned to Joe. 'Continue, young man.'

'Anyway, I've done everything Randalf asked of me,' he said.

'And more,' said Norbert, nodding. 'He's been marvellous!'

'But now I want to leave Muddle Earth,' said Joe. He smiled bravely. 'You're my last hope, Roger the Wrinkled,' he said. 'Can you send me home? *Please!*'

'That could be tricky,' said Roger the Wrinkled, shaking his head sadly. 'I'm afraid magic isn't simply a matter of waving a magic wand and casting a spell.'

'It isn't?' said Randalf, surprised.

'Gracious me, no,' said Roger the Wrinkled, giving him a wrinkled frown. 'Regardless of what you might have heard, Joe, wizardry is a highly complex enterprise, requiring great skill and heightened powers of interpretation. Not even the legendary Ian the Clever was able to perform more than half a dozen of the simplest feats of magic from memory.'

Joe felt his heart begin to sink.

'Accuracy is everything, you see,' Roger continued. 'There is, for instance, a wart-removing spell that is only two words and a whistle different from a turning-someone-into-a-pink-stinky-hog enchantment. You can see the danger.'

Joe nodded glumly. Henry whimpered softly. Randalf looked down at his feet shamefacedly.

'That's why we wizards have the *Great Book of Spells*,'

said Roger. 'To ensure the accuracy required. And even then it's not easy. Years of study, it takes, before an apprentice wizard can interpret its symbols, codes and diagrams, in order to carry out its instructions to the letter.'

'But *you* could, couldn't you?' said Joe, hope in his voice.

'I *could*,' said Roger the Wrinkled, 'if I had the book.' He sighed. 'Unfortunately – and don't ask me how – the *Great Book of Spells* has somehow fallen into the clutches of Dr Cuddles.'

'Hmm,' mused Veronica, glaring at Randalf. 'I wonder how *that* could have happened?'

'He keeps it locked up inside a heavy box secured to the top of a tall, oak lectern ...'

'Or Cecil, as he used to be known,' said the willow sadly.

'Poor, dear Cecil,' the hornbeam murmured. 'And now Oswald's going the same way.'

'Cuddles only allows me to read a word at a time from the spell book,' Roger the Wrinkled went on. 'And then, only from the particular spell *he* wants conjured. So you see, it takes absolutely ages to weave even the simplest magic.'

Joe sighed. Every time he got his hopes up, Roger the Wrinkled dashed them again. Not that Joe was about to give up. Not yet ...

'What about the key?' he said. 'If the book's locked up, there must be a key to *un*lock it.'

'There is,' said Roger the Wrinkled, shaking his head

sadly. 'Dr Cuddles wears it on a silver chain around his neck.'

Joe groaned.

'Oh, well, we tried our best,' said Randalf. 'Let's get back to the Enchanted Lake and have a well-earned cup of spittle tea.'

Veronica fluttered down from Roger's pointy hat and landed on his shoulder. 'Shut up, Randalf,' she said. 'We're not leaving now – are we Norbert?'

'Certainly not,' said Norbert.

'And as for the key,' Veronica went on. 'You leave that to me!'

'You'll find Dr Cuddles in his Giggle House over there, behind the privet hedge,' said Roger the Wrinkled. 'And if you do manage to get your hands on the *Great Book of Spells*, stick it up your jumper and bring it to me, and I'll be happy to weave you any spell you like, young man. Good luck, and don't you worry about me!' He waved a wrinkled hand airily.

The five of them turned and set off, Norbert, Veronica, Joe and Henry (back on his lead) in front, and Randalf trailing reluctantly behind.

Although most of the trees had been felled, Giggle Glade was not completely bare. The clearing was dotted with a number of small, pathetic specimens: a wispy willow sapling, a scrawny hollybush, a weedy elm . . . As they crossed the glade, darting from tree to spindly tree and hoping that they wouldn't be spotted, Joe noticed more teams of elves – each one being supervised by its own manacled wizard – constructing other sections of the massive tree rabbit.

'Isn't that Bertram the Incredibly Hairy?' said Veronica, flapping her wing at a tall, stooped individual, his features hidden behind thick, bushy tresses.

Norbert nodded. 'And look,' he said. 'Over by that huge back leg. It's Melvyn the Mauve.'

Joe kept quiet. The sight of the imprisoned wizards depressed him more than he would have liked to admit. If *they* had all been captured by the dastardly Dr Cuddles, then what chance did *he* stand?

'Cheer up, Joe,' said Norbert, as if reading his thoughts. 'It might never happen.'

They were crouched down behind the bushy privet just in front of the house waiting for Randalf to catch them up. Joe peered over the little gate. A path of stepping stones led up to an ornately decorated wooden cottage. There were pink roses round the door and every window had powder-blue shutters with heart-shaped peepholes.

'*That's* the Giggle House?' said Joe.

'The nerve centre of Cuddles's sinister operations!' said Randalf, panting noisily as he caught up.

'Not so loud,' whispered Veronica. 'He'll hear us.'

Just then, from inside the Giggle House, there came the sound of a door slamming.

Dr Cuddles stood outside Ingrid's chamber. 'She's

driving me stark staring bonkers!' he groaned. 'You'll have
to deal with her, Quentin. I've had all I can stand.'

'Oh, but, *sir*,' Quentin whined.

'That's enough!' snapped Dr Cuddles, his blue eyes
blazing. 'I'm going to my room and I do not want to be
disturbed. Do you understand me?'

Quentin nodded unhappily.

'Good!' said Dr Cuddles, giggling menacingly. 'It'll be
the worse for you if you don't.' He marched towards his own
bedchamber, walked in and slammed the door behind him
with even more force than before.

BANG!

'Someone's in a bad mood,' whispered Veronica to Joe. 'I'll just take a peek inside to check the coast is clear. Wait for my signal.'

Joe nodded grimly. The budgie flew off, a bright flash of blue. He watched her fluttering through the air and round to a shuttered window. She landed on the window ledge, peered in through the heart-shaped peephole, then turned and beckoned with her wing.

'Come on,' said Joe. 'We're going in.'

Heads down and shoulders hunched, Joe, with Henry, Norbert and Randalf scurried over to the house and joined Veronica by the window. Their shadows were long in the light from the low sun. They crouched down. 'What can you see?' Joe whispered.

'Take a look for yourself.' Veronica nodded at the peep-hole. 'I think it's him.'

Slowly, cautiously, his heart thumping and legs shaking, Joe straightened up and peered into the room. It looked like a nursery, with toys and games – and there, lying on a bright yellow bed, was a small figure, all wrapped up in baggy robes. He was sound asleep, snoring softly. On a chain round his neck, a small, silver key glinted from the shadows; beside it, on a bit of old string, hung a rusty-looking whistle.

'It *must* be him,' Joe whispered. 'There's the key. But how do we get it without waking him?'

'Leave this to me,' said Veronica, flying up from the ledge and squeezing through the peephole. Joe held his breath as he watched her land on the pillow next to the sleeping figure and, taking care not to wake him, disappear inside the shadowy folds of his hood.

Dr Cuddles twitched, grunted and rolled over. 'That tickles, Quentin,' he giggled in his sleep. Joe held his breath.

The next moment, Veronica emerged from the hood, a silver chain clamped in her beak. With a flap of her wings, she launched herself into the air, flew across the room and out through the peephole once more.

'Well done, Veronica!' Joe whispered excitedly.

Randalf seized the key. 'It's not over yet,' he said. 'Come on.'

With their heads down, they stole round to the front of the house and, having peeked through the letter box to check no one was there, tried the door. It was open. They tiptoed in.

Joe peered round. Compared with the golden glow of the evening sun outside, the room he found himself in was bathed in shadow. Slowly, his eyes grew accustomed to the light. The rosebud wallpaper clashed with the powder-blue frilly curtains. The orange carpet was decorated with big bright daisies.

'Look,' Joe whispered urgently. 'Over there.'

Everyone turned to the lectern in the corner with the locked box secured to it at the top. Randalf nodded.

'Come on, then,' whispered Veronica. 'Let's unlock the spell book and get out of here!'

Keeping close together, they crossed the room and gathered in front of the lectern. Joe held Henry close on the lead and, finger on lips, reminded him to remain quiet. Veronica fluttered down and landed on Norbert's shoulder. Randalf stepped towards the box.

He raised the key. He slipped it into the heavy padlock. He turned it . . .

'*WAAAAARGH!*'

As the floor abruptly opened up beneath them, the five hapless intruders tumbled back into the darkness. Down, down, down, they fell.

'*WAAAA . . .*' The trapdoor slammed back into place.

There were cries of, '*Oof!*' '*Ouch!*' and 'Get your elbow out of my ear!' as, first Norbert, then Randalf, then Joe, then Henry landed one on top of the other on the stone floor of a damp, smelly, pitch-black room beneath the house.

Joe extricated himself from the tangle of limbs and stood up. He peered round. This time, however, his eyes did not grow accustomed to the light – because there wasn't any. Not a glimmer. Not a spark.

'Now what?' Joe murmured.

All at once, there was a *click* and a light came on. Then came the sound of rusty bolts being drawn back and the creak of a heavy door slowly opening.

Blinking in the brightness, Joe looked round. They were in a small, windowless cellar with water on the floor and green mould on the walls. In one corner was a pile of chains attached to large iron balls. In another was a staircase. The sound of heavy footsteps striding down a corridor echoed round the cellar.

'*Buffaloes' bottoms . . .*' Norbert hiccuped nervously. 'Someone's coming!'

Randalf hid behind Norbert. The footsteps got louder – followed by a voice.

'Honestly, Colin,' it lisped, 'how many times must I tell you not to tamper with the spell book?'

A pair of pointy shoes and glittery tights appeared at the top of the stairs, followed by a sparkly red jacket, a pale face, a floppy quiff . . . The figure froze and let out a little squeak. '*You're* not Colin the Nondescript!' he said.

'Quentin!' Norbert cried.

The thin, foppish figure gasped. 'Norbert?' he said.

Randalf stepped out from behind the ogre. 'Quentin!' he said. 'What are *you* doing here?'

Quentin fingered his quiff. 'I work for Dr Cuddles now,' he said.

'For Dr Cuddles?' Randalf said, his mouth falling open in astonishment.

'And it's all your fault, Randalf,' said Quentin. 'You dragged me here to Muddle Earth without so much as a by-your-leave. One minute my world was icing sugar and fondant crème, the next, you thrust me into that unflat-tering armour and talked me into going on that awful quest. And then!' he said indignantly. '*Then* you had the cheek to run away and leave me at the first sign of danger!'

'Sounds familiar,' muttered Joe.

'Thank goodness Dr Cuddles came along when he did,' Quentin went on. '*He* told me a thing or two about you.'

Randalf blushed.

'Granted, he may be an evil mastermind intent on taking over the world, but at least he appreciates me . . .'

'Running away?' said Randalf. 'I wasn't running away, my dear Quentin. I was executing a tactical flanking manoeuvre that we wizards call—'

'Saving yourself,' Veronica butted in. 'The same old story!'

'Oh, don't let's argue,' said Norbert. 'Quen-tin,' he said slowly, clapping his hands together and smiling happily. 'How *are* you?'

Quentin smoothed down his sparkly jacket and patted his quiff. 'Mustn't grumble,' he said. 'Thanks for asking, Norbert . . . Oh, but that Ingrid! She's a monster – and she never stops! From first thing in the morning to last thing at night it's all, "Quentin, do this!" and "Quentin, do that!" I don't know whether I'm coming or going.' He paused theatrically, then nodded towards the pile of shackles. 'But enough about me,' he said. 'Get your shackles on everyone, and follow me.'

Randalf snorted. 'And what if we don't want to, Quentin?' he said.

'Then I'll tell Dr Cuddles,' said Quentin.

'I'll be right with you,' said Randalf, hurrying across the cellar and securing one of the shackles to his ankle. Reluctantly, the others followed his example.

When they were all ready (even Veronica, who had a

tiny ball and chain of her own) they picked up their heavy iron balls and climbed the stairs.

'Where are you taking us?' said Randalf uneasily.

'You'll see soon enough,' said Quentin.

At the top of the staircase, they went along a narrow passage that led to Dr Cuddles's sunshine-yellow kitchen. There were decorated snuggle-muffins everywhere.

Norbert gasped. 'Quentin, you're an artist!'

'And you're a sweetie, Norbert,' replied Quentin, opening the kitchen door. 'This way, everyone -- and careful with that iron ball, Randalf!'

They followed Quentin out of the kitchen door and into the backyard of Giggle House. The yard was huge (the size of three football pitches at least, Joe thought) and full of hundreds of elves. In front of them was a long podium, upon which were seven wizards – each one with a ball and chain attached to an ankle – seated on seven chairs, and a lectern, with a short character dressed in baggy robes standing behind it. He had his back to them and was shouting in a high-pitched giggly voice.

'Quentin! We're all waiting!'

'I'm coming, sir,' Quentin shouted back. 'You'll never guess who fell through the trapdoor.'

'It can't be what's-his-name, he's over there,' said Dr Cuddles, turning round.

'No, sir, not Colin the Nondescript. Look!' He ushered Randalf and the others forward.

From inside the shadowy hood, two piercing blue eyes grew wide with surprise for an instant, then narrowed menacingly. 'Well, well, well,' said Dr Cuddles. 'If it's not Randalf the Wise! It's been a long time, Randy, my old friend. Far *too* long! Why, if I didn't know better, I'd have sworn you'd been avoiding me!'

Joe frowned. 'You know each other?' he said in surprise.

'Of course they do,' said Veronica.

'Shut up, Veronica!' said Randalf.

Dr Cuddles giggled. 'I'll enjoy having a nice little chat with you later,' he said. 'In the meantime, I've got bigger things on my mind.' He turned his back on them.

Quentin motioned to the wizards to move up and make room for the late arrivals. With much shuffling and grumbling and shifting of chairs on the podium, they got themselves settled, by which time Dr Cuddles's fingers were drumming impatiently on the lectern.

Joe and Norbert had managed to squeeze themselves on to the end of the line, Henry lay at Joe's feet, Veronica sat on Norbert's head, but Randalf still lingered at the foot of the podium, with Quentin fussing beside him.

'Come on,' said Quentin impatiently. 'Move along a bit there at the end, Colin. That's it, now Bertram the Incredibly Hairy and Boris the Bald can move over. Then Eric the Mottled can move on to that chair. Ernie the Shrivelled, move there; Melvyn the Mauve, there . . . Norbert, budge up next to Roger. *That's* better.' He mopped his brow. 'Right, now you can sit down, Randalf.'

'Oh, no need to bother,' said Randalf, with a nervous smile. 'I'll just slip back to the kitchen and wait for you all . . .'

'Sit, Randalf!' growled Dr Cuddles. Randalf did as he was told, perching next to Norbert. 'Right, well if we're *all* ready at last,' he said, eyeing Randalf sternly, 'bring on the tree rabbit.'

Hundreds of tiny elf voices chattered excitedly as the huge wooden construction was wheeled in through the powder-blue back gate.

Towering above the house, the tree rabbit had been fashioned with minute attention to detail. It had splendid wooden whiskers, huge wooden paws and a wooden tail carved to look fluffy.

'Quentin,' said Cuddles.

Quentin stepped forwards. 'Congratulations, my dear elves,' he said, his voice echoing round the glade. 'Your work here is done.'

'*O-oh*,' the elves sighed sadly in unison.

'It remains only for me to pass you over to that most demanding and unyielding of slave-drivers. The one, the only . . . Doctor . . . Cuddles!'

The elves burst into applause.

'Thank you! Thank you!' said Dr Cuddles, raising his arms and staring round at the great gathering. 'I have worked you hard!' he said. 'Days of backbreaking toil and ceaseless endeavour, just as I promised . . .'

'More! More!' cried the elves.

'And today, I make you this pledge,' Dr Cuddles continued. 'There will be many such hard, gruelling, thankless tasks to come.'

'Hooray!'

'Noses to the grindstone, shoulders to the wheel, fingers worked to the bone!'

'*Hooray!*'

'But for now I declare the holiday here in Giggle Glade over!'

Quentin stepped forwards. 'Please leave in an orderly fashion,' he lisped, 'taking care to take all personal items and luggage with you. Thank you.'

As one, the elves stood up and set off back through the forest. 'My aching back!' said one happily. 'Lovely!'

'And I've got *so* many splinters in my fingers!' said another, his face creased up in a grin.

'Can't beat a good bit of heavy toil,' said someone else. He tutted. 'It's back to sewing in Goblintown for me.'

'All good things come to an end,' said yet another with a wistful sigh.

'All work and no hard labour makes Jack a dull elf,' replied his companion.

The elves filed out of the powder-blue back gate and skipped off through the forest, trilling at the tops of their voices.

'Glad to see the back of the little squeakers,' grumbled

a hefty ash tree.

'Yeah, good riddance!' shouted a spiky pine.

'And don't come back!'

Elfwood was quiet once more, the only sound, the wind in the branches and the distant babbling of a brook. At the top of the oak tree, Brenda opened one eye. She looked down. Her face relaxed.

'Sniffy,' she said. 'I think they've gone.'

In Giggle Glade, Dr Cuddles was still holding court. With his elf audience gone, he turned to address the wizards and captured visitors behind him.

'They said I was mad,' he announced.

'You are,' Randalf murmured.

'They said it couldn't be done. But I, Dr Cuddles of Giggle Glade have proved them all wrong.' He turned and gestured towards the great tree rabbit.

Joe looked. It was absurd, with one ear longer than the other, giant outsized paws and a lopsided expression on its face. A trapdoor at the base of the wooden creature hung open, a set of steps leading down to the ground from it.

'I have tried everything to breach the walls of the Horned Baron's castle,' said Dr Cuddles. 'The singing curtains. The enchanted wardrobes . . .'

'I told you Dr Cuddles was at the bottom of them,'

Veronica whispered to Joe.

'But this time,' Dr Cuddles went on, 'I shall succeed with deception where brute force has failed!' He paused. 'Inside this tree rabbit is a secret chamber in which shall be concealed an elite squad that I have prepared,' he said, giggling gleefully. 'The tree rabbit shall be left outside the castle walls as a goodwill offering from me to the baron who, suspecting nothing, will take it inside. Then, as the clock strikes midnight, my squad shall leap out and . . .' Cuddles's blue eyes flashed madly. '*I* shall become the ruler of Muddle Earth!'

He turned to Roger the Wrinkled. 'Roger, the spell of animation if you please.'

Roger climbed to his feet, looking oddly unperturbed by Cuddles's speech and stepped forwards. The other wizards looked at one another and muttered under their breath. Roger stopped at the front of the podium, looked up at the rabbit and raised his arms. He intoned a long and compli-cated incantation. The next moment, the wheels at the four corners twitched and the tree rabbit trundled forward.

Joe gasped with amazement.

'Yes!' cried Dr Cuddles triumphantly. 'It's working! I am a genius!' He looked round, wild-eyed, and fingered the rusty whistle around his neck. 'The time has come,' he announced, 'to enter the tree rabbit!'

'Not so fast, Cuddles!' came a voice behind him, as a huge, pink, stripy cat bounded over the powder-blue back

gate and raced towards the podium, with a warrior-princess
– blades glinting in the bright morning sunlight – on its back.

'Sniffy!' cried Joe.

'Brenda!' shouted Randalf.

'*Eeeek!*' screamed Quentin, jumping up on to Norbert's
lap, as Brenda somersaulted from Sniffy's back and landed
in front of Dr Cuddles. She brandished her huge two-
handed sword.

'Release these people, fiendish sorceror!' she roared.

'Never!' cried Dr Cuddles.

'We'll see about that,' said Brenda, striding forwards. In
a blinding flash, her blades sliced through the air. *Swish,
swish, swish.* Dr Cuddles's robes fell in tatters to the floor.

Standing before them, was a short pink teddy, with
blue eyes and stubby paws. A gasp of surprise went round.

'What?' said Joe, scarcely able to believe what he was seeing.

'Haven't I seen you somewhere before?' said Roger the Wrinkled thoughtfully. He turned to Randalf. 'Isn't that . . . ? Didn't you once have . . .'

'Shut up . . . Oops, pardon me, sir.'

'Typical,' said Veronica. 'Still trying to keep things quiet. When *are* you finally going to come clean?'

Brenda was circling Dr Cuddles, a look of bemusement on her face. 'Strange,' she was saying. 'Are evil sorcerers meant to have pink fur and big blue eyes? Is *this* the fiendish Dr Cuddles you were so afraid of, Rudolf?'

'You're a fine one to talk!' said Randalf. 'Falling to bits at the first sight of an elf!'

'Yes, well,' said Brenda, blushing and turning her attention back to Dr Cuddles. 'You're an extremely naughty teddy and I'm going to have to box your fluffy pink ears.'

'And rap him on the paws,' said Bertram the Incredibly Hairy.

'*And* spank his bottom!' added Ernie the Shrivelled.

'And . . .'

Dr Cuddles scowled. 'You think you're pretty tough, with your big pointy weapon and your big stripy battle-cat, don't you? Well, I've got news for you . . .' He took hold of the small rusty-looking whistle hanging round his neck, put it to his lips and blew hard.

Pfeeep!

For a moment, nothing happened. Everyone looked round at everyone else. Then, with a loud *crash*, the door of Giggle House burst open and a dozen identical teddies – exact copies of Dr Cuddles in every way – marched over to the podium.

'My secret weapon!' Dr Cuddles roared. 'The Tickle Squad!'

The wizards all began muttering at once. 'Whose work is this?' demanded Roger the Wrinkled. 'Only a wizard can perform a spell like this. As if one Dr Cuddles wasn't bad enough!'

'Not me,' chorused Bertram the Incredibly Hairy and his brother, Boris the Bald. 'Nor me,' said Eric the Mottled, Ernie the Shrivelled and Melvyn the Mauve.

Roger looked sternly at the wizard on the end of the line. 'Oh, Colin!' he said. 'How could you!'

Colin the Nondescript winced unhappily and shuffled his feet. 'I'm sorry,' he said softly. 'I just wanted to be noticed.'

Brenda chuckled. 'Never mind,' she said, tightening her grip on her sword, her muscles rippling. 'Just leave them to me.'

The teddies marched towards her, their big blue eyes staring fiercely.

'I've grappled with ogres and wrestled with hags. I've battled with the warty gutguzzler of—'

Suddenly, the squad split into two. Six of the teddies

pounced on Brenda and six on a startled Sniffy. Brenda stumbled backwards. The teddies started tickling.

'Oh, my word!' she giggled, dropping her huge sword. 'Stop it. *Tee-hee-hee!* Get off me! *Ha-ha-ha . . .*'

Meanwhile, the other six were rendering the great battle-cat as weak as her mistress. Within seconds, the pair of them were helpless with laughter, rolling around on the ground, gasping for breath and with tears streaming down their faces.

'Tie them up,' Dr Cuddles ordered.

Brenda was shackled to four enormous sets of balls and chains, while Sniffy was trussed up like a chicken in what looked suspiciously like Dr Cuddles's sitting-room curtains.

Cuddles was triumphant. 'Nothing shall stop me now!' he giggled. 'Muddle Earth shall be mine!' And he threw back his head and giggled loudly and unpleasantly. '*Hee-hee-hee-hee-hee!*'

'Tickle Squad, atten-*shun!*' Dr Cuddles shouted.

The Tickle Squad snapped to attention, their pink fur glowing in the bright sunlight; their blue eyes glinting. Dr Cuddles walked along the line, straightening up an ear here, flicking a bit of fluff from a shoulder there.

'Excellent,' he giggled. 'Excellent!'

One or two of them giggled with anticipation. Dr Cuddles reached the end of the line and stepped back.

'Tickle Squad!' he shouted. 'You are an elite force and you must show no mercy. You are to conceal yourselves in the great tree rabbit which, by means of magic, shall be transported to the Horned Baron's castle. Once inside the castle walls, you are to wait until darkness, observing complete silence at all times. That means no giggling, Number Seven!' The seventh bear along stifled a giggle. 'On the stroke of midnight you are to burst from the tree rabbit and take over the castle. Any resistance is to be met with extreme tickling – to the death, if necessary!'

The bears nodded impassively, not a trace of emotion registering on their pink, furry faces.

'Good luck, Tickle Squad,' Dr Cuddles cried. 'To the tree rabbit!'

Turning smartly, the bears set off in a line, marching in step to Dr Cuddle's barked commands. 'Lef', lef', lef' right, lef'!'

Joe watched helplessly as the Tickle Squad approached the great tree rabbit. 'Is there nothing we can do?' he said. 'Brenda? Randalf? Roger?'

Brenda rattled her chains and shrugged. 'I'm sorry, Joe, they took me completely by surprise,' she said.

'I knew this was a bad idea,' said Randalf, shaking his head. 'We should never have come on this hopeless quest. Why, I could be at home right now tucked up in my king-sized bed if it wasn't for you lot.'

'Shut up, Randalf!' said Veronica.

Joe turned to Roger the Wrinkled. 'Can't *you* do something, sir?' he said. 'As the most powerful and important wizard in Muddle Earth.'

Roger's face wrinkled up into a crinkled smile. 'Don't worry, young man,' he said reassuringly. 'I already have.'

'But I can't help worrying,' said Joe. 'If Muddle Earth is taken over by Dr Cuddles, how will I ever get home?'

The first pink, blue-eyed teddy bear of the Tickle Squad approached the steps leading up into the giant tree rabbit.

Dr Cuddles followed, Quentin by his side.

'To think, Mildred,' said a nearby chestnut tree to her sister. 'They cut down Edna and Deirdre to build that great big wooden rabbity thing.'

'It's a disgrace, Millicent,' came the reply.

'Well, if it means we've seen the back of Dr Cuddles,' said a great spreading tree behind them, 'then it'll have been worth it.'

'You've got no heart, Bernard,' trilled the chestnut trees. 'You're as hard as mahogany.'

The first bear was halfway up the stairs. The animated tree rabbit's wheels twitched, eager to set forth. Joe's heart was pounding loudly. Any moment now, the whole Tickle Squad would disappear inside the tree rabbit, Dr Cuddles would secure the trapdoor and they'd be off – off to the Horned Baron's castle.

Just then, Joe heard a little sigh. Looking down, he caught sight of something glinting by his feet. He looked down and gasped. For there, tapping lightly against the side of Roger the Wrinkled's hogskin high-heeled bootees, was a tiny teaspoon.

Joe recognized it at once!

From the ornate curlicues on its handle, he knew it was the one he had retrieved after the cutlery stampede; the one he had seen again amongst Margot the dragon's treasure. Now it was here. But how? And why?

Roger the Wrinkled's face creased up. 'Just in time,' he said. 'Where are the others?'

The teaspoon sighed and did a little pirouette. It tipped its bowl back the way it had come.

'Look!' cried Joe. 'There they are!'

Emerging from the surrounding woods, a great army of cutlery was advancing. Knives, forks and spoons there were; cleavers and ladles, graters and tongs – all clattering across the clearing in a cloud of dust, their silver blades, bowls and prongs gleaming brightly in the noonday sun.

Roger the Wrinkled turned to the teaspoon. 'It's up to you now,' he said.

The teaspoon sighed softly, tripped lightly down the stairs from the podium and climbed on top of a rock. It tapped lightly, bringing the swelling ranks of cutlery to attention. Then it performed a short dance, nodding first at the tree rabbit and then to the Tickle Squad, before leaping down and leading the army of cutlery in a charge.

The knives clashed their blades menacingly, the forks twanged their prongs and the spoons clattered their bowls together as they raced towards a startled-looking Dr Cuddles and a terrified Quentin.

'Tickle Squad!' screamed Cuddles in a high-pitched wail. 'He-e-elp me!'

The squad tumbled back down the steps and formed a tight cordon round their leader. At the front of the ranks of cutlery, a line of steak knives advanced menacingly, while a horde of assorted forks and soup spoons swarmed round the back. The egg slicer led the cake forks and fish knives on one side, whilst a tiny silver toothpick (engraved with the name *Simon*) marshalled the kebab skewers and heavy ladles on the other. The Tickle Squad was surrounded. And, with every attempted escape swiftly repelled with a poke of a knife or a prod of a fork or a rap on the back of a furry paw by a spoon, there was nothing they could do.

From the centre of the tight huddle of teddy bears, Dr Cuddles's voice rang out. 'I'm not finished yet!' he shouted.

'I think you'll find that you are,' said Roger the Wrinkled from the podium. He turned to the teaspoon. 'Take them away,' he said.

As one, the great circle of cutlery moved towards the back door of the Giggle House, pushing, prodding and poking the Tickle Squad along with them.

'Come on, everyone,' said Roger the Wrinkled. 'Pick up your balls and chains and follow me, or you'll miss all the fun.'

They followed the cutlery into the house and crowded round the kitchen doorway, looking into Dr Cuddles's richly furnished sitting room. In the middle of the daisy-covered orange carpet, the army of cutlery surrounded the Tickle Squad, which was clustered before the locked spell book lectern like shipwrecked sailors in a sea of shiny metal. In the corner, a group of heavy ladles had Cuddles and Quentin pinned to the wall.

From the doorway, Joe watched, intrigued. All of a sudden, with a neat double back-flip, the tiny silver toothpick (*Simon*) jumped up on to the locked box and began picking at the lock.

'No!' shouted Dr Cuddles. 'Don't do that!'

The trapdoor opened. The Tickle Squad tumbled down. The trapdoor slammed shut.

'Hooray!' shouted Joe above the sound of Henry's excited barking.

'*Pork pies and custard!*' bellowed Norbert. 'I mean, hooray!'

'Bravo!' cried the wizards. 'You haven't lost your touch, Roger.'

'Well done, sir!' said Veronica.

'Allow me to

add my humble congratulations,' said Randalf. 'I never doubted you for a moment, sir.'

'Oh, it was nothing,' said Roger the Wrinkled modestly. 'It was Dr Cuddles who gave me the idea.'

'I did?' said Dr Cuddles, from the corner.

'You wanted something bright and shiny to tempt a dragon, remember? What better than the baron's own silver cutlery?' Roger smiled, his face a mass of wrinkles. 'Oh, you thought you were so clever, allowing me to read only one word at a time from the spell book, looking over my shoulder the whole time. You were so busy fussing over the *Great Book of Spells* that you didn't notice the little spell of my own that I was working on.'

'No, I didn't,' said Cuddles, darkly.

Roger cleared his throat. '*One teaspoon to rule them all, one teaspoon to heed them, one teaspoon to bring them all to Giggle Glade and lead them!* I give you . . .' He finished with a flourish. '*The Lord of the Teaspoons!*'

The wizards broke into applause. The little teaspoon by his feet gave a soft sigh and bowed.

'Curses!' muttered Dr Cuddles.

'So, you see,' Roger the Wrinkled went on, 'the moment he sent the cutlery off, his fate was sealed. Of course, they took their time getting here, but all's well that ends well. And as for you!' He rounded on the pink, starey-eyed Dr Cuddles. 'You should be ashamed of yourself,' he said.

'It's not my fault. I had a terrible childhood,' he said, glaring at Randalf.

'He's mad!' said Randalf, turning bright scarlet. 'Quite mad, I tell you.'

'You don't know what I went through,' said Dr Cuddles. 'Dribbled on, dragged about by the ears, forced to sleep in a tiny bed . . .'

'Bonkers!' said Randalf. 'Completely bonkers! And I'll have you know it's a king-sized bed.'

'That's enough,' said Roger the Wrinkled sharply. 'Hand over the key to the spell book, Cuddles, and we'll put an end to this nonsense once and for all.'

'The key?' said Dr Cuddles. His paw went to his neck. 'Er . . . I appear to have mislaid it.'

'Another one of your tricks, Cuddles?' said Roger the Wrinkled.

Randalf reached into his pocket. 'I think *this* is what you're looking for, sir,' he said.

Roger the Wrinkled frowned. 'Why, Randalf,' he said. 'I'm impressed! How did you manage that?'

'Oh, like you, sir, I have a few tricks up my sleeve!' beamed Randalf.

'On your head, more like!' said Veronica, perched on Randalf's pointy hat.

'Shut up, Veronica!'

Roger the Wrinkled crossed the room to the lectern and put the key in the lock. Instead of turning it, he tapped it three times with his forefinger. There was a soft *click*. The trapdoor remained shut.

'It's all a matter of technique,' said Roger, as he opened the box and removed the *Great Book of Spells*. 'At last,' he said reverently as he hugged the book tightly to his chest. 'Now I shall be able to restore some order to Muddle Earth.'

A murmur went round the room. Randalf shuffled awkwardly.

'Now you're going to be for it,' Veronica whispered in his ear.

'Shut *up*, Veronica,' Randalf hissed.

Roger the Wrinkled placed the book down on the lectern and opened it up. Joe moved forward for a better look. The *Great Book of Spells* had a battered blue cover with a ruled box in the middle, in which was written, *Roger the Wrinkled, Head Wizard, Enchanted Lake, Muddle Earth. Subject: SPELLS*. It reminded Joe of one of his school exercise books, only five times the size.

Roger turned the yellowing pages, which were all covered in strange black symbols and squiggles, intricate annotated diagrams in red, green and gold, and words laid out like verses in a language Joe had never seen before.

'*Warrior-Hero-Summoning Spell*,' said Roger, looking up at Joe. 'You see, I haven't forgotten, young man. Now where are we?' He turned a couple more pages. '*Walking Rock Spell* . . . *Wardrobe Spells; various* . . . Ah, here we are. I . . .' He took a sharp intake of breath. 'But what is this?'

'What is *what*, sir?' asked Randalf innocently.

'The very page I require has been torn,' said Roger the Wrinkled. 'Half of the spell is missing. What is the meaning of this?'

'Will you tell him, or shall I?' said Veronica.

'Tell him?' said Randalf. 'Tell him what?'

'Randalf!' squawked Veronica. 'I've covered up for you long enough! I'm warning you, I'm ready to sing like a canary!'

'Oh, all right!' Randalf cried. 'I admit it! It's all my fault.' He reached into his pocket a second time and pulled out a folded square of parchment. He opened it up carefully and handed it to Roger the Wrinkled.

'It's the missing bit of the spell, Randalf,' said Roger. 'Perhaps you'd like to explain yourself.'

Randalf grimaced. 'It was while you were away at the Dress Convention in Goblintown,' he began. 'You remember, sir.'

'Yes, yes,' said Roger quickly. 'Well, what of it?'

'Well,' said Randalf. 'I . . . I . . . I couldn't help myself, sir. It was just lying there on the table. So I picked it up and opened it . . . and . . .'

'You didn't,' said Roger, his voice hushed and full of dread. 'You used the *Great Book of Spells*.'

'I did,' said Randalf, turning red. 'I . . . I had a go at a spell of animation.'

'Oh, Randalf,' said Roger the Wrinkled. 'That was far too advanced a spell for a beginner.'

'I know that now, sir,' said Randalf, with a sniff. 'I . . . I tried it out on . . .'

'Don't tell me!' said Roger. 'You tried it out on that childhood toy of yours, Charlie Cuddles!'

'I prefer *Doctor*, if you don't mind,' said Cuddles stiffly.

Randalf nodded shamefacedly. 'Yes,' he said. 'Yes, I did. How could something so soft and cuddly and cute-looking turn into such a monster?'

'Magic can be a tricky business,' said Roger the Wrinkled, nodding sagely.

'He was mad!' Randalf went on. 'He grabbed the spell book. I tried to stop him. We had a bit of a tug-of-war. All I remember is a tearing sound, and falling over clutching that page. When I looked round, the *Great Book of Spells* was gone and I was left with half a warrior-hero-summoning spell. I think you can guess the rest.' Randalf hung his head. 'But I tried to put things right. Honestly, I did.'

'And made things worse and worse in the process,' said Veronica sharply.

'Yes, well,' said Roger the Wrinkled gently. 'Don't be too

harsh on him, Veronica. I think Randalf here has learned his lesson, haven't you, my boy?'

'Yes, sir,' said Randalf meekly.

'And you must be the *oldest* wizard's apprentice ever. I think it's high time we gave you a houseboat of your own, Randalf, and made you a *real* wizard at last. What do you think?'

'Oh, sir!' said Randalf. 'Me, a real wizard! With a houseboat of my very own. Did you hear that, Veronica?'

Veronica managed a smile.

Just then, there came a piercing screech from the chamber at the back of the house. 'Cuddles! Quentin! Where *are* you?'

Dr Cuddles trembled. Quentin swallowed nervously. 'Oh, deary me,' he said, shuddering nervously. 'I'd forgotten about Ingrid!'

'Bring me my breakfast!' she demanded. 'Scented tea and icing-sugar waffles. Now!'

'I can't,' Quentin muttered. 'I just can't take it any more . . .'

'If you'll excuse me for just a moment, Joe, I'll take care

of this,' said Roger the Wrinkled, flicking on through the pages. 'My word, it is good to have the spell book back.'

He stopped at a *Sleeping-Beauty Enchantment*, raised his arms and, reading from the yellowed pages, started intoning a brief spell under his breath.

'Cuddles, I won't tell you again!' Ingrid was shrieking. 'Quentin! Quen—' The voice abruptly fell still and was replaced with a low, rasping snore.

'There,' said Roger the Wrinkled. 'Fast asleep. And so she will remain until she is awoken from her enchanted slumber by the voice of her loved one.'

'Loved one! The Horned Baron!' said Dr Cuddles crossly. 'Ransom note after ransom note I sent him and he didn't reply to a single one. I did him a favour if you ask me.'

'I *didn't* ask you, Charlie Cuddles,' said Roger the Wrinkled calmly. 'In fact,' he added, returning to the spell book, 'there is only one thing I have to say to you.' He raised his arms once more and uttered a second incantation.

'It's not Charlie Cuddles,' protested Dr Cuddles. 'It's *Doctor. Doctor* Cuddles, do you hear? Doctor Cuddles of Giggle—'

Suddenly he stopped. His pink fur lost its lustre; his blue-eyes lost their sparkle. He tumbled to the ground, where he lay, motionless, silent . . .

For a moment, no one made a sound. The next, the Giggle House exploded with whoops of excitement and cries of joy.

Dr Cuddles was defeated!

Muddle Earth was safe!

Quentin bent down and picked the teddy bear up off the floor and held it up in front of him. 'I've been such a fool,' he said. 'But I, too, have learned my lesson. It's snuggle-muffins and iced decorations for me from now on. Norbert, can we be friends again?'

Norbert smiled. 'You'll always find a welcome in my kitchen,' he said.

Randalf stepped forward, his arms outstretched. Quentin handed him the teddy. 'Charlie Cuddles, I had no idea you thought of me like that. It really isn't healthy to bottle up all those negative feelings, you know,' Randalf said thoughtfully. 'But in the spirit of reconciliation, I'm prepared to let bygones be bygones – though from now on, you're sleeping in the cupboard along with Tracy and Mr Hiss.'

Roger the Wrinkled's face creased up happily. 'We muddled through, eventually,' he said, and the other wizards all nodded in earnest agreement.

'Excuse me, Roger, sir,' said Joe. 'The spell, remember?'

'Ah yes, forgive me, Joe,' said Roger the Wrinkled, smiling down at him benevolently. 'Step over here and I shall send you back.'

'One moment,' said Joe, hurriedly. 'I just want to say my goodbyes.'

Roger nodded understandingly.

Joe looked round at Veronica and Norbert, and at

Randalf (who, even though he had proven not to be a proper wizard, would always be Randalf the Wise to him) clutching the now harmless teddy bear tightly in his arms.

'Oh, sir,' said Norbert, rushing forwards, tears welling up in each of his three eyes. He wrapped his great arms around Joe and squeezed tightly. 'I'll miss you!' he wailed.

'I'll ... miss ... you ... too ...' Joe gasped as the air was squeezed out of him.

'Let him go, you great lug,' said Veronica. She fluttered in front of Joe. 'Farewell, Joe,' she said. 'It has been a pleasure and an honour knowing you.'

'And you, too, Veronica,' said Joe as the budgie perched up on the brim of Randalf's pointy hat. He looked down into Randalf's eyes. 'Goodbye, Randalf,' he said.

'Farewell, Joe the Barbarian,' said Randalf. 'Finest warrior-hero ever in Muddle Earth.'

Joe smiled. 'How many times do I have to tell you?' he said. 'I am not a warrior-hero. I'm just an ordinary boy who—'

'Oh, but you are, Joe, whether you like it or not.'

Joe turned to see Brenda and Sniffy standing in the doorway. Brenda smiled, stepped forwards and clasped Joe's hand in her own.

'You *are* a warrior-hero, Joe,' she said. 'The best kind. For your heroism, Joe the Barbarian, comes from within.'

Joe looked down at the floor bashfully. Maybe there was a little bit of the warrior-hero in him after all.

'Come on,' said Roger, taking him by the arm. 'It's time to go home.'

Joe followed Roger the Wrinkled back to the lectern, where the wizard returned to the torn page, smoothed it flat and inspected it closely. 'I see,' he said. 'I see.' Then, a moment later. 'Yes, I see . . .' He turned to Joe and Henry. 'It's really rather simple.'

He raised his hands, closed his eyes, threw back his head and bellowed a single word.

'*HOME!*'

For a moment, Joe thought he must be joking. 'Home?' What kind of a spell was *that*?

But even as he was about to say as much, he noticed something strange beginning to happen. His whole body – from the top of his hair to the tips of his toes – tingled and crackled with silvery strands of electricity. He heard slow, mournful music, and his nose twitched at the smell of burnt toast. The air shimmered and wobbled; it was as if he were looking through water.

There were Norbert and Quentin holding hands. There was Randalf with Veronica perched on his pointy hat. And Brenda and Sniffy and the wizards – and Roger the Wrinkled . . .

'Right,' he was saying, his voice sounding distant and echoey, 'all that remains now is a little unfinished business with that tree rabbit . . .'

And that was all. As his voice faded, so too did his face

– and everything else in Muddle Earth. Joe gasped as he found himself tumbling headlong down a long, pulsating tunnel. The strange music grew louder; the smell of burning more pungent until . . .

CRASH!

Joe opened his eyes and looked round. His armour was gone and he was back in his old clothes, sitting at the centre of a great, dusty rhododendron bush. Henry was beside him, his tail wagging uncertainly.

'We're back!' Joe cried out. 'Henry, we're home!'

Henry barked excitedly.

Together they scrambled out of the bush and headed off across the grass. 'Come on, boy,' Joe shouted. 'They're going to be so worried!'

As he went through the gate and up the path, Joe felt himself trembling. It was all so familiar, yet strange – like those first few minutes after returning from a holiday, only more so. He ran round to the back of the house and into the kitchen.

'Mum! Dad!' he shouted. 'I'm back! Hello Ella! Hello twins!'

Ella shook her head and left the room, muttering under her breath. The twins looked at one another and giggled.

'Did you have a nice walk?' asked his mum, switching

off her vacuum cleaner, which only seemed to make the sound of his dad's electric drill even louder.

'Yes,' said Joe, puzzled. No one seemed to be at all worried. 'But I've been away ages!' he said.

'About half an hour,' his mum said. She smiled. 'Tea'll be ready at six. Why don't you pop up to your room and get that homework of yours done. What was it again?'

'An essay,' said Joe. '*My Amazing Adventure.*'

'Have you got any ideas?'

Joe nodded, a broad grin spreading across his face. 'One or two,' he said.

Back in Muddle Earth, the great tree rabbit had completed its long journey to the Horned Baron's castle. Benson – who had noticed it standing next to the gates – had gone out to take a look. He had found a letter clutched in one of its enormous forepaws and taken it to the Horned Baron, who was busy with a spot of moonlight-gardening in the vegetable patch.

'What now, Benson?' the Horned Baron snapped, waving his trowel at the manservant irritably. 'If I've told you once, I've told you a hundred times, not to disturb me when Fifi and I are tending to our turnips.' His eyes narrowed. 'Particularly,' he added, 'if you're about to tell me you've received another blooming letter!'

Benson held the envelope out. 'This one's different,' he said.

The Horned Baron opened it up and began reading. The expression on his face turned from mild irritation to unbounded joy. 'Oh, but this is marvellous news!' he exclaimed. 'Listen, Fifi. It's from Dr Cuddles. *Apologies for all my recent tricks . . .*' he read out. '*I've decided to retire. Please accept this little gift as a token of my friendship.*' He turned to Benson. 'What little gift?' he said.

'It's outside the gates,' said Benson.

'Then bring it in, bring it in,' said the Horned Baron.

'As you wish, sir,' said Benson. He left the vegetable garden, returning a moment later with the great tree rabbit trundling slowly beside him.

'Ooh! A garden sculpture!' cried Fifi. 'It'll look lovely over there by the wall, *and* it'll scare all those naughty, greedy tree rabbits and stiltmice away from our turnips. I love it, Horny! I absolutely love it!'

'So do I,' said the Horned Baron. He gripped Fifi's hand. 'And I love . . .'

Just then there was an ominous *creak*. It seemed to come from the tree rabbit. Benson, Fifi and the Horned Baron looked up to see a trapdoor at the base of the rabbit drop down, and a huge, pudgy leg appear.

'Walter?' came a voice. '*Walter!*'

'Baroness?' said Benson.

'Ingrid?' gasped Fifi.

'*AAAAARGH!!!*' screamed the Horned Baron.

Joe Jefferson sat at his bedroom desk, pen poised. It was still noisy. Ella's music was pounding above him, the electric drill and the vacuum cleaner were battling it out below, while the twins were fighting just outside his door.

Not that Joe noticed. Eyes down and head full of memories, he started writing.

Night was falling over Muddle Earth. The sun had set, the sky was darkening and already two of its three moons had risen up above the Musty Mountains. One of these moons was as purple as a batbird. The other was as yellow as an ogre's underpants on wash-day . . .

As the three coloured moons of Muddle Earth sank low in the sky, they shone across the Musty Mountains and the Perfumed Bog, across Goblintown, Trollbridge, the Enchanted Lake – and a dusty track, along which two figures were hurrying. One of them was Fifi. The other was short, bandy-legged and bald . . .

'Oh, Fifi,' he was saying. 'Free at last! We'll be together now for ever and ever, growing fields of turnips beyond compare.'

'You and me, Walter. You and me,' said Fifi, squeezing his hand tightly. 'After all this time . . .' She turned to him. Oh, Walter, you're as handsome as you were the day I first met you. For shame, hiding those rugged good looks under that horrid horned helmet for so long!'

'It's such a relief not having to wear it any more,' Walter admitted. 'The weight, the heat, the burden of responsibility – all gone. I feel a new me!'

Meanwhile, back at the castle, a light was shining from a window in the West Wing. Voices floated out from it into the night sky.

'Ooh, it does suit you. Promise never to take it off. You look magnificent, Benson!'

'Do you really think so, Baroness?'

'Oh, Benson, you're the Horned Baron now, remember!' A girlish laugh filled the air. 'You can call me Ingrid!'

Paul Stewart has written books for young readers of all ages, most notably the bestselling Edge Chronicles. He lives down the street from Chris Riddell in Brighton, England.

Chris Riddell, cocreator of the Edge Chronicles, is an award-winning illustrator and political cartoonist. He lives down the street from Paul Stewart in Brighton, England.

Paul and Chris first met at nursery school. Not theirs, but the one their sons went to. For some strange reason, which they can't quite remember, they decided to work together. That was over ten years ago. Since then, they have created several books together, including those in both the Edge Chronicles and the Far-Flung Adventures series.